■ God's Peculiar Care

Patrick Roscoe

MAINSTREAM
PUBLISHING

Edinburgh and London

First published in Great Britain 1991 by
MAINSTREAM PUBLISHING COMPANY (EDINBURGH) LTD
7 Albany Street
Edinburgh EH1 3UG

British Library Cataloguing in Publication Data

Roscoe, Patrick
    God's Peculiar Care
    I. Title.
    823.914 [F]

    ISBN 1-85158-304-1

The publishers gratefully acknowledge the financial assistance from the
Scottish Arts Council in the production of this volume

Printed and bound in the United States of America on acid free paper ♾

For all those who have struggled and lost,
but never in vain.

F.F.
1914 – 1970
R.I.P.

■ Considerations

Jane Bowles, The Canada Council, Toni Childs, Rickie Lee Jones, Jessica Lange, Carson McCullers, Joni Mitchell, The Ontario Arts Council, Jean Rhys, Ardith and Michael Roscoe.

■ Acknowledgements

Excerpt from "Living It Up" by Rickie Lee Jones. © 1981 Easy Money Music (ASCAP). All rights reserved. Used by permission.

Excerpt from "Pirates (So Long Lonely Avenue)" by Rickie Lee Jones. © 1980 Easy Money Music (ASCAP). All rights reserved. Used by permission.

A brief scene on pages 165–166 was partly suggested by "Skeletons," by Rickie Lee Jones.

The chapter titles "The Last Station Near Home," "Where's the Ocean," and "Zimbabwe," as well as several images in the last, were originally created by Toni Childs in her work, *Union*.

Portions of this novel first appeared in the following publications: "Without the Desert No Oasis Would Emerge" and "Lights! Camera! Action!" in *Canadian Fiction Magazine*; "How Far Is the Journey From Here To a Star" in *The New Quarterly*; "Menthol Cigarettes" in *Mental Radio*; and "Zimbabwe" in *The University of Windsor Review*.

■ A Factual Note

In Los Angeles, California, 1943, immediately prior to the beginning of a long period of incarceration in various mental institutions, an actress named Frances Farmer worked on an autobiographical novel with the hope that its composition might ward off gathering clouds of darkness. Upon her eventual release from hospital care, she found that the uncompleted manuscript had vanished in what might be interpreted a mysterious fashion, and all efforts to locate it failed. That the following pages bear the same title as Frances Farmer's missing manuscript could be called coincidental, except that under the peculiar care of God there are no accidents: every dream of love and loss is the same, and similarly real.

■ God's
Peculiar
Care

Starring Roles

Frances Farmer, a fallen star
Emily, a sojourner
Frank, a bartender
The Boy, a survivor

Madeleine, a searcher
Sister Mary, a sidewalk preacher
Sam, a movie-theatre operator
Ethel, a worshipper

Supporting Roles

Ingrid
Jeanette } hotel residents
Sally
Rita } corner characters
Blue
Nina, a beautician
Annemarie, an absent friend
Lucille, Sister Mary's sister
Joe, a desk clerk

Harry, a disabled bartender
Stella, a suburban lady
Slow Burn } more corner
The Pilot } characters
Señora Sanchez, an emotional
    woman
Reeves, a boy who stays behind
A Messenger who wears shapeless,
    colourless clothes

Bit Parts

Steve, Frank's part-time help
Fingers, Frank's piano player
Nick, yet another bartender
Ginger, a barfly
Lolita } further corner
Eddie-Jane } characters
A Woman who knits on a staircase
A Jovial Young Bus-driver
An English-Speaking Gentleman
A Thin Little Black Girl
*Two Companions Enjoying Something
    Cool*
*A Heavyset Man Who Has Been
    Wounded by the World*

A Young Couple Who Dance
Lino Moreno, a lonely man
Robert, Stella's betrothed
Mr Carson, a pharmacy owner
Bettye Jones, a waitress
Dorothy, an aunt
Kaye, another aunt
Three Native Boys
A Daytime Desk Clerk
A Young Man Who Lives in a Park
Mabel, a shopping-cart pusher
Baby J, a corner labourer
Michael, a missing brother/uncle
Harrod, an equestrian owner

Contents

■ Part One

". . . I began to figure out that if God loved all His children equally, why did He bother about my hat and let other children lose their mothers and fathers for always? I began to see that He didn't have much to do about people's dying or hats or anything. They happened whether He wanted them to or not, and He stayed in heaven and pretended not to notice. I wondered a little why God was such a useless thing. It seemed a waste of time to have Him. After that, He became less and less, until He was nothingness."

Frances Farmer, 1931

■ Angel Dust

Ghosts of Frances Farmer and other fallen stars whisper to the boy, but can't be heard and wander lost beneath the noise of traffic and music and shouting in the street. Frances Farmer sense Devil sneaking up behind boy and scream: Run away! There's a place somewhere for us!

Ambulance answer a call for help too late, drowning out a million other cries, including boy's silent questions (run where? run how?) and Frances Farmer's indistinct reply. Siren fade away with daylight and sun's warmth and boy's cranked-up high. Slide way down, then further down. Sidewalk squat on HB, switch on LA. Back against a message on a wall, left foot on Gene Tierney's star. A sky tremble neon and cars coast west. See them going, going, gone. . . .

Bleach-blonde headlights shine black pussy pulling switchblade. She slice her knife and say: Bust ass, white boy, you on my star. Blade carve down back of boy's jacket but don't touch his inside skin, he ain't more hurt.

He move it onto Judy Garland, kill a minute watching moon fake the sky. Busted brunette safety-pinned together strike a match and ask the way to closest launderette. Need to be clean, want to wash it all away. Cigarette flick arc above Montgomery Clift, fall deep down curb. It cold beneath the Hills, cold parking lots and bowling alleys and barred-up pawnshops cul-de-sac a Hollywood scene rehearsed to death before. Lookit, the midnite matinee. . . .

Now Fatbelt has a fifty to buy some time so prop the boy: Wanna go with me there for cab fare back?

Cab drive on high gear these hard time days, say boy.

How high is high? wonder Fatbelt as he fumble with a ring.

Depending on the ride, speak boy from far away.

I listen a twenty buy front seat backstreet trip to 69th.

Boy shake his head: This cab clean and new, cost five

3

of spades and splash of sweet mad dog red.

Wait here, say game. He shuffle off to Handymart in search of spirits, leaving boy beside a parking meter without a car to drive away. Chords swell sweet from open door of T-Shirt Shoppe and promise all boys: Everything go, come back again.

Down the street stars falling from the sky. Smash in slivered glass that first burns with the glow of lost Heaven's fire, then with the red and blue of cocktail signs. Winking blinking eyes. Angels who've caught free rides down from Heaven leap lightly from the glass and waltz away, looking over padded shoulders for boy to follow. He gives chase, cutting feet on glass and leaving tracks of blood for other boys to know the way. How all angels hide inside bars and dancehalls and cabarets, where it's warm and dark and crowded. Beneath halos of burning cigarettes and behind slits of smiles they tell the boy the only way to find a night train hidden deep inside the city. They offer false directions and broken promises and touches that come from the frozen sky but burn hot. Flesh that brands and tattoos, names and marks. Then like the fallen stars the aging angels splinter, glow and finally burn out.

Boy wander out from bar into street grown quiet as some graveyard. In the distance night train whistle goodbye, so long, see you in my dreams. Cold air come through tear in boy's jacket like a hand running down his back. He shiver.

Snap finger, heel turn around the corner and over Jennifer Jones. Meet Baby J who work a stoplite on the Strip, hot corner burning like cool deuce a shift. Baby swing it up to boy and say: Where you going, there ain't no place to go.

Mabel and her shopping cart fade into view. Lipstick open and words slide out: Bad boys, do you know how bad it is to hope for rides in this bad city? The bad things they do to you I've seen. (She dip her arm into cart and stir around a stew of empty cans and torn newspapers where every accident she's witnessed is smudged in black and white.) Like a knife in your heart and a body cut to pieces then thrown beside a freeway. Where's your home?

Baby flash a blade and warn: Push it on, granma. She roll away talking to her trash.

Now angel dust floating down through big black sky, shining white like softest snow and making the city not so dark. Please PCP with me a little, plead boy to Baby J. I ain't seen snow for so long now. Look, it's falling on your head, it's melting on your hair like way back when.

I got to go back to work before this town die some more, speak Baby J to boy.

Black car cruise up and boy get inside.

Where you going? say driver.

Frances Farmer smile inside her heart.

■ Part Two

"I had no idea what the picture was all about all the time I was making it. I never did find out . . . It was a long sweet nightmare. . . ."

Frances Farmer, 1936

Part Two

■ Without the Desert No Oasis Would Emerge

"Do you worship?" inquired the heavy-set woman who settled with a sigh into the seat beside Madeleine when the bus paused to take on new passengers in another small town in the middle of the night.

"I used to," Madeleine replied, turning eagerly toward the woman. "But recently I retired. You see, I found that after some acquaintance any God I placed my faith in turned into only another foolish clown."

"Some people give up too easy," remarked the larger woman. "I could have abandoned Her a million times or more and spared myself. Those without faith like to mock the ones who have it, they toss the Christians to the lions. I could have spared myself the trouble of this bus trip, for instance. I'm not a traveller by nature. But I feel an obligation, especially now that so many have fallen by the way and She is nearly forgotten. Frances, I mean. Frances Farmer, The One and Only. I call Her by Her first name, we're close as sisters. Why shouldn't God have a Christian name, when you think about it?"

The large woman spoke easily and loudly to the young blonde, disregarding the possibility that other passengers might be trying to rest, as indeed was the case. Most of them had been on the bus a considerable time. At the start they had all chattered like chickens about the amazing fact that every one of them had California as a common destination; this seemed the first indication that from now on life would take the shape of one long, unending miracle. Bottles were exchanged with Christian names, campfire songs with infinite choruses were loudly carolled, and very quickly the small dingy towns from which the travellers had fled were forgotten. Those who had already been to California offered information to those making a virgin voyage. Rich words concerning orange groves and palm

9

trees and Beverly Hills gushed like oil wells, flooding
the interior of the bus with a thick, liquescent substance
which seemed to stick the passengers together more
firmly. Madeleine, for her part, had been a kind of
ringleader of the gang, stating that she had been to
California so often she felt at home in a swimming pool
the way other people did in a kitchen. She passed up
and down the aisle, sitting on laps, throwing her long
blonde hair this way and that, batting her eyelashes,
ending every sentence with a punchline. She gave out
the addresses of those movie stars who were her particular soul-mates and hinted that recently she had de-
clined a seven-year contract with MGM on the advice of
Elizabeth Taylor, who said that Louis B. Mayer had suf-
focated genius in the old days and things hadn't
changed much since then. Everyone peered out the windows, expecting the Pacific Ocean to emerge around
each bend in the road. They calculated miles and minutes and impatiently imagined the moment when they
would finally step off the bus and into a state of grace
with a capital city named Sacramento. Whenever the
bus paused in a little town, the whole troop had disembarked to stretch legs and to comment upon how the air
already seemed fresher, softer and more delicately
scented.

However, conversation had long since languished.
People tried to sleep in awkward positions and insufficient space. Their legs cramped, their necks stiffened.
Some remained upright with closed eyes and mumbled
prayers, as is commonly done during times of extended
suffering. It was recalled exactly how little money wal-
lets and pocketbooks contained. Now and then words
such as *Palm Springs* or *Malibu* or *Santa Monica* were
slurred in the most hopeless of despairing tones. It
seemed that at present the bus was travelling across a
desert of unlimited breadth and width, and there were
no bends or rises in the road to add variety to motion or
even to suggest that the bus was moving at all. Only

Madeleine had persevered in straining to see beyond
the blackness that enfolded the bus—when she was not
otherwise engaged with freshening her lipstick, lighting
cigarettes, or composing rhymed poems which all began
with the line, "Without the desert no oasis would
emerge."

"Ethel's the name," offered Madeleine's new travelling companion, extending a hand but avoiding a glance
into the girl's face. "I don't have a nickname, I'm afraid.
Some people have them and some don't, and who on
earth knows why? Life is full of mystery and we're all
explorers, that's the truth. Take this Jesus fellow for
starters. They say he's still pretty popular these days,
though I do understand he's slipped some in the polls.
If he's managed to hang onto even one follower after all
this time, I say all the more power to him. Ethel doesn't
begrudge him a bit. But I must say it strikes me just a
touch peculiar. How long did he suffer for our sins?
Thirty-six hours or so? In my books he got off easy. A
few days, a few nights—what's the big to-do? A week-
end in Vegas or on the cross, take your pick. Such a
thimbleful of suffering wouldn't begin to atone for the
sins of my next-door neighbours, never mind those of
the folks down the block.

"Oh, there's something fishy in the whole business
and I'm not the least partial to seafood," Ethel sailed on,
as though Madeleine had given her the slightest encour-
agement—when in fact the girl had remained silent,
with only a sulky, stubborn expression forming on her
face. "Could this Jesus fellow have stood the suffering
that Frances bore? Tell me only that and I'll die a satisfied woman. Thirty years She spent on Her cross. Yes,
they took Her down from the silver screens where everyone could see Her spirit shining in the darkness, illu-
minating all the pain and sorrow and suffering in this
world. It was the ones with money and power who
were responsible for Her crucifixion. They are the ones
who cause the earth's heartache and profit from it. They

are the ones who know they can't be saved and out of
spite wish to keep others from salvation. They are the
ones who don't want the truth to flower in fields where
they have sown their crops of lies. So what did they do?
First they locked Her up in a small dark cage, and for
five years they kept Her naked and hungry, cold and
dirty. They injected Her with drugs and they seared Her
with a steady stream of electric shock. They thought
they could blow out the lamp in Her heart, but Her light
sustained and shone no matter what they did. Until they
cut into Her brain and with one small slice made Her
unable to remember the message She had been given to
spread and made her unable to shine and dazzle like a
star in the night that people may pray to and wish upon
and draw comfort from all through the darkness until
dawn. Yes, at last they let Her free to stumble upon the
earth with no idea of who She was and no knowledge of
where She was going or what She hoped to find there.
Thirty years She wandered with empty eyes. Thirty
years She tried and forever failed to recall how She had
flickered in the vast cold heavens and eased the fear of
us all here below. So She did take a little drink now and
then. So what? With nails driven through your feet and
hands, with a crown of thorns cutting into your forehead always—wouldn't you feel in the mood for a stiff
double or two from time to time?"

Madeleine decided not to answer this question. She
felt the crazy lady beside her tremble and shake, and
she tried to edge away slightly so this vibration would
not affect her. Unfortunately, the lady was large and the
seat was small. Glancing slyly over, Madeleine noticed
that Ethel's hands were clenched into fists so tight that
most likely her fingernails cut painfully into her palms.
"I used to play hooky from Sunday school," Madeleine
said in a bored tone of voice. "I preferred to use the time
practising juggling and tightrope walking."

"Then they played the cruelest joke of all," Ethel continued bitterly. "Sent Her out to Minneapolis to wait for

the early end that comes to a body worn out by suffering. How can anyone rise from a graveyard in Minneapolis? It can't be done. I can't believe She's really buried there. I know She's still out in California. So every year around Her birthday I take my week off work and make this trip. It isn't much, but it's the best I can do. I find a room in an old hotel down in Hollywood and every morning I go to a certain alley behind the old Paramount lot. There I spend the day among the starving cats and skinny scarecrows and nickel riders, and I feel Her presence. It fills me until I overflow. When the sun begins to set I place the bouquet of flowers beside one trash can or another and leave the darkening alley. I go to the movies at night and wait until I am with Her again the next day. I can't help but think that no one in their right mind would rise from a grave unless they felt someone welcomed their ascension. Why lift yourself up only to face the old troubles in the shape of a new cross? Some mornings I can't rise from bed, so I call into work and say it's that old arthritis acting up again. But it's really something else. Well, after my week in Hollywood it's back home to work in the drugstore another year. I look past the displays and out the windows at the snow that's always falling from November until April there. It covers the earth six feet deep. I hang Christmas decorations all around the drugstore, then the ones for Valentine's Day. Then the ones for Easter, then the ones for Mothers' Day and Fathers' Day. The seasons pass on by. I get along. Her spirit sustains me. People call me names but I pay them no mind."

"It must be quite a relief to have belief," sang Madeleine in an artificially high voice. "I don't believe in following such an easy route myself. I find greater challenge, spiritually speaking, in continuing my search without any fixed idea of where I'll end up or who will wait for me there. Let's just say I'm keeping my options open, as the businessman would advise. You never know, do you? The most unlikely stranger could turn out to be your saviour, and every intelligent, open-minded human being must be prepared for just such an event."

Ethel's back stiffened. "My," she said. "It must take you quite some time to fiddle with cosmetics and bleach those roots each day. But of course we must all look our best when we meet our saviour, mustn't we? And I suppose a girl like you would paint her toenails too before she thought of climbing the stairway to Heaven."

"But those poor nuns and monks!" Madeleine burst out laughing. "Safe behind their holy walls and in their narrow beds! They would ignore His knocking on the gate if the Ascension occurred outside visiting hours."

Ethel gritted her teeth and reminded herself that every moment upon this earth we are put to the test. Pure devotion is not easy and neither is travelling on a bus when you suffer motion sickness and the company of a flighty blonde. To soothe her nerves, Ethel began turning over in her mind every item in the drugstore and how much each one cost. She knew them all by heart. Murmuring brand names of shampoos and toothpastes was one way of seeking sleep and counting sheep another; there are a million ways to make it through another night, and each one is holy if it leads back to the light.

Madeleine remained anxiously awake. Several lines appeared on her face as she became more tired. The bus rolled and rocked through the night. The fat lady snored beside her. Madeleine was torn between a desire to keep what little distance she could from this stranger's body and to seek the warmth of its touch. The other passengers muttered and sobbed and cried out, lost inside the maze of nightmare. They were people afraid to fly or unable to drive; they did not have the means to own a car or to buy a ticket to take them swiftly through the sky. Where were they all now? Did the driver even know? Still somewhere on a desert where only cactus grew and no cold clear water could slake a thirst? Madeleine was afraid to fall asleep, for then she might waken and not know why she was on this journey rather than still safe inside her mama's eyes. "Without their separation, no lines would converge," she murmured, adding a second line to her rhyme. Like all poems, it was really a prayer.

■ Lights! Camera! Action!

The bus on which Madeleine had been riding for three days and three nights pulled into a depot, and even before it came to a complete stop the other passengers crowded anxiously up the aisle. Apparently they were unaware or unconcerned that this city was not quite Hollywood and that no orange groves or swimming pools were in sight. Madeleine made no move to rise from her seat. "Ethel must have gotten off somewhere at dawn," she thought idly, as if this fact were scarcely worthy of notice. "Anyway, in a metaphysical sense, I've moved beyond Hollywood years ago. Certainly I'm old enough to know that California is but a state of mind."

The driver, a jovial young man whose cheerful manner had endeared him to a good many of the passengers, stood at the front of the bus shaking hands and exchanging well-wishes. He was looking forward to a good steak dinner. Seeing the blonde girl still in her seat, he frowned and called back: "This is the end of our journey together. It has been a lot of fun, but now it's over. All good things must come to an end. Enjoy this fair city and look after your health. When you have your health, you have everything."

Madeleine did not respond. She pretended to look out the window when she saw the driver approach down the aisle. Just before he touched her shoulder, she looked up and quickly said, "I want to go farther west."

"Can't unless you fly or float clear across to Japland." The driver flapped his arms comically but continued to frown.

Through the window Madeleine noticed, without surprise, a dozen members of a chain gang milling among the suitcases and waiting travellers. Though freed, they were unused to liberty and by habit stuck close to those who had shared their toil and pain. They shuffled stiffly and slowly with eyes fixed upon the ground, as though in search of lost tickets they had no real hope of finding. It was only too clear that they had no place to go and yearned only for the time when they would be back in irons.

Madeleine blinked, then her own reflection covered the window. She noticed with relief that in spite of everything she still possessed her youth and sex appeal.

The driver coughed in an obvious manner. Sighing and stretching, Madeleine murmured, "This seat is so comfortable I could sit here forever." She cast a considering eye upon the driver, who was turning as purple as a grape. "Tell me something, my good friend. How many passengers does this bus carry?"

"One hundred and forty-four."

"Fancy that!" Madeleine marvelled. "Could you believe it? They put the care of one hundred and forty-four souls into the hands of a fool! One flick of your wrist and you could have killed us all. And, if that weren't enough, your uniform doesn't suit you in the least."

"See here," began the driver.

"I never wanted to drive a bus," said Madeleine loudly. "Even as a child I had no such dream. People in uniform bore me." She flounced by the driver, her hair falling over one eye.

Madeleine walked from the depot and followed where fancy led. The street was wide and dirty and not crowded. A few people loafed in front of movie houses, studying news of coming attractions. Others, idling at bus stops, pretended they had some place to go. An old man dug deeply into a trash can. None of them would have any idea of west or east or where the land met the sea. Fortunately, Madeleine was one of the lucky souls who knew that every strange city is the same, alas.

A skinny little black girl began to follow Madeleine. "Mama, where's home?" she asked in a high tinny voice. "Take me home." Madeleine looked severely at the child and proceeded to walk more quickly. "Did you bring me presents, Mama? That what you got in them big bags?" The little girl ran with small steps beside Madeleine and pulled at her sleeve with surprising strength. "Where's home?" she whined.

"Please go away, little girl," said Madeleine. "I'm afraid I can't help you."

The child stopped and began to cry. "I got to find my mama. Help me, please. She needs me, my mama does."

Madeleine walked hastily away. She turned, somewhat disconcerted, up a narrower street which at first seemed a bit more cheerful and lively. After only a few steps, however, Madeleine had the strange feeling that this street was a careful copy of some other street not quite worth imitating in the first place. The people and cars appeared to go busily about just to flesh out a stage of cardboard buildings and painted sky; with some uncertainty they seemed to be trying to follow the conflicting orders given by a director who stood out of sight. "False fronts," thought Madeleine, looking with crestfallen eyes at the buildings before her. She had an urge to push them over and reveal that nothing but empty space was concealed behind them. That the street rose sharply to the sky before her only added to the pilgrim's disheartenment.

When her bags grew so heavy she could walk no farther, Madeleine stopped and looked up. The streetlights blinked on, as though answering a cue. There, before her very eyes, was the Holiday Hotel.

At that precise moment Madeleine knew finally and surely that she had found her haven. "My travelling days are over," she said to herself. "I have escaped the doom of the restless, discontented wanderer who believes always that his Eden lies forever beyond the next mountain. Here I can bask in peace and flourish under the care of God."

The honest truth was that for some time Madeleine had been travelling from place to place, establishing residence in all the international capitals, acquiring foreign languages as easily as bad habits, rubbing shoulders with the masses, acquainting herself with the ways of the world, living always by whim and only for pleasure. She had used bus tickets for Band-Aids and based her religion upon the concept of the fresh start. But recently she had grown weary of the careless life; its charms had gone stale. Old bread is sold cheaper than new bread; but knowing Heaven is not to be found in the bargain basement, Madeleine had decided to devote herself to certain spiritual matters, et cetera. Before it was too late.

All the signs were favourable. This she saw immediately upon stepping across the threshold, entering the lobby and speaking three minutes with the desk clerk. For example, the hotel was large, yet not too large, and neither old nor new. Secondly, it was situated exactly in the centre of the city, which was extremely ironic. How could she have ever guessed that she would find her peace amidst all the hustle and bustle? On one side of the hotel were shabby streets, a neighbourhood quaintly known as The Tenderloin where the homeless lay dead drunk at noon. On the other side rose clean new office buildings filled with those blinded by the false glitter of gold. A Chinatown, an Italian area and a chic artistic community were all located but a stone's throw away. And of course the sea was just beyond. This was part and parcel of the hotel's charm. Each day she could visit any number of different worlds according to impulse and mood and the demands of her mission, without straying too far from home. It's true when they say that variety is the spice of life. But how much more true that no place is quite like home.

What pleased Madeleine most was the hotel's clientele. It did not cater to the driven traveller who rests only one night before hurrying on. Most of the hotel's guests lived there for months on end and some, attracted partly by the sizeable reductions given for lengthy visits, stayed on for years. A certain number of the inhabitants were older people living on one kind of fixed income or another. The rest were young and still to make their way through the world.

This was nothing short of ideal. There would be no danger that Madeleine would become infected by the travel fevers, yet there would always be a few fresh faces to add a pinch of zing into her life. She could strike acquaintance safe from the threat of imminent goodbyes. While the older citizens would offer advice and teach the wisdom of patience and time, the younger ones would share with her their dreams and hopes. The hotel's atmosphere was a rare and precious combination of change and sameness, Madeleine realized at once. She paid a month's rent in advance.

"No tricks or trade," warned the heavy-set woman who was perched on a small stool behind the desk.

"I'm sure we will become beautiful friends and share all the secrets of our hearts," said Madeleine. "What's your name?"

"My legs too tired to climb them old stairs. You can see the room yourself. Your eyes is in your head."

"Let me guess. Is it Linda or Susan?"

"Bathroom down the hall, no guns or funny stuff allowed." The woman slapped down a key with more force than was actually called for, then buried her face in a newspaper.

"I see you are looking at the want-ads," ventured Madeleine. "That is surely a curious coincidence, because I'm looking to buy a radio, good but not expensive, for my new nest. Maybe it's more than a coincidence, who knows? Some people say that things like that occur only in the movies, but more and more I wonder. I like all kinds of music. I'm not biased one way or the other, though maybe it's more a question of taste than bias. There's sugar and there's spice, but it's all music in the end, isn't it?" All at once Madeleine felt very tired. She looked softly at the woman's hair, which was crinkly and grey.

"I'm looking for no trouble is what I'm looking for," replied the woman, angrily rustling her newspaper. "What's wrong with you? Get on now."

"If you ever feel sad or lonely, we could have a drink together. Only if you want to. I believe in neither force nor persuasion. That's because I'm a pacifist. What's your name?"

"I feel I want to look at my paper. Ain't the drinking kind and ain't never sad or lonely." The woman came from behind the desk and began pushing about the furniture of the dingy lobby. Because the particular shape of the room did not permit its furnishings to be arranged with any kind of satisfaction, the woman's efforts were largely unrewarded. Breathing heavily, she looked with sadness at the room until suddenly, as though pushed, she plopped onto the floor. This did not appear to upset or surprise her, for she sat calmly with her fat legs shooting straight out before her and her dress hiked up around her knees. She carefully examined the carpet on which she sat. Only when Madeleine began to move discreetly toward the stairs did the woman look up.

Madeleine's eyes were hard and very bright. "Why did you lie to me?" she asked quietly. "I smelled it on your breath. Whisky."

The woman looked quickly down again. Her finger slowly traced the faded pattern on the carpet, the faint lines of a map on which her little girl somewhere wandered lost.

In all honesty, Madeleine's heart fell slightly when she first saw her room. It was small, dismal and dirty. There was a sink, a bed, a small table before a mirror and one hard-backed chair. Because the only window looked upon a gloomy air shaft, the room would be as dark in day as it now was at evening. A pile of wet garbage lay at the bottom of the air shaft three stories below. Many other rooms shared this same view, but their inhabitants chose to draw curtains against it.

Madeleine lay on the lumpy bed and smoked a cigarette down to the filter. "I must work to make this place my home," she thought. "That's the first step. Who needs the crimson carpets, the velvet drapes?" Her eyes glided about the room without resting on any particular object. Many miles and months she had searched for a place that looked like home, and now that she had found it God would know her address. "General Delivery is such an unreliable way of receiving Word," she thought.

Several hours later, remarkably refreshed, Madeleine stood in the shabby hallway with a bright smile fixed upon her face. Her goal was to find friends or acquaintances—she wasn't fussy—for was it not the comfort of human companionship that kept away the nightmare fears and the travel fevers? She strolled up and down passageways, searching in vain for signs of life. Because the rooms were not numbered, it was difficult to know which door hid a bathroom, which a linen closet, which a small home. Madeleine had the funny feeling that every room contained someone who was holding breath, waiting for her to pass by, dreading discovery. When her floor offered nothing but closed doors and complete silence, Madeleine climbed up to the next one and then the next one after that, until finally she found herself on the seventh storey.

At the far end of the corridor stood a figure half hidden by the dim lighting. Madeleine casually approached what turned out to be a small hunchbacked old man who seemed to be attempting to open a locked door. An expression of sweet friendliness played upon her face as she watched him fumble with a key. Surely he could tell her tales of the old seafaring days when treasures and continents waited to be discovered by anyone brave enough to leave familiar land behind.

"Excuse me, but are you having trouble with your key?" asked Madeleine. When the old man did not answer, she continued: "Perhaps you are holding the key upside down. I've done that myself. Or maybe you are using the wrong key. That's a mistake just as easy to make. Why, I've even tried to unlock the wrong door in instances like this, when the light is so poor and all the doors are so similar in appearance."

Still ignoring her, the old man shuffled to the next door and fiddled with his key as before. Madeleine looked on in sympathetic silence. At last the old man spoke. "I don't know who you are or what you want, miss, but we people here have no time for gabbing in the halls. We frown on gossip and chatter because they always lead to troubles. Our motto is: stay in your room and make sure the door is locked and don't open it if anyone knocks. There are murders and muggings in this neighbourhood, also."

The old man scurried sideways to the next door and recommenced his efforts. "You look like nobody's daughter, either," he called back to her. "At night we call and cry for our lost children, but we don't cry for you."

A gust of cold, damp air rushed down the hallway, as though a door to a dungeon had opened. Madeleine leaned against the wall and lit a cigarette. Although the old man had disappeared into the shadows, she could still hear the rattle of doorknobs and keys.

"What a droll character," thought Madeleine as she walked slowly back to her room. "I know I should feel discouraged after such an episode, but I don't." A whisper of the old feeling brushed against her, like the feathered wing of a bird flying south.

"Is anything the matter?" asked the tall slim girl who was standing at attention by Madeleine's door. She was the Pre-Raphaelite type, and her pale face gleamed in the darkness.

Madeleine's heart turned over with the force of excitement and fear. "Nothing," she replied, "except that I have had a strange adventure which I do not fully understand. Have you been waiting for me here?"

"Yes," said the dark-haired girl in the kind of very soft voice which can be an annoying strain to hear even when your ears are especially sharp. "My name is Ingrid and you are Madeleine. I'm your neighbour from upstairs. I once had a doll named Madeleine, but I gave it away because it made me feel too worried. I felt responsible for the thing. You should move to a higher floor where there's more hot water and fewer bugs. I never dared dream you would resemble Napoleon so distinctly."

Madeleine chose to believe this a compliment offered in the pure spirit of friendship. "Thank you. I thought he had dark hair. Marlon Brando was such a handsome Napoleon, wasn't he? But let me make one thing perfectly clear: I will never move from my room. Cockroaches be damned! My roots are planted and nothing can dig them out. Really, I feel quite passionate about my home."

Ingrid bit nervously at her fingernails but, unlike most people, made no attempt to conceal her vice. Her black slacks were obviously made at home and in a hurry—they had crooked seams, loose threads and were somewhat too tight. "I meant that if Napoleon were a woman with long blonde hair alive today, then he would look exactly like you. I think Napoleon was really God, only French."

"Thank you again. Of course," continued Madeleine, "I don't believe in worshipping movie stars, never mind world leaders. What kind of care did your Napoleon take of his men? Is leading innocent youths to frozen death in Russian winters an act of love? But let us step inside my little home. We can chit-chat more comfortably there."

Ingrid looked away from Madeleine and down the hallway, as though she could see something there. Madeleine glanced at the empty darkness into which her new friend was gazing and quickly became irritated. She felt that Ingrid was practising wiles. "Short men aren't my type," she said. "I make them buy me meals and drinks."

Ingrid turned bewildered eyes to Madeleine. "Every night I have to work at the Dollar-A-Dance place to pay for the university classes I attend during the day. I should be waltzing around in the arms of an old man this very moment while he tells me the colour of his dead wife's eyes." Again she turned away.

Madeleine roughly opened the door of her room and snapped on the light. "Hurry up. Are you coming in or not?"

"I can clean this place up for you, if you want," Ingrid offered immediately, her eyes brightening as they darted from the dust to the carelessly unpacked bags. "Please don't think I'm criticizing. Your concerns must fly far above the daily grimes. Do you enjoy a cup of tea in bed at morning? Say at roughly ten A.M.? Lemon or milk?"

Madeleine noticed a pleading look on her new companion's face. "Wouldn't it be too much trouble? Now tell me the truth. We know each other too well not to be frank."

"No, no," exclaimed Ingrid with excitement. "No trouble at all. I have a handy electric kettle that boils water very quickly. In fact, it would be an honour."

"Surely, though, you have your own star to follow, so to speak," suggested Madeleine generously, while a greedy light shone in her eyes.

"I live by the stars. Will you permit me to tell you your fortune? I'll guarantee in advance that it will be a wonderful one. I've already sensed a good deal. For example, I bet you speak French."

"You're right," admitted Madeleine. "I used to speak them all, German and Spanish included. Still could if I cared for it. But I don't, they make everything sound like a lie. Fancy talk and Frenchisms, that's not my style. Keep your Paris."

"I agree with you a million per cent. Excuse me." Ingrid executed a clumsy pirouette, then left the room.

She smiled shyly upon her return a few minutes later with assorted disinfectants and cleaning products over-flowing from her arms. "I can't talk while I'm working," she apologized to Madeleine, who lay upon the bed with a bemused expression playing across her face.

Once Ingrid had straightened the room, she began to scrub and scour with an alarming fierceness. The harder she worked the dirtier the room appeared, as is often the case when years of settled grime is tampered with. The extreme tightness of Ingrid's clothing added to the difficulty of the task. Very quickly her pretty curls were stuck with sweat upon her forehead, and her face grew flushed around eyes that drowned in pools of panic.

Madeleine stuffed a hand in her mouth to contain her laughter. Controlling herself, she waved a languid arm. "Pray sit down. You may finish that at some later date. Now I would like to hear something of your life."

Ingrid remained standing in such a way as to suggest that further orders were expected or a general's inspec-tion was imminent. "Napoleon could read French with one eye and German with the other. At the same time," she faltered, staring fixedly at Madeleine. "I sit in class all day long waiting for the part about Napoleon. But the professor goes backwards instead of forwards. We began with the Spanish Inquisition and now we're at Cro-Magnon man. Where's Napoleon in that? Are we supposed to read the texts from back to front, like the Chinese do? Napoleon could do that too."

"That isn't what I meant," said Madeleine unsympa-thetically. "What is your favourite colour and who is your favourite movie star? That kind of thing."

"I only go to school because I'm so lonely," said Ingrid.

"Yes, yes. I know all about history. Wars and treaties, et cetera. I would help you with your work but for the fact that I have only recently discovered my own calling in life. It's something in the line of—well, I'm not really at liberty to discuss it at present. At any rate, it will occupy all my hours and then some." With extremely diligent motions, Madeleine began to sharpen a number of pencils with a small device made for that purpose. It was fashioned in the shape of a frog, from whose mouth shavings of wood spat rudely upon the floor.

Ingrid stood with locked knees and spoke in a singsong voice. "It gives me such a funny feeling. The wallpaper is dark and faded, and the floor is shiny with wax. The room is too big, making the chairs and couches pushed together at one end look lost. The music echoes. We crowd around the bathroom mirror, applying make-up and spraying perfume and arranging dresses. Girls poke with elbows and pinch with sharp fingernails to get the best places before the glass. Then Mrs Reid comes to look us over. No pants or tipping or booze, she warns every night as if she's never said it a million times before. You can smell the coffee turning thick and black, heating up the air. My girls are nice girls, says Mrs Reid remindfully while we whisper and giggle around the sink that's stained yellow. Then she opens the door at nine P.M. sharp."

Ignoring Ingrid's recitation, Madeleine began to hum quite loudly while she sharpened her pencils.

Ingrid dreamily addressed the wall: "They rush in like it's a race with a million-dollar prize for the winner. It's a private club, they're regulars, you know their faces. All the old men. The quick, smart girls grab up the promising ones. I get the retired salesmen who've come out west to die away from the cold. I know they've been sitting in their rooms all day, preparing for

the Dollar-A-Dance Club. Polishing their old shoes,
ironing their shiny suits. Watching the clock. In the old
days things were made to last, they tell me as we turn
around and around to the music. Reid plays the same
songs in the same order every night; if she didn't, the
men would complain. I'm always afraid they'll fall on
the slippery floor and break bones too brittle to mend.
So I hold them tight, they start to breathe a little anxiously. Let's sit this one out, I say.

"We balance on the edge of a couch, you have to or
you fall into the hollow where it sags. The springs are
broken. We drink coffee from paper cups while he talks
about his dead wife and his wars. Look at this, he says
and gives me a yellow photo of a girl in an old-fashioned dress squinting at some sun. I look at her a long
time, to see if she resembles me. Then I turn to see him
staring at the other girls. We watch together. Their
smooth faces are always laughing at the old men they
pull around the room like balls and chains. When they
get bored the girls play tricks, like dancing so fast the
men huff and puff until they fall wheezing onto a chair,
their faces gone all grey. Suddenly Reid pokes me in the
back and hisses: 'Having fun, lovebirds?'"

Madeleine stopped her humming and pencil sharpening to interrupt. "This doesn't sound like you at all,
Ingrid. Surely you of all people must know that
Napoleon didn't let old men into his army. Mr
Napoleon was far too busy to think a second about old
men, never mind lead them or look after them. It's history."

"That's just it," said Ingrid slowly. "I can't understand
why I have such powerful thoughts about Napoleon
while I'm at the Dollar-A-Dance. All the time."

"Speaking of time," said Madeleine, "I haven't slept
for ten years and urgently require some rest. Run off
and dance your heart out. This has been most enjoy-
able." She pushed Ingrid toward the door.

"I know you have important matters to attend to,"

said Ingrid. "I'll be back tomorrow with your tea.
Sugared or plain?" She hovered wistfully in the doorway and demonstrated the coded knock by which
Madeleine could know that a friend and not a foe had
come to call. Then she was gone.

"It's so close," thought Madeleine as she rearranged
her golden hair upon the pillow. "I must not let these little setbacks discourage me." For some reason her encounter with Ingrid had disappointed her more than
those with the little black girl, the desk clerk, or the man
in the hall.

Madeleine turned off the light and worked on her
memory exercises, as she was accustomed to do for one
hour prior to sleep. The purpose of the procedure was to
recall random pieces of the past and extract any little
lessons that might lie in them, thus preparing for a more
perfect future. By forcibly training her mind in this direction, Madeleine hoped to conquer an evil habit; that
was automatically falling into a state of hopeless, unanswerable prayer the moment she found herself alone in
the dark. The difficulty of the exercise rose out of her inability to recall any but the choicest pieces of the past,
while knowing full well that in her case the sour had
outseasoned the sweet by far. "My life has certainly not
been all days of wine and roses," she murmured
drowsily and cast her mind back into the darkness
where tough, hard nuts of nights waited for their morals
to be chewed from them. As usual, however, her mind
just naturally skipped forward to the come-what-may,
that delicious darkness where endless courses of
savoury suppers were waiting for her to dig in. Dressed
in a spotless white shirt and a well-fitting suit, God
would stand discreetly by her left shoulder, keeping her
plate piled high.

■■ Frankly Speaking

As usual Frank woke to find he'd been clutching his pillow so tight in the night that his arms ached like hell. He opened one eye and looked suspiciously around the bare bedroom of his apartment before opening the other. "Bed's too damned wide," he thought and threw the pillow across the room, where it fell to the floor with a grunt. It was the middle of the afternoon, it was time to get up. No rest for the wicked.

A year ago Frank had hired a young guy to open and tend the bar during the first few hours of afternoon, so he could catch a little more sleep. There wasn't much business then, only a few regulars who'd still be drooping on their stools come closing time. For ten years Frank had dreamed of sleeping until he was finally good and rested and ready to bear the weight of the world on his back. But he found he didn't enjoy the extra hours in bed like he thought he would. Didn't feel any better for them. "Guess I'm just used to being tired," he thought, rubbing his eyes with a fist.

He opened a beer from the fridge and went into the bathroom to shave. Glancing into the mirror, he grimaced—then wiped the glass clearer before slapping water and smoothing cream on his grey skin. This was the best part of his day. Quiet, peaceful, no one around. He got to thinking, things kind of stretched way back to when he'd sit on the edge of the tub and watch his daddy shave. "Your time will come," Frank's father always promised. "You just wait and it'll come."

Maybe it had. His own man, his own boss, his own bar. The days and nights were pretty much the same, but there was always some little thing to puzzle over until it wasn't so little any more. Not much of a personal or home life, though. His apartment was OK but he'd done hardly a thing to fix it up; he didn't spend much time here, it wasn't important. The Shanghai was

important. It was his. It told strangers straight away and
plainly what kind of man he was, what he believed in.
On the face of it neither the customers nor the bar was
anything much. Nothing fancy, kind of shabby and dim
and sad. Yet it felt right that way, he wouldn't turn the
bar into some shiny, slick place you couldn't get a grip
on especially if your grip was none too strong to start
with. ("Get a grip on it," Frank would say to some
chump crying at his counter, then he'd pour the fellow a
shot of something on the house.) "Sure," Frank liked to
say, "I run a bar and a hotel and a clinic and a church.
Jack of all trades, master of none. That's me."

From the age of eighteen to thirty-five Frank had kept
bar for other men. Did a good job, never missed a night
of work, always set some money aside. When it came
time to move out on his own, he'd looked around and
thought things over quite a bit before finally starting up
the Shanghai. His friends and business acquaintances
advised against the location. He had enough to afford
something better in the main shopping part of town just
a few blocks east. But he felt it was the right thing to do
to start up on that beat-up block. He didn't know exactly why. Seemed like there was more of a need there.
A need for booze or for something else? Well, every man
can only do what he can and maybe that's not enough.
It was pretty plain that his friends thought he didn't
know what the hell he was doing. During the first few
years Frank was putting in a lot of hours getting the
place on its feet, and there wasn't much chance to see
the old crowd then. "Stop in for one or two sometime,"
he'd say when he ran into this guy or that guy on the
street. But they never did come into the Shanghai and
now they walked past Frank like he was some kind of
stranger. Which he guessed he was. A stranger to them
and to himself both.

Frank pulled the razor across the mask of white lather
on his face, making paths and patches of clear skin.
Often he was unaware of the motions his hands were

making or it was like he was watching someone else, such as his daddy, shave—until he cut himself and swore out loud. There were days when he'd look in surprise to find the job all done and to see his own features laying there before his eyes like countryside that had been hidden beneath deep snow all winter long, emerging at springtime as something forgotten yet familiar both at once.

It was springtime again. A season for change. Sometimes Frank paused before a store on his way to work and looked into the window. "What do I need?" he asked himself. "What do I want? There must be something missing. What?" he didn't need anything for the apartment, he was happy with his clothes, the Shanghai was fine as it was. A contented man? It looked that way. Now and then he'd talk about taking some time off work. Going away on a holiday like other people did. Some island in the sun somewhere. Never had been out of the country—hardly left the city, come to think of it. He'd stop by a travel agency and pick up a handful of brochures printed on shiny coloured paper. Tahiti, China, Finland: a million places. Customers at the bar would have their various ideas of where he should go; they all knew what was best for him. He listened and he thought, then after a while he found himself sticking the pamphlets behind the cash register. "Guess I'm staying right here," he'd tell himself, throwing them out a month or two later. "Guess the world would fall apart if I went away for a week."

A good woman, maybe. Someone to care for who would care for him back. Dammit, he was forty-five, the bed was wide, it was way past time. And a couple of kids to follow him around and ask him questions he couldn't answer. "Your time will come," he'd tell the boy who sat on the edge of the tub and watched him shave. The Shanghai was no gold-mine, but he didn't know any way of living except quietly and there was money in the bank, more each year. Soon he'd find

himself wandering the streets and giving it away to
strangers. Begging beggars to take it. "Help me out,"
he'd plead.

Frank took a step back from the mirror. He was
strong. Strong arms, strong back, strong shoulders.
Strong enough to take care of someone else? His face
was half lathered and half clear, neither one nor the
other. Two minds. He'd known a few good women in
his time; it had been kind of nice and kind of strange,
how the rest of the world fell away like it had never
been there in the first place. Something happened to end
each of those good times, though for the life of him he
couldn't figure out what. All he knew was that he was
alone once more and that the world came creeping back
through the door like a cat you've kicked out into the
cold. Now there was always some baby at the bar asking him when he got off work, waiting around while he
tried to close up. Yet most nights he took care of the
cash, locked the door, walked home alone through the
streets quiet and nearly empty at three A.M. Foghorns
calling from the bay. The pleasure of cool clear air after
the smoky din inside the bar. On the odd night Fingers,
his piano player, came back to Frank's place for a drink
or two. They rolled the dice and once in a while one of
them said something the other just let hang in the air
until it passed away on its own. Like last night. Frank
touched his forehead, winced, reached for the beer. The
hair that choked the dog's throat.

He pointed the razor at his reflection like a teacher in
a classroom. The thing was he couldn't think of taking
anyone on. When he left the bar each night there was a
weight upon his shoulders heavier than a sack of cement. Waking up, he felt it still there. Frank threw back
his shoulders, shrugged them. Yeah, it was there all
right. What? The people who came into the bar. That
was it. He'd tell himself it was just a business, not the
best one in the world but something he was comfortable
with. Of course he shot the breeze with his regulars,

knew their names, the stories of their lives. Their troubles. He had no choice; they talked. They came in, sat down, and before he could pour their first double J & B on ice they were off and running. Their man had left them, their woman was sneaking around behind their back. They'd just lost their job or a bundle at the races or their last hope on earth. A million things went wrong in the world every day and Frank heard about every one of them.

Right from the start he'd made a rule about not socializing with his customers while off duty. Sure, most of the time he was working anyway, and it hadn't really happened that he was ever asked to come along for a cup of coffee or a drink or to the movies. Still, he had this rule and he meant to stick by it. His bar was not his life. What was his life? Shaving, that was it. Almost forgot there for a minute.

"Who're you trying to kid?" he accused the sleepy face in the mirror. The truth of it was that most every night he came home alone, poured himself a drink, turned off the lights, and sat over in the big easy chair. Then he turned over in his head the characters he saw every night. Played them like a deck of cards, their faces clear as photographs. All the kings and queens and jokers. Cheating each other, trumping each other. Trying and failing to win every hand. Solitaire was the name of the game he played, yet it wasn't lonely. There were faces near to him in the dark.

Like Billy The Bettor with his lottery tickets and racing forms he went without eating to buy, always counting the number of steps it took to cross a room or the number of people he passed on a block, always searching for the lucky number. He'd die the day he found it, there'd be nothing left to live for. A girl named April with a mean scar running clear down one side of her face; every two minutes she was taking a compact from her purse and patting more powder on the mark, as if that helped one bit. Some guy named Lenny who still went over and over the day his wife had run off with a piano tuner seven years ago—what he'd had for breakfast, if the sun had shone, how the traffic had been on the bridge that day—hitting and hitting the same few notes like some day his life would get back on pitch that way. Mary-Jane, kind of a quiet girl, didn't say one word all night, just stared at the same person from opening till closing, you felt something burning your face like acid. The next night she stared at someone else—but was it with hatred or longing or love? Who could tell? Who could tell with any of them? And there were dozens of them. It seemed they were anxious to give away their secrets yet frightened to let them go at the same time. Sometimes Frank would close his eyes a moment as he stood behind the counter. He looked down on the city as though he were up in a helicopter, and below him were a million ants scurrying from their little holes and moving toward the Shanghai from all directions. There were faces he'd seen only once and never again. Those faces were as clear as any of them.

Frank sighed, rubbed fresh lather on his face, and began to shave again. He was just another of those ants himself, wasn't he? Yet there was something about some people that made others think they could trust them. Tell them everything. Maybe it was how some guy looked kind of quiet yet also alert. Interested in what was around him but not too curious about what wasn't his business. Something in how he stood? The arrangement of the features on his face? Eyes that looked like they could understand? Pools large and deep enough to contain secrets, confessions, fears? "And pools that are also bloodshot," Frank frowned, seeing the irritated streams running into the corners of his eyes.

Some of them interested him more than others. Take that black lady who called herself Sister Mary. She was getting old, her hair was turning grey. Looked tired but also like she still had some fight left in her. She dragged around a kid's wagon with an old apple box fixed on it.

The crate was covered with a piece of shiny red cloth, and perched on top of the whole rig was a cross made from cardboard wrapped up in silver foil. Sister Mary went up and down the sidewalks of the neighbourhood with this thing, parking it on the corners and preaching to the loafers and homeboys and beggars gathered around. "The Lord! The Light! The Overflowing Cup!" she cried. Or she beat on a tambourine and sang about no more crime in our lifetime, she hollered about some place called Zimbabwe. Sometimes she rolled on into the Shanghai. The first few times Frank feared she'd cause a scene, disturb his patrons with some spiel about The Spirit while they were drinking to forget that kind of thing. But all Sister Mary did was come over to the counter and ask for a glass of water. "Spreading The Word is thirsty work," she'd say, taking a refill. Then she'd roll away. What did she do at night? She was never on the street past sunset. Did she sit in some small ugly room with loud angry noises coming through the thin walls? Did she close her eyes, bow her head, press her hands over her ears and think about the new dawn coming?

When he turned over these various characters like cards, Frank didn't hope that if he kept playing long enough they'd somehow turn out different—happier, stronger, richer. That wasn't winning to his mind. All he hoped was that maybe the cards would fall into a pattern they'd never known before. Jokers would still be jokers but they'd turn up in places that were right for them. Where they felt peace. Where they fit. Where they belonged.

Frank shaved more quickly the second time. This joker had to get a move on. Dressed and out the door and down the street to where he belonged. He'd have lunch in a café, reading the newspaper while he ate. Tip the waitress, pay the bill, move off toward the Shanghai. There he'd pause in the doorway a minute to squint at the darkness until he could see what it contained. The

slow-motion sippers of afternoon. Fingers waking up
with a cup of coffee over by the pinball machine. The
new guy, Steve, behind the counter. Frank would talk
with Steve while the man got ready to go home. How
business had been, whether things had run rough or
smooth. Then he was alone behind the counter, straightening bottles, checking the beer fridges, making out his
stock-sheets. Letting the place settle in on him slow. The
dimness, the clink of ice in glasses, the faces like faded
moons in the night. Soon he'd be a part of the place, so
that anyone who walked in the door felt Frank had been
there all his life. Was born there, would die there.

Suddenly he thought about the girl who'd taken to
coming into the Shanghai pretty steady these last few
weeks. New in town, he guessed—though she tried to
act like she'd been around forever, chatting up all the
old stand-bys like they were her friends from way back
when. Funny girl, he didn't know her name yet. She had
a way of looking at him slyly out of the corner of her
eye while ordering her triple Johnny Black on ice. Like
she knew he was onto her act or like they had some secret, silent understanding. Hell, understanding was the
last thing he had. What do you make of a girl who
speaks now in a high little-girl voice, now in a fancy
way no one can make head or tail out of, now in the
most rough and low and weary drawl? One minute
she's dancing around the place like someone audition-
ing for a Hollywood talent scout, then before you know
it she's sprawled on the counter and about to slouch
herself off the world. Always slipping in and out of
roles, nervous that none of them fit, forgetting who or
what she's supposed to be. Fresh from the country or an
old survivor of the street? Frightened or friendly or
fancy-free? Frank had the idea that if anyone touched
her, just a warm hand on the shoulder, she'd scream out
like a ghost had kissed her in the dark. A good looker,
too. Young and blonde. But not that young, Frank bet.
And breaking up pretty bad and fast by the look of

things. The kind that carries on until one day before you know it they can't carry on another second. They fall apart on you. You see them shuffling along the sidewalk with a sort of surprised expression on their face, as though unable to believe that this has happened not to someone across the bar but to them. Not sometime later, but now.

Hell. The final thing—the thing that crouched in the corner of the bedroom when he searched for sleep at dawn—was that none of them really knew him or cared to know him when you got right down to it. "How's things, Frank?" they asked, sliding onto their stool. Before he could answer they were off to the races about that son of a bitch of a landlord who threatened to throw them into the street on their ear. What would he answer if they let him, anyway? Things are OK. About the same as usual. The answer wasn't the point. The deal was that though they went on about how he was their very favourite bartender, their best buddy, the only one who really cared—why, they wouldn't know him if they bumped right into him on the street. "We're all the same to them," thought Frank, drying his cleaned face on the towel. Every bartender and desk clerk and waiter. All the same face, the same voice. We're the ones who watch. Part of the background scenery, along with the neon and the rainy streets and the lonesome lamp-poles on the corners. Props on the stage they stumble over while always looking and never finding. Something to grab onto to keep themselves from falling into the gutter. That's all.

That's a lot. There was Harry, the bar-keep over at the Starlite Lounge. Joe, who clerked up at the Holiday Hotel. Sam at the Hollywood Palace. Funny how he hardly knew any of them except as a familiar face to nod to while he waited for a light to change from red to green. How what they had in common kept them apart: the secrets they were given to hold onto and to protect. Frank wouldn't mind talking with Harry or Sam or Joe;

maybe they could help him figure things out. Understand everything or at least something. They were good boys, all of them. Good at their work because they cared about it. Proud of doing a decent, honest job. And that was to take care of the broken-down winners on these streets. "That's what we're here for," said Frank, looking evenly into his own eyes.

■■■ Mythical Beings and
Several Mere Mortals

■■■ i

"Where are you going?" asked Ingrid.

Several short weeks had passed, and already Madeleine's life was rich and full. Any fool could see that. She smoked more cigarettes and drank more bottles of liquor than anyone, to begin with. Children walking on stilts had less elevated spirits than Madeleine; kite-flyers would have let their strings go in a second if they were given half a chance to be like her. But they weren't.

"The Shanghai Saloon, the Hollywood Palace, the Starlite Lounge. And the corner," murmured Madeleine.

"The corner of what?" asked Ingrid.

The two young women sat before Madeleine's mirror while Ingrid helped her friend ready herself for the street. These preparations were especially painstaking because Madeleine felt that the much anticipated breakthrough in her work would occur on this very day. While Ingrid brushed the long blonde hair, Madeleine gazed into the glass and addressed the shadow that wavered there. "They're waiting for me on the corner," she said.

"They? Who are they?"

Suddenly Madeleine laughed. "I saw you on Sixth Street yesterday. Why do you walk with your legs so stiff and your eyes stuck to the ground? You looked quite comical." She picked up her red vinyl purse and walked out into the hallway.

"I feel so far from home," explained Ingrid.

The two girls looked down the dark hall. At the end an old woman was sprawled on the first step below the landing in such a way that anyone wishing to use the staircase had to squeeze painfully past her. She sat there day and night, knitting pale blue wool with two long sharp needles and violently cursing everyone who rose and descended around her. No one ever saw her sleep and she made no visible progress with her handiwork, perhaps secretly tearing out as many stitches as she put together. "If we only knew why she hated us so," bemoaned Ingrid.

"Let her serve her penance for her crimes," Madeleine said matter of factly. With more emotion she asked Ingrid, "Will you still be here when I return?"

"Where would I go?" Ingrid walked toward the other end of the hall, where another flight of stairs led to the upper floors of the hotel.

Madeleine called after her. "I'm meeting this fellow who has a car. We're going to drive along a freeway fast and you'd only feel scared. You'd best stay inside. Don't you remember what happened the last time?" Sometimes Madeleine really did ride with racing-car drivers, but only on days when she wasn't feeling brave.

"Outside means the opposite of inside, after all," she thought, descending the stairs. "One thing and one thing make two things, not one. Mathematics can explain anything."

At the hotel's entrance Madeleine paused until her eyes adjusted to the bright, slanted sunlight. For a moment she looked happily surprised, as though she had just remembered that this was her day to ride up to the moon. Springtime filled her eyes, colours fell across the pavement, the world commenced to spin round and round. Then Madeleine's mouth tightened. The blocks falling sharply before her had recently brought her considerable joy; she had passed her first weeks in the city on them, to the exclusion of other locations. Yet now the sight made her heart tumble down the slope to land bruised and battered at the bottom, and there seemed no choice but to traverse this path of pain if she wished to retrieve that very essential organ.

The street was filled with tourists who thronged around trash restaurants and souvenir stores. Seeing Madeleine, they ran up and danced around her. Some mistook her for a movie star attempting incognito and pointed at the red polka-dotted dress and fancy heels which comprised her outside costume; others shoved maps in her face and demanded directions. They pushed around her, arms laden with Kodaks and popcorn and babies, each desiring to do and to see the most, feeling Madeleine to be a tourist attraction that should not be missed.

Madeleine, in no mood to lead parades, jabbed the tourists with her elbows and stepped neatly through them. They were the least of her worries—here today, gone tomorrow, using up places as quickly as cigarettes, five minutes of pleasure and nothing left behind but a trail of ash. What concerned her and distressed her were those who made this street their home seven days a week and with whom she could no longer linger. They felt they were the soil from which Madeleine was nourished, despite the fact that there was nothing but cement as far as the eye could see. This place of recent shelter now looked like a crazy kindergarten from which she had graduated long ago. Madeleine put on dark glasses that might allow her to slip along without seeing too clearly those who played games in which she could no longer join. She stared straight ahead and tried not to listen to the ones who stood motionless in the swirling crowd, watching her and calling her name. That she could have chosen a different route of descent, thus avoiding what was becoming a daily trial, was not quite the point.

She couldn't help but see them. There was the old woman who worked a little ventriloquist act on the sidewalk in front of Woolworths, and she called out to Madeleine in a croaky song accompanied by a shuffling dance. There was the man who operated a flower stand across the street, also a friend to Madeleine; he held out a daisy he wanted her to fix in her hair. There were the gents in oversized suits who always gave to her the dimes they begged from others. There was the man who sold sweet buttered corn, the one who painted water-colours on the sidewalk, the juggler and the blind man and all the others who waited for her to appear before their eyes every afternoon at four o'clock. There they were, and she passed them by, feeling the gaping wound where once her heart had beat a full, rich song of these friends. She remembered how they had shared with her their cigarettes and time, and how she had run from one of them to the other, making jokes and playing games and helping with each little business, until all the work was done and the night was long fallen. She had stayed with them, sitting on the curb, resting their heads upon her shoulders, even when the cries of night had begun, those calls from all across the city that waited to be answered, that finally told her she could remain with her old friends no more.

Now a brown-skinned woman dressed in black ran through the crowd with heavy steps and reached for Madeleine's hands. Sister Mary's grip was warm and steady and strong. Often Madeleine had helped the missionary push her little portable pulpit up or down the block, according to the need for The Word.

"Where you going so fast you can't say hello to your own people?" Sister Mary asked sadly. "They all say for me to speak to you 'cause they all troubled. They waiting for you all day and then you walk right on by. It ain't Christian. And I don't hardly speak of myself, who prays for you every night before sleeping."

"You of all people should understand, Sister Mary, because you too have work that takes you far from all you know and love. You go where you are needed and so do I."

"All souls need the same, these folks just as much as Chinese folks." Sister Mary reached out and brushed the hair away from the girl's eyes; then she held Madeleine's chin and made the girl meet her own un-flinching gaze.

"I can't stay here, Sister Mary, but not because I don't want to. After all, a pilgrimage is somewhat more diffi-cult than a Hawaiian holiday." Wrenching away from Sister Mary and her sad dark eyes, Madeleine felt her heart pinched by some cold hard instrument, such as a pair of pliers.

At once she perked up. She remembered all that waited before her in the area located several blocks far-ther west, known for its particularly raw and carnivo-rous character. Searchers stood in doorways there, when not sleeping on the sidewalk. All who were strangers to the expansive life feared these blocks because of the vio-lent and holy acts which occurred upon them, witnessed yet unseen; furthermore, the locale and its inhabitants were called by wicked, evil names.

Madeleine proceeded along, protected within the ar-mour of her dream, and even those with crank-crazed eyes saw her light shining as clearly as a spotlight on an empty stage. It was there in The Tenderloin that they, the only they that mattered, waited for Madeleine as well as for summer to arrive. She saw in her mind how they would be waiting with loose, empty hands and asking eyes. This thought caused her to feel oppressed, so she began to skip along to induce a sense of exalta-tion. When this ruse failed, she wandered from arcades and cafés to bowling alleys and bars, delaying briefly the moment for which she longed.

If it seemed that everyone in the streets already knew Madeleine, this was possibly because she journeyed tirelessly through them day and night, placing no limits upon the scope of her activities; also, she had years ago decided that shyness was a luxury that she could not quite afford. She was unlike other outside people who feared that the one place they knew best would vanish or change its features the moment they strayed too far away. Madeleine had a trick way of strolling hither and thither, looking in windows and conversing with strangers, as though all the time in the world belonged to her and all the cares to someone else. It was amusing to pretend that she was going anywhere but to her special place and—an even better joke—that when she reached the corner it would be empty. The punchline was that she knew they were waiting for her, like lungs for air. Slow Burn and The Pilot; Rita, Blue and Eddie-Jane; Frankie and Freelance and Cee. As well as assorted others.

Lighting a cigarette and skit-skatting deeper into the heart of where she wished to be, Madeleine envisioned the corner and how she had found it several days before. Hundreds of people passed the site every day without seeing its unique charms. For them it was exactly the same as any other corner: a fire hydrant, a lamp-pole, a parking meter, a phone booth, a bench. They were unaware that it was a place where magic happened—real magic dependent upon neither illusions nor tricks—and they could not perceive the lucky ring drawn around it like a snare to catch unsuspecting disbelievers; they saw only cracks in the sidewalk.

In its every aspect the corner held significance, although Madeleine did not care to articulate these points. For example, the first day: one minute she had been standing in the awkward position of a saviour without sinners; that is, leaning against a lamp-pole, painting her nails and watching people walk quickly by. Then, suddenly, a woman had pushed her into an alley and said, "What's your game, Vanilla Child? You working?"

Madeleine had wished the woman's face were not so very near her own. "I didn't enjoy those games they made me play when I was a little girl," she had replied quickly. "Hopscotch, jacks, hide-and-seek, red light-green light: they all bored me and I never tried to win. I preferred conversation then as I do now. Why don't you and I go around the corner and have a heart to heart over something cool. This time I'll treat. Also, I wish to ask you where you bought your skirt. It's elegant."

What happened next, on that first day, was a blur. The woman, whose name was Rita, had taken Madeleine to a café where they had exchanged confidences for a few minutes but no longer. Then Rita had brought her back to the corner, upon which other people had since gathered. "Check this one out," Rita had said. And ever since, Madeleine had belonged.

"How can a place with no walls, no roof, no furniture and no drapes be a home to me and, more than that, the only place where I feel safe and warm?" Madeleine had asked Ingrid only yesterday. "Safer than behind ten locked doors?"

"You don't need locks if you have nothing worth stealing," Ingrid had pointed out, looking betrayed. "This hotel is where you sleep and where you keep your clothes, not to mention where you brush your teeth. Are your roots no longer embedded here?"

"It's not so much a question of roots as it is of the sap which rises from the roots," Madeleine had begun to answer; then she stopped, realizing that despite all her excellent qualities Ingrid was incapable of understanding certain broad principles which must guide any truly spiritual quest.

As she neared the corner, Madeleine's thoughts whirled more quickly. For example, any time she met one of her co-believers away from the corner everything was altered in a way which would have dismayed someone less steadfast than herself. Once she encoun-

tered Blue and The Pilot experimenting with chance and
skill in an arcade with several boys who didn't belong.
Although Blue and The Pilot had exchanged pleas-
antries with her, the words were different than they
were on the corner; likewise, the tone in which the sylla-
bles were spoken. Perhaps there had been a secret sign
hidden behind their eyes that only she could see.
Perhaps Blue and The Pilot had not desired these
strangers to know the true nature of the bonds existing
between those who belonged together. Her soul-mates
had laughed and joked when a free game was won, and
to the naked ear and eye that was all. The harder she
looked at them, the more they had participated with the
alien youths in that kind of playing which resembles
fighting. The flashing lights and ringing bells, the black
balls clicking on cues and the tired juke-box singing—all
these things had swum around Madeleine, then pulled
at her with drowning arms of no little strength. For an
instant she had almost thought that Blue and The Pilot
had no yearning for her to rescue them. Then she felt
her mission still carved deeply by a switchblade upon
her heart.

More peculiar yet was how circumstances with Blue,
The Pilot and the others would be as ideal as ever when
they all reconnoitred on the corner later that or any afternoon. They would all be together once more, blessed
by their union; and it was as if they had always been so
inextricably woven, and would remain forever this way.

Because she saw them so clearly in her heart, the actual sight of her compatriots on the corner struck
Madeleine still; she feared double vision. Then she
rushed toward them with a cry. She began to skip
around them, as was her habit, swinging her purse and
composing songs on the spot. Usually they laughed
when she flounced about in this manner, and in doing
so encouraged her to more extreme modes of behaviour.
A slender gang of lost tourists and rat-kids often gathered to watch Madeleine pose and slouch and drape

herself around a lamp-pole or a boy—in spite of the fact
that her movements, while intended to suggest abandonment, were in reality somewhat awkward.

Unhappily, on the present afternoon Madeleine's
companions were not distracted by her little airs. She
passed around cigarettes to buy some time until inspiration should arrive. Fortunately, it came on schedule, and
she addressed the group at large: "Dearest Friends, I
know this hour of afternoon can be unsettling.
However, I have an intimation of how we might enjoy-
ably pass this time. If we proceeded to the Hollywood
Palace and attended a double feature, it would be dark
by the time we emerged from the theatre. Subsequently,
we could continue on with our quests."

Freelance and The Pilot hunched inside the phone
booth and whispered behind glass. Rita walked away.
"If I get anything, I be back," she said, but did not
sound hopeful.

Madeleine tried again. "Remember all those illumi-
nating afternoons we've had at the movies? Please recall, too, how instructive they were. The entertainment
today will be equally rewarding, if not more so; on this
you have my most sacred vow. And Sam, who owns the
Palace as we all know, is an admirer of mine. I sense that
he would let us all in free of charge if I were but to kiss
him. I don't want to, but I would for the sake of you, my
friends. Apparently Sam believes I resemble a deceased
movie star, which is half a compliment and certainly
better than none at all. You know that they always
kissed with their mouths closed, those old stars. It was
the law."

Madeleine halted and considered the boys scattered,
each one apart, among discarded cigarette butts and
slivers of broken glass. For the first time she noticed that
they looked sick and weary and very alone. As moments passed without her being acknowledged,
Madeleine became increasingly nervous. She screamed
with terrified laughter, pranced amidst the boys, sashay-

ing and spitting and flicking the hair from her eyes.
From one boy to another she danced and shook and
shimmied. She tickled Eddie-Jane and pouted secrets in
his ear; but he only shivered, shrugged one shoulder,
and turned away.

Frankie looked at Cee and said, "I'll try across South
Side, but there ain't no game left there no more."

"Games, games, I've got a surprise," sang Madeleine
in a quivering tone. "Guess."

"She ain't got nothing," said Blue. Slowly all the boys
walked away, and their dying eyes steamed like coals
fallen into the deep blue sea.

"They'll be back for me later," Madeleine thought
calmly. "When it gets dark."

■■■■■ ii

Five blocks north a woman stood every day and all day
on the crowded sidewalk before a large, expensive department store. One hand held a transistor radio to her
ear while the other, outstretched, clasped a small tin
cup. No sound carried from the radio and the cup was
always empty. The woman was middle-aged, slightly
built and dressed in shapeless, colourless clothes.

Through winter and through summer she stood motionless by the main entrance of the store. When given
an especially vigorous push, the door would hit the
woman's side; but she did not react in any way to the
blow. She held no umbrella against the rain and wore no
hat against the sun.

Despite the tin cup, the woman was unlike the pan-
handlers of the city. She did not speak to the tourists,
shoppers and office workers who passed her by, nor did
she seek their eyes with an imploring gaze. She looked
nowhere and said nothing, and she was not approached.
She had stood in this spot for longer than anyone could
remember, but not a single person knew her name or
age or place of birth, and no one knew if she were
happy or sad. Although so silent and small and

unassuming, she was noticed by all who passed her and she was a cause for wonder. Yet people quickened their step and averted their eye upon nearing the woman. They did not wish to see her or to speak with her. They feared her.

And though too frightened to give them voice, people had numerous and various thoughts about the woman. Some thought she was deaf and blind; and it seemed to them that she heard less than the deaf, saw less than the blind. To others it appeared that the woman's lips were pressed together to hold back a terrible cry that once begun would never end, but would go on and on like the cry of the sea. She knew everything that happened around her, some supposed, all things good and all things bad; but they were not certain to which use she would put this knowledge. Perhaps her stillness was the stillness of the storm's centre, perhaps her silence was the silence that precedes or follows catastrophe. It was believed that she awaited only the voice of someone known and loved and lost long ago; it was also believed that any greeting, from friend or from foe, was her worst fear. There were those who said that beneath her clothes the woman's body was covered with scars and disfigured with wounds yet bleeding. Still others suspected that she was serving a lifelong penance for a crime too appalling to imagine, for a sin too awful for words to speak. But whether this error was committed by the unknown woman or by themselves, they did not know.

Yes, every day and all day the woman stood before the department store, and she did not seem aware of the passing of time, the changing of seasons, the flowing of life. And all who passed this woman recognized in her their guilt and saw in her their shame, and they bowed their heads before her and they carried her image inside themselves as they walked away.

Then one day everything was different. Instead of the radio the woman held in one hand a sheaf of pages. The other hand hid inside a pocket. She was trembling and shaking, and everyone could see her fear. This way and that way she turned her head to look longingly and searchingly into every stranger's eyes; and her own eyes glittered and burned, as falling stars flame with lost heaven's fire. When the people saw her anxious face, they became more frightened of the woman. They crossed the street to avoid her presence and they felt a new kind of fear.

During all the morning and during part of the afternoon the woman watched the people pass. Then, all at once, she stepped forward and stopped a younger woman who was walking by. For a long time she talked to this girl in a low voice that no one else could hear. It seemed that the woman had many things which needed to be said, for she spoke quickly and fearfully, as though worried that the girl would leave before all the words were uttered. But the girl simply stared with amused or troubled eyes at the woman, while her fingers played with the single feather which adorned her pirate's hat. From time to time she seemed to nod her head in agreement with the woman's words. People paused as they stepped around the two women or they stared at them unguardedly.

Pressing the papers into the girl's hands, the unknown woman for a moment looked hard into her eyes. Then she turned and walked quickly away, and she did not look back. She never returned to her place in front of the store, and never was she seen again. No one knew where she had gone.

■■■■■ iii

Sam walked quickly down the sidewalk, so absorbed in his thoughts that he nearly bumped into other pedestrians several times. However, the owner of the Hollywood Palace did notice that blonde girl who had recently taken to attending his movie house pretty often, usually accompanied by a gang of young trouble-makers, but

sometimes alone. The girl was listening as an older
woman spoke to her. This older woman also looked familiar to Sam, though he couldn't place her. The blonde
glanced in his direction, her eyes gliding by him as they
would any stranger. He guessed she didn't recognize
him.

Sam turned into the Starlite Lounge, sat on a stool and
ordered a whisky. He knew the bartender, Harry, but
not well. In a careful, savouring way Sam lit and
smoked a cigarette. After he had stubbed it out and finished his drink, he took several folded pages from his
pocket and began to read.

Dear Mr Brodey,

*I don't know why you're asking questions about the
Farmer woman, but I'm tired of questions. You say it's
out of personal interest that you ask. What is personal
interest? If I knew anything, I might not tell you it,
but since I don't it doesn't matter, I guess. It was a
long time ago, and sometimes you can't tell what you
remember and what you dream. Or at least I can't.*

*Yes, it's true that I was working at the
Knickerbocker in 1943 when Frances Farmer was
staying there. I was making the rounds of the studios
then, but without much luck. That was the time when
a lot of girls were busing into Hollywood from everywhere, from every little dot on the map, looking for
work, for a chance, for a way out. I wasn't so different
from any of them, chambermaiding on the side to pay
the bills, waiting for my own lucky break to fall my
way.*

*What I remember about Frances Farmer mostly is
that she never left her room and that she was trouble. I
worked mornings, but I'd hear from the night girls
how there'd be screaming and carrying on in her room
when it was late. The funny thing about it was that
she would be alone in there. I guess she used to throw*

the empty bottles against the wall and scare the wits out of the people in the next room. There were complaints, sure, but what could the management do? Even if she was on the skids, she was a star, or had been, and that still meant something in that town then.

How I know about the bottles is because I was the one who cleaned her room every morning. Room 315, some things just stick in your mind. Broken glass all over the floor, sometimes she'd cut her feet on it. There she'd be, bleeding a bit, but acting like she didn't notice it. Her blonde hair falling over her face kind of wild. Maybe it was that there were too many other things she was worried about to pay her hair or feet any mind. I didn't think it was my place to offer to fix up her cuts. Especially when I got to know her a little, I knew she'd just fly off the handle if I tried to help.

So, yes, I saw the glass, but never any shouting or anything like that. I don't mean that she wasn't upset, because she was, always. Tense, nervous, scared—use any word you like, use all of them. But she was quiet, too. As soon as I came in she'd start talking, and once or twice I wondered if she'd been waiting for me. I heard that no one came to see her. There was something she wanted me to know, something she wanted to convince me of. That's what I felt, listening to her. But no shouting, there wasn't time for that, or energy. She would look tired after not sleeping all night, maybe she took pills like they said she did. I didn't look for any. But the bed was never slept in.

Half the time she talked I didn't have a clue what she was on about. Sometimes it was things from her life. Crazy stories, about the trouble she fell into down in Mexico, strange stories. Talk about people who were out to get her, the studio chiefs and the press, some pretty big politicians, the FBI. They were scared she'd tell something, expose them, I don't know. Like I say, I didn't have half a clue what she was spilling. I'd try to tell her that I had to get the room cleaned fast, there were other rooms to clean. She'd say for me to sit down and listen, put my feet up, she'd clean the room herself later. So she'd pour us both drinks and then begin talking up a storm. I must say I always felt funny sitting there and was glad to leave. I couldn't help but think who she was and wonder why she didn't have anyone else to talk to. I suppose you've seen pictures of her, so maybe you know what I mean.

Of course, I'd heard all the dirt they were dumping on her around town. You know the kind of thing I mean. But she did me no wrong. She was in some kind of deep trouble and looking for a way out. I felt sorry for her. And you know, sometimes she'd ask me questions, not like how are you and how's the weather, but about where I'd come from and what luck I was having with agents, and so on. It wasn't what she asked me that I remember so much, but more the way she asked. Like she was trying to find something out about me that she needed to know. Or I needed to know. She'd tell me to go back to where I'd come from, back home, to forget about Hollywood because it was garbage. She tried to give me the money for a bus ticket, but I couldn't take it, not when I knew how she wasn't rolling in it then.

Sometimes she'd tell stories from a book she was writing. I'd see the pages flying all over the room. I can't remember much about it. It was hard to follow and the drinks she poured were tall and strong. All I remember is that it was about a girl named Mary or Maude, some name like that, and was called God's Peculiar Care. Sometimes even now I'll be sitting up with some sewing in front of the Late Show and those words will pop into my head from nowhere. God's peculiar care.

Anyway, I came in for work the morning after they took her away. Stories were flying all around the staff room, about the cops dragging her down the hall, and her kicking and swearing and screaming and crying. Everyone was pretty excited, so I was able to run up to her room and grab up all the pages I could find. Then I beat it out of that hotel, out of that town. I guess it was stealing, but all I could think was that the last thing she'd have wanted was for them to get their hands on those pages. By "them" I mean the cops, the studio bosses, the newspapers. I never read all the pages, her handwriting was poor, and what I did read made no sense to me. I can't remember. I just wanted them to be safe.

I lost them, who knows where or when. After leaving Hollywood I didn't go back home. Instead I moved from place to place, waitressed a bit, did a few other things I want to forget, finally found myself here up north. I could have lost those pages anywhere, you lose things when you move around.

Sometimes I'd catch something in the papers about her. They were full of her for a while. It made me pretty sick, I didn't want to know, I wanted to forget. Then for a long time there was nothing, no word, and I didn't know what had happened to her, figured she was dead or something. Now I wish I didn't know. But what could I have done? There was no way I could have helped her. It was hard enough getting by myself. What did you do to help her?

But I'll tell you something. Some strange things happened later on. I got a letter from Frances Farmer, after they let her out of Hell. She said she was looking for that manuscript, she thought it had been stolen. I replied, telling her what had happened, but never heard from her again, and why should I? God knows how she found out where I was.

But she did, and so did some others, and so did you. I got a letter one day, saying how I should forget about Frances Farmer, as if I had the chance. It wasn't quite a threat, but there was a little of that to it. No return address. No name. There were other letters like that.

Remember Willa Baines, that actress who OD'd in the fifties? Well, someone wrote and told me that it was no suicide, that anyone who cared about what had happened to Frances Farmer, and why, would be interested in the Baines case because it was part of the same thing. It has nothing to do with me, I said. I said that also to a man who came to see me, wouldn't say who he was, but I'll lay odds he was a private snoop or something in that line. He tried to sniff me out about Frances Farmer, asked all kinds of questions, I couldn't figure out what he was getting at. Told him to beat it, lay off, I knew nothing.

It was nothing to do with me and it was a long time ago, anyway. Leave me alone, please. Don't write again. I've probably told you more than I intended to, more than it's your business to know. But I'm tired of the whole mess. I've worked hard all my life and now I'd like some peace to tend my garden and my broken heart, and to forget.

Irene Jordan

Sam folded the paper without making new creases in it. He stowed it in his coat pocket, looked up, and saw Harry standing with his back to him. The bartender was taking stock. He measured how much was gone from each bottle in order to know if new ones were needed. Several times he turned toward Sam and held a bottle up to the light, the better to see what was inside it. Then he wrote what he discovered on a little pad. Sam couldn't tell from Harry's expression if the bottles were nearly empty or nearly full.

Sam had known Harry for years. He saw him several times a week, either here in the Starlite or over at the Palace. The buildings were situated only a couple of blocks apart. Slipping out from the Palace for a quick drink, like now, Sam would head for the Starlite without thinking. The two men also met on Harry's nights off, when he often took in a show at the Palace. Sam knew the bartender's taste ran to romantic comedies, especially ones starring Fred MacMurray. But he knew little else about the man. A bartender with a bum leg. How had it happened? Was Harry born a cripple? Had he suffered some accident as a baby, a boy, a young man? Was his left leg really real, or was it made of wood or plastic or something else? Did it hurt him always, or was he so used to the pain that he forgot it? Sam just didn't know. Come to think of it, he knew Rita Hayworth better than he did Harry.

Sam didn't like to bother a bartender who was working; he knew what it was like trying to earn some kind of a living. So the only time the two men talked at length was when Harry came out from a show at the Palace. Then he would usually stand at the front door of the theatre and smoke a cigarette with Sam. As the customers filed out of the place and into the night, the two men would talk about the show just ended, how business was, the weather. Although Harry was a friendly guy and seemed in no hurry to rush away, he always left as soon as his cigarette was smoked. Sam often gazed after him as he walked away with a bobbing, jerky gait down the street, his hands in his pockets. He couldn't tell whether Harry was on his way home, off to somewhere else, or just strolling. Limping. After switching off the marquee and closing up the dark Palace, Sam would walk in the same direction Harry had taken. Kept his eyes open for a man with an uneven walk. Got in the habit of noticing every cripple he came across, felt amazed at the number of disabled people who stumbled through the world. Like Harry. And, sure, like himself. The only difference was that his own limp was invisible. Unseen, but the same. Six of one, one half dozen of the other. Take your pick.

Although Sam always had this feeling he and Harry would run into each other one night on this street, it had never happened. So the two men had never become

good friends, and things had gone on too long for them
to change. Sometimes things just seemed to work out
like that. Now, looking at the bartender's back, Sam
tried to imagine what Harry did at home in his apartment or wherever it was he lived. He guessed Harry
lived alone, though he had no real reason for thinking
so. But you could usually tell a thing or two about a person just by looking at him.

Like Harry's clothes. He always dressed neatly in a
suit, grey or brown, when on the street, though in the
bar he took off his jacket and worked in shirtsleeves
rolled up at the elbow. He wore the same suit when he
came to the Palace on his nights off, but with a different
coloured shirt and tie. His clothes were a little loose, so
you couldn't say exactly what size he was. Sam wondered if Harry deliberately chose them that way, or if he
just put on whatever some woman, a sister or an old
friend, picked out for him. Not a wife. Did he look out
the window as he knotted his tie or did he have to stand
in front of the mirror to make sure it was straight?

Harry handled the bottles easily and lightly, as
though they were unbreakable. He went into the back to
get some fresh ones, stopping on his way to play the
pinball machine. After the game was over he stood
looking at the pattern of lights for a moment.

Most of the people who came to the Hollywood
Palace Sam could read right off. It was easy. They were
the kind of people whose secrets had been stolen from
them by too much poverty and loneliness, people who
had long ago grown too tired to try to hide anything.
Maybe that was why they seemed ashamed. It wasn't
the kind of life they led that bothered them, but that others could see so easily into them. They'd slip by Sam at
the door when they bought their ticket, as if going to the
movies were the one private thing they had left, the last
secret they could protect. Sam would feed them lines,
trying to liven them up a bit with little jokes about Jean
Arthur's size-three shoes or with impressions of little-

known MGM contract players. But he could see that
they thought he was making fun of them.

Harry finished taking stock and limped over to the
window. He winced. His game leg was complaining,
saying it was tired; Harry shifted his weight off it. He
looked up and down the block, or perhaps only across
the street. Then he turned and looked around the bar.
The place was quiet. "Want another?" he asked Sam,
who never had more than one drink.

"No thanks. Got to get back. I've got My Man
Godfrey playing Thursday. With William Powell. He's
pretty good. You should try to stop by for it."

"Thanks. I might."

"So long."

■■■■■ iv

Sister Mary's voice was failing her as the sun went
down. She had been preaching since the middle of
morning, first on a bustling business street, then over in
the shopping district, and for the last several hours here
on the sidewalk before the sorry old Shanghai Saloon.
She leaned against her pulpit and cried out hoarsely
about The Light that would surely shine on anyone who
believed with all their heart; but there was no audience
before her to receive this message, and Sister Mary felt
despair. All day long she had been unable to draw lis-
teners, except for a while at noon when several secre-
taries had sat nearby, nibbling sandwiches from brown
paper bags in the spring sun. Now darkness drew near
in the slow sure way it does when summer is right at
hand, and Sister Mary was weary.

Some days the words soared strong and true from her
throat, and with joy Sister Mary would hear them flow
through the air, those words of belief and hope and
promise, and always then a crowd of lost lambs would
gather near to listen to this song. Then there were times
like today when her voice seemed to bounce off the
scarred brick walls and echo mockingly in her ears.

"The Light? The Spirit?" she heard a doubtful, questioning voice repeat, and this was her own voice and this
was her own doubt.

The street was nearly empty. The night owls were still
in bed and the early risers were already getting sleepy
in the bars. Only a few swingshift whores stood on the
corner, filing their fingernails and flicking their hard
eyes past Sister Mary. The sun had moved beyond the
tops of the buildings and the pavement lay in deep
shadow. "Let us hook up to the train that waits for one
and all and let us ride the glory train together," Sister
Mary urged. "Let us meet in the station named Grace
where the conductor will find room for everyone on
board." But there were no potential passengers on hand
to catch the tickets she sent spinning through the air,
and Sister Mary was tested.

In warmer times such as now the broken ones forgot
the cold that entered their bones on every winter night
passed on cardboard beds in doorways. They forgot
how they would then gather around Sister Mary as
though she were a fire and how they would stretch out
their hands to receive her warmth. And with her words
Sister Mary would console them and with her song she
would comfort them; then she would lead the needy
ones through the wet, dark streets, her pulpit rolling
along like float in a parade, and she would bring them
to the Mothers of Mercy who always had a warm bed
and a plate of hot soup for a friend of Sister Mary. She
would leave them in the Shelter, so they could eat and
sleep and thaw themselves enough to hear her words
tomorrow; but when Sister Mary returned to the Shelter
the next day, they would be gone away to wander in the
rain again, their fingers raw and their faces red and
chapped and their souls still not saved.

After the spring rains ceased it was always easier for
the homeless ones to lie in the park beneath the stars
and dream their dreams of Jupiter and Venus. Then the
cold seemed as long and far away as childhood, and

sunshine seemed the only Light needed to see an old friend's face. Sister Mary gave thanks to God's sun for easing the pain of those on which it shone. Yet this was the hard time for Sister Mary and this was when she was filled with doubt. For while she sang insistently about the shepherd who cares for his flock, the exiles from Eden swam like fish through the sunshine, floated lazily into the dim bars where they could always hook a dollar or two to set them up for Happy Hour. And then Sister Mary questioned if her preaching served a purpose and then she felt that her mission was not easy. "Hallelujah!" a suffering soul would slur, strolling by in the sun. "Praise the Lord," a broken-hearted boy would mumble from the bench where he sat basking. And this was when Sister Mary's voice would begin to fail her and when she would stare down at her pulpit, seeing where the red velvet had run in the spring rain, leaving paler streaks of pink where once this colour had been rich and strong.

And this was the season when Sister Mary wished she were two people. She dreamed that when she grew weary a fresh strong Mary could step out strongly from her shadow and call away in clear ringing tones, allowing the tired Mary to go on home to her room, take off the pinching shoes, move bare-footed across the cracked linoleum, fix some supper on the hotplate. (Warm, rich smells rising, her face bowing down toward the savoury steam, her eyes closed and a smile on her mouth.) Food, then sleep, to make her strong again and ready to take over when the second Mary grew weak and weary.

But there was only one of her and she had to be enough. Her ragged raspy voice told her it was time to stop preaching for the day, but Sister Mary could not leave her duty until she felt that at least one needy being had heard her and received her. Just one. Sometimes in the middle of her song Sister Mary would see a lost lamb throw his bottle down the curb, look up at her with cleared, brightened eyes; and she would go to her room that evening filled with The Spirit. "One by one," she would think as she lay her tired bones upon the bed. That was how it would work. One would tell another, who would tell another, and in this way a single one would swell into a multitude and their voices would be many and their song heard all across the land. A chain would grow and grow until it stretched all the way around the world, and it would weave back and forth into a net that linked every heart to every other heart, connecting them all forever in belief and hope and strength.

Then the next morning Sister Mary would see the soul she had touched the day before cradling a bottle on the curb once more, his head drooping sadly below his knees, and she would wonder if yesterday the bottle had been thrown away only because it was empty and if the eyes had brightened only at the thought of a new full bottle. And then Sister Mary would know that the world is a place of sadness and that the earth is a place of loneliness, and she would have to close her eyes to keep firm her vision of the bountiful valleys and the clear-running streams and the gardens growing green. She would wish for her voice to sound rich as rum and sweet as Southern Comfort and to fill the street until it overflowed with spirit holier than the oldest whisky. And she would open her eyes to see the angry words painted with spray upon the walls and the doped boys falling in tears upon their knees, and the doubt would rise like a lump in Sister Mary's throat and it would choke her song. And she would need to go into the sad Shanghai Saloon and ask for a glass of water.

"Don't drink to forget and don't dope yourselves to forget!" Sister Mary cried out now, bringing on a spell of coughing. "We must remember what has gone before and this memory will show us the path that lies through the forest ahead." And Sister Mary tried to remember her own life before The Light had fallen upon her five years ago and she would try to see into the darkness of

the past. Once Sister Mary had been a woman called
only Mary who looked at the TV, went to the launderette, and did some part-time cleaning when the spirit
moved her. She had lived with a sweet weak man
named Harold who left her when The Spirit suddenly
fell from a star and entered her human heart. Harold felt
jealous of Jesus even when Sister Mary told him that
now her heart was only larger and now there was room
enough in it to cherish Harold's weakness in addition to
his sweetness. But Harold had gone away and she had
never seen him moving along the avenue toward a corner where she preached, she had never seen him in his
shiny suit and favourite hat, coming back to her. Mary's
blood sister, Lucille, who knew the ways of the world
and the workings of offices, had got Mary on the
Assistance that paid for her room above the pawnshop
and for her butter and eggs and tea. Mary had sold all
her worldly goods to Fair Freddy in the store below, and
this included the banjo painted with a moon and five
stars which Harold had left her in place of alimony. She
had used the money to buy this wagon and to make it
into this pulpit, and as Sister Mary she had taken to the
streets to spread The Word six days a week during these
five long years, resting always on the seventh.

Sister Mary looked down at the silver cardboard cross
fixed upon her pulpit. It had become bent in an accident
which occurred just past noon, over on the South Side.
A messenger on a bicycle had lost his balance and come
crashing into Sister Mary out of nowhere, falling upon
her cross like a sacrifice. Mary reached out to straighten
the cross and she wondered if her mission were truly
useful and truly righteous. She had found The Light in
His own good time; God had shone upon her when she
was ready to take Him into her heart. Maybe she was in
error to try to make Him shine upon others and maybe
she should better let them find The Light on their own
appointed day. Sister Mary thought of all the millions of
words which had flowed through her throat and faded

into nothing, while the sirens still screamed and the street still strangled on its sobs and the lonely ladies of the night still wept into their pillows at break of dawn. What good was it? What did it all amount to? Sister Mary pictured the vast deserts made from endless grains of sand, and she felt fear. Soon night would come again and the city would switch on its false, blinding lights once more and in her room above Fair Freddy's Sister Mary would listen to the shouts and cries of the desperate streets below, and she would pray for strength.

"Just about done for the day?" asked the man who owned the Shanghai Saloon, approaching his doorway.

"I just done and you just starting," said Sister Mary.

"That's right," said Frank. "The changing of the guard." He stood a moment there, jingling the keys in his pockets, then stepped through his shadowed doorway.

Sister Mary stood a while longer on the sidewalk, but she could not sing and her voice was silent. This was the first day she had ever felt that all her hours on these streets had come to nothing and that she had failed. She looked before her and hoped to see into the years ahead, when better times would come for all; instead she saw that poor lost girl who went by the name of Madeleine cross the intersection, a sheaf of pages cradled like a baby in her arms, her hair flaming golden in the last light of the sun. The girl disappeared from sight and Sister Mary stood alone. She looked up at the sky, then set her shoulder against her pulpit. "Let's go on home," she said, pushing it into motion. "We all done for this day now."

■■■■ v

Weary after her long, fruitless wait for her friends on the corner, Madeleine kicked off her shoes, threw down her hat and dropped the pages she had been given. She flopped onto her bed, which elected to sag.

For several minutes Madeleine felt the immense distance separating her and the oasis. After only a few refreshments, however, her thirst was slaked and her natural spirits revived. She paced her room, addressing herself aloud as was her custom and ignoring the bangs of her overly sensitive neighbours upon the cardboard walls. "Frances Farmer. Surely this is the name of a sensible, healthy country girl rather than of a saint who suffered for us all. Where have I heard this name before?" Immediately she recalled that this was the name endlessly incanted by Sam, the owner of the Hollywood Palace and one of Madeleine's million admirers. He was attempting to enslave Madeleine to the silver screen and to induct her into the service of this very Frances Farmer. However, Madeleine balked, remaining true to her principle that supplication and popcorn do not mix. "Jesus did not go to Hollywood," she reflected.

Acting against every instinct in her mind, body, as well as heart, Madeleine picked up the pages from the floor. A strange smell, as of burnt flesh, hung over them and spread through the room. The pages were ninety-nine in number, stiff to the touch, and aged as golden as the basin beneath the dripping tap. At first Madeleine suspected that the script, here childishly scrawled and there tightly cramped, was some code, hieroglyphic or invented language. The words slanted this way and that, rose above and fell below the ruled lines; for the most part the ink was faded as a trail lost in time, yet some phrases stood out jagged and black. Madeleine deduced that quite possibly the manuscript had been written by a number of different people in various moods and at various points of history. "Chicken-scratch," she decided, summoning all her powers of linguistic interpretation upon the task at hand. The words finally trailed off into nothing, obviously before the story ended.

However, Madeleine had read more than enough. She threw the manuscript across the room in disgust and

commenced to stride up and down the small space between her bed and the window, rubbing her fists into
her eyes all the while. Suddenly she grabbed a bottle of
perfume from the little table, then sprayed scent over
herself and the pages, and into the air. "My sweet, sweet
saviour," she crooned, rocking herself back and forth.

A torn face stared at her from the mirror. Madeleine
hastily applied another thicker layer of make-up. There.
If she didn't look much like herself, at least she looked
less like someone who has finally caught a glimpse of a
long awaited god, only to see this deity appear as just
one more lost soul. Fortunately, the whisky bottle was
still more than half full. "Divine intervention," laughed
Madeleine through her tears. The first two shots she
drank quickly; the third one she nursed, along with the
frightened child inside.

In a little while it was better. There was her own face
in the mirror, there was her room that she loved, there
were all the precious things she carted from city to city
to remind herself exactly who she was. Photographs and
charms and glass jars and golden chains and . . . and
two small pictures of silver ships riding brilliant blue
waves in black velvet seas. Was that music coming from
down the hall? Yes, it was. Party music. Someone was
having a party in their room, and there was dancing and
singing, no doubt, as well as more. Much, much more.
Of course she had been invited to this party herself; but
receiving so many invitations to parties and other social
affairs each day the way she did, she could not possibly
accept every one. Just like Jesus with his disciples, she
had to pick and choose. "Oh, yes, the world seems a
rosy place when I'm inside my room," she thought,
breathing deeply. "I'm as happy as a hen. I am, I am."

Some while later Madeleine woke to find the light off
and her body upon the bed. Three times during the
night she turned on the light and looked at the pages
scattered on the floor. However, she did not reread the
words of Frances Farmer at this time, fearing eye-strain

and even blindness when at last her God stood shining before her.

■ Annemarie Across the Sea

For one week Madeleine did not appear upon the streets. From somewhere there arose a rumour that she had departed for Honolulu for an indefinite or even permanent stay; almost immediately this point of destination was challenged and that of Maui offered in its place. There were, of course, people who wondered who would go anywhere in Hawaii during summer except someone who would also take swimming lessons in order to learn how to drown.

In actuality, Madeleine spent this period of time inside her room, admitting through her doorway only Ingrid and the morning tea. "I am embarked upon a retreat from the world," were her only words to this friend. "I may be with you here in body, but in spirit I am very far away indeed. Call it a transcendental vacation, if you wish." She appeared pale and withdrawn, and her hair went uncombed and her body unbathed during this phase of inner travel. A sign of her deep commitment to the voyage was her strict abstinence from whisky, cigarettes and other sources of pleasure or relief. "The flesh is weak," she sometimes murmured, taking a sip of plain water then twisting her face in distaste. Every morning at four o'clock Joe, who manned the hotel desk during the graveyard shift, saw her slip stealthily through the lobby, returning some minutes later with a bag imprinted with the name of a nearby convenience store which remained open all night. In her room Madeleine quickly and voraciously ate various foodstuffs from this bag, afterwards carefully brushing away crumbs and all other signs of feasting.

On the seventh day Madeleine hunted through her jumble of clothing and selected several items from the bottom of the pile. After bathing at the end of the hall, she carefully clad herself in a long purple skirt, a plain white blouse, a black tie with thin strings and black velvet ballet slippers. Upon her head she arranged a black beret and upon her wrists she slid numbers of silver bands, which clinked together whenever she waved her hands. Studying her appearance thoughtfully in the mirror, the artiste made several minor adjustments to this new costume, then kicked the red polka-dotted dress, the fancy heels, and the shiny purse into a corner of her studio. Lastly, she pushed her wide assortment of cosmetics and scents to one side of the small table, clearing a space large enough to hold pens and paper. Only then did she light a cigarette and pour a drink; obviously, these were tools for labour rather than toys for pleasure.

With a deeply serious expression Madeleine sat before the desk and composed a letter to her dear friend, Annemarie, who was at present residing in Berlin.

> *Sweet Annemarie,*
>
> *It has been some little time since last we enjoyed the pleasures of our mutual company. We have both been called away. As you must know, I have made a hejira to this delightful city in order to embark upon my life's work. I have discovered that it is much more challenging to face the demons in such an ambiance as I now enjoy. Each morning I waken with the words "to work! to work!" ringing around my brain. And this, of course, is something you share so completely with me. Remember the times we sat amid candlelight and incense and toasted to fame and fortune? Recall also our vows that no obstacle would we leave unsurmounted. We were children then, I think.*

Oh, the flame that burns inside us! We, the chosen ones, must follow the mountain path that climbs high above the easy comforts of family, employment and civic responsibility. Not for us the counting of hours, the suppers at six. By nurturing and obeying the secret flame through each and every day—that is how we shall rise like cream to the top. Onward! Upward!

Of course, there are times when we wonder if the flame we serve burns for us or for our worst enemies. It is only natural that there occur moments when it seems we save others only to damn ourselves; or, worse yet, that the whole business is some ghastly joke played by a crazy puppeteer. But I am just spitting in the ocean: these fears are only to be expected and pass quickly enough. They are small and heaven is large. After all, this matter of divinity is something more than a game of darts.

Now you, my dear, are in the Old World, surrounded by the symbols of history and civilization. Surely they are signs which point straight in the direction we seek within our hearts. Do you remember the time we drank and drank, then in early morning discovered an empty shopping cart at the end of a one-way street? First I pushed while you, my heart, rode inside the Safeway buggy. Please recall how we raced and rolled through the dark sleeping streets, and how we laughed all the while. Then it was your turn to push while I rode inside. Somehow, accidentally, the buggy crashed against a curb and I flew out upon a grassy lawn. You were so worried that I was hurt, even when I told you I wasn't hurt at all. I can't remember what happened next, but I do remember so clearly how the grass felt all wet with dew. . . .

Madeleine paused and chewed contemplatively on her pen. The letter seemed unfinished, but in a way that she could not quite understand. She wished to say something more about the times Annemarie and she had passed together before the fevers had struck down her friend.

Casting her eyes around the room, Madeleine noticed the pages of Frances Farmer still scattered on the floor beside the bed, where she had dropped them a week before. She lit a match and picked up the manuscript, then brought the pages near the flame.

At once Madeleine noticed something of an unusual nature contained within the pearl of flame. A girl dressed in white was standing by the edge of a sea on a stormy night. Lightning struck the ground in a circle around the girl. Trees waved beside her, heaving in the wind. Something seemed to be falling from their branches, something white, like snow. It melted when it hit the sea. The girl in white did not seem aware of either the lightning or the snow falling all around her. She stared out at the heavy, churning waves.

"Annemarie?" asked Madeleine. She strained to see inside the flame, then whispered again. "Frances, is it you? What do you see?"

The match burned Madeleine's fingers. She shook her hand, wiping out the flame and the vision. Dropping match and manuscript, she buried her head in her arms.

A noise out in the hallway disturbed her meditations. She flung open her door to find Ingrid whispering cronishly with an older woman who immediately scuttled down the hall. "Yes?" inquired Madeleine. "What is it?" She squinted through the smoke of her cigarette at Ingrid, whose tentative stance suggested that she too was considering flight. "It's long past the time for tea in bed. That is morning and this is afternoon, two entirely different things."

"What are you doing today?" asked Ingrid, looking wonderingly at Madeleine's new costume but making no comment upon it.

"Any old thing. I have some affairs of business which require my attention, but not for some time. You may enter and sit down. Close the door, also. And please tell me who that woman was out in the hall and why she ran off the way she did."

"Her name is Sally," said Ingrid. "She heard about you and wanted to see what you looked like. She's curious about people but afraid of them, at the same time. She locks herself in her room. When you knock on her door you can hear her bumping about and talking to herself inside, but she won't open the door. When you bring the matter up later, she denies she was at home. I think I should tell you that although you do not know Sally now, and may not become intimate with her for some time, the cards have informed me that eventually she will play an important role in the unfolding of your destiny. So perhaps you should remember her name. It's not Jane and it's not Nancy. It's Sally."

"I see," replied Madeleine, then abruptly took up her letter to Annemarie and held it closely before her face.

As was her wont when not performing small services for her friend, Ingrid sat stiffly and expectantly on the rather comfortless, hard-backed chair. She gazed silently at Madeleine, who was sprawled out on her unmade bed. Ingrid intermittently pulled a fringed shawl more tightly around her shoulders and shifted in her seat.

Very soon after the two girls met, Madeleine had seen it her duty to educate her friend. "End this schoolgirlish toe-wetting and plunge into the pool of life," she instructed, and at once Ingrid had dropped her studies at the university. Then she gave up her job at the Dollar-A-Dance, also upon Madeleine's advice. "You must choose your load wisely," the latter had explained. "While I've no doubt that those old men are as pitiful as pity, it's immaculately obvious that you could carry the burden of a dozen young souls far easier than you could a single spirit weighed down by decades of sin. If he were alive today, Napoleon would be an extremely old man."

In her final week at the dancehall, Ingrid was hardly able to take two turns around the floor without feeling faint. The thought of towing an endless string of leaden weights high into an infinite, empty sky exhausted her. The elderly men, lacking the strength to drag her poundage in time to music, had ceased requesting Ingrid as their partner. She had sat in a corner, shaking in suspense of the moment when Mrs Reid would sneak up behind her, pinch her hard and hiss, "Smile, dance, life is gay." Between pinches Ingrid watched the teetering men being hurled around by the young girls, who after the dancehall closed made their partners take them out on dates, buy them dinners and dresses, and write them cheques.

Now, unless she ventured into the streets with Madeleine, Ingrid did not leave the hotel. She wandered aimlessly through its hallways for short spells and spent the rest of her time in her room with a radio of which she had grown very fond, enjoying both the AM and FM frequencies. She mentioned Napoleon and her mystic visions less often. Propped up by pillows in bed, she read movie magazines and fooled with crossword puzzles. The days were long and the nights longer still, but then that was life, wasn't it?

Presently Madeleine observed Ingrid's fixed eyes upon her and said, "You must forgive me. I am not myself today. My thoughts are only of my dear friend, Annemarie, who is the only person I respect in all the world."

"I understand," said Ingrid.

"There is more," continued Madeleine, somewhat severely. "Sometimes I worry that Annemarie will lose her way. She is less strong than I and less sure, besides."

For a moment she considered Ingrid closely, as though seeing a piece of handiwork anew. "Here," she said, filling a tumbler with a healthy dose of whisky. "Drink."

"Oh," faltered Ingrid, who was less acquainted with spirits than Madeleine. However, when her friend pushed the glass into her face, Ingrid had no recourse but to swallow. Instantly she turned paler.

Madeleine fished beneath the bed for another bottle and the opium. She filled a bowl, smoked, then handed the pipe to Ingrid. "Your turn," she said roughly.

Ingrid moaned. Even as she was still choking on the smoke, Madeleine pushed a freshened drink into her hand. "Two's more cosy than one," she spat.

Ingrid began to laugh helplessly. "I saw the funniest thing this morning. It was hysterical. Do you know the area at the back of the hotel, where the narrow hallways are always dark because someone keeps stealing the lightbulbs? Well, I was strolling there when I heard a moaning sound. A door on my left was ajar, so I glanced inside. There was a little boy, surely not more than six years old, sitting on the edge of the bed. His arms were clenched around his naked body, which itself looked as tense as iron. With closed eyes he rocked himself back and forth, moaning over and over again. *Why me, why me*, I think it was. Like a song. And do you know the funniest part? There was no one in that room other than the little boy, and I had the feeling he'd been left by himself for quite a while. Weeks." Ingrid screamed with laughter.

"Yes, that's a funny joke," agreed Madeleine, a bit peevishly. "But people like that shouldn't leave their door open. You can keep your door open if you're having a party, but not otherwise. It isn't polite. Do you know any other jokes?"

Ingrid didn't hear her. She had fallen off her chair and was crouched in a little ball on the floor, whimpering to herself.

Seeing her friend was no longer sociable, Madeleine lay back on her bed, smoking cigarettes and twisting strands of hair around her finger. Several times she glanced nervously at the manuscript pages which Ingrid had fallen upon.

Woken by fear, Ingrid crawled across the floor as though trying to make her way through a low tunnel. The wall stopped her. She propped herself against it, gazing in a kind of mute terror at Madeleine, who appeared lost in thought.

"Four o'clock!" Madeleine suddenly exclaimed. "What am I doing here, wasting my day?" As she brushed her hair and applied fresh lipstick, she said kindly, "Why don't you see if your friend Jeanette is in her room? Perhaps she is in need of company. Or maybe that Sally."

Ingrid lurched across the room and grabbed at Madeleine's hands. "Please don't leave," she cried. "Please don't go, for your sake and not for mine. I have a premonition that something terrible will happen to you if you leave the hotel this afternoon. Something that will completely ruin your life forever. You must believe me."

With some difficulty Madeleine freed her hands from Ingrid's desperate hold. An ugly, bitter smile appeared on her face. "All right," she said lightly. "I'll stay. Pour us both another drink." Madeleine lay back on the bed again, while Ingrid messily served more whisky.

The two girls drank in silence. Each time her friend's glass became dangerously empty, Ingrid leaped up to refill it. She worried that Madeleine would become bored and go out wandering the streets after all. When Ingrid had accompanied her on these walks, she had on each occasion become confused by the changes which came over Madeleine upon stepping out the hotel's door. Outside, Madeleine spoke in a different pitch and tone of voice and used phrases which Ingrid had not heard before and could not understand. She would neglect to introduce Ingrid to her friends and sometimes seemed to forget her presence entirely. What was worse, she had a habit of disappearing down alleys or through crowds, leaving Ingrid alone in various unsavoury and dangerous locations.

"You could use this empty bottle as a candle holder," Ingrid said, breaking the long silence.

"Keep it yourself. A gift from me to you. I insist,"

replied Madeleine. "I don't need them any more," she muttered, pushing the beret more firmly onto her head.

"Who is them?" asked Ingrid.

Madeleine didn't answer. She remembered the last time she had seen her corner friends. It seemed just yesterday that she was returning to the hotel with the manuscript pages feeling heavy in her hands. The words of the woman who had given them echoed around and around her ears: "Her tears are the rain, her eyes the stars, her smile the sun, her breath the wind." Suddenly, Madeleine had seen her corner friends straggling down the sidewalk toward her. They were falling in and out of one another's arms, stumbling in circles, walking backwards and forwards, and screaming high. They had seen her and they had called her name three times. "Madeleine," they called, and she looked at them in puzzlement, feeling strangely that it was someone other than herself they called. They did not stop, her corner friends, but moved together once more, laughing harder than ever. As they turned and disappeared around a corner, Madeleine had felt something twist inside her.

"I don't need them any more," she repeated.

Ingrid lay prone upon the carpet. Her pale face shone in the gloomy light of the room and her skin appeared as smooth and cold and hard as marble. Sweeping cigarettes and manuscript pages into a string bag, Madeleine stumbled over the body and from the room. "No doubt Ingrid will enjoy a peaceful sleep, then wake up refreshed and lively," she thought. "But those of us denied the release of the unconscious must seek our solace elsewhere."

■ Dark Angels and Dim Bars

Fortunately and conveniently, the Shanghai Saloon was situated just around the corner from the Holiday Hotel. It was as dark as any bar could and should be during daytime. Large paintings of hunters and fishermen adorned the walls. The patrons enjoyed looking at these, and they took pleasure also in choosing between stools in front of the counter, little tables covered with red cloth, or booths which afforded a measure of privacy. Madeleine spied a half-dozen acquaintances whom she slipped past in favour of an empty table near the back. "There is much work to be done here," she told herself, rolling up the sleeves of her white blouse and spreading pages over the table. "But first I must take something to give me the mood."

Musing and mulling, she sipped several whiskies in a contemplative style. It was with a sense of dread that she gazed down at the alarming number of sheets covered with nearly indecipherable handwriting. "I must gather together all my strengths for this task, for what else have I to hold onto in this world besides my art? All I need do is alter some of the words and tack on a happy ending to lend the story an inspirational slant." She made a fussy business of choosing the pen that would most exactly meet her needs.

In the corner of the bar a boy stood before a pinball machine, which he played with great seriousness for a long while. It was difficult to tell from his expression if he were winning or losing. Finally he appeared to run out of interest or luck or quarters, and stood idly beside the coloured lights that blinked in patterns beneath the glass. Madeleine noticed a jagged tear running down the back of his black leather jacket. Through the rip she could see his shirt, and through a hole in the shirt gleamed skin.

When he saw Madeleine spying in his direction, the boy immediately looked away. He lit a cigarette and played little games with the match. "Why, what a nervous boy," thought Madeleine in surprise. "Most boys like him aren't the nervous type." She stared fixedly at his back, but the boy's darting eyes would not meet hers.

Madeleine turned her powers of concentration upon her drink once more. Emerging from her thoughts some while later, she started with the shock of finding the boy seated at her table. What was more, he was frankly reading a page of her manuscript, or so it seemed at first. "Sometimes," began Madeleine, "my luck at games improves when I have a drink. I find, surprisingly enough, that my reflexes quicken and my concentration deepens." In a voice less shrill she added, "You look thirsty. Would you care to join me?"

The boy didn't reply, but rather continued to look at the page before him. Madeleine noticed that he wasn't actually reading it, but what disturbed her more was that he didn't even pretend to move his eyes along the lines. He had dark hair and dark eyes, and Madeleine suspected that this had something to do with it. At last he set down the page and nodded his head.

"Besides, writing is a lonely business. It makes me appreciate any company." Without a word or a smile the boy gazed over Madeleine's shoulder, a curious look in his eyes. When he neglected to thank her for the drink, Madeleine quickly said, "This book I'm writing is going to be a big one, I can tell you that much. Already I've written hundreds of pages, thrown out just as many, and that's only the beginning. This worries me because I know publishers don't really welcome long manuscripts. Things aren't as they used to be and paper is too expensive, or so they say. But what can I do except slave away from dawn to dusk, a prisoner of my art? There's no easy way to fame and fortune—Schwab's Drugstore or no Schwab's Drugstore—and that's what I'm after. I'll admit it frankly to anyone who cares to hear the truth in this deceiving world. I for one have nothing to hide. My greatest problem is this: every day I have new adventures and meet new people all so interesting that I feel compelled to include them in my work. I haven't the heart to leave them out, I'm not one of the tattooed ones who steal you away then abandon you in some strange place from which you can't find your way back home. You're alone with an empty bottle and barely half a cigarette, it's last call on Saturday night, the lights go on, and where is your pirate and where are you? I wouldn't wish that fate even on the stealing kind. Please don't think it's you I'm accusing, because it isn't. I'd tell you if it were. What do you think? I know what you're thinking: why doesn't she stay in her room and stop with all the adventuring until the job is done? I would if I could but I can't, as the fellow says. I'm called by my blood. Water runs downhill, but blood is thicker. What can I do? Give it all to the Red Cross? Blood is not tomato juice. Don't you agree? They call them Bloody Marys, but what's in a name? Nine times out of ten, people don't use their real names anyhow. A baptism is just another cocktail party and names are changed as often as socks. Who but their owners have soiled their names? Tell me that. My name is Madeleine. The bartender here is named Frank. What's your name?"

Before the boy could respond, Madeleine proceeded: "Actually, a friend of mine started the story and I'm just finishing it up for her as a personal favour. The gods were against my friend and, it's a pity, she let this cloud her vision. There's no money in clouded vision these days, so I'm adding little jokes and sayings to brighten it up somewhat. Do you know any?"

Madeleine peered into the boy's dark eyes for the answer that suddenly seemed to lurk behind them. As certain memories involving both the spirit and the flesh overcame her, the room spun sickeningly around. Madeleine looked at the still boy until the fear quieted within her.

"No," he said. His eyes were either very clear or very blank.

Madeleine showily waved her ink-stained hands so her bracelets would jingle. "Sometimes I fear I'll never be able to string the story together. Every day it changes shape. Once it was simpler and purer and closer. When I was a little girl." Madeleine's wistful tone sharpened: "Of course, I've considered chopping it up into short stories, but then stories really don't sell unless they're optioned by the studios or you're already famous. Let's say I'm infamous and leave it at that. Let's say it's a mean, tough business, selling bits and pieces of yourself to the highest bidder."

The boy's eyes clouded. "Isn't it kind of dark in here for writing?" he asked slowly.

"Well, yes, it is a little. You adjust though. That's why man is not extinct. And naturally I have friends. It goes without saying. Half the people in this bar are my friends and maybe more. They know, however, not to interrupt me while I'm working. Now and then I'll call this one or that one over to my table to share a drink and a chat. But they understand my working habits."

Madeleine paused and an uncomfortable silence grew. "He certainly is a quiet boy," she thought. Quickly she ordered more drinks. "Do you live in a house, an apartment or a hotel?" she inquired brightly, to draw him out.

The boy's hand wrapped more tightly around his glass. Shifting in his chair, he looked toward the door that led onto the street. Then he stood up.

At this moment Frank, who had been observing the scene carefully from behind his counter, made a move as if about to approach Madeleine and the boy. Then he shook his head. He'd seen the blonde go off with strangers any number of times, returning to the Shanghai the following day full of rhapsodies on this latest romantic interlude and with a black-and-blue face.

Hell, it was her business. Frank stayed behind the
counter and took another sip of his coffee. While continuing to watch the blonde intently, he also remained
aware of what was happening in the rest of the bar.

"I see I've touched a sensitive nerve," Madeleine
laughed nervously. "You must excuse me. My line of
work requires that I lose no time forming fellowships,
and sometimes I proceed roughly. Maddening
Madeleine, my mother called me. She claimed that one
hour of my company would drive any perfectly sane
person straight to Sunnybrook Farm, where they would
spend the rest of their life playing shuffleboard in the
sun without keeping score. You see, my mother viewed
my taste for conversation as a flaw rather than a talent.
We had a serious disagreement of a philosophical nature
when I was twelve years old. At that moment we both
realized that the only sensible thing would be for us to
go our separate ways, with no hard feelings on either
side. And I haven't seen her since. I don't know where
she is or even if she's still alive. Often I've imagined en-
countering her unexpectedly in a bar exactly like this.
She'll be sitting alone in the shadows across the room,
gazing at the ice floating in her drink, now and then lift-
ing the glass quickly to her mouth. She won't be glancing around the bar and therefore she won't see me.
Really, it's only on the chance of seeing her here that I
frequent this bar at all. Heavens, it's certainly not my
style."

The boy turned to leave. "Stay for one more drink,"
invited Madeleine in her most persuasive tone. "It's
early yet, too early to begin the night and too early to
end the day. Secretly, I hate this hour. Please reconsider."

She clutched the boy's sleeve. "I know what it's like to
walk around from place to place without a home. It's
hard for you to talk because everything is so unfamiliar."

As the boy pulled away, Madeleine pushed pages into
her bag and hurried after him. "Listen. You can stay

with me at the hotel until you find your feet. It won't
cost you a penny. And we can live it up when we're not
too busy doing other amusing things."

Exiting the bar with the boy, Madeleine touched him
cautiously and chattered. She tried to recall who had
told her that the angel of death can appear just as beautiful as any other angel. Something told her that this
warning had come from either a friend or an enemy—
but from which she wasn't certain.

■ Summertime When the Living Is Easy

This was the beginning of the perfect times. Madeleine
felt a new kind of peace and became a homebody. No
longer was she pulled out into the streets against her
will, no longer did she need to discover what hid
around every corner and behind every closed door. The
old days when she used to hang around the depot and
look hard into the face of every person who climbed
down from the buses seemed very far away.
"Everything I need is right here in this room," thought
Madeleine, and she traded a bottle of Jack Daniels for
the housecoat of a shut-in who lived down the hall. She
wore this faded, shapeless garment, along with fuzzy
slippers and a rag in her hair, during all the long, tran-
quil hours she spent with the boy in the hotel room.
Often she flicked a duster across various surfaces while
humming tunelessly beneath her breath.

Of course, she still left the hotel every afternoon at
four o'clock, but more from a sense of duty than anything else; she was not the type that abandons friends
the moment fortune calls. However, she did limit her
outside expeditions to a period of several hours, and
these adventures took on a more earthbound quality. All

during June she laboured at darning a certain sock of
the boy's wherever she happened to be. Wearing the
shorts, halter and sandals of any girl next door, she muttered stitches and frowned at her needle in the park, at
the corner, in the bars.

It was summertime when the living is easy, and many
of the city's inhabitants departed on well-deserved va-
cations, leaving those unable to holiday behind in the
streets as a kind of skeleton maintenance force. Every
day was long and warm and sunny, and even the most
desperate souls seemed content to relax with a can of
cold beer in the park. Sister Mary sometimes sang show
tunes instead of hymns before her pulpit, Sam showed a
series of undemanding Doris Day films which went
over very well at the Palace, and Frank kept the air conditioning turned on full force in the Shanghai Saloon.
Madeleine herself seemed scarcely aware of summertime, perhaps because she had dreamed of it with such
longing that its actual occurrence came as something of
an anticlimax. She spoke often of the coming fall and the
recently passed spring instead. "Remember when," she
would begin many sentences, recounting a minor incident of May as though it had occurred in the distant historical past.

Her associations with her corner friends and other
outside acquaintances acquired a settled, practical tone;
she seemed during this time to delight in the exchange
of plain words between one ordinary being and another.
"I'm only human," she took to saying, and kept her eye
open for items on special at the corner store. She enjoyed a very nice conversation with Frank concerning
the financial details involved in setting up and running
the Shanghai. She strongly recommended to Sister Mary
a home-remedy, made from honey and garlic and other
everyday ingredients, which would definitely soothe
the preacher's sore throats. With Sam she discussed at
length the difficulties in keeping the floor beneath his
theatre seats free of spilled popcorn and soft drinks,

offering several excellent suggestions which the Palace owner immediately put into use.

Even as she readied herself to venture outside each afternoon, Madeleine already imagined her return up the hotel stairs, arms laden with food and cigarettes and bottles. She looked into the mirror as she applied the sparing paint and shadow of a *hausfrau*, but saw only the boy on the bed behind her. There would be no need to place her key in the lock, for he would open the door and let her back in. She would unpack parcels while telling him how the summer grew hotter every day, yet she longed only for the room's cool dimness; how every stranger encountered on the street made her wish only to look into familiar eyes. Madeleine reported to the boy everything that happened in the outside world, though he never asked for such news.

In fact, he rarely left the room. It seemed he had the weariness of someone who has walked an extremely long distance without rest. "I was once like him," thought Madeleine, recalling the ancient days of her arrival in the city. Mostly the boy rested on the bed, smoking cigarettes and looking up at the ceiling with half-closed eyes. The rest of the time he slept. He had a way about him that did not allow Madeleine to ask where he had come from and what he had done there. He spoke slowly when he spoke at all, pausing between words as though his thoughts were broken up and needed to be seamed together before being uttered. When Madeleine attempted to initiate conversation, he usually closed his eyes and pretended to fall asleep. Consequently she knew very little about her partner in life.

Aware that you can learn a good deal about a person by watching him sleep, Madeleine acquired the habit of gazing at the even rise and fall of the boy's chest, of listening to the soft sound of his breathing. It seemed sometimes that by studying the way his arms and legs lay carelessly forgotten over the bed she was very close to learning the truth about him. While she observed most intently, the boy would invariably open his dark eyes, glance at her, then close his eyes again, seemingly with the single purpose of showing he knew she watched him. But he did not roll over upon his front or turn his face to the wall.

During the hour before she left the room each day, the boy seemed to become more nervous. He was then prone to pacing up and down, lighting fresh cigarettes even while others still burned in the ashtray, quickly repeating questions without waiting for answers. Madeleine wondered if he had friends in the city and if they missed his company or searched for him. She had seen him turn his head quickly, the way people do when they hear a call from far away. "We're all free as birds," she told him. "Please don't stay inside on my account. You can come exploring with me or go your own way if you prefer." When the boy replied that he would rather remain inside the room, Madeleine was secretly pleased.

Upon returning home in early evening, Madeleine would pause outside the room, thinking she might gather information about the boy in that way. But no sounds carried through the door and she would quickly open it to find him still lying as though chained upon the bed. His nervous phase would be behind him. He listened to her tellings with a peaceful, clouded look upon his face.

He was always there when she went to sleep, and when she awoke her hair would be wrapped tightly around his hand, like a rope. Thinking the boy still asleep, Madeleine would lie very still and count her blessings. Then he would begin talking or moving beside her, still without opening his eyes.

The small room did not seem cramped by a second occupant; on the contrary, it felt more comfortable and cosy. There were few visitors, especially since Ingrid had been informed that tea was no longer required of a morning. Madeleine felt that she had magically melted into the background of a stage and she practised her most discreet manners. A *Do Not Disturb* sign hung permanently outside the door. Only Sally, the shy yet curious woman from upstairs, disregarded this, knocking then running quickly away before the door was opened. "This is just her way of saying a neighbourly hello," thought Madeleine, brimming with understanding and tolerance, "as swearing is the mode of greeting practised by the old woman who knits on the stairs." Madeleine listened to the sounds of the hotel as it went about its daily routine and she knew that she had found her niche in this little world.

While the boy rested on the bed, Madeleine sat at the small table before the window. She was working steadily on Frances Farmer's book. Occasionally she asked the boy for a word: what is the word that means you are homesick for a place, but don't know where or what it is you miss? The pencil scratched against the room's silence like a hand soothing a troublesome itch. The bells of streetcars out in the avenue sounded faintly in her ears. A beam of sunlight somehow managed to slant down the air shaft and fall through the window. These were the hours when Madeleine breathed softly and wrote carefully, lest the spell break and the boy awaken.

Sometimes during his naps she slipped up to Ingrid's room to share some conversation. Ingrid was worried for her friend, and with no tea to bring time weighed heavily on her hands. Madeleine, for her part, was rather disappointed that Ingrid had not replaced Napoleon, university, the Dollar-A-Dance and mysticism with new and more worthwhile interests, refusing even to take Madeleine's advice to suntan. The girl remained pale and solitary in her room. "When will I meet him?" she asked. "I see him when I come to your door, but he is always sleeping. I have passed him on the stairs and in the halls, but he doesn't look at me or speak to me, and he wears such a sulky expression."

"He's only a little bit shy. You see, when he's lying on

the bed with closed eyes he's not really sleeping. He's only focusing his thoughts and forming different plans. This is a very trying time for all the world. You just have to pick up any newspaper to realize the issues and problems which abound. Of course, I don't believe in world or even national news. My grandmother taught me that much, poor woman. She said that the papers are printed just to make the fat cats fatter and the frightened mice more frightened. Why, she said, there would be no headlines or heartaches if people would but cease abandoning home and birthright without proper reason. That's the biggest issue and the biggest problem: people wandering the planet without due cause."

"Should I simply introduce myself?" puzzled Ingrid. "Perhaps he and I have something in common. What is he interested in?"

"Serious things. Maybe one balmy night we can all go out together on the town. We could make it an occasion. And listen, could I borrow a bit more money?"

"Do you ever speak to him of me?" asked Ingrid as she pressed the bills into Madeleine's hands.

■■■ Where's the Ocean

"Hey, stranger, where you coming from?" asked Frankie.

"Don't ask me any questions, please. And move over." Madeleine settled on the bench between Rita and The Pilot and took out her knitting. Her present project was the composition of woollen caps for her corner friends; she worried what would happen to them when the fine summer ended and the cold rain came to visit.

Madeleine pointed with a knitting needle. "What's the matter with him?" Blue was squatting by the lamppole with his arms viced around his knees. One hand scratched the other arm, which was red and torn.

"He OK. We all going to find a man. Someone got to stay here for to take care of Blue. You watch over him?"

"I'd be glad to. But I can't stay long. There's someone waiting for me."

"We pass back right fast," said Rita. "Come on." She slid away with Frankie and The Pilot.

"What's the matter with Blue-boy?" asked Madeleine. She touched his shoulder, which felt cold in spite of the sun's considerable warmth. Her knitting needles and his chattering teeth clicked together in a little song.

"Madeleine," said Blue.

"What? Here, have some gum." She put a stick in his mouth for him. "It's funny," she mused. "I start knitting one thing, then it always turns into something completely different."

"Madeleine," said Blue.

Suddenly she spotted, right across the street, the boy whom she had left lying on the bed an hour earlier. She was about to call to him, but something in the way he stood silenced her. Beside him, also waiting for the light to change, stood a taller, larger man who wore a tie and a business suit. The boy dragged on his cigarette and looked sharply this way and that to see whatever was hidden in the side streets. Madeleine could tell he was in one of his nervous moods by the angle at which he held his head. The taller man spoke to the boy, who seemed to nod in reply.

The light changed to green and the pair crossed the street. Madeleine crouched down beside Blue and wrapped her arms around him. She hugged him as tightly as she could, so tightly that she might almost press him back together again, if only for a little while. "The others will be back soon. Everything will be all right. Can you manage by yourself?"

Blue didn't answer. Madeleine stood up, looking away from his frozen eyes. "Here. You need a new piece of gum. That old one must be stale by now. Perhaps you had better keep the whole package. I have to go."

"Madeleine," said Blue.

She followed the man and the boy. "It's better this way, far better for everyone," she told herself. "And thank Christ he has some respectable friends. It would be tragic if he spent his free time alone and sad in bars or, worse yet, with the kind who seek narcotic release from their blues."

The man and the boy turned into a bar. Madeleine was about to follow when a doorman said, "I'm afraid you can't come inside, lady."

"Why not? My dearest friends are inside."

"Rules. Beat it. Junkie whore."

Madeleine walked slowly away. She entered the Shanghai Saloon, which happened to be empty except for Frank. He looked quickly up from the newspaper spread before him on the counter. "How you doing?" he asked.

"A whisky, Frank."

"You got it," the bartender replied brightly. He neatly poured the drink, then watched Madeleine expectantly.

"Frank, I have to think now. We can talk later."

"Sure," he said, trying to mask his disappointment. He methodically turned the pages of his newspaper and kept Madeleine in the corner of his eye.

She pondered. "I've known all kinds of boys in my time. Shy boys and sly boys and lover boys. Mean boys and funny boys and wise boys. Since I have no particular type to place limits upon the focus of my attractions, I have known every kind of boy in the world. And then some.

"Perhaps," she meditated, "I have become detoured from my path, mistaking a dead-end alley for a freeway leading toward forever. Or possibly I have been sailing with only one other passenger on a ship meant to carry a multitude across the sea."

She ordered another drink and lit another cigarette, trying to ignore the suspicion that someone watched her from the shadows at the back of the bar. She turned her head several times, but too slowly to catch a glimpse of the figure lurking in the corner of her eye.

Madeleine looked up to see Frank staring at her. "Ever hear of Frances Farmer?" he asked abruptly. "You can sometimes catch her movies on the Late Show. Sam's a big fan. What brings this up is that just an hour ago this old character comes in and says he'd given this Frances Farmer a ride in his taxi once. Forty years ago, down in Hollywood. Says she cried in the back seat and didn't know where she wanted to go. The meter kept clicking and she kept crying, then suddenly she threw a twenty at him, jumped out at a red light, nearly killed herself. This old guy has a glove he claims Frances Farmer dropped in his cab. Wants me to trade him a double J & B for it. Can you beat that?"

Fingers entered the bar, nodded to Madeleine and Frank, and sat at the piano, warming up the keys in preparation for the night. His music always drew a big crowd; people like to have something live in the background while they sip. Some customers sang along with Fingers when they were feeling especially good, although Frank didn't encourage this, not everyone being blessed with perfect pitch. Fingers flexed his hands and played slow songs without names. The music sounded strange in the nearly empty bar.

"Did you make the trade?" asked Madeleine.

"Sure, why not? Hell yes, not that I believed him. But he was a funny old guy and it was a good story. What am I going to do with one glove? I say to him. Do I look like a glove-wearing kind of man to you? And it's all ripped, with missing buttons. Here, take it." Frank tossed a soiled white glove onto the counter.

Fingers doodled around the keys, singing in a voice that sounded like the echo of a ghost:

> *Oh, Wild and the Only Ones*
> *Tell me where you are . . .*

Madeleine and Frank listened in silence for a moment.

"I think I'll join you," said the bartender, then poured himself a shot.

"How long until Happy Hour?" Madeleine asked anxiously.

Frank raised his glass and threw back the shot. "Just wait. It'll be here soon. Moment or two the door will open, the gang will string in, out for a good time, a few laughs, a few drinks. The same old story. I should be getting those peanuts into bowls right now. Stick around and join in the fun."

Madeleine slipped the glove, which was very small and obviously suited for a child or a dwarf, carefully into her purse. A wan expression appeared on her face as she struggled against a longing to nestle into the Shanghai for the night. "Some other day," she replied finally, and tousled Fingers' hair as she walked away.

Madeleine wandered through streets unfamiliar or unremembered. Dusk began to fall, and the day's heat sank with a sigh into the pavement. It was the hour when some cars have headlights on and some drivers feel no need for such illumination yet. Businesses were closing and their workers were free to rush home or to loiter in lounges; some stores remained open to serve evening shoppers. The streets rattled and rang and Happy Hour hummed.

Madeleine turned from the busy streets. She walked past dark buildings and closed parks and empty alleys, past a boarded-up church with smashed windows. She walked up and up the climbing street, until the colours and sounds behind her ran together like a painting washed by evening. When she reached the top of the hill, Madeleine paused. Below was the harbour, the lights of ships and docks, the ocean stretching into blackness beyond. "Not yet, not yet," she thought, then turned and started back downtown.

Now store windows blazed, marquees flamed and neon flashed. Taxis rushed by with honking horns and squealing tires, carrying passengers to dinners and parties and shows. In the cabs' back seats they leaned toward each other, amid the flashing of jewels, the scents of perfume. They glanced out windows at those who could not afford to travel like swift stars through the night, who walked slowly with heads bent to side-walks leading to rooms too dark or too bright, who stood mutely before store windows with hands hidden in empty pockets. Madeleine walked slowly and looked at the city around her with puzzled eyes, as if she had just arrived there.

As always, the boy was resting on the bed when she returned to the hotel. The bare lightbulb seemed very bright. The boy looked as though he hadn't left the room all day; Madeleine could almost see the haze of lazy peace drifting up from him. She glanced toward the pages of her book messed upon the table. "Move over," she said to the boy. "I feel tired. I got lost and had to walk the long way back home."

When she woke later the room was dark, but the boy's eyes were still half open. He was humming a song Madeleine did not recognize, but she knew that this tune wasn't what had ended her dream.

■ Across the Lake

One day Madeleine could not get out of bed. She lay with the covers pulled over her head and worried that, like Annemarie, she had been struck down by the fevers. From somewhere far out in the streets a clock tolled four times like a church bell chiming, but Madeleine was unable to leap up to answer its call. A closer sound made her cautiously uncover her face.

From beneath nearly closed eyelids she saw the boy rummage quickly through her things, picking up clothes and keepsakes then tossing them aside. He searched carefully through her beach bag and looked at length at the soiled white glove. With an anxious expression he traced a small circle in the middle of the room. Going to the table by the window, he leafed through manuscript pages.

"Did you lose something?" asked Madeleine, rising from bed and wrapping herself within her housecoat. "It happens all the time, doesn't it? You move from place to place, leaving something behind in each one. I left a blue kimono in Tokyo and a silver wedding band in Paris. A little bit of me is scattered in every city upon the globe, I feel I'm everywhere at once."

Madeleine poured herself a drink and stood by the table, looking down the air shaft. She turned to the boy, who had taken her place upon the bed. His face was pressed into the pillow. "Shall I read you a story?" she inquired. "Perhaps you've been wondering precisely what I've been doing here at my little desk these long days." She picked up a sheaf of papers, shuffled them nervously, cleared her throat and moved onto the edge of the bed. "Now please listen carefully because no one will ever read to you quite like this again."

She breathed deeply and began:

As God's eye closed and the summer light failed, two children toted ten large stones from the water's edge and arranged them in a circle on a clean patch of sand. Then they hunted along the shore for driftwood that was old and dry; the small pieces would be used for kindling, the larger ones thrown on the fire once it was burning strong. They rolled long logs close to the ring of stones to serve as benches. In the wood behind the beach grew thin green shoots which made perfect roasting sticks once trimmed smooth and clean with the sharp kitchen knife. Lastly, marshmallows, wieners and buns were fetched from the cabin. Everything was ready. As soon as it got dark they could light the fire, but not before.

While they were working Frances and Reeves heard the ferryboat cross back and forth. The lake was nearly one hundred miles long, and at this narrow point the ferry connected one shore to the other. It was a small boat that ran on cables, and carrying ten cars it was completely full. During summertime it ran twenty-four hours a day, but in the still dark night there was very little traffic; people around there lived quietly in those days and were long in bed before the moon travelled far. Often the boat rested on one side of the lake or the other for an hour or more, waiting for a car to carry across.

The humming of the ferry's engine was a sound so familiar that Frances and Reeves noticed it only when it stopped. Then something was missing. Fish might jump and tugs might drift by, but the ferry was always there, with the mountains and the lake. On long drawn summer evenings, when lake and mountains melted slowly into quiet darkness and then disappeared, you could tell precisely the first moment of night: the captain of the ferry switched on the lights. Green for starboard, red for port. Boats coming in late from fishing were warned away from the cables which lifted out of the water during a crossing, and the ferry rose from darkness like a coloured constellation.

Stars came out. Ten hot dogs and two bags of marshmallows vanished. It was still early, and Frances and Reeves were full and sick and bored. What they needed was a good smoke, but punkwood was difficult to find during daytime; at night the search was nearly impossible. The best and scarcest pieces were made of a light hollow wood aged and cured by sun and water. If a finger could not dent it, then the punk was no good.

Frances and Reeves hunted the shore with bent backs. Now and then there sounded the shout of a discovery, followed by a muttered _shit_ when the piece proved no good. If only a good storm would blow down the valley and wash fresh pieces upon the shore or at least carry some of the poor ones away. At last, after much searching

and many false alarms, they came up with several good
finds and returned to the fire to smoke. It was fine
punkwood, with an old sweet taste to it. Reeves and
Frances sat with sand in their shoes and smoke in their
eyes. The fire was strong because they fed it. Their backs
were chilly, but their faces glowed orange and burned
hot.

Clear calls sounded from far across the lake. Other
children were jumping off a wharf somewhere near the
point, splashing and laughing in the dark. Their voices
became tuned to a strange sharp pitch during the journey over water, as though reaching from a distant part
of the world where sound and time are bent into shapes
unknown here.

Frances and Reeves coughed now and then. "I'm
bored," said Frances. "I'm so bored of everything."

"We can do anything we want," said Reeves. "We can
go across the lake and get Grace and Jeannie. We can
hitch-hike down to the drive-in and sneak in free. We
can go ganker-shanking at the campsite. Anything."

They were free during summers at the lake because
the aunts left them alone then. It seemed for those several months that Frances and Reeves were not each a
child of two of the four sisters, but belonged to them all
as common property and could be regarded without
maternal intensity. The four sisters wished to be left un-
bothered to drink and play cards together. During hot
days they brought the card table and patio chairs right
down to the edge of the lake, so they could keep their
feet wet and cool during their endless games. They
played for nickels and dimes or a penny a point, each
keeping her winnings in an old peanut butter jar or jam
pot. Sometimes one woman would shake her treasure
chest and wonder if she had enough coins to buy a fur
coat or a trip to Las Vegas. The card table was always
crowded with big tumblers of gin and tonic in which
floated boats of lemon and ice. The sisters laughed and
swore and toasted brown, and they did not miss their

husbands who had to work in town all week long. They did not mention Michael who still lay at the bottom of the lake, never found. If the children came around, they were put to work keeping score or fetching more ice from the cabin. The sisters slept in two sets of bunk beds there, while the children camped on the sand or in a tent pitched among the pines behind. Or they broke into railway cars stalled upon the sidings and dreamed all night that they were riding away, never coming back. Until September everyone could do and dream as they pleased.

But now it was the end of July and everything had already been done a million times before. Though only half-way through, the summer seemed nearly over; every few days the children calculated with sinking hearts the number of weeks left before their mothers repossessed them with narrowed critical eyes and moved them back into town for school, closing up the cabin for winter. Every morning it was harder to decide what to do with the day. Often Frances and Reeves spent the whole day up in the treehouse trying to plan how best to use their liberty, until it was too late to do anything at all.

"I'm so bored of everything," repeated Frances.

The fire was burning down into coals. Suddenly yet slowly Frances and Reeves rose as one and without a word walked in separate directions from the fire. Returning with laden arms, they flung wood on the fire and sent sparks flying upward. Immediately they left to gather more fuel. Soon they were running and carrying and throwing faster and faster and faster. Then, as abruptly and silently as they had begun, the children stopped. The fire was taller than a giant and too big to put out.

"Frances! Reeves! You kids come here right now!" Dorothy screamed from the sundeck of the cabin. "They're attempting to burn down the world," she said to her sisters.

"Run!" hissed Frances, and they raced for their lives
across the sand, laughing so hard they tripped and fell a
dozen times. Breathing wildly, they reached the ferry
just before the ramp was cinched up and the boat began
to move. Dorothy stood in light on the sundeck and
peered into darkness. She called them three more times,
but they were safe in the middle of the lake, riding
across the cold deep water, floating above long plants
which reached up toward the current from their still
dark bed. One day, Frances believed, a hand would
break above the water and she would see emerge her
laughing uncle whom she had never seen before.
Michael would take her away with him. They would
ride the rails with hobos south to California. They
would become tap-dancing movie stars who gave inter-
views to fan magazines.

On the lake's other side Reeves and Frances walked
down the dusty road that ran beside the tracks. The railway didn't keep its fences mended as they should, and
every winter a few horses were killed by trains. After
crossing the wooden bridge over the creek, the children
turned up the hill and climbed high into the pines.
There was no sky there in the forest where bears lived,
and deer and pheasant too. No God could see what happened among the dark trees, but the children weren't
alarmed by owls that cried or branches that creaked or
thunder that echoed through the valley. It wasn't
through fear that they bounded back down through the
long grass, jumping like deer over the sweeping breast
of the hill. Though they could not see their footing, they
leaped high and fearlessly. The night was now so dark
that Reeves couldn't see Frances, but only hear her
breathing light and strong. Or maybe this was just the
rustling of the grass.

At the bottom of the hill old man Harrod's pastures
stretched for miles in every direction. No one knew how
many horses he owned; some said it was close to a

hundred, others spoke of half that number again. No one knew except for the children of the valley. The old man couldn't tend the animals the way he should. Fences were broken and horses escaped up into the hills, where they lived wild in the pines; some younger ones had yet to feel the touch of a human hand. In winter, when deep snow covered grass, the older horses would lead the younger ones down the hill to Harrod's big barn, where there waited hay and bran and oats.

In years gone by the old man had operated a profitable trail-riding concern. Now, with all the saddles broken and the horses gone wild, business had fallen off to nearly nothing. Harrod let any child who could round up a few horses in morning ride free for the rest of the day. It was hard work, for the horses knew every trick of capture and wisely preferred the cool shade of brush to a hot day's labour. Children chased them around and around through buttercups and thistles, the hems of their jeans becoming soaked with morning dew, their foreheads wet with sweat.

Night was different. All you need do was stand still and whistle, and horses would come out from the darkness one by one. At night they moved quietly and peacefully. They seemed lonely for the sound of a human voice and liked to stand near and warm, nuzzling and brushing even a body that brought no carrots or apples or sugar. The horses made low sounds that had to do with the night and the open fields and the lake beyond. Frances and Reeves knew every horse, gave names to the youngest ones, remembered the older ones from summers passed. They picked burrs from manes and whispered into listening ears. When the hour grew late and a dog barked from far across Sutter's farm, the children left the pasture. A long line of horses followed them to the edge of the field, as polite hosts show their guests to the door. Even while the children walked away the horses stood still and watching by the fence.

Frances and Reeves returned along the road that ran between berry bushes and apple trees. A late large moon had risen, and shadows fell sharply upon the gleaming dust. They crossed back over the stream they floated down on the hottest days of summer; its water was always so cold you didn't feel the hurt when you bumped into rocks. The children didn't speak all the way back to the ferry landing, for their secrets had been left behind with the horses.

The boat was resting on the other side of the lake. Their home side. A car could flash its headlights to signal the boat to cross the water; children could only shout and cry with their loudest voices. But no matter how long and hard they called, the boat would not budge for them. It seemed certain that everyone in the valley could hear them, that their voices travelled far across the mountains and deep into the lake. Well, people knew the captain of the ferry slept on duty and drank too, but they didn't care.

It didn't matter. Frances and Reeves walked over to the Carpenter place and pulled big beach towels from the clothesline. On a warm summer night they could sleep dressed and covered with towels without feeling cold. It was best to sleep outside anyhow because then they woke with dawn and the day seemed longer than any day ever dreamed.

Dorothy leaned heavily against the railing of the sundeck. The lights of other cabins were scattered like glowing cigarette tips discarded along either shore. A tugboat travelled slowly down the lake toward the mill, straining under its heavy load of logs. Dorothy gathered up beach towels already cold with evening dew and hugged them in her arms, pressed them against her burning face. "One afternoon my brother went fishing for trout and never came back," Dorothy breathed into the darkness, listening to hear how the night would receive her words. The tugboat passed. Now the ferry, crowded with cars returning home from the drive-in movie, began another journey across the lake.

Turning and looking through glass, Dorothy saw her sisters hunched over their game. They threw cards down soundlessly and had the strained look that comes with playing too many hands for too long. The world had shrunken smaller and smaller until it was no larger than the table upon which the cards were scattered, and the players' eyes were smaller too. Soon Kaye would begin to blame the others for her bad luck and not just with cards. She would accuse them of cheating and meanness and of being poor sports who ruined all her pleasure. Then she would accuse them of ruining her life. Hours later one of the sisters would look up to see dawn sneaking over the mountains and she would swear with irritation.

Dorothy lingered on the deck. The lake breeze was cool. It was getting late and God only knew where the children were. Running around like wild animals, living on stolen plums, hiding. They were sly and full of secrets, always looking past you and sliding away before they could be spoken to. "They're safe," thought Dorothy.

Suddenly an owl hooted nearby. Dorothy started and turned quickly inside the cabin. She closed the sliding glass door behind her. Beneath the naked light her sisters looked pale in spite of their dark tans. The room was full of cigarette smoke and the smell of gin bottles left carelessly open. Her sisters glanced at Dorothy and asked what was the matter, annoyed that she had forced them to look up from the cards. "Hurry up, it's your turn to play," she heard them say. "We've been waiting on you as usual."

"I thought I saw Michael standing behind the big old pine," said Dorothy. "I thought I saw his shadow on the sand." She looked at her sisters with tears in her eyes and the towels clasped forgotten in her arms.

"You've had too much to drink," said Kaye. "I bid

two spades. Are you going to bid or pass?"

As always Reeves feel asleep quickly, just when Frances
most wanted to talk. He was younger and needed more
rest. Frances snuggled close beside him and let her
thoughts mix with the breeze that came fresh off the
lake. Reeves's face was blurred though near. A calm
face. "He will stay in the valley," thought Frances. "He
will remain where it is safe, living among trees that are
always green, snow that is always white, summers that
are always blue." He would stay and she would go.

Frances looked across the water and saw the lights of
their cabin. With no one to feed it their fire had died
away long ago. The other side of the lake looked so
close. Surely someone strong could throw a stone across
the water. Or reach across the water. Several times each
summer a spell of adventure fell upon some of Harrod's
horses. Late one night last week Frances had been
woken by a disturbance that was not the ferry, not the
sisters laughing, not an ordinary summer noise. It was a
sound of splashing. She was lying in her sleeping bag
upon the sand where it sloped downward before the
cabin toward the water. Looking up, she saw three of
Harrod's horses swimming across the lake. Their necks
were stretched out flat upon the water, their legs
churned the lake and made it foam white in the moonlight. It seemed that they were swimming straight toward Frances, but then their path veered south. The
water was cold and deep and dark, with a strong current
pulling south. What made these three horses and none of
the others wish to cross the lake? Say they were wandering through the pasture and saw a path of moonlight appear before them and beckon them toward the unfenced
shore. Say they had stood upon the beach during a thousand days and looked across the water and with flaring
nostrils received strange scents from the exotic other
side. Say they heard a voice calling from the lake.

Far below the horses, beneath the pull of current, Michael lay on the lake's flat bed, his face as still as the face of the smiling young man in the photograph album. The little brother who had grown tall and strong, who took his sisters to Kinsmen dances in town or rowed them across the lake to moonlight picnics on the bluffs, where Benny Goodman sang up into the stars. Who rowed alone one late summer afternoon to catch trout for supper because Dorothy had a sudden craving for tasty rainbow trout, she would die for them.

What happened? The horses escaped across the lake and for one day they had a fine time trampling through gardens and wandering down the highway. Then old Harrod fetched them back where they belonged.

Frances saw a figure come out onto the deck of the cabin and gather up beach towels draped over the railing, wave them like flags, press them to her breast. Then the figure returned inside. The ferry approached across the lake, but Frances didn't waken Reeves. It was too late to return home tonight. It was so late that soon she would hear the two A.M. train coming down the tracks, twisting along the cliffs above Sunshine Bay, shining its lights into the trees. After the ferry landed and its cars drove off, the valley settled into the quiet country night. Then every sound seemed an echo from somewhere else, and this somewhere called to Frances like the church bell on the mountain. Atlas countries as blue as sky, as green as grass. The current would pull her south and Reeves would stay safely behind with Michael. Yes, she would go alone.

Suddenly the world seemed to tilt more sharply on its axis and several stars fell into the lake. They floated beside the lights of the ferry. The moon was just bright enough to illuminate little waves which washed against the Carpenters' wharf. Frances held her breath and waited for the stars to return to their rightful place in the sky.

"Isn't that funny?" cried Madeleine. "I laugh every time I read it. There are parts twice as funny, but I lost them."

The boy grabbed his jacket and in one movement was at the door.

Madeleine dropped the pages onto the floor and sprang after him. "Wait!" she cried.

"What?"

Madeleine clutched his sleeve. "You can't leave with that tear in your jacket. Let me sew it up for you. A few small stitches and it will be as good as new."

The boy shrugged out of the jacket and walked out the door.

"Reeves! You're crazy!" Madeleine screamed after him. "I didn't write that story. A friend of mine didn't even write it. Only an insane person who is also a pathological liar would think up such a thing. It has nothing to do with me."

Madeleine stood shaking in the doorway.

▆▆▆ Heart To Heart

"He's gone. I knew this would happen. He is running away like a thief in the night. He has stolen all your secrets and will sell them to the first pawnbroker he meets for far less than their true value."

Madeleine turned and saw a girl with mouse-coloured hair and thick spectacles standing close beside her. "Who are you?"

"Don't you know me? I'm your neighbour, Jeanette. We have met briefly on several occasions, I believe, through our mutual friend, Ingrid."

"I can't remember."

"You seem troubled. Why don't we enter your room and talk together for a few minutes. This will make you feel much better, I promise."

Jeanette chose to sit on the small hard-backed chair. With hands folded primly on her lap and feet planted squarely on the floor, she looked coldly at Madeleine, who appeared slightly dazed.

"Now, although we are not as yet intimately acquainted, I have a favour to ask of you. I do not hesitate because it is not for myself that I ask. It is for the good of others."

Jeanette continued: "You may or may not know that I am engaged in certain scientific investigations of great importance and far-reaching ramifications. I will not bother you with all the intricacies. Suffice to say, my study involves a group of people of whom, I understand, you have a degree of knowledge. I speak of the blind beings who have been led astray from the light. They inhabit an area several hundred yards west of this hotel. You know to whom I refer?"

Madeleine stretched her mouth into a hideous approximation of a smile. "Do stars drown or can they swim?" she asked in the bright voice of a child posing a riddle.

"I will rephrase my question. Do you know a certain group that may be classed together, sociologically speaking, by reference to their dependency upon the city streets? My preliminary findings suggest that these subjects derive, if you will, a kind of pleasure from said streets—a pleasure not unlike that which the addict feels when under the influence of various narcotic substances. I speak now of the vagrants, the drifters, the petty criminals, et cetera."

"I thought I had the strength to pull them up into the sky where they belonged."

Jeanette raised her voice. "The favour I ask is this: since it is essential for my study that I become intimately acquainted with these specimens and since my efforts to form such association have thus far met with nothing but rebuttal, not to say hostility, I am therefore in need of a go-between. That is you."

Madeleine laughed bitterly. "I thought it was me. I thought it was me who could carry them between the shores."

"No one is asking you to be a boat," said Jeanette, becoming exasperated. "Simply introduce me to your friends and nothing more. Adopt a casual manner which will allow me to ask them a few small questions in a relaxed atmosphere, as it were. They seem very hard to get to know."

"They are my finest friends," intoned Madeleine like an automaton whose button has been pushed. "They need me and I need them. They took me in their arms when no one else would, and they gave me courage. They will never walk away from me and they will always be there."

"Hmm, yes," replied Jeanette sceptically. "But that is not quite the point. Granted, they do seem to exhibit particular behavioural patterns. But do you have a drink? We can discuss this and other topics more freely over a few highballs. The relaxed atmosphere is very important to my work, as I say."

To Madeleine's surprise, Jeanette threw back her glass of whisky, widened the distance between her legs, then smacked her lips loudly.

"Booze," said Jeanette, pouring herself another portion. "Now what about this Ingrid, eh? What a case. She has her heart set on Hollywood and valentines, knows nothing of the world. You and I understand one another. We have seen a few things and we are alike. We know that life is more than a tap-dance across a shiny floor."

Jeanette leaned confidentially toward Madeleine. "We would like to help her if we had the time, but we're busy running the race of life. Ingrid is still in the starting blocks. She has quit the university and, as significant as that is, it is far more important in the symbolic sense. You can see that she has fallen under evil influence and is falling without parachute or wings. Remember this, I tell her: the gutter lies a scant two inches below the sidewalk. She told me I reminded her of Winston Churchill, but I wasn't flattered."

Jeanette talked on for an hour, freely replenishing her glass without, however, offering the bottle to Madeleine. Unlike most people, Jeanette did not relax under the influence. Instead, two lines on her forehead deepened and she became increasingly anxious.

"I'm a serious person," she explained. "I spend my days on the street interviewing various characters and my nights writing up the day's work. I have no time to sunbathe. The problems of the city weigh heavily upon my white shoulders. They excite my nerves and worries. I can't sleep. There's a crazy lady who lives in the room next to mine. For weeks on end I neither see nor hear her. The light in her room is always off and her door is always closed. Then, suddenly, her room becomes crowded day and night with many people who drink and argue and laugh, but in the least amusing way. You know these thin walls, so you can imagine the commotion. Then, just as suddenly, the parties cease and a third phase begins during which the crazy lady stands at her open door and says in a loud and bitter voice: someone was knocking on my door, someone was knocking on my door. She repeats these words over and over, calling out into the empty hallway all night long. I suffer headache. She wears gold sparkles beneath her eyes. Then the first phase begins again, and so on. Systematic craziness is the worst kind of all. This only makes me feel more sick at heart and exhausted. Charity begins at home, but I live alone. The government sends me monthly cheques to support my research. I feed greedily off the tragedy in the street, but still I'm always hungry. And thirsty." Jeanette gulped another drink. "While they lie sick and drugged in the gutters, I have my comfortable room and my three meals a day."

"This is not an expensive hotel," pointed out Madeleine.

Jeanette didn't hear her. "I'm getting paid several

dollars for every misery and death. Even while the crazy lady sits quietly in her room, I can still hear her voice calling down the hallway."

"Jeanette, if you weren't receiving this money surely someone else would. Is this true or is this false? Regardless, there would still be heartache if all the seas dried up and turned to desert. Let's go out and forget the world's blisters for a while. You have earned your night of fun."

"All I do is scrape at their bleeding sores with my questions. No one asks me questions. My class voted me Girl Most Likely To Be Lonely. No one knocks upon my door."

Without warning, Jeanette lurched up from her chair and staggered to the door. At the threshold she said, "There now, don't you feel better after our little talk? But beware of boats, girlie. They sometimes sink. They will trick you with yellow scarves and golden earrings until you are unable to distinguish between the blue sea and the black dungeon. Then one sunset you find yourself wrapped in chains upon the plank."

The door closed. Madeleine carefully gathered the fallen pages from the floor. She stared dully at them, for the life of her unable to recall what the story she had just read had been about. "How strange. I too have heard a voice calling down the hallway. Perhaps it should be comforting that someone else has also heard this voice, but for some reason it isn't." She placed the pages on the little table and righted the empty bottle. The room seemed very empty and somewhat cold. Madeleine looked at the boy's black leather jacket, but she did not have the spirit to play seamstress at the moment. She put on the jacket, still torn, then crawled into bed. Her always difficult memory exercises now seemed impossible: she could not recall even the most significant events which had occurred one year ago, and the more distant past had fallen into blackness. "What is my name? Where was I born? In what year?" she wondered wildly. Her mind slipped gratefully toward the future. "This is but a small setback," Madeleine decided. "Who knows what will happen tomorrow?"

▆▆▆ All That Glitters Is Not Gold

The following morning Madeleine wakened to see Ingrid placing the tea tray on the foot of the bed. "He's jumped ship, hasn't he," said the girl in the rough, careless way of speech she seemed to be developing. "I knew it all along. What did you expect? It was fated. I guess I'll bring you tea in the mornings again. What the hell else is there to do?" She handed Madeleine a folded note. "I found this slipped under your door."

Madeleine silently read:

> *Dear M. Last night I lay awake until morning worrying only about you. I would be a false friend if I did not spell out my concern in black and white, and a false friend is far more dangerous than the most evil enemy. I could not live with myself should anything happen to you, so I will speak with the bluntness of a godparent in hope that these words will guide you through your day and perhaps beyond.*
>
> *In this city many fall victim to their environment; that is, the idle life. Case after case illustrates just this and, believe me, I have figures and data to back up my point. The paths to ruin are many, but the trail to Eden is overgrown and difficult to follow. It is easier to leave than to return. The only way to avoid these traps is through worthwhile labour. Think, please, of the many excellent charitable organizations crying out for the help you could so easily give. Or there are countless employment opportunities in various fields*

*which would provide you with a decent, respectable
wage. One can always find pride and satisfaction in
honest toil. Don't you agree? You will discover,
through work, a purpose and pattern to your days,
and this will save you from such destructive influ-
ences—one is named Ingrid—as are all around you.
Remember: humble makes pure.*

*Please consider these options carefully before you re-
ject them willy-nilly. Finally, you must keep in mind
that although God's care may at times seem provided
in peculiar ways, it is always there for those who look
to see that glitter contains only false gold. This last
point I cannot stress too strongly. J.*

Madeleine sighed. "Jeanette probably wrote this early
in the morning when she was feeling tired and grim,"
she thought. "If she would rise at a more relaxing hour,
as I do, she would feel less worried and realize that such
things have but little relevance."

She spoke to Ingrid. "It's from him. He was detained
by business last evening, but desperately desires that I
meet him in a nearby café where we may speak together
about important matters. I haven't a moment to lose."
Madeleine tore up the note and dropped it out the window, turning away before the pieces fluttered to the bottom of the air shaft.

"What? You mean to say you're not going to drink
this tea?" asked Ingrid in the kind of tone which often
leads to argument. While Ingrid made the tea things rattle loudly, Madeleine hastily dressed in torn jeans, the
boy's black jacket and dirty sneakers. "Oh, I forgot," she
said over her shoulder, leaving the room. "Lock the
door when you're done cleaning."

Outside the street was sunny and cheerful, and
seemed to greet Madeleine like a long lost friend.
"However, even the best friends change," she thought,
walking quickly for several blocks, then strolling to a
slower beat. Although it was a weekday, Tenderloin

people had no pressing business to distract them from
the demands of the leisure life, and the area had a holiday air to it. Madeleine avoided her corner. She watched
her reflection float across store windows. Two men
drinking rye in a doorway invited her to join them.

She stopped in front of a store she was very fond of
looking into, though she never bought anything there. It
was a pawnshop, and behind its barred windows was
displayed an interesting assortment of watches, radios,
cameras and guns. Though crammed to a bewildering
degree, the window was arranged with great care. You
could look into it forever and never see everything that
was there.

A woman sidled up beside Madeleine. "See that
banjo? There, in the corner. I have my heart set on it. If I
had that banjo, my life would be full and I'd want nothing more for the rest of my days."

"Banjo music is nice," commented Madeleine.

"I'm saving for it," said the woman. "Each week I put
a little aside. I got Fair Freddy's word he'll never sell it
to nobody but me, but I like to check by every day to
make sure it's still here. With that banjo I'll be the life of
the party."

Madeleine noticed that the woman's hands were red
and cracked and that her knuckles were severely
swollen. A reflection darkened the window and a voice
spoke her name. Turning, Madeleine greeted Jeanette.

"You see how it is, Madeleine. They pawn their hearts
and souls for a dollar, then lose the ticket. They throw
down their lives like dice, so careless it's a crime."
Jeanette spoke in businesslike tones and made no mention of the previous evening's chat or of that morning's
note.

"Have you met my friend here?" Madeleine gestured
toward the woman beside her who was, however, gazing into the pawnshop window with such concentrated
longing that all else around her was excluded. The banjo
was painted with a moon and five stars.

Jeanette shifted files and papers in her arms. A pencil
was tucked behind her ear. "Where are your other
friends?" she asked. "I require them desperately for my
study, which without them will come to a complete
standstill." A pained and envious expression crossed
her face.

Madeleine closed her eyes. She saw Frances Farmer
sitting carefully upon the edge of a star, looking down
through miles of clear summer sky, intently observing
the globe below. Madeleine could see Frances Farmer's
face clearly, but couldn't tell if she watched the world
with concern or compassion or coolness.

Jeanette began to speak with false animation. "Oh,
friends! Why did you bring up the subject? I used to
have more friends than anyone in the world. At the university I belonged to sororities, clubs, all kinds of
groups. There were endless parties and dates with boys.
I didn't sleep for four years I had so many friends. Rich
ones, poor ones, friends of all sizes and shapes. They
used to grab my hands and never want to let me go.
They still write begging letters and extend invitations
for me to visit. Some send bus, train or airplane tickets.
But, of course, now I have my work."

"Really?" inquired Madeleine politely. There was a
cocktail lounge that revolved thirty storeys above the
city. She would have a nice quiet drink there and look
down at the turning world below, seeing what Frances
Farmer saw.

"Oh yes, I was quite the girl in my time, flirting with
the devil, too frivolous for my own good. But I was
never tempted by parts of town like this, as you so obviously are. I simply fail to understand the attraction." A
few characters gathered around to watch the scene, for
Jeanette was speaking in a loud, passionate manner.

"They are my friends. I feel at home here," Madeleine
reminded Jeanette patiently. "Besides, getting murdered
is the very least of my worries."

"Friends! Those men at the corner, all those boys.

They are incapable of friendship. Their environment and way of life prevent any real human relationships. All my research points straight to that conclusion."

Jeanette paced up and down the sidewalk, her hair slipping from its serious bun. Madeleine looked neutrally into the pawnshop window while Jeanette outlined points. "One: you are, or were, sharing your room with this certain boy without knowing who he really is. I have heard the stories and they are not pretty. Two: that Ingrid foolishly follows you into the snare, and under your direct influence does nothing but sit inside her room with wasteful, trashy magazines. Did you see her new dress? It's exactly like one of yours. Three: you are playing with your life and not as a responsible adult. You aren't nourishing your soul or moral character with these people, this life."

Despite the summer sun, Madeleine pulled the boy's jacket more closely around her. "I've been in jail two times," she thought, "though on neither occasion was I guilty of breaking a law. I was simply outnumbered. Their strong hands encircled my wrists and pressed into my shoulders and prodded my back. They threw me into a cell, the metal door clanged shut, a key turned in the lock. Then they walked away and it was very quiet. I had always thought jails were extremely noisy, chaotic places, but it was like being alone in space."

"You've been living unoccupied for some time," declared Jeanette. "That you can't deny. I know the patterns. You are exactly typical of most girls in this district."

"This is a trial time for me," said Madeleine, smiling softly. "I need my friends nearby to keep away the blues."

"Blue and red and black. Those are colours. Life is not a paint-by-number. My God, the stories I could tell."

Frances Farmer leaned precariously over the edge of her star, the better to see below. Madeleine looked up at the empty blue sky, still smiling. "Some stories are best left untold and unwritten. Some stories can never really be finished and you shouldn't try to impose an ending upon them. They go on and on."

"They don't make pens and pencils just to chew on," snapped Jeanette. She pointed to the woman who still stared through the window. "You there, what's your name and how are you supporting yourself?"

"I have to meet someone," said Madeleine. "I promised." She began to walk away, but not in the direction of the Cloud Nine Lounge. The world was spinning fast enough without turning towers and cocktails.

Madeleine didn't glance over her shoulder to see Jeanette follow her with longing eyes. Nor did she see the other woman, now with her face and hands pressed against the pawnshop window.

■ The Last Station Near Home

Madeleine turned the corner, and all at once the sidewalk was crowded with people, mostly young men, passing to and fro and every other which way. It looked like several parades, approaching from opposite directions, had collided, mixed together, then forgotten where they were supposed to march, and why. There was singing and dancing and waving bottles and jackets swinging lasso-style above heads. Young men threw caps into the air, then ran away before they fell back down to earth. A boy and a girl rolled and kissed in the gutter, encircled by a ring of swaying, cheering spectators. Another laughing barefoot girl was being chased by a gang of whooping boys. The revellers pushed out onto the street and stalled traffic. Some drivers were leaning on horns, while others had abandoned their cars for the fun.

The throng behind pushed Madeleine against the wall
of people ahead. She tried to walk more quickly, hoping
to escape the crowd, and in her haste bumped into others several times. They did not become angry, but tried
to pull her deeper into the confusion. At last Madeleine
pushed to where the crowd thinned and traffic moved
once more.

"Slow down, girl." Rita caught her arm. It took
Madeleine several moments to recognize her friend. Rita
stood at the sidewalk's edge and glanced sharply into
every car that passed.

"What's happening here? Why are there so many people in the street?" asked Madeleine.

"No reason. Them sailor boys done left their ships
and land makes them crazy. They don't know what they
like or where they going. They just walking back and
forth, interfering with my business." Rita waved to a
passing vehicle, but it continued on without stopping.
"Madeleine, I been looking for you all around. We all
been looking for you. Why you been hiding out?"

"I'm so glad to see you, Rita. I was just thinking about
you. How wonderful that we should meet like this."

"Listen, baby. I would love to chat with you, I really
would, but I working. Lately seems I always working
and always getting poorer and poorer. Say, you got a
boy working for you?"

"What kind of a boy?"

"Just a boy in one big hurry. He come up to me and
talk like he know who I is. Then he give me some cash
and say I should pass it to you. Here." Rita fished into a
boot and pulled out a wad of old bills, which she
handed to Madeleine.

"I think I know who you're talking about. Did he
leave a message for me, too? It's quite important."

"Said he got to go away for two, couple days. He be
back soon, that all he say."

"When? Which way did he go?"

"I don't know, sugar. He be back soon is all."

A black car pulled up to the curb. Rita smartly opened the door and slid inside. She turned to wave goodbye to her friend, but Madeleine was already running quickly to the sea.

She had not ventured there before, as the moment had not seemed right for harbour-haunting—the rightness of moments being one of the few things in which she still placed faith. But now she ran and ran, up the hills and down the hills and past the new stores along the shore where tourists shopped. She didn't stop until reaching an area where warehouses, cranes and wharves loomed together.

Thick fog hung over the water, swallowing both the big bridge that ran over the bay and the farther shore it connected. With a sinking feeling Madeleine watched cars, their headlights turned on against the fog, venture upon the bridge then disappear into grey. At the point where land met sea the fog cleared suddenly, creating a line as mysterious as the border between two countries. Madeleine shivered. A chill, damp breeze blew in from the sea. Sometimes it carried wisps of fog, which Madeleine brushed away from her face, like cobwebs.

She spied a young man sitting upon a wall which enclosed a little park. Excepting him, the waterfront was deserted, and no seagulls flew upon the sky.

"It's a nice view, isn't it?" the young man called, while with one arm he waved to the gloomy docks. His voice carried farther and more clearly than might have been expected. "Look over there, at those lights in the middle of the bay. That's the boat that carries commuters across the water. They live over there on the other side and work here in the city. Because it is late afternoon, the boat is crowded with passengers returning home after a long day's labour. They sell drinks on board and a little band plays, so you can imagine the merriment. They say the pilot himself takes a sip or two now and again."

The young man stopped talking as abruptly as he had begun. Madeleine saw the little boat reeling and dipping through the waves, often disappearing beneath them for a moment before rising to the top again. The boat seemed somewhat small for such rough water.

"I can see you've studied this scene quite carefully," said Madeleine.

"I have. I live here in this park, so naturally I find myself looking out at the bay fairly often. There's always a lot of activity going on. Ships anchor and unload and load again. Sailors come ashore on leave, then return to ship with all their pockets empty. Kids fish off the wharves. There's always something or other going on."

The young man took a bit of bread from his pocket and began to eat it. Madeleine suddenly felt very hungry.

"Ever since I was a little kid, I wanted to go to sea," the young man said between bites. "I tried it once, but it wasn't for me. I just felt sick all the time. It's not much fun when you feel sick." He finished off the bread and neatly brushed crumbs from his clothes.

"I suppose they must have a lot of stowaways," remarked Madeleine.

"Sure they do. Everyone wants to ride on the ships. Fellows are always loafing about down here, looking for a chance to work on board. It's a good life, if it doesn't make you sick."

"You must have a good life yourself, here in this park beside the sea."

"I do. You won't hear me complaining, though it can be chilly at night. I have the pleasures of land and sea at the same time. Is anything the matter? You seem to have run here from a long way."

"I heard about a ship that sails away this afternoon. A friend of mine was supposed to be on it and I wished to wave goodbye. It's always more pleasant when there's someone waving goodbye from the land you're leaving, don't you think?"

"But the ships don't dock right here at the waterfront.

The water is too shallow. They anchor out in the middle of the bay and little boats carry the passengers out to them. Your friend is somewhere out there in the fog right now, I would guess."

The small commuting boat had vanished. Madeleine watched the waves for a moment, in hope that its lights would appear above them once more. When they didn't, she said, "There's no point in waiting here then. Goodbye."

She began to walk away. The young man followed several lengths behind. Happening to see him, Madeleine halted in order that he might catch up to her. But when she stopped, he stopped also, thus preserving the distance between them. "Would you like to walk with me?" she called back at last.

He didn't answer. "Of course," thought Madeleine. "He lives a lonely life of compromise here by the docks. It's natural that he should desire company. He's just like everyone else, after all." She started back toward the young man, with a look of great tenderness.

At once he turned and retreated quickly toward the park. "I didn't tell you everything," he called over his shoulder. "Sometimes children give me the fish they catch. I make a little fire under that tree over there and roast the fish over the flames. Goodbye."

The young man disappeared into shadows thrown by the warehouses upon the water like great blankets against the cold. Just at the moment when his back vanished, Madeleine felt a wave of something powerful and heavy roll over her and she wanted to run after the young man.

After she fought back up to the surface, Madeleine took a deep breath of chilly air. Then she walked back into the city.

■ Living It Up

Several evenings later, when night was fallen and the streetlights bloomed a thousand moons, the old mood came back to Madeleine out of nowhere. The boy also returned without rhyme or reason or explanation. Madeleine took one look at him, sent him out for wine and roses, and changed into an emerald green cocktail dress.

Running up to Ingrid's room, she shouted excitedly through the door. "Quick! Bring your radio and candles and cards. We can have a party in my room. The night is just beginning and I feel the old joys a little."

She stood impatiently outside the door, waiting in vain for it to open. She knocked firmly and more than several times. There was no doubt that Ingrid was home; music played distinctly inside the room. Also, Madeleine knew Ingrid would never venture from the hotel after sundown, despite Madeleine's taunts about an overcooked spaghetti spine. Ingrid said that bad things lurked outside, but refused to say what these things were.

No light showed under the door. All at once Madeleine feared that Ingrid had taken up icon-adoring ways again. She turned the handle and the door opened.

Several points of light burned like jewels in the darkness, but with an unnatural brightness. Soon Madeleine realized that these were the illuminated dials of Ingrid's radio. "Ingrid?" she called. "Where are you?"

The radio was playing a song concerning moons and love and stars. "Ingrid?" called Madeleine again. She could not determine exactly what the dark shapes around her represented. Reaching out, she inched forward until her progress was abruptly halted by a dresser or some other obstacle of furniture. "Ingrid, are you sleeping?" she asked, trying to sound playful. Yet to her ears her voice held a frightened note. The song ended and an announcer's voice began to murmur.

"No, I'm listening to my radio," came Ingrid's low, clear words. As her eyes accustomed themselves to darkness, Madeleine made out a shape on the bed. Ingrid was lying, fully clothed, with her face pressed to the wall.

"And in the dark!" snapped Madeleine. "It's not good for you. Haven't you heard about cancer?" She groped the wall for the light switch, then flicked it on. "Hurry up. We're going to have a party in my room."

"Just a minute. This is my favourite song."

Madeleine tapped her foot, muttering about jargon, cant and propaganda. At the song's climax she snorted in disgust. Ingrid sat up quickly and switched off the radio. Blinking like a shortsighted owl, she looked around for her shoes. A sullen expression crept upon her face.

"The radio," reminded Madeleine. "Bring it. In a party setting it's a different cookie, isn't it?"

Ingrid scowled, picked up the radio and carried it like a baby down to Madeleine's room.

There Madeleine arranged and lit candles, laughing and giggling to herself. Sitting with hunched shoulders on the floor, Ingrid did not seem fully awake. Upon the boy's return, Madeleine jumped up and danced around him, causing the air to rush and the candle flames to shake. "A toddy for the body," she sang as she twirled and spun. Ingrid was forced to press against the wall, since the room was small for exuberant dancing. Madeleine's arms were stretched up and her hair was flying like a flag. In the middle of a movement she broke off her dance and rushed to the small table, where she applied more rouge to her liberally painted face. Frowning at the pages of her book, she ran back across the room and dug a small vial from her purse. "Oh, my black, black beauties," she chortled, swallowing three black capsules.

"How was the holiday?" Ingrid asked the boy. But he

was watching Madeleine, who suddenly fell laughing on the bed.

"Holidays, holidays and more holidays," she screamed, seizing a bottle of perfume and pumping scent into the air. "More wine," she cried. Looking anxiously around the room, she rubbed her hands vigorously together. "This is more like it. I insist that everyone have fun."

Ingrid drained her glass and grabbed the boy's hands, addressing him in an aggressively psychic tone of voice. "Very interesting hands. Has anyone ever told you that before?" She pressed his palms in a professional manner. "I'd like to do a reading. In private."

"But where is Jeanette?" loudly interrupted Madeleine. She dashed out the door, then dashed back in, dragging the bespectacled girl by the hands. "We will have so much fun, you must come along," she was pleading.

The boy removed his hands from Ingrid's grasp, then went to the window. "Napoleon had hands just like yours," said Ingrid, staring fixedly at a candle flame. "He also didn't like people holding them. That's why he hid them in his coat."

"What in the world are you talking about?" demanded Jeanette. She was plainly hurt that she had missed the beginning of the party and sat stiffly on the hard-backed chair.

"I don't think Ingrid meant to perplex you," said Madeleine. "She was only making conversation."

"I see," replied Jeanette icily. "Conversationally speaking, I can't stay long." She looked suspiciously at the boy, whom Madeleine had neglected to introduce her to. "I see everything is very cosy here tonight. You are having a fine time, but I have work to attend to." She tapped her foot impatiently on the floor.

"Wait," said Madeleine breathlessly. "Everything is just beginning. This is the first time we have all been together, and I strongly feel that we shall spend many more evenings just like this. Please, Jeanette, stay with us a while. We've saved a bottle of wine just for you. This is very important to me."

"We could ask Sally to join us, but she's reluctant to leave her room," said Ingrid, staring at the boy.

"Sally? Who is Sally?" shrieked Madeleine. "I am tired of hearing about this Sally, who buzzes like an unsociable bee just off-stage while the thrilling drama of my life unfolds." The boy looked at Madeleine with a slight smile.

At last they were ready to leave for the bar. They tramped noisily through the hotel hallways and thundered down the stairs, Madeleine leading the way.

"Fingers!" she shouted as she tumbled into the Shanghai. "Where have you been?" Madeleine rushed up to the unhealthy looking man who was banging on his out-of-tune piano, dressed in an Oriental costume. A sign announced that he could play 'many more than twelve hundred tunes, plus all the latest hits.'

"Give me a title, my old friend," he greeted her, hitting the keys without pause.

"I can't think, I can't think. Please, please, give me a drink," sang Madeleine. "I feel so decidedly gay. But what does this exact moment remind me of?" she addressed no one in particular. Putting her hand to her forehead, she closed her eyes.

"Shall we find a table and order a round of drinks?" suggested Jeanette.

"Of course. Naturally," said Madeleine. "You three find seats in a dark corner. I have something to say to Fingers in private." She watched her friends thread their way into the darkness of the bar.

As soon as they were gone, she approached a nearby table where two youthful-looking ladies were staring into tall, exotic-coloured drinks. "Excuse me, but are you ladies drinking for festive reasons or everyday ones? Also, are you straight or exactly how?"

The more vivacious looking of the two women turned

to Madeleine and in a voice of great weariness said,
"There is no such thing as a straight line in this natural
world of ours. Next time you stand at the prow of a ship
in mid-ocean, notice this: although the horizon may
seem a straight line, this is merely an optical illusion.
Science has proven that the world is a curved place built
solely and exclusively on the notion of curves, and so
there is nothing more natural than two women companions sharing a few cool drinks in a bar."

"Well," Madeleine replied shrilly. "That is the freshest
thing I have heard in many a day. It goes without saying
that a full-figured girl such as myself thrills to have her
share of male company. But if ever I desire an easy
pleasant evening, I naturally turn to my girlfriends as a
matter of course. We discuss general themes and share
our little visions of life. I too adore science, but I'll tell
you what, girls. In truth, I have a cute boyfriend who is
waiting for me at a nearby table right now. He feels sad
in the afternoons, so is apt to act somewhat unsteadily.
He can't help it, but I really shouldn't leave him alone
for any length of time. As much as I would dearly love
to share opinions with you, I must get back to him."
Madeleine smiled intimately down at the women as she
swayed unsteadily to the music. The two ladies looked
alarmed, and gathered their furs and purses together.

Instead of leaving, Madeleine sat down at their table
which, as it happened, was scarcely large enough for
two. She glanced nervously around the bar and seemed
oblivious to the joys of feminine companionship. A ma-
ture woman wearing grey curls and a golden crown sat
alone at a table across the room. She bowed her head to
Madeleine with dignity and in recognition.

"Of course," Madeleine cried suddenly. "Now I remember." She paused politely to offer her new friends
the chance to inquire what it was that she remembered.
However, the two ladies only peered fixedly at the ice
melting in their tall drinks. "Heavens," thought
Madeleine. "What kind of company am I enjoying?

Have they no notions of social interest?"

Madeleine spoke with feeling: "I remember what this moment reminds me of. On summer nights when I was a girl we used to drink beer around a campfire beside a lake. There was drinking and kissing and hugging all night in the sand. One morning, as the sky lightened with dawn, we all trooped over to the Honeymoon Hotel, where it was possible to rent kayaks by the hour. Each person paddled his own boat; we floated in a long line along the shore. By chance I found myself separated from the others. Suddenly thousands of little fish began to jump all around my kayak, throwing themselves up to catch the morning sun. I stopped paddling for fear that I would frighten them. How still the lake was at that hour! I couldn't say how long I watched, but all at once the fish were gone and I was tired. I paddled slowly back to the hotel. And the next day I left that lake place, never to return there again."

Madeleine looked at her new friends, anxious that they should see the significance of her story.

"But what is the connection?" asked one of the ladies.

"The connection to what?"

"The connection to this place. You said that this place reminded you of that long ago incident."

Madeleine laughed uproariously. "This place! What am I doing? I've been sitting all these minutes in this place and not one person has bought me a single drink. Frank! Tequila!" she called to the bartender. "Tequila and lemons and beer!" She lit a cigarette and puffed energetically into the air. The two companions glanced at one another, then rose as if to leave.

"Wait," said Madeleine, touching one woman on the arm. "You must understand. What I was talking about just now didn't really happen to me. It happened to someone else. She's dead now, but I am committed to tell her story to the world. I was simply trying it out on you because you seemed such sympathetic and large-hearted people." She looked at them with open, child eyes. "I didn't mean to trick you or upset you. Please believe me."

Madeleine looked at the ladies with such urgency that they felt it was a choice between sitting down again or creating a scene. Selecting the former course of action, they grimly recommenced to sip their drinks.

Madeleine imbibed with flourish and gusto. Again she looked around the bar. The piano music rattled on and the patrons melted like ice cubes onto the tables. Seeing, at the back of the bar, the dark figure of the boy, Madeleine felt a twinge of worry, but reminded herself that she must allow him to meet people and socialize according to his own light. She couldn't see Ingrid or Jeanette, but estimated that they also had their own mixing to do. Madeleine drank and smoked until the bar's din faded into a pleasant hum.

When at last her mind turned from her drinks, she noted with surprise that the two companions had vanished. "I expect they became a bit tired," she suggested reasonably to herself. "But where is the boy? How could I forget him when he relies upon me so? I will have one more quick drink, then find him before he indulges in his habits."

Outside the street was nearly empty. It was late, the air was chilly with approaching autumn. "I must remind myself that this is earth, not heaven," Madeleine muttered to herself. "What should I do now?"

Three young women, with arms linked over shoulders, rounded the corner and bumped into Madeleine. "Excuse me," she said politely. The three girls shrieked with laughter and fell over one another down the sidewalk. Madeleine stood on the corner alone.

Not quite alone. An old man slept on a step, with a little dog beside him. The dog was still awake. He rested his head on the old man's knees and looked patiently before him. "Hello, Charlie, hello," Madeleine called softly. She remembered this dog from long ago. She remembered the pale green ribbon tied around his neck.

The ribbon was made of silk, and it was soft and worn.

Music from a nearby bar flooded the street. A spirit seized Madeleine, kicked off her shoes, danced her round and round in circles, threw her into the air. Her arms stretched out wide and waiting.

"Hey, sister," called a sad voice from an alley.

The pavement felt hard and cold beneath her feet. Madeleine looked in the direction where the sea must roll. Over there: across rooftops, down fire escapes, out windows, through alleys, beyond land.

The streetlights were being extinguished one by one all along the avenue. The party was over. Madeleine picked up her shoes and ran lightly and quickly, as though late for something. She followed Frances Farmer, the one who blew out the lamps.

■ The Party's Over

Madeleine was sunk in a swamp of despair at a certain table of the Shanghai Saloon, where she had more or less been living for the past week. On but a single occasion had she gone to the Holiday Hotel to regard her room mournfully, and neither hide nor hair of the boy or her neighbours had she seen during this visit. Her face was swollen and puffy, her eyes were bloodshot, and the green cocktail dress, worn constantly throughout these days and nights of desolation, now shone less brightly than an emerald, in fact being soiled, wrinkled and in two places torn. The party was most definitely over.

During this phase of hopelessness Madeleine had buried her face in a drink whenever anyone approached her table and in a bitter, accusing voice conversed aloud only with herself. When she became weary, she would nap on a bench in the corner of the bar; after the

Shanghai closed she slept beneath a tree in the small park by the shore without, however, ever seeing the young man who resided there. Frank had frequently considered speaking with the blonde, to encourage her to pull herself together; but always in the end he left her alone, only slipping needed nourishment, in the form of celery, olives and nuts, in her direction and looking often with concern toward where she suffered on her cross.

The bar was quiet in the middle of the afternoon. Madeleine gazed down at the manuscript pages before her, which floated in a shallow pool of spilled whisky that blurred their ink and further mystified their meaning. She wearily took another sip of her hemlock. It was time to take stock, whether she wanted to or not, and to see if the cupboards of her soul were really as empty as they seemed.

"By now," she thought, "I should be accustomed to the suddenness with which a dream can turn into a nightmare. One minute you fear waking will end your visions of Heaven, the next you long only for such a waking to erase nightmares of Hell. Certainly I have taken two steps back for every one step forward on my path, and an undeniable fear of failure hangs heavily in the air of this sad bar.

"However," she continued, "I may be the kind of pilgrim who stumbles upon salvation when least expecting or prepared for it. Night is darkest just before dawn; my new day will be something I will create with, of course, assistance from a more powerful Creator. Possibly I am, like Marilyn Monroe, the kind of artist who achieves her most valuable accomplishments during hours apart from aesthetic concerns. It could be very likely, also as with Marilyn, that I will inadvertently provide salvation for others even while I seek and fail to find my own saviour. I must steel myself for such a possibility with whatever means lies close at hand."

Madeleine took another swallow of her drink. "And

while it is not my place to question the worth of my duty, I may at least ask myself who, after all, Frances Farmer was and in what way her life of suffering differed from that of anyone in this very bar. Neither physical, emotional nor spiritual pain may be measured on a scale and given exact weight. Conceding the fact that she was raped by gangs of jeering, drunken soldiers on a thousand and one nights, one might very well say that Frances Farmer was blessed in having a rich, full romantic life. Ours is simply not to say.

"There is no doubt that I have committed several sins since arriving in this city, and to be punished for them is something I must not only expect but also anticipate with longing. By doing such penance I am, in the end, assuredly paving the way for an extremely lucrative reward; for example, free and easy entrance to Heaven. If I can only keep this in mind, it would enable me to sustain my vision and proceed onward with my search. In any event, there is really no option for me since I did not volunteer for this mission, but was chosen."

Madeleine looked up from her drink for the first time in a number of hours. Frank had just come through the door for his evening shift, and following behind him were a number of customers who rubbed their hands in expectation of Happy Hour. Fingers would show up any minute now. Madeleine felt considerably better for meeting her demons face to face, to the extent that she was empowered to repair the ruins of her mascara. Even while accepting that the party was over, she ordered another drink to celebrate the spiritual hurdle over which she had just leaped.

■ Another Station of the Cross

"Hey, sister."

Madeleine looked up from her second celebratory drink at a man who sat across the bar. Something about the man had puzzled her when she had noticed him enter the Shanghai several minutes before, but now she could not remember what this was and she suspected that even at the moment it could not easily have been defined.

"Are you addressing me?" she asked, wondering if he had a nearer relation on hand.

"I hope you're not a jazz baby."

"A what?"

"A jazz baby. The kind of girl who crosses over to or from the wrong side of the tracks. They like to drink in bars and don't mind at all if they're the only woman among many men. In fact, they prefer it like that. You know what I mean."

"I'm not sure I do," Madeleine said a clear ringing tone; it was necessary to speak quite loudly in order to be heard across the room, though the bar was still virtually empty and silent. Happy Hour had not arrived, unaccountably and despite the fact that its time had certainly come. "Of course, I appreciate music as much as the next person. Do you disapprove?"

"You would if you were me."

"Tell me about it. That is, if you'd care to join me."

Madeleine tried again to recall what had initially disturbed her about this gentleman as she watched him thread his way with some difficulty through clusters of tables and chairs. He sat down heavily and perspired visibly.

"But you forgot your drink," pointed out Madeleine helpfully.

For a second it looked like her new friend would either cry or break some chairs. Instead, he looked

craftily at Madeleine, then in a childish voice said, "I
didn't like that one anyway. I forgot it on purpose. Hey,
pal," he shouted to Frank. "Two whiskies."

Madeleine wisely said nothing, for this was the kind
of large, big-boned man who can do much damage
without giving it a second thought. For several minutes
they sipped their drinks in silence.

"See this table top?" asked the man abruptly, peering
through the slits of his red eyes. "Pretty tiny, ain't it.
Well, once I had a baby who could sing and dance on
table tops no larger than this one and that was when she
was pie-eyed."

"Was she talented?" asked Madeleine.

"Hell, yes. It's warm in here, wouldn't you say?" The
man loosened his collar. "Though not as warm as last
month. Things were cooler in the old days. Sure, she
could have gone straight to Hollywood and I mean right
to the top. A big star, everyone said that. But she was
rich or spoiled or maybe a bit of both, the kind without
the ambition it takes to be a star. She preferred to drink
and carry on in hotels and bars."

"Once I joined a circus," said Madeleine. "Only it was
just pretend. A high-wire act, with two partners. We
would dress the same and do the same tricks at the
same time, except in reverse. Like three swans swimming on a glass lake. It was pretty."

"It's an old, old story. Thousands have everything in
the world that it takes. Plus a little craving that caves in
their skin and eyes and voice. Believe me, baby, I've
seen it happen a million times or more."

"Haven't we all. A circus came to town and every
child on the block flocked to see the acts. For a while we
all wished to dance on horses or fly from trapezes or
juggle flaming torches in the air. There was one girl in
the circus who had beautiful long red hair and the
strongest teeth in all this world. I felt inspired when I
saw her climb up a ladder to the very top of the tent,
so high that she looked like a little glass doll. To the

accompaniment of a drum roll she bit into a golden cord, and there she hung a hundred feet above the crowds. Only her teeth lay between the beautiful girl and a messy death, for no safety net waited to catch her if she fell. As the coiled cord unwound, she spun faster and faster, her arms curved above her head, her hair whipped around and around, her white throat looking up at Heaven. I watched her spin six nights in a row, but was not there on the seventh night, when the red-haired lady fell to her death."

"That's a sad story, but mine's sadder. You see, we loved each other all along, as sweetly as one child loves another. It was the drinking that made her act ugly and take up with mean fellows. But with me she was different. It was to me she always came the morning after, when her head hurt and the silver slippers lay all busted beside the bed."

"They said it was an awful sight. They said the circus tent was as still as could be that night the glass-doll lady fell and crumpled upon the sawdust. No one screamed or cried or fainted when they watched her die. The audience just filed slowly from the tent, then went their separate ways into the cold, starry night."

"She lay there in my arms, those mornings after, and cried and cried. I didn't ask her where she'd been or who made her cry, I knew even then that children need secrets. Later she turned ugly from the drink and dope, and only came to me for money. I gave it to her. Yes, I gave it to her. When she danced on table tops in bars, no one watched her any more except for me. One night she didn't show up at the bar, but even I didn't care by then. My sorrow drowned while the lifeguard watched drunk from shore."

Madeleine looked into her glass, as a seer looks for shadows of lost days. "Her name was Annemarie," she whispered.

"Later, there were different stories, the same old stories. Some said she died in the gutter or alone in an unpaid hotel room. There was talk of the needle, the razor, the lonely park bench. But they were all stories. You could pick any ending and it could be just as true as any other."

Madeleine seemed to hear the man for the first time. She leaned toward him. "What ending do you believe in?"

"Well, I heard from this guy that she made it out to California, just like she said she would. He claimed he ran into her on Hollywood Boulevard and she looked happy and alive. Of course, that guy never told the truth, but what the hell. Who cares."

"Maybe she joined a circus," suggested Madeleine.

The man looked at her suspiciously. "I know your type, sister. The kind that sets a trap then walks away without bothering to see who she's captured."

"Excuse me," Madeleine replied somewhat politely. "You are mistaken. Perhaps you confuse me with another lady."

"All the same, all the same," shouted the man. Suddenly, he rose and threw the table onto its side. One leg nicked Madeleine's ankle and a trickle of blood began to run into her silver shoe. The man turned and walked heavily from the bar.

Madeleine felt a trifle foolish, sitting in the middle of a room with no table before her, so she picked up her lamé evening bag, stepped adroitly over the broken glass and slid onto a bar stool.

"What got into that joe?" asked Frank.

Madeleine rested an elbow on the counter. "Oh, the poor man has been wounded by the world. Pour us both a drink and let's forget what ails the heart."

Frank was relieved that apparently the blonde no longer felt so under the weather, but he was too delicate to comment upon this change. "Say," he said, "whatever happened to that kid you used to chum around with?"

"People come and go and nothing ties them down. I haven't seen him for a while. You see, I'm not his anchor."

"I saw him over on Twelfth just the other day. Or at least I think it was him. He pretended not to know me and he looked kind of different."

"Different how?" asked Madeleine.

"Just different," replied Frank uneasily; it was obvious that he was concealing something. "I recognized the two characters he was with. They're bad news, take my word for it. I suggest this: if you see that kid again, look right past him like you don't even see him. He's no good, though it's none of my business."

"It's not, and I think you're wrong. But let's not us quarrel, Frank. It's so important that I be good friends with the man who makes my drinks. We are good friends, aren't we?"

"Sure we are." Frank turned his back and poured liquids back and forth between bottles. He hummed a tune that Madeleine didn't remember, if she had ever known it at all.

"I never dreamed it would turn out like this," she said, but only to herself.

■■■ Painful Pleasure

Several minutes before, a thoughtfully dressed woman with short curled hair had entered the Shanghai. It was obvious from her indecision at the door that the place was unfamiliar to her. She had chosen a stool two down from Madeleine and ordered an Old-Fashioned. For several minutes both women gazed silently at Frank's back.

"Pardon me," said the woman, rather abruptly, "but I couldn't help but overhear your little discussion. I like to share views as well, but it almost seems a lost art in these modern times of ours. Now, you people have had heartache, that I understand. But, my Lord, who hasn't lived and suffered in this world? I have found a certain

measure of consolation in the wider view. Science, time,
world famine, et cetera." She looked wisely around the
bar and a merry smile flowered on her face. Playfully
she swung her legs, which were crossed neatly at the
ankles.

Frank turned and looked at the plump woman, with
an expression of great dislike. Madeleine was shocked
to see him roll his eyes, unguardedly enacting a pan-
tomime to show he thought the woman crazy. However,
the little lady smiled as brightly as before, and with an
inviting air patted the empty stool between Madeleine
and herself. It was evident that she was enjoying herself
immensely.

"Thanks," said Madeleine. She changed stools with
difficulty, and in the process a little blood dribbled from
one high-heeled silver shoe. "Well, I hear what you say,
but how painful it is to see the stars, the endless horizon. Try this and see if I am not right: gaze into the
starry night or beyond the moon, and you will feel great
pain and loss. Only inhuman creatures take pleasure
from the sunset, the stars, the far off vistas."

The plump little woman was enchanted. "Stella," she
said, extending her hand. "Now, isn't that lovely. I also
am no star gazer, though I do read my horoscope faith-
fully. I owe myself that much. But when my mind is not
too occupied with world concerns, I also find pleasure
in the smaller things of life. Just this morning I looked
around my kitchenette and thought: this is joy!"

A shadow passed quickly across Madeleine's face. "I
don't think I said precisely that," she corrected Stella.
"The little things offer only painful pleasure, but at least
they are known and familiar and cause no unforeseen
fear." Her voice trailed off and she stirred the ice in her
drink with the index finger of her left hand. "Frank,
make me something warm and soothing. So tell me,
friend, do you live in a house, an apartment or a hotel?"

Immediately the stranger beamed more broadly.
"Why, I have a cute one-bedroom on the third floor of a

new apartment complex. You should come and see it sometime—it's a distance from the centre of the city. There's some nice furniture, some nice plants and a lot more. I'm pretty proud of the way I've fixed up my home."

"I suppose you have a TV, a stereo and all the rest of it?"

"Sure I do," replied Stella. "My friend Nina says to me: Stella, I don't know how you do it. She can't believe how well I manage my money now that I'm no longer officially employed. But I think of my apartment as an investment, for I hope to catch a working man. I just invite the fellows over for a drink and they fall for the place. Most gals don't know how much a working man yearns for a real homey spot to hang his hat. At this moment there are five working men making me offers. Good offers, too. But I'm taking my own sweet time. Not that I'm waiting for Frank Sinatra to come along. It's just that important decisions can't be made too slowly." She eyed Frank and fussily ordered another drink. "And I like 'em strong," she told him with a wink.

"Working men are hard to find," commented Madeleine.

"That's the truth, my friend. You see, I've worked hard all my life—something in the business line—and to tell you God's truth, I didn't care for it. Not that I have a lazy bone in my body, I don't. But the business world is foreign to me. Of course they frown on it during these troubled times, but nothing gives me greater pleasure than to turn up the stereo really loud and go around my rooms with the vacuum. I'm the kind of woman who likes to spend a lot of time at home and it doesn't shame me one bit. When I'm away from home I get a sort of blue feeling."

"Well, it's a pleasure to meet someone who knows exactly what she wants," said Madeleine.

"It's a shame to admit it, but even this fancy bar

makes me nervous. It's nothing to do with you, son,"
Stella said to Frank. She pushed her curls and smiled at
some private joke. "Yes, as I was saying, I feel tense
when I'm away from home and tend to drink too much
in bars like this to compensate. But a friend of mine told
me working men have been known to come here, and
you know I'm always looking."

"Are you the shy type?" asked Madeleine, warming
up to Stella.

"No, neither shy nor antisocial. Heavens, I have more
company in my place than anyone else in the building.
Everyone likes to come over to my place, I've decorated
it so nice. We play cards around the kitchen table, and
naturally we have snacks along with our drinks. Oh, it's
a fine time. No one ever wants to leave my place."

"It certainly sounds like a centre of enjoyment," said
Madeleine. "I haven't played cards for years."

"They're not so much in vogue lately, though it's all
beyond me. What's gayer than a group of friends and a
good game of hearts? You can talk and socialize all you
want, there's music in the background, whatever your
heart desires."

"That does sound attractive," said Madeleine with an
envious light in her eyes. "I have a room here in the city
that was once home to me. Just last week I was in this
very bar with a large collection of friends. But something always happens. If I may speak frankly, of late my
room and my life here have been something less than
ideal."

"Well, listen, honey. I don't even know your name,
but I'll take you in all the same. My friend Nina is away
and I can use the company. So if you won't mind my
boyfriends and my card games, your home is with me."

"It sounds perfect," said Madeleine. "I'm sure I will
be completely happy there."

Frank watched pensively as the two women walked
arm in arm toward the door. "Madeleine, you haven't
finished your drink," he called.

She laughed lightly into Stella's curls.

■ Part Three

*Judge: Is it true that you were in a fight
at a Hollywood nightclub?
Frances Farmer: Yes, I was fighting for
my country and myself.*

Trial transcript, 1943

Part Three

▰▰ A Crown of Thorns

The rain began. Children returned to school, tourists left town, and home-dwellers withdrew from the city of summer into tightly shut and sealed houses. Those who could not so easily escape only exchanged the streets for bars and cafés and hotel rooms. Each afternoon darkness fell a little sooner, colder, harder. Coloured neon cried and quivered on wet pavement; alleys were empty save for starving, shivering cats. Even here beside the sea, when the cold was never severe enough for snow, it was felt that the time ahead would be difficult and long. There were many people who feared the falling rain and there were many who were uneasy during this season.

On or off duty Harry of the Starlite Lounge had felt the rain coming long before anyone else. His bad left leg began to ache steadily and sharply even while the rain was still falling only through the future. I should become a fortune-teller, thought the man when the rain inevitably arrived. Then his face was set stiffly into a mask as he fought to forget the ceaseless complaint screaming between his left toe and shin, as he struggled to keep his mind on pouring drinks, making change. Customers who didn't know the bartender wondered at his stillness and silence; when they saw him lurch from one side of his counter to another, they believed him drunk. A sympathetic response to the natural world, Harry sometimes thought grimly as another ball of pain fell through his knee like a drop of rain. He closed his eyes and didn't want to open them upon drinkers' grey faces sprinkled amid artificial, decorative stars. Yeah, guess I'm just a sympathetic kind of guy. But not pathetic. No.

135

■■■■■   iii

For a while Sister Mary persisted with her sidewalk preaching, for this was the time when she was most needed and this was when her voice could not fail her. In a yellow raincoat she stood before her pulpit on the corners and sang in harmony with the splashing of taxis through petroleum puddles, and above this sound she heard the whistle of the night train drawing near. "It's coming," she called, seeing her breath hang like smoke in the air and hoping her words could be seen and recognized as clearly. "But till you get on board listen to me and hear me. There's a warm bed, hot food and dry clothing for one and all. There are helping hands and we must reach out and take them. The Lord Above understands how hard it is to hear His Word when your shoes are wet and when your belly grumbles. He understands and He hears, and the night train is coming to carry us all away.

"It will be here soon," cried Sister Mary; but something happened to her voice when the rains began to fall, and now her throat was more hoarse during the first fresh hour of morning than it had ever been in the final weary hours of afternoon. Slowly through September Sister Mary's call became a sound that could not be understood and it became a noise to be ignored like the screaming sirens. At first it seemed that Sister Mary was calling in a foreign language or that she was singing songs she had learned in Zimbabwe long ago; then it seemed that she was not singing words at all, but only crying sound like any animal in pain who cries on and on and who will not cease crying.

And through the falling rain people who before had gathered around to hear Sister Mary now hurried by with folded newspapers over their heads in place of hats. And then it was that several people who cared for Sister Mary became concerned. They worried that the long arm of the law, which before had only waved to Sister Mary in understanding and in greeting, now would reach out and take Sister Mary away. And she would be confined with all the others who cried out in words not of this world, and from this place there would be no leaving for Sister Mary and there would be no cure for her.

And so one day a Brother came by and he spoke to Sister Mary and he looked into her eyes until Sister Mary stopped crying and ceased shaking on the corner. Then the Brother helped Sister Mary lift her pulpit up three flights of stairs and carry it into her room above Fair Freddy's pawnshop. They set it in the corner, by the stove where there was space. Later, when Sister Mary could stand looking at the idle pulpit no longer, she tore off its cross of silver cardboard and she covered the box with a white cloth embroidered with pink pansies, and she used it as an everyday table.

And from this time Sister Mary did not cry out in words of this or other worlds and she was silent. Sister Mary did not leave her room except to walk to the corner store and back again, and it was believed by some that Sister Mary had left the city for good. She sat beside her window and looked down upon the streets. She looked also at what had been her pulpit and she prayed for strength to preach again one day. Sometimes she wondered if the Lord could find no more use for her and if her work was done. And she wondered if it was time for her to go to her rest.

Often Sister Mary would look up from The Word and she would believe that the rain had stopped falling, that it had finished washing the world clean, that its work was done. But as soon as she listened for the rain she would hear it beat upon her roof once more, drowning out the long-drawn whistle of the night train that was leaving with the saved ones on board. Drowning out the cries of the ones who were left behind in the city, in the rain, in despair.

■■■■■■   iv

The banjo in Fair Freddy's window vanished. One day a woman stood for an hour or more looking at all the goods behind the glass. She could not see her banjo there, yet she could not believe it gone, for Fair Freddy had given his word that he would sell it to no one but her. Every day the woman returned to the pawnshop to remind Fair Freddy of his promise and to ask about her lost banjo and to wonder where it could be. She haunted the sidewalk in front of the store, she huddled in the doorway to keep dry. She followed Fair Freddy home from work and to his regular café for lunch and to his favourite Happy Hour bar. "Where's my banjo?" she would ask again and again, dogging his footsteps and plucking his sleeve. At last, one October afternoon, Fair Freddy formed a plan and he told the woman that the banjo had been returned to him. Now she could have her banjo and now she would want nothing more for the rest of her days. Fair Freddy showed her another banjo which resembled the original one only slightly. "But where are the moon and five stars?" sobbed the woman. "They were what I loved and longed for. Without them this banjo means nothing to me. It's not the same."

■■■■■■   v

It was already dark by the time Frank left for work in late afternoon. At first he moved quickly between his apartment and the Shanghai, as if the distance between the two places frightened him. Scared that if he didn't keep moving fast he'd forget where he was headed, would wander lost in the rain for the rest of his life? "I live in darkness," Frank thought suddenly, the words seeming to fall like drops out of the big black sky. Turning up his collar and bending his face toward the sidewalk, he walked more quickly.

Yet it took him longer to reach the Shanghai these days. He couldn't seem to walk at a steady pace any more; his hastened step would slow. He'd find himself stopping before a store window and gazing blankly at a display of furs or furniture or children's toys—then shaking himself back into motion without knowing how long he'd been standing there. He paused on a corner and looked at length in every direction, like someone unsure of his way who can only guess which avenue before him leads to his destination. Lighting a cigarette, Frank stood in a doorway to smoke. His grey eyes narrowed and looked into faces approaching from both ways along the sidewalk. Was he searching for a particular face? Frank tossed away the half-smoked cigarette and walked on. He passed the Starlite Lounge, and through its window glimpsed a dim blue-lit space around which figures floated; it was like looking into a fish bowl. He moved quickly past the Hollywood Palace, noticing that another letter had burned out in the sign. He glanced into the doorway of the Holiday Hotel and observed that Joe, the graveyard clerk, wasn't on duty yet. It was still way too early for Joe's shift to start; Frank was late for his own shift. He didn't know why he'd lately taken to walking this particular route each day—what he hoped to glimpse in store windows and strangers' eyes, his reasons for always pausing at certain mysterious points. Another kind of Calvary.

He didn't make it in through the door of the Shanghai till evening was well under way. Steve, his part-time man, looked at Frank and noticed that his grave face was for once unshaven; the stubble made the man look older. "Feeling a little under the weather," said Frank, avoiding Steve's eyes. "Can you stick around a while longer? Think I need something to set me up."

Frank carried a half-full snifter over to one of the small tables. This was the first time he'd ever sat like a regular customer in his own bar. A broken rule, he thought, taking a sip of brandy and feeling the good warmth slide down into his belly. Did the bar look larger or smaller from this angle? Smaller, he thought.

From behind the counter you could see from one end of
the room to the other; your eyes could sweep across the
crowd, settle upon any face, move onto any other. Here
he could only see the faces nearest him. Couldn't see the
area over by the pool table, had to turn around or look
over his shoulder if he wanted to see the door. Smaller,
sure. Smaller, sadder, dingier.

The place was just starting to fill up for the night.
Frank recognized most of the faces around him. Noticed
how they kind of looked at him in surprise. Wondering
what to make of his sitting here among them. Should
they ask him over for a drink or would he invite them to
his table for a few? What the hell was he doing, anyhow? Spying on them? The drinkers nearest Frank took
on guarded expressions, lowered their voices slightly,
quickly glanced toward then away from him. A ripple
of uneasiness washed through the room.

All he wanted was a little pick-me-up because he was
feeling kind of low. Low and tired; he had trouble sleeping lately. But why not pick himself up behind this
counter? Why was he sitting here on the other side all of
a sudden—across a boundary as definite as the border
between two alien nations? Maybe he wanted to know
how it felt over here. So the next time he was behind his
counter, in the country where he belonged, he'd have
some sort of lead into what he saw happen night after
night in this strange land and what he could never
understand.

Had the past summer been so puzzling? Anything
out of the ordinary? Frank couldn't seize upon one particular thing that stood out. A few fights, a few tears, a
few laughs. What else? What mysterious vision had he
glimpsed that he hoped would become clear if he sat
with a drink here at this small table covered with cheap
red cloth?

For a dozen years he'd felt good about the Shanghai.
Felt it to be a worthwhile use of his time. Yet what did
those twelve years mean if he couldn't even begin to

explain the worth of the bar and his time inside it? Something to do with taking care of others—that was it. That was why he was here. Helping anyone at all to make it through a tough night, a hard week, a hot summer. Helping, not harming.

Yet thinking it over, Frank couldn't light on one thing that showed he really helped at all. If he and his bar weren't there, these drinkers would be somewhere else—probably over at the Starlite with Harry—that served them more or less the same. Frank glanced again at the faces nearest him. Faces that paid him little attention now. Faces of people who'd been forced to adapt to a thousand sudden changes at the blink of an eye, who'd already become used to his face being here among theirs. All the faces. All a little more lined and grey and broken up since he'd seen them for the first time way back at the dawn of history. Sure, things change, people change. These people would keep coming around till one day he'd suddenly wonder what had happened to So-and-So. Come to think of it, he hadn't seen So-and-So for quite a while. So-and-So was gone, he would never see So-and-So again. What the hell, so he'd helped So-and-So make it through a long night, a bad week, a lonely summer. To what purpose? So some other Frank, Joe or Harry in some other town could help So-and-So make it through the next night, week, summer. Until there were no more next times for So-and-So. But Frank, Joe and Harry were lucky guys, there was always another unlucky So-and-So to assist through another season, the work of some lucky guys was never done, there was an endless supply of unlucky So-and-Sos, so don't you worry, son.

Slow down you lucky Such-and-Such, Frank told himself. Take it easy and take in the scenery. Yeah, he guessed the bar did look different from this angle. You noticed different things. Besides the cigarette burns on the table cloths you noticed the cracks in the vinyl seat covers and you noticed the stains on the worn-out

carpet and you noticed the drinkers in a way you'd
never noticed them before. How one or both hands are
always clutching the glass, even while it rests idle on the
table a hand always encircles a glass, as if the glass were
in danger of running away or floating up to the ceiling.
Stay a while, glass, don't go and leave me all alone.
Then the hand lifts the glass with a purely automatic
motion. A secret signal has whined through the smoky
air and triggered a nerve in the brain, issued a curt com-
mand: lift glass, open mouth, tilt glass, swallow, lower
glass. Same with cigarettes. Same with tears and laughter, smiles and frowns. Jerky mechanical motions.
Puppets. Manipulated by whom?

Frank felt a chill, a wave of something colder than the
November air outside, pass through him. He took
another quick sip of brandy. Funny, his glass had been
empty a minute ago; now it was full again. Never mind.
Lift glass, open mouth, tilt glass, swallow, lower glass.
Hell.

So a few people had come and a few people had gone,
and now the summer was over for sure and so was
autumn too. Big deal. And the Shanghai Saloon was his
contribution to world peace and harmony or something
like that. What did he want, for Christ's sake? Visible
proof. That's what he wanted. Verifiable evidence that
the bar and his time in it added up to something solid,
something real, something that couldn't be washed
away by rain. Failing that, maybe he'd settle for a little
peace. Frank felt the warm brandy flicker through his
veins, heard the rattle of Fingers' piano start up. A little
piece of peace. That's all he and a million other sons and
daughters of bitches wanted. Him and Madeleine and
Sister Mary and every other name you could find in the
phone book. And don't forget the ones with unlisted
numbers, pal, the ones seeking privacy as well as peace.

Well, he'd never gotten the blonde's number, that's
for sure. How many hours had he watched her out of
the corner of his eye? Flirting, frowning, flouncing

about. Always falling. Yet he didn't have a clue what made her tick. If she ticked. Madeleine had made it through another summer here and now she was or was not making it through another winter somewhere else. Helped by another Frank, Joe or Harry. Where? A town exactly the same as this town. They shot a hundred movies on the same sound stage, called the same city a hundred different names, made an ingenuous audience believe that Berlin was Paris was Rome. Madeleine was in Chicago or Montreal or New Orleans. So what, so nothing.

Before it had always been enough for him to watch and to wonder and to pour the drinks. He'd felt he had a place in the whole crazy business, that he was woven into the pattern in a certain spot because he was meant to be in that spot and nowhere else. Now he wasn't so sure. Now he felt maybe there wasn't any pattern. Maybe there was only someone knitting without any clear set of directions and without any idea of what they finally hoped to weave together. A coat of many colours? A blanket large enough to warm all the world? And maybe someone always tore out the stitches before the thing could ever be finished, ripped them out because the stitches were flawed or because there'd been a change of plans or for no clear reason that anyone on earth could know. The ball of wool became tangled and twisted and it would never again be a smooth round globe that could be knitted into a pattern that was beautiful and true, into something that was strong and solid and real.

And for another dozen years he'd watch and wonder and pour the drinks. Over and over he'd learn the same small lesson: there is no pattern, the world will never be woven together, the loose strands will not be joined into one. The Shanghai Saloon is not an oasis in the middle of a vast desert where all the thirsty, weary searchers can rest and drink and gather strength enough to cross the last miles of burning sand that lie between here and—what? The ocean?

Union.

Frank gazed down at the table top before him. When did this new glass of brandy arrive and how had it gotten here? Frank looked up and saw Steve standing with folded arms behind the counter, standing very far away. The table top was nearer. Frank's finger moved from one cigarette burn on the cloth to another. Join-the-dots. What shape would emerge if all the dots were connected? What face? That of the chief knitter? The big puppeteer?

Lift glass, open mouth, tilt glass, swallow, lower glass.

It was like someone had suddenly turned up the volume of a film's soundtrack. In one moment the bar seemed to have become much noisier. Louder voices, looser laughter, broader chuckles. And it was like the film was playing at a different speed now, both faster and slower at once. People seemed to float between tables, eyes seemed to glide like fins around the room. Expressions melted one into the other, time blurred into a liquid mass without divisions.

Frank blended into the bar, but not as he'd always blended in when behind his counter. Then he'd been woven into the outer edge, as part of the strong border that holds the thing together. Now he felt woven right into the centre of the pattern and held there by stitches on every side of him that were connected to every part of him. Now he knew why he'd crossed his counter and entered this other liquid land. Now he knew what he'd always watched and wondered about while over on the other side. He lifted his glass and looked around the bar. A dozen other glasses lifted at the same time. Union.

███ vi

A change came over the Hollywood Palace, but for some weeks Sam tried to ignore it. He kept busy. He continued to screen five different shows a day, beginning in morning and ending at midnight. There were tickets, candy bars and popcorn to be sold. Films had to be ordered, projected, then returned to distributors. Turn on the neon, then turn it off. Open, close. The routine of twenty-four years carried him through the hours at the Palace, and as soon as he arrived home from work Sam fell into a deep long sleep. However, at morning he woke more tired than rested, and with flickering, shadowy memories of dreams. Sometimes it seemed he'd spent the whole night watching something awful occur right before him which he could neither try to stop nor close his eyes to. At other times he felt that through the night he'd been trapped himself inside the awful occurrence while someone else viewed it and did not try to halt it. As he moved through the early days of December a cold haunted feeling came over Sam whenever he stopped to think.

One night after the last Janet Gaynor show was over and the crowd had gone away Sam sat at the back of the empty Palace. Red velvet curtains were pulled across the screen. The threadbare crimson carpet was a sticky mess of spilled soda pop and popcorn. Sam hummed a movie theme, but in the dark vacant theatre his voice sounded small and scared. He rubbed his hot eyes. Thoughts about the changes occurring in his theatre crept out from the blackness around him and sniffed him like cautious mice.

Ever since the rains had begun things had been different. Usually Sam felt that only real fans came to his place to watch the shows. But he knew that more and more the true believers were being replaced by people who didn't give a damn about the movies. They just wanted a dry place to sit where no one would bother them. Each morning they dragged themselves through the lobby, sat or slept in their damp clothes until midnight, then dragged themselves back out into the dripping streets. Sam continued to stand by the front door of the Palace, entertaining everyone who entered or left the theatre with his imitations and funny stories of the old stars. But he couldn't make these customers laugh.

To some extent this happened every winter. In previous years Sam had turned up the heat and there had been no problems; the audiences waited quietly and peacefully for spring to return, when they could sit on benches in parks or at bus stops again. But this winter wasn't the same. Now it seemed that no matter how high the heat was turned on these people would never feel warm. They looked like they would stay cold and wet until one day without warning they would all rise to run screaming through the streets. Sam tried to choose with care the pictures he screened, selecting light comedies and dancing shows, avoiding images that might be the least bit disturbing.

Still there was trouble. Earlier that evening there had been a scene and it hadn't been the first, either. Janet Gaynor was dying in the arms of the man she was too proud to love and an old lady in the audience suddenly started to scream. "I'm Janet and Janet is me. She isn't dying and I'm not dying. It's a lie, a lie!" cried the old lady over and over. Nothing could quiet her down. When Sam tried to soothe her, she climbed under her chair and crouched snarling down there. Finally Sam had to call the cops. It took them quite a while to pry her hands from the legs of the seat; as they dragged her away, the old lady didn't seem to know who or where she was. There was a look of triumph on her face.

But the funniest thing was that no one in the audience paid any attention to the old lady or her screams. It was almost as if they didn't care what happened on or off the screen. Sometimes Sam stood at the back of the house and watched the audience. It was difficult to tell which viewers were awake and which were sleeping. No one laughed at the comedy on the screen. It was when the audience was most quiet that Sam felt a kind of fear and felt somehow closest to the memory of his dream.

He tried to push these worries from his mind. He was

absorbed with a project that was more important than anything he had ever done in his life. It was something he had dreamed of for a long time and at last it was coming true. At last he would show them all.

After five years of searching Sam had managed to get his hands on every one of Frances Farmer's pictures. They came out of vaults where they had been hiding beneath dust for thirty years. They came from secret rooms with locked doors and lost keys. They came from dark corners of attics and from the bottom of broken trunks and from other places where long-forgotten things lie. They were pictures which certain people had felt nervous about other people seeing. Now Sam would screen them all and he would give everyone the chance to see. Frances would speak to them. She would tell them the truth that they were waiting to hear. Sam didn't know what would happen when they saw and heard her. Maybe she would make the cold sleep-walkers feel peace and calm and able to make it through the winter. Maybe the pictures would make them angry and mad as hell, make them smash store windows and riot and loot and set cars ablaze in the streets. Sam wasn't sure what would happen, but he knew something would change. He knew he had to do this.

He rubbed his eyes again. All his hours in darkness bothered them. He felt obliged to watch every show that ran in his house to make sure scenes hadn't been cut or placed in the wrong order by some sloppy distributor who didn't give a damn about his work. Lately Sam had begun to feel that all the movies he'd ever watched were stuck in layers upon his eyes. All he could see were a million images burned and blurred into one crazy picture that wouldn't go away no matter how he blinked. Just the other day he'd sat half-way through a picture before realizing that it was Joan Crawford and not Rosalind Russell who laughed and cried before his eyes. And there was that time last week when he was walking through what seemed to be the empty midnight streets

of a Norma Shearer tragedy. Only after he'd stepped off
the curb and been woken by brakes and horns did he
see that the street was filled with rush-hour traffic and
that Norma was not crying in a doorway by a lamp-pole
in the rain. Maybe it was some mixed-up movie he saw
in his dreams, where black is white and white is black,
where comedy is tragic and tragedy is funny.

Though it was around two in the morning, Sam didn't
feel like going home to dream. He walked up the aisle
and climbed the stairs to the projection room. Putting on
one of the Gaynor pictures, he climbed back down into
the theatre and took a front-row seat. He had seen this
picture many times before. Its dialogue and action were
so familiar that Sam could let his thoughts wander yet
still follow the show. He sat there in the dark, feeling
like an old friend was very near.

███████ vii

Jeanette bought a bottle and drank alone in her room.
She turned to gold and from her window waved like a
flag to people down below. The empty bottle fell five
storeys and crashed upon concrete, causing a passerby it
nearly hit to scream he'd call the cops. So Jeanette went
wandering in the streets until she lost her way, and soon
she couldn't feel the driving rain or see armies of fire
escapes running naked to the roofs.

Slow Burn and The Pilot were looking for the man
who owed them one they needed right away. They were
lost and cold beside the freeway and didn't know just
what to do. Stalled like cars backed up from an accident
far ahead: windshield wipers slapping raindrops,
exhaust hanging like hairy creatures in the air.

Out on the overpass they found Jeanette waving to
cars that crawled below. Wind blew from the sea and
tore her words away somewhere: north to where cars
were heading, headlights hitting lost fog that huddled
above the city; through the night insomniacs would wait
and pray for a morning sun to burn it all away.

They helped her to the other side and parked on a stone bench while deciding what to do. With blind eyes Jeanette saw nowhere, hands twisting broken glasses on her lap. "Get Madeleine," she said, trying to light a rain-spoiled cigarette. The wind wiped out the match flame until Slow Burn and The Pilot gathered round. People under umbrellas eyed the trio, then quickened steps. Fog horns boomed like church bells drowning in the bay.

Slow Burn turned and saw The Pilot was needing bad. His clothes and hair were soaked, a smeared look was on his face. Jeanette stumbled between the boys until they found their corner, where Rita was hiding in the phone booth without a dime to call back home. She scrawled a lipstick message on the glass for anyone who wished to find her, help her, carry her away.

"Get Madeleine," said Jeanette, so they walked to the hotel.

"I done told you people she don't live here no more," said the lady behind the desk. "That right, just stand there dripping till you flood my lobby. Then you be happy, I suppose."

"Joe?" asked Jeanette.

"Do I look like any joe to you?" asked the desk clerk. "Joe work here nights so not to have to mess with daytime trouble like I got to do."

"Where's the key to your room?" Slow Burn asked Jeanette.

She smiled and looked through pockets until her smile grew sad. "I don't know. I gave it to a man crying across the bridge. He said he needed it to unlock all the imprisoned hearts around here. Then he sang a song he made up just for me and said The Lord will provide."

"I provide you to leave here right now. Shoo," said the woman behind the desk.

"We can take her to the avenue room and sleep until the rain lets up," said Slow Burn to the others.

"There something wrong with that boy. He ain't

well," said the desk clerk. The Pilot's teeth were chattering and his knees and hands were shaking.

"It just the cold. He don't like the cold," said Rita.

"And I don't like people losing keys. There a five-dol-
lar charge for lost keys. You got five dollars, sugar?"

"She ain't got nothing," said Slow Burn, looking at
Jeanette. "Why don't Madeleine look after her friends?"

■■■■■ viii

Five floors above the hotel lobby Ingrid climbed into
bed and under covers, hoping to be warmed. On the
floor, within easy reach, stood her radio. She stretched
out an arm, felt for a dial, turned it in search of favourite
songs. They were always one station away.

Through the afternoon Ingrid remained in bed, pulled
in and out of sleep by familiar music, by unfamiliar
voices. As the hour grew late signals reached farther
through the cleared, emptied air of night, and more stations appeared audible on Ingrid's radio. Now voices
reached her from the Rocky Mountains and from the
great Central Plains beyond and from far down in the
desert. There was darkness all across America and
everywhere there were voices speaking in the darkness,
clear and uncoded connections: crossing miles of flat
fields where the lights of only one farmhouse interrupted the darkness; climbing thickly forested mountains where no lights burned at all; traversing all the
blank spaces on the continent that still waited to be discovered; offering information about what it was like to
be alive in Saskatchewan and South Dakota and Kansas
City and Quebec. It was raining all along the Pacific
Coast and it was warm and dry in the southern interior.
A cold front was moving in over the northwest, a high-
pressure ridge was building to the east, and heavy snow
was falling upon Minneapolis.

Ingrid was carried from song to voice to song through
the falling night. Waking stranded in strange places, she
would not open her eyes, but waited for sleep to come

and carry her away again; and for music to seep into her dreams and to fill them with images of love and loss. The gulf between waking and sleeping gradually narrowed until the two shores of these separate countries were within sight, then bridged by singing voices, choirs of angels, hosts of hard-faced disc jockeys. Ingrid stood upon the bridge and looked down at a cushion of fog that rested on grey water far below. The beckoning grey of angels' eyes. She leaped and fell.

"Who is it?" Ingrid's eyes opened to find her room in darkness. "Madeleine? Is it you?" The signal died away, became lost beneath crackling, buzzing static.

Ingrid put on a home-made dress patterned with red polka dots and went out into the street. She walked east for several miles, then stopped. Music sounded faintly from behind the door before her. Shivering in the summer dress, Ingrid stood at the entrance of the Dollar-A-Dance. But she did not knock upon the door and it did not open; Ingrid's pale face gleamed as it turned away. Nearby a sax player blew mournful riffs that went nowhere. The cold made his fingers clumsy. An open case at his feet contained several pennies. When Ingrid walked past without adding to his earnings, he stopped playing and swore at her.

Her eyes were fixed upon a figure that stood beneath lamplight across the street. Ingrid looked both ways before stepping off the curb and walking in a straight line toward the man who whistled on the sidewalk opposite, his tune travelling like a secret signal through the night, a sound that she could follow with closed eyes, without ever stumbling, without becoming lost. "At last," she said, nearing the man and seeing his hard unsmiling face, his flat grey eyes. "Napoleon has finally arrived."

He looked at her quizzically, then shrugged. "Why not?" he asked, taking her arm.

"Elba was always only across the water," said Ingrid, walking with her face glimmering up toward the man, feeling the secret warmth that travelled through his clothes.

"Take it easy, baby," he laughed.

Ingrid pressed against the only angel who smiled from behind a stranger's eyes. Of course, historical records had forewarned her that he would not be tall; nevertheless, she could not help but feel disappointed. "How lucky that I didn't wear my heels," she thought, walking away with him through the rain.

████ ix

One or one thousand miles south car pull off Boulevard and idle by sidewalk curb. It ain't supposed to rain on this town, but most things happen like they shouldn't. So boy approach and look through rolled-down window at man caught behind blank space inside.

You know a canyon? ask the man. You know a dirt road in the canyon, we drive up there you and I together, we drive up there you and me, and I get out and I lie on the dirt road wearing what?

What you wearing I don't know, reply boy. He watch the man rub hand up and down himself like afraid your own body can leave you: what a dream.

Looking lites of 2doors wander up and down Boulevard eyeing sighing tricks.

I wear nothing and the road is dirt, say man. You drive the car where?

Here the street dark and quiet like children never played on it and everyone moved away.

Where do I drive? ask boy.

Over me and on me and through me.

Give me a twenty for to find someone else to drive your car, say boy, I don't like driving in the dark.

In boy's shirt pocket bills are bandage that don't stop the bleeding but slow it down a little.

Fuck what is left are gas stations and liquor stores and bars where angels lie.

■■■■■ x

Two hours later it was just another gig played for cash
and coke at first. Then the trick lay bleeding in the
empty kitchenette. Lolita and Eddie-Jane threw on
clothes and beat it down the stairs. Lolita ran to the
phone booth on the corner, but Rita's message was too
smudged to read. Eddie-Jane hunted for the others in
bowling alleys and bars, but by the time he found them
it was too late to say goodbye. The eastbound bus with
Lolita and Eddie-Jane on it pulled from the depot at the
same moment sirens began screaming where the trick
had left off.

■■■■■ xi

The game was called off by rain before it could be won
or lost, at least at that place, in that time. The corner was
empty. The lonely lamp-pole seemed to say that everyone had been driven south to some warmer place or to
wherever moths go when winter comes and flames die.
The last trace of Rita's message disappeared too, leaving
the booth's clear glass waiting for the next call for help,
although the phone itself was broken. There would
always be another message and another corner; but, if
anyone had cared enough to watch, it would have
seemed that everyone had vanished, never to play
again.

■■■■■ xii

"I can't believe you're really going," said Reeves.

"Maybe I'm not," said Frances lightly. "Maybe this is
all a dream."

They stood on the corner of Bay and Cedar avenues.
It was early evening and snow fell slowly from the sky,
wavering in the still air, dreaming down to earth. Lights
from store windows and streetlamps lay in silver or blue
paths upon the snow, and Christmas carols washed
through the air.

"Come with me, Reeves. They'll make you into a new

Gary Cooper."

"What if I don't want to be a new Gary Cooper?" he smiled.

"Everyone wants to be a new Gary Cooper," Frances laughed. "Don't tell me. In reincarnation you'll come back as yourself again."

"Will *you* be coming back?"

"Only as a snowflake. Do you think they'd let me come back as myself?" Frances tugged nervously at the fingers of one white glove. "You know what they're like. Once I step onto that train the gates of this town will be closed against me for good." She reached out to brush snow from Reeves' hair. Dark eyes, dark hair. "Will all my lovers have dark eyes and hair?" she suddenly wondered.

"Buy yourself a hat, my friend."

Reeves kicked the sidewalk with his shoe. "Is that a fashion tip from the A La Mode Boutique? Would you advise a vanilla, chocolate or strawberry one? Aren't you taking anything with you to Tinseltown? Where are your bags?"

"At the station. Dorothy insisted upon packing them herself. I'll have more flannel underwear than any other girl in Hollywood."

She stood tall and straight before him. A strong girl of seventeen. Her blonde hair was tightly braided and coiled around her head; her clear grey eyes darted quickly about as though in search of escape, then came to rest upon Reeves' face. This couldn't be goodbye. She couldn't really be leaving. In a minute she would burst out laughing and confess that it was all a joke. She would take his arm and lead him to the Silver Bell Café, where they would slurp sundaes and spin endless fantasies of an escape for Frances, safe in knowing that such flight wasn't really possible.

Reeves wasn't sure what was or wasn't possible any more. "I'm perfectly serious," Frances would say to him or to anyone else during the past three years. "My calling in life is to become a Hollywood starlet. I'll be the girl who stands in the background behind the big stars, uneasy because she's afraid she'll blow her one and only line." Reeves believed that Frances had to have some good, valid reason for seeking this particular route of escape and he felt that something was not right when the reason was kept secret from him. Unspoken messages no longer carried clearly and easily between Frances and himself; once they had, like breeze across a lake. He wasn't sure about Frances or himself or anything else any more. He was fifteen and from now on he would grow a little less sure each year.

After she turned fourteen Frances had refused to spend summers up at the lake; preferring to remain behind with her father in the Columbia Avenue house, she spent the long days flirting with lifeguards at the town's public beach, which was situated where the big cold lake narrowed into a tamer, more tepid river. Once she told Reeves that she didn't belong among the mountains and pines any more; she had become exiled from the lake, estranged through discontent. And removed from Reeves. Each winter in town he and Frances journeyed farther apart. They had separate friends and were in different grades. He would meet her walking with a group of girls in the high-school hall; she turned her face quickly toward him, rolled her eyes, then continued on with her friends, nodding over-emphatically to their words.

Reeves remembered how Frances had been before. Watching her at fifteen and sixteen and seventeen, he could almost see her struggle to fit herself into the demure dress of a pretty town girl, although this dress clearly wasn't her size. He saw her become the Apple Blossom Queen who in her swimsuit saunters serenely across the stage, only the slightest flicker of impatience in her eye; he watched the cheerleader whose enthusiasm might be seen as exaggerated to a point of irony only by means of a microscope's lens. Reeves felt that

Frances was always aware of the minutes remaining
until she could leave town; he would swear he saw her
lips move as she counted off several million seconds
beneath her breath. As long as she was trapped in the
town she would take advantage of the sentence by considering the difficulty of fitting inside tightly prescribed
limits as an acting challenge. Watch me be unremark-
able! she sometimes seemed to dare, chatting about the
weather or exclaiming over the season's blossoms with
town ladies on the block. Yet inevitably the role would
bore her with its lack of range and she would let a sharp
word drop in a store or on the street. She would slam
the screen door behind her, Dorothy's car keys in hand,
and go racing off into the night, collecting speeding tickets as well as corsages. A small flurry of talk followed
her, trailing behind her swift movements through the
town like the subtlest scent. In a corner of the locker
room Reeves heard older boys speak her name in low
voices.

He would see her behind the window of the A La
Mode Boutique where on Saturdays she advised town
ladies which suits would best fit the narrow contours of
their lives and earned the money that eventually would
buy her one-way ticket out of town. He saw her in
Dramatic Society plays, a vivid flame upon the stage,
but one that wavered unsteadily, without control. Even
while applause still echoed through the auditorium she
would be hastily scrubbing off the heavy make-up, then
running out the rear entrance of the Civic Hall to go
driving with one of the Carpenter boys. The car lights
twisting along the winding lake road, Frances throwing
the empty bottle out the window, her laughter waving
like a scarf across the cold black water. Wasn't she
always laughing? Yes, because that was the safest thing
she could do in that place; that was the best camouflage
for her ironic, judging eyes.

She had a secret life at which Reeves could only
guess, unknown perspectives from which she coolly

watched. Reeves would find books hidden under the cushions of Dorothy's chesterfields—Chekhov, O'Neill, Stanislavsky. "Oh, Dorothy's turned intellectual on us," Frances would lightly lie. Reeves had seen her sitting before her mirror when she thought no one watched. Earnestly examining her face, carefully touching the skin above her cheekbones, peering into her own narrowed eyes. Without the slightest trace of a smile. That was the real face, Reeves thought. That was the face she would openly reveal as soon as the train pulled from the station, as soon as the camera's eye found her.

Now shoppers laden with Christmas purchases stepped around Frances and Reeves still standing on the corner. The eight o'clock whistle sounded from the plant up on the hill. "I have to go," said Frances, anxiously pressing her hair beneath her hat. "This town is small and ugly and mean. People here are suspicious and cruel toward whatever they don't understand—which is just about everything. Even now I have to watch every word I say, so Mrs Smith or Mrs Jones won't be scandalized into her grave. What would happen after ten more years of holding my tongue? I wouldn't be able to say one honest word if I wanted to. I'd hate myself and you'd hate me more."

"Maybe I would," said Reeves. "Still, you might surprise yourself by feeling homesick."

"It looks all right now," said Frances sharply, the left corner of her mouth tensely twisting. "The snow is pretty and white and everything ugly is covered up. But this snow suffocates me too. I dream of snow falling on me and burying me alive. I can't breathe here."

"You can breathe up at the lake."

"Once I could. I'll always be at the lake. The real me will always be there. It's only some foolish Frances who's taking the train south. It will be some foolhardy Frances you see up on the screen at the Royal Theatre. Listen. Whatever you might hear about me, next year or ten years from now, remember that I always knew exactly what would happen. And whatever happens to me won't matter so much because my essence will always be at the lake."

"Essence?" grinned Reeves. "This conversation is becoming kind of lofty for a small-town boy like me. I guess that means it's time to say goodbye."

"Yes," said Frances. "The station will be a nightmare. I think Dorothy's hired the town band to send me off in its usual inimitable style—half a tone flat."

"Take care of yourself, cousin."

"If I were braver, I wouldn't have to leave," Frances said quickly. Then she began to tap-dance upon the icy sidewalk. "Remember your promise: you're to give me away when I marry Cary Grant. We'll waltz at my wedding."

"Sure," said Reeves. Then he walked away.

■■■■ xiii

They did not leave the city, but only moved east across the bridge. Slow Burn, The One-Armed Bandit, Rita, Blue and all the others: sat over styrofoam cups of coffee in cheap cafés, played nurse to call-liquor cocktails in low-rise saloons, looked across table tops onto their new home streets. From fifth-storey windows of low-rent singles they peered down at wet pavement or up at jagged rooftops. The ghosts of summer tried to call them down and out once more, but they could hear only the TV, the juke-box, the click of black ball on cue. They stayed inside and watched visionaries and missionaries cross intersections alone, searching for followers.

At first word of Madeleine spread slowly. There was nothing new about someone disappearing. Up and down the streets the story trailed, then back and forth again. Several times it nearly became washed away, like sidewalk pictures drawn in coloured chalk that run with rain down the drains. Then its faint traces were picked up once more, and the story changed form with each retelling. It was said that Madeleine had encountered fortune and escaped as an heiress or a honeymooner or the jackpot winner of a lottery. Some said she had been jailed for a misdemeanour or a felony, and was denied appeal, bail or the chance for parole. There were those who said it would be smart not to look in alley trash cans or in back seats of abandoned cars. She'd bought a ticket on the night train, some stubbornly insisted over and over again.

Then new stories hit, and these ones spread as quickly as news of a narc. Someone heard that Madeleine was singing the blues in a southside pit; another guy said he saw her jazzing a juke-box joint with a big stain of vermouth upon the front of her dress. Big Nose claimed he was there when she was hustled from an all-night coffee club by two house dicks. A nameless hunchback whispered that she'd become a marker's moll and was holed up in a mansion built with laundered money. Numerous stories passed from bar to bar. They helped to pass the time, these tales of a girl in trouble. There was talk of looking for her and bringing her to the new neighbourhood. Sometimes they vowed to save her.

But they didn't look for Madeleine in the end. There was a rumour that this blonde in danger was really a brunette and this story was the one that was finally believed true. They feared what might happen if they went to look for her. They could not leave their street, their corner, their bar. Not again, not so soon.

Yes, they spoke of saving her. Then someone would enter the bar and a blast of cold air would follow behind. Rita would quickly hustle up enough for more drinks and new cigarettes would be lit. When those inside saw the ones who ran in panic through the streets, searching for the night train, they turned and looked away.

████ xiv

"Attention shoppers!" Ethel announced into the microphone that was rigged up at her cash register. Her thumb pressed a button which cut off the music—something called "The Chipmunk Christmas Album"—that her employer, Mr Carson, insisted be played continually in the drugstore through the holiday season. The customers didn't seem to notice this sudden silence; they wandered slowly up and down the gleaming white aisles, apparently picking items off shelves at random, appearing interested only in filling their baskets with anything at all. "They look like sleep-walkers," thought Ethel. "They need to be woken up."

The long line before her counter began to mutter and shift. Ethel's thumb still pressed the microphone's control, but for the life of her she couldn't remember what she wished to call to the attention of these shoppers. She didn't want to point out that certain items were on sale and she didn't want to remind that the drugstore's hours of operation were extended during these last few days before Christmas. What was it she needed to say? Previously, when her mind went blank this way, Ethel would find that words came to her out of nowhere; she would listen in amazement to a loud, strong, superhuman voice boom through the drugstore, saying the most extraordinary things, speaking words she didn't quite know the meaning of. She'd hear the word *sustain*.

Of course there had been complaints. Customers said that they didn't have all day to listen to Ethel's improvisations and that cashiers weren't MCs either. Mr Carson had spoken to Ethel several times about this matter and had instructed her to use the microphone at certain set, specified times and only then.

Ethel set the microphone aside and began ringing in the items of the first customer in line. She muttered numbers pertaining to dollars and cents beneath her breath and stabbed cash register keys without a single glance in their direction. Everyone knew she was the most experienced cashier in town, what with all her years here in the drugstore plus all that time over at the diner. But even the best and quickest cashier can handle only so much traffic, especially when she's without a bagger, and this was the Christmas rush after all. If Mr Carson were so concerned about his customers' happiness, he could hire a part-time girl over the holiday season—there was a second register standing idle right behind Ethel's back—or he could put down his girlie magazines, descend from his office on high and punch some prices himself. Yet he wouldn't. He wanted to push Ethel till she quit. He was itching to get rid of her, but he didn't dare. Not yet.

High on the back wall of the drugstore was the window through which Mr Carson could look down from his office and observe the entire store. When he wasn't ogling his magazines he was watching out for shoplifters or he was spying on Ethel; thinking himself some kind of God Almighty, he regarded the world without the slightest expression of concern upon his face. Ethel could feel his small eyes upon her this very minute and she tried to hurry things along, attempted to bag and to make change nimbly. However, her arthritis was acting up worse than usual this winter and her fingers turned against her like clumsy enemies—dropping pennies, fumbling to fit anything into a bag. They ached and burned and cried out for a rest; but Ethel didn't dare pause with this line-up before her. She needed this job, there wasn't much work around town any more, especially for a woman her age, and no one could survive on that Assistance.

To take her mind off her woes and her work, Ethel listened to the chipmunks light into the first chorus of "It Came Upon a Midnight Clear." She couldn't fathom why Mr Carson demanded that this particular record be played all the time—he'd switched off the speaker that was hooked into his office, she'd noticed. It wasn't at all festive in her opinion, seeming the kind of thing designed to drive anyone out of their right mind. Were they real chipmunks who'd been taught to sing in English or were they ordinary human beings who sang through their noses and only sounded like chipmunks? Ethel didn't know and she wasn't sure she cared to.

What had she been about to say into the microphone, anyway? Usually she felt something all of a sudden—a rush of energy, she supposed you'd call it—then found herself speaking to everyone in a voice so loud it couldn't help but be heard. Almost someone else's voice, almost a stranger's voice. Whose? What *had* been on the tip of her tongue a minute ago? It would come to her if only her hands would quit complaining, her knuckles loudest of all.

The line moved slowly. Ethel rang in nuts and candy and chocolates, decorations for trees and shiny wrapping paper for presents. Of course, people ran out of toilet paper and toothpaste at Christmas same as any other time. Still, this was supposed to be a holiday and why didn't people seem more cheerful? She saw an awful lot of fretful mothers slapping at crying children. "You have a Merry Christmas now," she said as she handed over change to old-timers with faces she knew as well as the back of her own hand and to strange young people who lived out in the new suburbs. Her head saw pictures of children unwrapping toys and couples forgetting differences and grandparents coming over for a big meal. A day of grace.

Well, her Christmas wasn't quite like that. She had to work until nine on Christmas Eve, and if she was a penny out on her cash she'd have to stay around for hours trying to find out exactly where that penny had gone, promising Mr Carson that such a mistake would never happen again. Suddenly it seemed to Ethel that lately Mr Carson had been dropping more than his usual number of hints regarding young blood and quick fingers and so on. It seemed to her that he'd get rid of her before she could turn around, all her experience notwithstanding.

All at once there were no more customers before her counter and the store itself, filled with a throng not fifteen minutes before, was as empty as a tomb. It always happened that way; the business came and went in waves. Like Pacific Ocean waves, thought Ethel, like the waves at Santa Monica which she would see again in springtime when she made another pilgrimage to California for the sake of Frances Farmer, for the sake of her own soul.

The chipmunks started in on "Silent Night" again and Ethel took a moment to glance around the store before the next rush hit. She'd done the decorations herself, coming in early on her own time to hang the coloured globes and silver tinsel, the wreaths and candy canes. She took pleasure in the sight, especially since she hadn't bothered to decorate the trailer. It wasn't worth the effort when there'd be no one but herself to enjoy the vision. And she worked such long hours during the Christmas rush that all she did was drop and die the minute she set foot in the door: a dead person doesn't notice the decor. Besides, the place was cramped enough as it was, having hardly room for an extra hair; Ethel always said she couldn't afford the luxury of gaining an ounce while she lived in that trailer. Still, she was used to it and it was all she could afford. And a roof was a roof.

She'd be so tired by Christmas that the day off would pass in a blur, broken only by her brother's phone call. Fred always called her Christmas afternoon. She'd hear the babble of voices in the background, she'd almost smell the bar across the wire. There'd be pauses while he tried to think of something to say, tried to remember why he'd called. A sad, lonely man. Where was it he was living now? She could hardly keep track, he drifted so much. And she could never write him; before a letter reached him at one place he'd have moved someplace else. Her only living flesh and blood. A brother was a brother.

She'd sit in the trailer and look out at the snow and think about Frances. Sometimes it felt like the spirit of

Frances was distant during winter. As if She had turned away and left the world to make its own way through the cold. As if it were all She could do to survive until spring Herself. Ethel would look out at the flat white plain stretching before her the way it did there at the edge of town and she would wonder if Frances could see the trailer buried in the snow, camouflaged the same white as everything around it. She would look at the images of Frances placed about the trailer—that face more familiar to Ethel than her own—and she would think that Jesus wasn't the only saviour born on Christmas Day and that saviours were born on any ordinary Monday or Tuesday at all. And she would think that Her message would be the same on Christmas Day as it was on every other day because it was a clear strong message that you could follow through all the four seasons and always be well guided. Sustain, it said.

Sustain through suffering and through sorrow. Sustain through thick and thin and one day winter will turn to spring. Hadn't Frances's voice sounded muffled and thin this winter? Or was it that Ethel's hearing was getting worse along with her arthritis? Didn't it seem, during all the silent nights she sat alone in her trailer at the edge of town, that Frances's voice reached her less clearly, more weakly, with greater difficulty—as though Her words had to cross a mile of sky or pierce thick blankets of snow? As though She were not near, but very far away?

Out of the corner of her eye Ethel saw Mr Carson approach across the drugstore. Her hand reached blindly for the microphone, her thumb pressed the control button hard. The chipmunks abruptly ceased squeaking about the three kings from the orient and Ethel heard her own voice echo through the empty store. "Frances, can you hear me? Frances, I know you're listening." Mr Carson walked steadily toward her, a pink slip fluttering from one hand. "Frances, I need you. Frances, help me."

■■■■■   xv

Heavy snow was falling upon Minneapolis as the eastbound Greyhound pulled into the depot. It was
Christmas Eve and the bus was crowded with travellers
trying to reach home for the holidays; those not continuing east disembarked with presents as well as luggage
and looked around in search of familiar faces that might
be there to greet them. The last person off the bus was a
slight middle-aged woman who wore shapeless, colourless clothes. She carried no luggage or gifts. Quickly
passing the scene of welcomed arrival, she walked from
the station and into the street.

She entered the first café she encountered. The place
was nearly empty. Christmas Muzak played softly. A
grill cook sat over a cup of coffee, a cigarette and a
newspaper at one of the back tables. A young waitress
with rings beneath her eyes pushed a damp cloth
wearily across a Formica table top.

"You want something?" she called to the woman who
paused inside the doorway. The waitress glanced at her
wristwatch. The graveyard girl was late. She herself had
to make it home across town in this snow, pay off the
sitter and wrap the kids' presents before she could fall
into bed. A badge on her white uniform said that her
name was Bettye.

The woman crossed the room and stood before the
waitress. "Yes," she said in a low clear voice. "Can you
tell me the way to the cemetery, please?"

"New in town?" asked the waitress without much
interest. "You got someone buried there? Join the club.
Sure I know where the graves are. One of them belongs
to my Billy. They put him in the ground last spring,
while I was carrying Danny. Danny came a month after
the funeral. They said it was an accident. The cops
didn't mean to kill my Billy at all. It was some other guy
they were after. There was an APB out for some guy and
my Billy got shot instead. He was on his way to the corner store to buy me some pistachio ice cream. I craved it

all through carrying Danny. He was almost home when they shot him by mistake. The guns woke up Susie, my second girl, who was a year then. We're very sorry Mrs Jones, they said afterward. The ice cream melted on the sidewalk in the sun and got mixed up with the blood. The cops sent a big wreath of flowers to the funeral. Beautiful flowers. They said they were very sorry."

"Is the cemetery far from here?" asked the woman.

"No, it ain't too far," replied the waitress, with a laugh. She gave directions to which the woman listened intently. "You can walk there if you want," the waitress said. "Myself, I'd take a cab with all this snow."

"Thank you," the woman said, then left the café.

It was snowing heavily on Minneapolis. There was no wind and the snow dropped straight from the sky. Nearly all stores and other businesses were closed, and the city was quiet. The woman bent her head toward the sidewalk and walked steadily through the centre of the city, then continued beyond.

The iron gate at the entrance to the cemetery was closed and locked. A dim light burned in the watchman's room at one end of a maintenance building. The cemetery was empty and silent. The woman bended between two bars of a fence, straightened, then walked quickly into the graveyard. Soon she was beyond reach of the lights at the entrance and at the watchman's room. The cemetery lay in darkness but seemed illuminated by the snow already resting on the ground and the snow still falling. There was shadow where the ground was hollowed and shadow thrown by anything that rose from the ground.

The paths between the rows of crosses had not been cleared for several days and the woman moved through several inches of new snow, making footprints which were soon erased behind her. She began to lean over crosses, brush the snow from them and peer at their inscriptions. Sometimes it seemed that she could not read these words and had to feel with her fingers what was etched into the stone, like a blind person reading braille.

She appeared to have some idea where the grave she wanted was situated, for she remained in one area of the cemetery and left the paths to move through deeper snow immediately around the graves there. Sometimes a drift of snow would suggest the presence of a grave where the earth was in fact unbroken; sometimes the snow concealed a grave and the woman would find one where she had not expected to. The piled snow upon the crosses and headstones blunted their shapes, blurred their edges and robbed them of definition.

The woman could not seem to find the grave she was looking for. Her movements gradually became more frantic; as they hastily uncovered epitaphs her ungloved hands scraped roughly against stone. Blood dropped and in the white snow crystallized as something black. The woman's limbs apparently grew weak and she began to stumble as she moved from grave to grave, in the manner of a small child or a drunk. Once she paused to look up at the black sky splintered with white; her eyes blinked as falling snow floated into them. Then she continued searching; but now her motions were as slow and clumsy as a dancer's in a dream. When she finally fell, a shout of laughter came from her mouth, sounding like a muffled gunshot through the silent snow.

She made no move to rise. Settling herself against the stone by which she had fallen, the woman sat in the snow and with clear, calm eyes looked before her. The cemetery appeared more flat from this angle and graves loomed unnaturally tall. The shadows from the graves seemed more numerous, long and dark. Once the woman's hand reached out as though about to brush snow from the grave she leaned against; then her hand stopped in mid-air, withdrew into her lap.

Snow continued to fall heavily upon Minneapolis through the night. At morning, when children wakened early to discover what was hidden within gaudy paper, the snow fell more slowly and its flakes were less large. By this time the woman in the graveyard was hidden beneath several inches of new snow. It covered her body completely and she was camouflaged. The contours of her shape were blunted in the same way as were those of graves and crosses. From a distance above the earth an eye would have been unable to discern that a woman lay in a graveyard or that a graveyard was there at all: the cemetery would have seemed a flat empty space of white. The snow fell steadily and in a silence that was broken only once, by a passing train which had been travelling westward through the night.

■ Part Four

"You have to realize that they were out to get Frances and she knew it. Who? The cops. Why? The political thing. The migrant thing. You name it. They wanted to bust that kid wide open and they finally had the opportunity."

Dalton Trumbo

■ The Stella Story

Prior to disappearing, Madeleine removed some clothes and sundry necessities from her hotel room and left a note for the boy in the event of his return there, explaining that she had found herself in need of a short rest and luckily an old friend had come by in the nick of time to save the day. She also left money for future rent at the desk with Joe, to keep the room for the day she herself might return. Then she and Stella travelled by commuter train out to the suburbs, where all the streets were straight and all the houses identical. "How delightful!" commented Madeleine, looking with rapture out the window.

What might have been an awkward arrangement worked out wonderfully well, perhaps because life at Stella's centred so firmly around the nightly card games. Stella and Madeleine would spend the morning tidying up from the previous evening. The two women each took a room and called back and forth as they dusted and polished. If they cared to, they would sing along with the stereo. In spite of her plumpness Stella moved quickly and lightly about her chores; often a gaiety came over her and she would dance gracefully in the morning light.

Coffee came next. Neighbouring women would drop in with coffee cake and other baked items. Over their cups the women discussed events of the previous evening and speculated upon the coming night. At the beginning, when unfamiliar with this new world, Madeleine only listened silently and marvelled that such happy home life could flow and wash around her. Stella wanted for nothing. "I haven't a care in the world since I quit the office," the contented woman was fond of saying. "I have my boyfriends, my bowling, my entertaining. We must join you up to the League—you do bowl, don't you?"

In afternoon they went to the mall to buy various articles. "We have it all right here, everything you could
want," Stella explained. "There's less cause to go downtown than there is to fly to the moon. You have your
safety, your neighbours, your patios and your lawns.
The free parking at the mall makes life worth living just
in itself." They stocked up on hard candy and pretzels
and nuts. Usually Stella bought some knick-knack or
other for her bedroom. Most people skimped when it
came to furnishing their bedroom, without asking themselves if this really made sense.

The late afternoons were the perfection of bliss. They
sat together on the sofa with a fashion magazine spread
across their knees. Everything was ready for the
evening's festivities, and this time of waiting was peaceful and exciting at once. Madeleine always finished
looking at a page first; then she would wait for Stella,
letting her eyes wander in wonderment around the cosy,
comfortable room. When Stella finished the page she
looked in Madeleine's eyes for a long moment. "Are you
done, dear?" she would ask gravely. After Madeleine
nodded, Stella would lick her finger and very slowly
turn the page; the sound of rustling paper shivered
down Madeleine's spine and caused the lids of her eyes
to feel as heavy as a sleepy child's. Every new page was
shiny and had a clean, inky smell. There would appear
large coloured pictures of fashion accessories, latest
improvements in lip gloss and marvellous new shampoos which could be bought at the mall the very next
day. Ella sang softly in the background. "I'm a modern
woman, as up to date as any," Stella always said. "But
my daddy raised me on Ella and I'm not one to deny my
roots."

Night would come and the lamps would be lit.
Madeleine and Stella dressed and made up before the
latter's large mirror. Each helped the other decide on
hairdos and co-ordinations of colours. It had been
understood at the start that none of Madeleine's clothes

suited the suburbs, and for the time being Stella generously lent her friend flowing kaftans, pastel pant suits
and also hostess pyjamas which, though not quite
Madeleine's size, were in keeping with the local atmosphere. Madeleine altered her make-up and hairstyle to
suit these garments; her manner seemed to transform
itself on its own. Now the young woman seemed
unusually shy, with a soft voice and a tendency to blush.
Stella gazed at her fondly in the mirror, then sprayed
scent into the air above their heads. It fell like rain upon
them both. A moment later the doorbell rang, ahead of
schedule as usual, because Stella's guests loved her parties so much they always arrived early.

A wide variety of people came to Stella's affairs,
which was one of her secrets of success. There were singles and young marrieds both. There were men who
worked inside at real estate, insurance or education, and
men who worked outdoors at construction, recreation or
grounds maintenance. Stella herself leaned toward the
men who worked outside; they were so much more
healthy and satisfying. All her special boyfriends
worked in the fresh air. Every evening they brought her
flavour-filled chocolates which Stella passed among the
guests. Far from being jealous of each other, Stella's
favourites were firm friends who harboured no ill feelings of competition; in fact, they were especially loyal
amongst themselves, in the way that members of a private club so often are. But all the company knew each
other well, and there was constant laughter, joking and
reminiscence.

The guests agreed unanimously that Madeleine was
the quickest learner of cards that they had ever met. She
absorbed like a sponge the rules to all their games:
Pennies From Heaven, Hollywood Canasta, Streets and
Alleys, Up and Down the River, Persian Rummy, Spit in
the Ocean and Forty Thieves. They played for nickels
and dimes and pennies a point. To prevent greediness,
Stella ruled that all winnings go into a pot that was used

for purchasing the next party's refreshments. Everyone enjoyed themselves to the fullest degree. They laughed and chatted and only laughed harder when they lost their dime. Or they let a gambler's fever rob their blood and played a winning streak for all it was worth.

After several hours, when everyone was on their third or fourth drink, the game began to die down of its own accord as one by one the guests counted themselves out for a hand and moved to the living room, where a space was cleared for dancing. The lights were turned lower and the group performed its favourite step, the mambo. When the hour grew close to midnight guests began to leave; they were working people who needed their sleep. Stella's boyfriends generally stayed slightly longer than the others, until she pushed them gently out the door. "Boys, you know I need my beauty sleep. Come over again tomorrow night and we'll have the same amount of fun." Then Stella and Madeleine would turn out the lamps, yawning all the while. The dirty glasses and ashtrays could wait until morning to be cleaned.

So the days passed quickly and uneventfully, and that there were no sudden surprises seemed a special gift. Stella did not seem inclined to discuss the future and the possible changes it might bring to life, and for her part Madeleine was grateful to live from day to day for once. Stella also showed no fondness for analysis of the present or the past; in this aspect she was like her friends, neighbours and beaux. Madeleine was often struck by the fact that from the moment she set foot in the suburbs no one asked her a single question about what she had done before taking that step. Everyone seemed to accept her as one of themselves as a matter of course, perhaps feeling so thoroughly satisfied with their lives that they couldn't believe that other destinies might be wished for, never mind achieved. This automatic acceptance at face value seemed to Madeleine a remarkable thing and she felt that before such unquestioning eyes she might for the very first time dare to reveal her true self. On the other hand, she was in no great hurry to rock the lifeboat.

"I've heard before that Stella means star," she said one afternoon, "and now I know it's true. This is the home I've been trying to remember always."

"I'm afraid I don't follow you all the way," said Stella, dreamily biting into a piece of chocolate fudge.

"Think of it this way: whenever I swim in the sea my body becomes homesick. The motion of waves, the pull of moon on tide, the sensation of floating like a cork—all these things affect me powerfully. When I emerge from the water to lie on the beach, my body feels strangely heavy and awkward. The reason for this, I believe, is that certain of my cells recall the time, so many years ago, when man was an organism that lived in the sea. While most of my body has evolved into a land-lover over the centuries, some stubborn cells still remain from that aquatic phase. And whenever I swim they remember the home they yearn for with every step on land: the sea of love."

"That certainly sounds scientific. I like swimming in the sea too. Skinny dipping." Stella considered the last bit of fudge. "Yes, you fit in very well, my love. It's a gift, an honest gift." The fudge disappeared and Stella chewed with an absorbed, inward expression.

The next day Stella found a postcard hidden among the mail's free samples and flyers. "It's from my friend Nina," she cried in excitement. "Nina has gone on holiday to one of those countries where they speak Spanish and nothing else. I met Nina years ago in the Silhouette Salon. She does my hair twice a week and charges me only half the regular price. No one understands my hair like Nina. Since she's been gone it's been a mess."

"Your hair looks beautiful. What does she say in the card?" asked Madeleine.

"Let's see. There is sun and sand and sea, she is having a good time but misses my card parties, how is everyone here? Nina always was the one for adventures and so forth. She's holidaying with another girl from the Salon. Naturally I was her first choice as travelling companion, but I just told her: Nina, I said, I have my boyfriends and my card parties. How can I go away? My home is too precious for me to get up and leave even for three weeks. Madeleine, I don't care for travel, don't need it. My life is full enough. But it's a pretty postcard and will look fine on my refrigerator."

"I used to be exactly like your friend," said Madeleine, "until I realized that every place is more or less the same—or rather, different. One day I asked myself how any God could look after me while I was always on the run."

"I agree with you one hundred per cent," said Nina.

It was in every way a fine and carefree life until the troubles began. The first unfortunate occurrence was only a small wrinkle in their days and it concerned the record player. "Now, I want you to feel completely at home here, Madeleine." Stella stood with hands on hips, a look of mock severity on her face. Out of good humour she wagged one finger. "You must use the stereo whenever you care to. My theory is that if more people had record cabinets and the joy of music, there would be no more wars or murders."

So one day Madeleine purchased a record album at the mall. The clerk was annoyed that she paid with money from the card-game pot, since this was entirely in the form of quarters, nickels and dimes. Stella became indignant and began to shout at the clerk. "It's legal tender, it says so right on the silver, if you could but read." The clerk became more nasty and harsh words were exchanged from both sides without either claiming clear victory.

Upon returning home, the two friends had a celebratory drink in the living room to christen the new record and to smooth the edges off the incident at the mall. After a few minutes Stella said, "Madeleine, dear, why doesn't she sing the words more clearly? I suspect that

clerk sold us a defective album out of pure malice. I
can't make out the words at all." Stella fiddled with the
dials of the stereo, trying this and that to mend the
sound.

"That's the style. She's singing of the lost home, the
searching heart. The song's about Los Angeles, which
means *angels* in English. Listen."

So long, lonely avenue
So long, lonely avenue

A shadow passed over Madeleine's face and she
quickly lifted the needle to a faster song. Then she
snapped her fingers and scatted along. In her enthusiasm a large quantity of her drink slopped onto the
couch and created a significant stain.

The music seemed to make Stella nervous. She felt it
was unhealthy and somehow linked to communism.
With Ella she could hear the words clearly and understand their sense. Whenever Madeleine sat down with a
drink to listen to her record, Stella was apt to spoil the
mood by periodically shouting: "There! What do those
words mean? Sense doesn't require secrecy!" At this
Madeleine would be compelled to open her eyes and
explain once more about Los Angeles.

When Stella was not turning down the volume of the
stereo, she was switching on the vacuum cleaner or the
dishwasher, both of which made more than enough
noise to drown out Madeleine's music. She was forever
saying, all sweetness, "I think maybe we've already
heard your record once today, I guess we've already had
our foreign-language lesson for the afternoon, we don't
want to wear out the record, do we?" She began to say
other things, too.

Stella could not fathom the change that had come
over Madeleine since buying this record. The girl had
lost all her nice manners and much of her enthusiasm
for housework. It gave Stella a creepy feeling to see
Madeleine sitting for hours on end upon the couch,

doing nothing but staring into space and drinking up all
the liquor in the place. For the first time Stella began to
wonder exactly who it was that she harboured beneath
her roof. She would hover anxiously near Madeleine,
sneaking peeks at her, until the girl looked up with a
sulky expression; then Stella would quickly pretend to
be busy with slimming exercises. When Madeleine took
to locking herself in the bathroom during the card parties, Stella became more deeply worried. Also, it was an
inconvenience for the guests.

These were some of the troubles, but they were minor
compared to the final one. Stella had one special
boyfriend, a strapping young man with broad shoulders
and curly black hair. His name was Robert and he
worked as a game warden in a national park situated
some fifty miles from the city. Stella confided many
times that in the end this Robert would surely be her
choice; any man who drove fifty miles each way on
every day of the week just to see her had to be sincerely
devoted. Plus there was his natural health, his comfortable income and his pleasant manners. He was a working man any girl would grab; but Stella was confident
enough of her charms to take her own sweet time to reel
him in.

One night the card party became particularly gay and
lively. Madeleine's cheeks became flushed, her hair fell
down and her voice grew loud. Toward the end of the
evening, accompanied by her record, she did some
slinky dancing in the living room. The guests formed a
circle around her and clapped hands in time with the
music. Madeleine swivelled and swayed, fingers snap-
ping dangerously, head turned to one side, hair hiding
one eye. When she kicked off a high heel it accidentally
smashed an ashtray off a coffee table, leaving bits of
green glass scattered across the floor. Not since the days
at the corner or in the bar had the thrill possessed her
so.

Robert joined her inside the circle when she crooked a

finger in invitation. They danced slowly and apart, cir-
cling each other warily. Madeleine felt her face harden
and her stare become bold and blank. Anything might
happen.

Suddenly Stella stepped inside the circle. Her hands
clasped together at her chest, she made an announce-
ment which at first no one could hear because the music
was quite loud. "Dear friends," she said in a higher
voice, "the hour is late. We don't want to keep our good
neighbours awake and risk jeopardizing our future parties, do we? Please come back and come back soon, as I
miss you all when you are not here."

The party broke up quickly. Madeleine still swayed
with closed eyes in the middle of the room, a drink nes-
tled against her. A thought struck her and abruptly
froze her still. Opening her eyes, she looked in astonish-
ment at the room around her. The ease with which she
had strayed from the light into the darkness was shock-
ing; what worried her more, she had not noticed the
slightest dimming of vision. "You put on sunglasses,
then you forget to take them off," reflected Madeleine.
"But gods do not shine like flashlights whose batteries
wear out in just one day." She concluded: "Regretfully,
this is not my Shangri-la."

Madeleine regarded Stella, who was huddled at one
end of the sofa. Her floral-patterned pant suit looked a
sad and crumpled mess. One of Stella's hands clutched
a big tumbler of whisky, the other a quantity of sodden
Kleenex.

"Do you think that drink wise so late at night?"
Madeleine asked gently. "You know how your head can
hurt the next morning." Stella seemed slightly sad.

"Don't tell me what to do, missy. Furthermore, you
owe me more than four hundred dollars for the rent, the
food you've eaten, the liquor you've swilled—not to
mention all the rest. Four hundred minimum."

"But I'm afraid I don't have that kind of money," said
Madeleine. "I have my little income, but that is all."

"I took you in because you seemed such a pathetic thing, sitting alone in that bar, wearing those ridiculous clothes. I'm a full-hearted sharing woman, and I certainly don't require exotic dancing in my own living room. My friend Nina is returning on Thursday, by the way. You looked so funny I could just about laugh, if the sight of you didn't make me feel sick instead. Los Angeles indeed!"

"I have seen this before," thought Madeleine. "Certain people turn ugly when they over-indulge. Sometimes they call the police. I had better give Stella the chance to calm down."

Madeleine fetched her purse, make-up case and overnight bag from the bedroom, then tiptoed into the bathroom. A locked door could be a precious thing at a time like this. She searched the make-up case for a small box lacquered in brilliant colours. Afterward, when the roach was flushed down the toilet, she repaired her make-up slowly. A song came to her and she hummed as she read the labels of jars and bottles cluttered inside Stella's medicine chest. Then, sitting on the edge of the bathtub, Madeleine removed everything from her overnight bag, article by article, and in its turn studied each object with great care and consideration. After some thought she changed from the purple hostess pyjamas she had borrowed from Stella into her own stained, crumpled and emerald-coloured evening gown. She piled her hair upon her head, then topped it with a glass tiara. After slipping on silver pumps and elbow-length white gloves, she waited in the bathroom for what seemed a long time, for the face in the mirror to stop crying. Then she made up once again. "Hello, monkey face," she whispered into the glass.

The living-room lamps were still lit when she emerged from the bathroom. Stella lay on the sofa, the empty bottle by her elbow.

"Goodbye," Madeleine said to the living room as she tiptoed out the door. Only later, when half-way to the centre of the city, did she remember the record album and other little possessions left behind. "They will add to the quality of Stella's life and she will be the richer for having known me," thought Madeleine. "There is always some shining jewel that may be retrieved from the wreckage of our lives; this may be the final consolation." With a sigh she straightened her tiara, then continued to follow her footsteps back downtown.

■ How Far Is the Journey From Here To a Star

After three days and four nights of steady travel two young women climbed down from a battered bus. They were tired and dirty, and had more luggage than they could carry. Yelping dogs and chattering children spotted the dusty street; a number of local ladies, holding big bags stuffed with fruits and clothing, pressed tightly around the strangers. Emily, the slighter of the two travellers, tried not to cry.

"Excuse me," Nina, the other new arrival, called to a man sitting before a small café of which he was apparently the only customer. "What's the name of this place? I assume you speak English. You look the type."

"Welcome to Puerto del Sol!" exclaimed the man with an awkward flourish of one arm.

"Where is the hotel and where are the discothèques?" demanded Nina. "The brochures are right here in my purse—if they haven't been stolen, that is."

She spread brightly coloured pamphlets over the man's table. There were photographs of crystal green swimming pools, tall iced drinks in cocktail lounges, and tanned young tourists dancing with half smiles and closed eyes in a glittering discothèque.

Nina pointed to a picture of a high-rise hotel. "Our

room is on the sixteenth floor. It says right here in black
and white: stylish simplicity and understated elegance
in the midst of a sumptuous tropical paradise. All we
want are three weeks of dancing, drinking, and some
tropical romance with palm trees and moonlight and
waves. We're a couple of beauticians in need of a relaxing holiday and we're certainly not searching for com-
plications."

The three looked up from the glossy photographs.
Before them stood some poor makeshift huts, a few
straggling stores with nearly empty shelves, and an
architecturally unimpressive church that had been abandoned half finished. Plainly there were no discothèques
or high-rise hotels nearby, and even the café in which
they sat, seemingly the grandest place in town, was
actually a filthy hovel.

A cruel joke had been played. In that country three or
four towns were often given the same name; its citizens,
with an ironic sense of humour they delighted to
express especially at the expense of tourists, did not
bother to point this fact out even when it was clearly
leading toward confusion.

"We suspected something was wrong when they
made us switch from our train to that broken-down bus.
Nobody spoke a word of English and the driver didn't
know how to drive. But we imagined it must be a surprise, bonus attraction of the holiday: Enjoy a genuine
Latin American bus trip!"

"Well, ladies, there's no bus out of here at this hour."
The man chuckled heartily; he greatly enjoyed the chaos
of the country, feeling it to be a true expression of the
spirit of the world. "You'll have to remain here at least
until tomorrow and maybe longer. On days when he's
in a bad mood the bus driver goes right past this town
without stopping. Don't worry. I'm sure you can find
some shack or other to nest in."

"Is the driver often in a bad mood?" asked Nina.

The man laughed indulgently. "This café is terrific!

They're always out of everything, yet insist they're still open. They make little kids too short to reach the stove do all the cooking."

In just a few minutes night had arrived. Emily looked toward the figures that moved silently in the shadows of huts. "Does it always get dark so quickly here?" she asked.

The next morning the English-speaking man found the girls on the rocky shore, bikini-clad amid sunglasses, tanning lotions and paperbacks. They held coconuts chopped open at the top; white drops of sweet milk stuck to their shoulders and chins, attracting flies which crawled upon their skin. The girls didn't bother to brush these uninvited guests away.

"How do you like Paradise?" asked the man.

"Puerto del Sol," said Emily, staring raptly at the empty bay. "A port is supposed to have boats."

"This place is hilarious," interrupted Nina. "We were lying here, working on our tans, when a boy came by and started running back and forth on the rocks in front of us. We thought he would soon get sore feet or at least grow tired. But he kept running until another boy arrived and gave us these coconuts. The two of them sat here and stared at us while we ate. Suddenly they both ran into the ocean and started swimming straight out toward open water. First they became only small black dots, then we couldn't see them at all. And as far as we can tell, they haven't returned to land."

"Amusing," commented their recent acquaintance, pushing a pair of shattered sunglasses higher upon his nose. In spite of the considerable heat, he was dressed in clothing sufficient for a severe winter's day. "It's been so long since I've spoken English. You have no idea how much pleasure this gives me." He turned abruptly and gazed with unsociable longing at the sea.

The girls gathered up their things, then began to pick slowly across the rocky shore. The difficult terrain forced them to look down at their feet rather than up at the mountains or sky. The river had a strong, unpleasant smell where it ran into the sea, and crossing it wasted much time and trouble. The girls grew tired and sweaty; the sun became very hot and moved directly overhead. Behind, the English-speaking man watched the two figures, already pink from sun, until they were no longer visible.

Nina and Emily neared three boys wearing only shorts, who squatted on rocks at the edge of the sea and stared into the shallows. Hearing the girls approach, they lowered their faces closer to the water.

"Let me speak," said Nina, who had woken at dawn to study her Spanish dictionary; a fast learner, she had already mastered many basic phrases.

"*¿Qué hacen?*" she inquired.

"Dolphins are smaller than whales," replied one boy, not looking up.

"We're looking for a good place to swim," Nina said suggestively.

"Our friend has a car," said the same boy, still peering into the gurgling water. "Would you like to ride in it tomorrow?"

Nina turned to Emily. "Did you understand that? I'll tell them maybe."

The next morning Nina and Emily emerged from their *palapa* prepared for the outing. They waited in the little plaza, which at this hour was empty save for a small dog resting on a nearby bench. The girls watched him waken from time to time, look to see how far the sun had travelled, then move to whichever bench now offered the deepest shade.

"Where's the car?" asked Nina, when their friends finally showed up on foot.

"Today we'll eat beside a stream," explained the tallest boy.

In a file of five they followed a trail up into the hills.

First they passed through banana plantations where men sweated beneath the hot sun; then the air turned cooler, and trees with large wide leaves became numerous. Vines twisted and coiled; strange birds whistled and called. Emily's heart beat rapidly, and she felt dizzy from the steep ascent. "Exactly where are we going?" she asked Nina.

"I'm not sure," the latter panted. "They used some words I haven't learned yet."

Emily's eyes strayed to the butterflies drifting among the bright jungle blossoms. Not paying sufficient attention to the rough trail, she tripped over a stone and very nearly fell. After that she fixed her eyes on the bare feet of the boy in front of her, which stepped neatly over vine and stone. The party silently climbed higher into the jungle.

They reached their destination. A stream formed a small waterfall, which dropped into a shady pool large and deep enough for bathing. Immediately the boys took off their shorts and jumped naked into the water. Nina and Emily sat on a large rock situated in the sun. Spreading their skirts carefully over their knees, they watched the brown bodies splash in the shadows.

"I'm so itchy and dirty and that water looks so cool and clean," said Emily.

"It does," agreed Nina. "But we haven't brought bathing suits and I don't think it would be a good idea to take off our clothes. It might give the wrong impression."

Emily looked bright-eyed at the water. "Perhaps if we just wet our legs," she suggested.

They held up their skirts with one hand and waded. Minnows darted through the cold, clear water around Emily's toes, and her head felt hotter and heavier than before. "I'm going to get sick," she suddenly thought, wading deeper and feeling the water climb up her body like a snake. The boys emerged from the other side of the pool and sat together on a wide flat rock, drops of water falling from their skin.

Nina cried out as she stumbled over a stone on the pool's bottom. Her yellow skirt floated around her like a parachute. "It's wonderful," she shouted, splashing and kicking water at Emily. Soon both girls were swimming beneath the waterfall, where the water foamed white and a current tugged insistently. In the corner of her eye, Emily saw three brown bodies twist slowly together and apart.

All at once the water turned icy and drove the girls shivering from the pool. They stood with cotton skirts and blouses clinging to their skin, and looked silently down at the three mixed-up bodies asleep on the rock.

"I'm hungry," said Nina in a clear voice. "We passed a few *palapas* just over that rise. Let's ask there for food."

They put on sandals and walked to the huts. Five dogs barked loudly and a man emerged from a doorway. "My name is Lino Moreno," he said. "What are you doing up here in the mountains?"

"We're with some friends, but they've fallen asleep and we're hungry," explained Nina.

"Today's your lucky day. I've just caught an armadillo. There's enough for everyone."

The skin of a very small animal lay near Emily's feet. Beside it were neatly piled the inner organs. "Wait over there in the sun so your clothes will dry," instructed Lino Moreno. "I'll cook the meat."

Nina and Emily sat at the edge of a large cement area which resembled a basketball court. In a short time they smelled something cooking; then Lino Moreno brought two green leaves each holding a tiny piece of meat. "This is where we dry the coffee later in the season," he explained, gesturing with great tenderness toward the cement. "My wife is dead and now only my son and I live here in this hut. We're lonely all the time."

Nina and Emily nibbled. Before they could finish the meal, their three friends arrived. The tallest one grabbed the leaves and threw them angrily to the ground. "Why

didn't you sleep after your swim?" he shouted; then he
added more calmly, "My friends and I were going to
catch a hundred armadillos to eat beside the stream."

The five dogs were fighting over the bits of fallen
meat as the boys turned and started quickly back down
the path toward the lower regions. The sun had long
passed beyond the upper rim of the jungle, and the
clearing lay in deep green light. "Goodbye," said Emily.
"Goodbye, Lino Moreno, and thank you for the food."

"Fool! He doesn't understand a word of English,"
called back Nina, who had already started on the downward path.

"Now, Nina has a headache and that means I must venture alone," Emily told herself some hours later.
"Perhaps she'll feel better in a while," she added
vaguely, then forgot about her friend.

She walked down the dark dirt road, taking care to
avoid the piles of garbage strewn all about; it seemed
people here threw their trash from their doorway
straight into the street. Through open windows Emily
could see whole families sprawled messily on one double bed. They were all—grandparents, parents and children alike—looking at comic books. Several ladies
lounged in doorways, whistling at Emily as she passed.

The little plaza, so empty during day, was now
crowded and brightly lit. Children dressed in long pants
and clean skirts ran screaming with outstretched arms,
playing what looked like an airplane game. Unlike
women in some places, their mothers did not wait quietly nearby with knitting and gossip, but had their own
game, which involved much animated laughter, comic
expression and vivid movement. "It looks something
like charades," thought Emily. She settled on a bench,
expecting to be thoroughly entertained.

As soon as she was noticed, however, the games
stopped and a crowd formed excitedly around her.
Emily tried to smile, telling herself that there was nothing

threatening in their expressions or voices, merely the greeting of another language and culture. She found it hard to relax, though, because an older woman had chosen to sit very close to her, and Emily's own position at the extreme edge of the bench prevented even a slight shift away.

Without warning the lady screamed out with a great, theatrical show of emotion. At once the crowd ceased pulling Emily's legs and skirt and hair. When it moved back a certain distance, the lady turned to Emily and said, "Hello, baby doll, my name's Señora Sanchez. What's yours?"

"You speak English!" cried Emily.

"Sure I do. I used to live with my man up in old California. I was as happy as a fish there, but my man never could get used to the States. He just didn't care for things up north. So we moved back here and opened ourselves a movie theatre. We show all kinds, American ones every Saturday night. Also, they're very cheap."

"Really? Tell me something: why are there no teenagers or men about on this beautiful evening?"

"Well, the men mostly stay out fishing all night. They come in at dawn and give their wives all they've caught, then sleep the day away. We have our men well in hand, but take no unfair advantage. We give them enough money for beer. They like beer when they're far out at sea at night, and we don't like to deny them their pleasure. As for the young people, they take their own pleasure in the darkness beneath the trees."

"It sounds like you have a nice life here."

"We do. It's quiet and it's peaceful, not like some places. I'm adaptable, I can roost anywhere. When my man asked me to move with him to the capital, I told him. Go right ahead and move to the moon if that's what you want, I said. But you're a fool if you expect me to follow. You dragged me away from California, where I had my nice set-up and my gang of American girl-friends, and I certainly don't intend to move again. That was five years ago and not a word from him since, but men are like that and am I crying the blues? The answer is: no. One niece runs the movie house and another turns a tidy profit from a little restaurant I own. Oh, I guess I have my share of God's gifts."

Señora Sanchez pawed about in her purse, then took out a package of Partytime cigarettes. "Care for a smoke?" she queried. "I always do enjoy a good smoke in the evening. Helps quiet the nerves."

"I don't mind if I do," said Emily, although she didn't have the habit. They lit up and puffed away in silence.

"My nieces tell me I shouldn't smoke in public, I'll get cancer, all kinds of foolishness. I tell them: If I can't have my small pleasures, what good is it? These young girls don't know what it's like to be modern and happy—no offence to you."

"None taken. I have four aunts who travel once a year to Las Vegas for a spree. They stay up all night for a solid week, drinking and smoking and gambling. They leave their husbands at home so they can have some extra fun, like meeting men who take them to all the shows. They say I can go along with them as soon as I find a husband and a home. But not before."

"They sound like smart women. Those things are important. I'm a rich woman, that's why I can afford this jewellery, this perfume, these cigarettes in the plaza. Rich and smart both." Señora Sanchez took a green glass bottle from her purse and sprayed a little more perfume than was necessary upon her arms and neck. "Want a shot? The only problem with perfume is that it wears off after a while."

A great peace fell over Emily as she felt the strong scent drift upon her. Everyone else had gone home, and the plaza was still and silent. There was only the sound of dogs barking in the distance.

"They all go to bed early here. After they're asleep, I generally sit here with my reflections. Of course, in California they stay up late. That's where I formed my

night-owl habits. Would you like to sleep at my place
tonight? It's a cement house with rugs on the floors and
running water in the taps, hot and cold both. There's not
a more elegant home in town."

"It sounds lovely. I would love to sleep there," said
Emily. "But my friend is waiting for me in our hut. She
worries sometimes."

"I have a bottle of brandy that's more than half full,
and two empty guest rooms. I have a radio and a refrigerator and an ironing board."

Emily looked at the bats swooping around the lamp-
poles. "All right," she said.

By the time Emily returned to the *palapa* the next morning, the sun was already hot and high. Inside the hut
was dim, and the dirt floor felt cool beneath Emily's
feet. She wondered where she had left her sandals, then
dismissed the question as having but slim importance.

Nina was stuffing clothes in a string bag. The rash
which had erupted upon her skin the previous afternoon now looked worse, and in spite of the dim light
Emily could see that her friend's cheeks were an
unhealthy colour. "Where have you been?" asked Nina.
"You missed all the fun. Just after you went out last
night some men took me to a dancing place in the next
town. We drove there in a car and mamboed all night.
Everyone on earth was there, kicking up their heels and
having a good time. The music was just as loud and fast
as you could want. What's the matter?"

Emily was looking searchingly into her friend's eyes.
For a long moment she stood dumbly. "What about the
orange juice?" she asked at last.

"What on earth are you talking about?" demanded
Nina.

"The orange juice. Remember you promised that
when we stayed at the resort hotel a room-service
waiter would bring us freshly squeezed orange juice
every morning. We would drink it knowing that only

fifteen minutes before those oranges had been hanging from a tree in the sun."

"Emily! This is a million times better than any room service or high-rise hotel. Look around you! They have fields full of oranges and every other thing you could possibly want. Why, last night a Señor Ramirez, the wealthy owner of the largest plantation around, was seeking my favours. He begged to show me around his place. Says he'll give me anything I want: oranges, avocados, bananas, limes. You name it!" Nina began to pack more quickly.

Emily remembered when, a long time ago, she had hidden for an afternoon in an apple tree. They had called for her and called for her, but she would not come out from hiding. All around were white blossoms and bumble-bees; if you sat quietly, the bees wouldn't sting. More than anything in the world she had wanted to pick the blossoms, but she left the tree with empty hands when she saw a storm approaching through the sky. In the middle of that night she was woken in her bed by crashing wind and thunder. She ran in bare feet through the dark, holding her white nightdress up from the long grass with one hand. She ran to the apple tree. Blossoms were dropping like butterflies through the dark. And when she bent down, she could see that the blossoms which had fallen were lying stained and bruised upon the grass.

"Today Pedro and Alfredo are taking me to the capital city for a fish dinner," Nina was saying loudly. "There'll be air conditioning and drinks, then parties through the night. I can't imagine when I'll return here. Probably not for days and days, if ever. Days and nights of fun and more fun!" Nina insisted shrilly.

A loud strange sound occurred. "That must be them, here already. They told me about their car. The horn can play five different tunes. See you in the movies!"

Emily looked dully around the hut. Her head and throat hurt, for she was unaccustomed to cigarettes and drink. She curled up in the hammock and spoke to herself: "Nina is my best friend. She's the one who telephones me every night and goes with me to the movies. She's the one who says to the owner of the Salon: Get rid of Emily, you get rid of me, then we'll see who needs who. She's the one who invites me to join her on holidays. Nina is my best friend and I'm hers."

Several hours later Emily rested on the beach after a swim. The sun dried her body and hair, salt coated her like a new skin. "After all," she thought sleepily, "God might be cruel or He might just as well be kind. The odds are probably fifty-fifty, the same as with any person you don't know yet."

Music woke her. Surprised to find herself still on land, she observed that her skin had turned the colour of someone else. Above her, drained black by the sun's glare, stood a boy wearing red shorts faded by sun and sea. His shadow fell coolly upon her. When he sat beside Emily, she wanted to reach out and touch his smooth brown skin.

A small boat drew near the shore, with voices calling from it. The boy ran into the water, swam to the boat, and hands pulled him from the sea.

A bird fell into the waves. The tide turned and the earth reeled. Emily shut her eyes in hope that the glaring dizziness would pass. "Fifty-fifty," she murmured consolingly. Opening her eyes again, she noticed that the boat was far from shore and that the boy had left his radio behind. She watched the sea until it was as empty as the wide blue sky.

The earth evened on its axis until it was flat once more. The tide crept slowly up the shore. Emily waited in the sun, an anchor in her heart.

Señora Sanchez sat alone in the empty plaza. "Emilia," she called. "I have arranged a special treat for this afternoon. You are feeling sad because your friend has gone and left you all alone. Dry your eyes, the fun is just beginning."

"I'm not crying," said Emily.

"A truck ride will make you feel less lonely," counselled Señora Sanchez. She was wearing the same black dress as the evening before, and looked very warm. "We'll ride all the way to the capital in the back of a truck. It's a cool, fun way to go. There we can shop in the big department stores and perhaps have dinner in one of those fancy new restaurants. We can stay in the city overnight or, if we feel homesick, return here by moonlight. What do you think, honey?"

"Do you think we might eat fish in an air-conditioned place?"

"Sure! I'm easy. Air conditioning, menus, waiters, I like them all. I'm a modern woman of today. Where did you get that radio?"

Emily looked down at the radio she held forgotten in one hand. "At the beach."

"I lost a radio just like that one at the beach," Señora Sanchez suggested craftily.

"Someone gave it to me," admitted Emily.

"Ahah!" triumphed Señora Sanchez. "You have boyfriends who give you presents. You and me both. I have a spare room crammed with radios, ashtrays, alarm clocks, all kinds of things and all given to me by boyfriends, admirers, suitors. Don't use them, don't sell them. I don't even look at them or think about them. They're like the men who give them to me: sand on the beach I walk over with dirty feet. What I think about music is different," continued Señora Sanchez in her poetic way. "It's in my bones. It would be easier for me to cut off my toes than to forget about music, and I'm not ready for an amputation." For a long moment she considered her feet, which were housed in silver slippers curling up at the ends, like those of a wizard.

"Isn't he a fast driver!" Señora Sanchez enthused as the truck careered over the mountain road. She had insisted they ride in the open back, although there was more than enough room with the driver up front. "What fun!" she cried, not for the first time. A cold wind whipped her black dress about, revealing blue lines beneath the black hairs on her legs.

The road was a very twisting one indeed, and the driver seemed ignorant of the difference between right and left lanes. "Why does he always speed up when he spies a car ahead?" Emily asked anxiously, gripping the side of the truck more tightly. "Surely we're going fast enough as it is." The wind, however, tore her words away before they could travel any distance—or her companion chose to disregard them.

"Oh, I live for truck rides to the capital! I could happily pass the rest of my life doing just this: racing over mountains, turning around corners, climbing up from the sea. Altitude is so refreshing, I find. Don't you feel exactly like a bird?"

"No, I don't," said Emily, but only to herself.

Señora Sanchez noticed the tears which the forceful wind summoned from Emily's eyes. "Scaredy-cat," she said.

Just then the truck stopped and Señora Sanchez scrambled down to the road with surprising spryness. "Hurry up, honey," she said. Emily alit just before the truck roared away amid a significant amount of dust.

She examined the surrounding terrain. It seemed they were somewhere in the centre of the mountain range, for an alarming number of peaks rose in all directions. It wasn't possible to discern where the mountains ended or what valleys lay in which direction. No houses or other signs of human life were in sight; nor, suspected Emily, were they by any means close at hand. "Where is the city?" she asked.

Her friend seemed a little distracted. Señora Sanchez pulled at her dishevelled hair, which only succeeded in adding to its disarray. Suddenly she fell upon the road and began to cry. Her skirt was hoisted above her knees and her legs stuck out at awkward angles.

"Please get up quickly!" cried Emily, "or you will be run over by an oncoming car." Señora Sanchez continued to weep with a large amount of passion. Spying a sizeable stone at the shoulder of the road, Emily decided to rest upon it until her friend finished crying. The truck ride had worn her nerves threadbare. To make matters worse, it would soon be dark.

Fortunately, for the sake of Señora Sanchez, there was no traffic on the mountain road. Yet this only added to the desolate atmosphere. Emily glanced at the jungle which grew closely up to either side of the road. A small animal of some sort emerged from it, crossed the road, then disappeared into the growth of the other side. The sight of the creature restored Señora Sanchez to her natural good humour, and she pointed to it, laughing very loudly. Emily resolved to force somehow the first approaching vehicle to stop and provide her with a ride either in the direction of the capital or back to Puerto del Sol. At this point, she could hardly be fussy about her destination.

Much to Emily's relief, Señora Sanchez moved off the road. She sat on the gravel near Emily, but as her dress was already quite dirty this didn't matter as it might have. "Why were you crying?" Emily asked.

"I wasn't crying. I was praying."

"What were you praying for?"

"I was praying for your soul," answered Señora Sanchez, but in so automatic a manner that the subject was decidedly closed. She fished into her purse and pulled out a bottle of brandy. After tilting it to her mouth, she offered it to Emily. "Drink, drink," she urged impatiently. Emily choked. Señora Sanchez grabbed the bottle back and again drank deeply, looking up at the sky while she swallowed.

Emily was surprised at how quickly the bottle became empty. Señora Sanchez threw it onto the road, where it smashed. Staring intently at the surrounding scenery, she seemed to forget Emily's presence entirely. It quickly grew cold and dark. "There will be no more trucks tonight," announced Señora Sanchez, after gazing up and down the road. "Would you prefer to walk back to the village or on to the capital?"

"Which is closer?" asked Emily.

"They are both far," Señora Sanchez replied severely. She began to walk away, and Emily quickly followed. After several minutes Señora Sanchez stopped and turned to Emily. "It is easier to walk downhill than up," she said, although at this point the earth was even. By now it was very dark, and difficult to follow the road. Emily had no idea whether they were headed toward the capital or the village, and her friend seemed too preoccupied to discuss their situation.

She hoped to see a moon and some handsome stars, and to find comfort in them. However, the sky was dark and completely without light. This suddenly changed when a star fell quickly through the night. "Did you see that?" Emily cried. "A falling star."

"That wasn't a star. I saw it. It was a firefly. An orange firefly," stated Señora Sanchez firmly. "When you see a firefly, then it rains. We shall soon be very wet."

Emily concentrated deeply upon the sound of her friend's slippers flopping against the pavement, in hope that this would give her bearing and save her from wandering lost into the jungle. "It was a star, it was a star," she thought over and over like a chant; but she decided it might be better not to argue with her friend, especially over something which had already passed.

▬▬ Notes on a Survivor

Two women sat silently together, their eyes turned out the window and toward a man who was mowing the lawn across the street in the rain. Then Nina sighed and once more took up the subject under discussion. "I can't believe it, Stella. It frightens me to think about what has happened to that girl. Somehow I almost feel responsible, although deep down I know it really has nothing to do with me."

"Poor soul, you must feel terrible," replied Stella. "I knew from the start that Emily was a sly one. Her kind always are—though I dislike speaking badly about friend or foe."

Nina and Stella were having coffee in the latter's kitchenette. They wore suspicious expressions which made each look unfamiliar to the other. Both women sensed that tragedy had befallen the other, but neither wished to be the first to speak directly of her woe for fear that the other would not reciprocate with an equally sorrowful story. As a result the old friends were afflicted with nervous qualms. Nina's skin was brown and mottled with freckles, and since returning from her Latin American holiday she had developed an alarming cough.

"Do you see wedding bells for Emily? A Latin lover?" Stella suggested wisely. "That would explain everything, wouldn't it?" She swivelled her hand so the large diamond engagement ring on her finger could catch the light more strongly. She had not as yet mentioned her betrothal to Nina; she had no wish to rub it into the poor girl's face. At the same time, Nina's failure to notice or at least to remark upon the ring served to sharpen Stella's mood of gloom, heightening the mournful effect created by her black costume; apparently, her ring brought her no joy.

"That's just it," said Nina. "No mention of love at all. I feel in my bones that she's hiding something from me, though she affects such frankness."

"Her type always do," remarked Stella sharply. "Believe me, I know. I always wondered how you stood that girl for as long as you did, never mind in a foreign land. The strain must have been terrible."

"There's something peculiar about the whole episode. She has given up a perfectly nice apartment filled with furniture and dishes, magazines and clothes. Not to mention the Salon. And for what? A foreign land where they speak a foreign tongue and exist godlessly."

Stella walked heavily to the stove and refilled their coffee cups. The kitchen and other rooms of her apartment were crowded with crates containing new linen, dishes, appliances and furniture intended for the newlywed nest. As yet, Stella had not found the energy to dispose of her old belongings or to unpack her new ones.

Nina watched her friend squeeze with difficulty between two big boxes. "Would you like to hear the letter?" she asked. Taking several pages from her purse, she began to read in an incredulous tone.

Dear Nina,

I suppose by now you have returned to the city and to the Salon. This place must seem just as far from you as the city seems to me. How could it be otherwise when one and the same distance separates us? This is what they mean by physics, I believe. But lest I forget, before I continue farther allow me to say that I sincerely regret that we became separated as we did. Many nights I spend worrying about you to the exclusion of any other subjects.

I will not return to the city, at least not in the foreseeable future. Rather, I will remain here in Puerto del Sol which, incidentally, is not always as sunny as it was during the period of your brief visit. The day after you left it began to rain, and raining it has been without cease since. This is not unusual, apparently; they say it will rain more or less continuously for four months as it always does at this time of year. That it is an annual event and not a freak of nature puts the rain into an entirely different light, don't you think? It's not as bad as it might seem, for if anything it is hotter

*during the rainy season than the sunny one.
Naturally there are also more mosquitoes and other
bugs now, but then that's an entirely different subject.
A kind woman is allowing me to live in her house, so I
can keep dry or wet according to my mood. There is
sometimes a greater sense of luxury in the little
choices than in the larger ones, I have discovered. I
have grown accustomed to the rain and even to like it.
It's a change from the sunshine, if nothing else. Even
bitter old you must admit that much. The only draw-
back to the rain is the sleepy feeling it always leaves
within me. But I have decided that this weariness may
really be a kind of peace masquerading in another
form. Of course, I cannot be sure that the feeling is
even caused by the rain in the first place. Are such
sensations caused by latitude or altitude, perhaps?*

*I did not intend to waste so much space describing
the weather. In haste I will continue with the fact that
my friend is gone a great deal of the time. She lives for
her weekly trips to the capital city, where she does
much socializing and shopping. I accompanied her
once, but the venture was not a success, alas. I fear
that the excitement of the city is too great a strain
upon my friend. When she returns home to our little
town she is invariably tired and nervous. Despite this
fact she refuses to rest and with each succeeding week
actually spends a longer time in the city. Last week,
for instance, she returned here only to change her
clothes, then immediately left again. It has now been
more than a few days since I've last seen her.*

*This does not bother me overmuch because, as I say,
the rain leaves me feeling sleepy and warm. Plus, there
is a very comfortable chair of which I've grown
extremely fond and which affords me an excellent view
of the plaza. You might almost call the plaza the centre
of town—but certainly you remember how everything
is here, so there's no need to explain each feature down
to the last detail. It's very curious how people here*

*walk about and gossip in the streets as though rain
were not falling heavily upon them all the while. It is
my secret wish to be able to gossip on the corner in the
rain as the women here do for hours on end, without
holding umbrellas or wearing jackets or hats. To be
sure, they very quickly become soaked, but do not seem
to mind this in the least. I've thought I might work on
this project in stages: one day stay out for so long, the
next day for a little while longer, and so on. This
method would ensure a smaller chance for a great
defeat, I feel.*

*What is perhaps more curious than the women are
the games the children play in the muddy streets.
These are the same games that we played as children:
hide-and-seek, hopscotch, jump-rope, tag. Although
they cannot as a rule speak anything but Spanish, the
children play all their games in English. To fill the
time I have recently begun to copy down the rhymes
by which the children play. I write them in a pretty
blue book bought for me by my friend, Señora
Sanchez. I pretended not to notice that this notebook
was the kind in which only the very smallest child
would scribble, as my friend's feelings are easily hurt.
Did I tell you about her spells of sadness in the afternoons?*

*I meant to include a few of the rhymes in this letter.
In fact, I had intended them to serve as explanation for
my remaining here in Puerto del Sol. Dare I say I
hoped that they might even explain the larger workings of my destiny? I felt strongly that these simple
rhymes possessed the power to transport my motives
from obscurity into clear light. Now, however, I see
that their full effect is lost on paper. I am more than a
little embarrassed to admit that copying the rhymes
into the blue notebook has been my sole occupation
during all these weeks.*

*Perhaps it is not the rhymes themselves which affect
me so powerfully, but rather the clothes which the*

children wear while playing. Please let me explain.

The streets are deeply muddy, as is natural when rain meets dirt, and of course the children tumble about a good deal in the course of their games. As a consequence their clothes quickly become soiled. The very next day, however, the children come out to play in the same clothes they wore on the previous afternoon, but which have somehow, over the night, become spotlessly cleaned. How do the women, who spend all their time gossiping on the corner, find the chance to clean these clothes? It is a mystery. Do they have a secret method of eradicating deep stains swiftly? Another question is: why don't the mothers dress their children in older clothes for the muddy games and save the pretty clothes for special occasions? It gives me a strange feeling to see the children dancing like white butterflies over the mud each morning, when I know that very shortly they will become as dirty as the sky.

Every day they call to me, inviting me to come out and play with them; every day I call back that I'll come out and play tomorrow. Sometimes it is enough to watch others do exactly the thing you most desire to do—or maybe I mean that watching in itself can become an act of participation. Every now and then a thin, sharp-faced girl looks up from the games and waves to me without stopping until I wave back. I sense that she knows I would certainly come out and play, if it were not for the terrors which still afflict me and of which you, Nina, are all too aware. But in my defence I must say that now I'm almost certain that my fear of the dark has lessened. Of course, I cannot be one hundred per cent sure of this. But I am sure that the fear would leave me completely were it not for the speed with which night falls. If the light dimmed more slowly, it would make a difference. Don't you agree?

On the other side of the scale, I'm a little ashamed of my inability to learn more than the simplest words of the Spanish language. There are certain things about *the playing children which I would like to know. For instance, I wonder why they aren't in school more often. This bothers me. Is it because there are so many holidays in this sphere of the world, perhaps? I've tried to ask my friend about the children and the clothes and the holidays, but she pretends to misunderstand me when certain subjects are raised. As I've stated, she is very sensitive. What I hope is that my failure with Spanish will be cancelled out by my great improvement regarding the falling of night. But are such things ever balanced? I wonder.*

The days pass one by one all across the world. I have accepted my destiny. From a certain point there is no longer any turning back. I have my little window upon the plaza and I have my radio. The music here is such that I can sit in my chair before the window and listen to it for hours on end. At night I sleep with all the windows open, for the sake of a breeze that blows the scent of flowers up from the courtyard upon the rain. There are red and purple and orange blossoms, and a few yellow ones too. Though the rain falls hard, it doesn't damage them. Still, their scent reminds me of something . . . but what that is I can't remember.

Emily

P.S. Dear Friend, I don't want you to think that I'd persecute only you with such a sorry letter. I am writing notes of explanation to everyone I know, or at least to everyone listed in my address book. I started with the A's and am working slowly toward the Z's. That seems the most logical way to proceed. But I won't go on and on. What I wonder is whether you could send—if you have it—the address of that woman we met in that restaurant we used to frequent in the city. You must remember the encounter. She was sitting alone at the next table, wearing a hat piled with plastic grapes that looked good enough to eat. We talked with her for several minutes about various varieties of trout. I remember that she was quite knowledgeable on the subject. I also recall that her name began with an S. But would that be her first or her last name? I don't know. Though I've never seen or heard from her since that single meeting, I have a great urge to confess to her.

P.P.S. I notice, with great distress, that I have neglected to write about my feelings for the sea. The sea is as important to me as the children, and I meant to include it in this testimony. It is just as important as the promise you once made me.

The two women sat in silence. The letter contained no return address. Stella had recently taken to keeping all her house lights burning brightly throughout the day, and this lighting created an uneasy effect. "I'm a nervous wreck," said Nina. "You know how I usually sleep like sugar. But since this letter arrived, I've lain awake trying to understand what has happened to Emily. What can this nonsense mean?"

"I believe Emily is trying to upset you deliberately and meanly," conjectured Stella. "She knows your vulnerable regions. If I were you, I'd not read any more letters that might arrive from that direction. Burn them unopened or hand them over to the police as evidence."

"There ought to be a law!" Nina nearly wept with frustration.

Stella shook her head sadly but triumphantly. "I think her plot is clear. You and I can learn from poor Emily's misfortune the dangers of abandoning home and comforts. You escaped narrowly, but here you are and thank your lucky stars. As I see it, Emily has been deceived by some dream, and in revenge attempts to poison your bliss. Or perhaps she's found a kind of happiness unimaginable to you and I." Stella's voice turned doubtful. "What looks like misery in another's eyes might just as well be joy.

"No, Emily has fallen by the way that we will never know, knock on wood. If there's one thing I have learned through the years, it is this: we are not super-women. It's all we can do to look after our own happi-ness, never mind the joy of others. You could spend your precious life taking care of others, but where would that lead you? Bobbing for the apple of tempta-tion and gaining only water up your nose." Stella shook her curls in a serious, philosophical style.

"In the meantime, why don't we take in a double fea-ture down at the mall? There's no better way to pass a gloomy afternoon. To be quite frank, Nina, you look like you need some entertainment and, well, I can always enjoy a good show. And of course you'll come for cards tonight, won't you sweet?"

▄▄▄ It Is Easier To Leave Than To Return

"I'm back, Joe," said Madeleine to the desk clerk of the Holiday Hotel.

The long walk into the city from Stella's suburb had been an evil dream of dark streets and abandoned ware-houses and windy overpasses. They no longer built roads for walkers; everything was cars, cars, cars, and pedestrians prohibited. Shoes were the same or worse, an expensive crime against the pocketbook: witness the heel broken against a curb back on Sixteenth Street. The spattering rain and lurking molesters, desperadoes and other assorted heathens had added insult to the injury. "No wonder crusading is no longer so popular," reflected Madeleine, looking around the hotel lobby. Though as shabby as ever, it appeared to her now like the face of an aborted child miraculously come to life.

Joe threw her key onto the counter without looking

up from the column of figures with which he was wrestling. The page was covered with many patches of numbers and mathematical symbols leading in every direction, with scribbles to point out the mistakes. Madeleine noticed that Joe had drawn exquisite representations of birds in flight amidst the numerals.

"How is everything here?" she asked. "I bet a thousand things have happened while I've been gone. I have some stories of my own to tell, you know." Joe punched the keys of his battered calculator in a frustrated manner; he seemed involved with an especially tricky problem. "Well, you'll have to tell me all the stories later," Madeleine said after a short pause.

"Everything's the same," said Joe, still not raising his eyes. "Nothing has happened and there are no stories to tell, so don't ask."

Madeleine smiled as she ran lightly up the stairs to her room. Joe was the same as ever and his gruff manner didn't fool her one bit. He was a fine old character unsuited to dealing with the public, choosing to work the graveyard shift because less traffic passed through the hotel lobby then. As she turned the key in her lock, Madeleine was still blessing Joe for remaining the same.

Though the usual mess of clothes, papers, empty bottles and overflowing ashtrays cluttered the old room, it looked somehow different. It had that cold and empty aspect which rooms take on when left to their own devices for too long. Madeleine tiptoed around in search of signs of the boy. Amidst the jumble she found: one matchbook cover imprinted with the name of a bar in Los Angeles, California; a newspaper clipping that described the beaching of eleven whales upon the coast of Oregon; an outdated airline schedule listing arrival and departure times for flights between the Queen Charlotte Islands and Vancouver; the stub of a ticket for a fair in a nearby town; three used razor cartridges; and an old photograph, roughly torn from a magazine, showing Frances Farmer on her way to jail, complete

with untidy hair, cigarette and sneer. After studying
these clues carefully, knowing that the smallest nothings
speak fantastic words, Madeleine placed them in a shoe-
box she kept hidden beneath her bed. Only then did she
notice that some of the boy's clothes were gone.

"Ingrid!" she called at her neighbour's door. No one
answered however hard and long she knocked, except
several inhabitants of adjacent rooms who with small-
minded pettiness complained about rackets in the early
hours.

Next she tried Jeanette's door. After a few minutes a
voice from behind it cried, "Go away!"

"It's me, Madeleine," she called distinctly. "I've come
back."

"Yeah, well you can go right on back. In five seconds I
call the cops." This voice didn't sound like it belonged
to Jeanette or to anyone else that Madeleine knew for
that matter.

"This is certainly strange," she thought, returning to
her room. "Where can everyone be?" When she closed
her door behind her, a draught fluttered the pages of the
manuscript which had been gathering dust upon the
table during the time of Madeleine's absence. Nothing
else moved.

She sat on the edge of the unmade bed in her crumpled evening clothes and smoked a cigarette. With a
sigh she removed the glass tiara from her head.
Thoughts of the joyous homecoming and the docking
ship passed through her mind. She had often seen
groups waiting impatiently at airport terminals or ship-
side docks for their returning pilgrims. The welcomers
carried balloons, gift-wrapped packages and big home-
made signs scrawled with crayoned greetings. After the
wanderer was welcomed, the party would ride off in a
taxi to celebrate in some restaurant or other with cham-
pagne and kisses. The fatted calf was killed to feast the
prodigal sons and daughters. Even the pirate was
eagerly welcomed by the young girls he carried off to

sea. Such things happened every day all over the world.

Madeleine meditated. "It may very well be," she mused, "that all that has occurred to this point has been only preparation, so to speak. The chef may spend more time readying his ingredients than he actually spends at the stove. Possibly I have mistakenly believed I've been fully engaged in fighting a battle when in fact I've merely been cleaning and loading my weapons in anticipation of the first attack. My artistic efforts, by the same token, have more than likely been a groping in the dark so far. Given that my life is dedicated to spreading the teachings of Frances Farmer, it does not necessarily follow that I can offer such instruction best by repeating her painful experiences myself; in this aspect I might very well be only the tool that best serves its purpose by remaining hard and sharp and without feelings. Now that night is over and dawn has finally arrived, I suspect that my task will be completed very quickly. Yet I must also keep in mind that the Bible was not written in one day or even one week.

"Certainly I could easily move from this hotel to another, creating the illusion of renewed momentum by settling within walls of a different colour and beside neighbours with new faces. However, if Ingrid, Jeanette and the other characters from the first act of this passion play have disappeared into the wings, it may be for a very good reason and I must be prepared to stand on the stage alone. It seems to me that this is exactly the time to dig my trench and establish my position for either an attack or a defence. Certain experiences have transpired in this city; although to a cold, critical eye they might seem petty, insignificant and even without meaning, there is also the chance that they have all been the workings of fate. In short, I feel that the fight is only now beginning."

Madeleine picked through her wardrobe, sensing that the next stage in her destiny would reveal itself more clearly when she was appropriately attired. After some consideration she exchanged her evening clothes for a simple grey business suit with a black tie and very low heels. She scrubbed the make-up from her face and imprisoned her locks within a tight bun, then placed her manuscript pages inside a brown briefcase. While transforming herself, she came to feel that she could now face her duty squarely, soberly and briskly, and for a brief moment even considered the idea of climbing upon the wagon and riding it for a distance. However, as the first grey streaks of dawn dropped down the air shaft and into her room, Madeleine felt that it was just this kind of drastic measure she should take pains to avoid, and so sipped several short drinks.

With deliberate movements she left the room and emerged upon the street. There she moved quickly with men and women of business, on their way to responsible work, who also carried briefcases. She made her way to The Tenderloin, feeling that it might prove useful to remind herself where she had come from in order to know better where she was headed. The area was deserted at this hour, its residents only recently off the avenues after another long night. The corner was empty save for an old man sleeping on yesterday's newspaper. Madeleine considered the drugstore, the bus stop, the fire hydrant, and the cocktail sign flashing pink and green. She knew that these were signs, but it was less immediately obvious in which direction they pointed. Madeleine frowned at the unoccupied phone booth and bench, then glanced down. A circle of cigarette butts lay around her feet. She picked one up, read the word *Lucky* printed in a ring above its filter. Putting this butt into her briefcase, she smiled wisely and turned away.

Back at the entrance to the hotel she ran into Sally, the recluse who lived on the seventh floor and whom Madeleine had only glimpsed at a distance from time to time. "Where are you going?" she asked in surprise, knowing how seldom Sally left her room.

"Where else? It's Friday, and you know I'd never miss

a Friday at the post office. I'm not that far gone. Where there's life, there's hope. You're welcome to join me, if you like."

Madeleine hesitated. Now was the time to start choosing her acquaintances with more care and to select only those souls which would obviously illuminate rather than confuse her mission. She frankly doubted, from what she had heard about Sally, whether this woman could teach her essential lessons. "All right," she finally said against her better instincts, falling into step. "Sally, I've been away and I'm finding my return somewhat more painful than I'd imagined."

"Away? I wouldn't have known unless they printed it in the newspaper. Now, I read about a new café that's just opened up around here. They say it's a quaint place for an early morning cup of coffee. All the chic folk gravitate there, so the story goes. I thought I'd drop by and see with my own eyes what is what."

"Sally, can you tell me where my friends Ingrid and Jeanette have gone? I can't find them."

Sally sniffed. "It's none of my business. If girls want to vamp and vix and carry on with men, it's their own affair. Your friend Ingrid is moving from man to man around the city. Bed-hopping, dear."

"What about Jeanette?"

"I don't know. I've heard stories, but can't remember them. My mind is a doughnut. Everything slips through the hole in the centre. We'll have a doughnut or two with our coffee. Chocolate-glazed."

Madeleine glanced dubiously at Sally and recalled what she knew about the woman. Sally had been living in the hotel for three years; previously home had been a more expensive place across town. She was patiently waiting for a letter from her ex-husband, who was on the road somewhere. The letter had been due for some time now. Soon it would arrive, as Sally had always known it would, care of general delivery; Sally also knew that there would be a one-way ticket on the

Greyhound inside the envelope. A ticket south. Sally
had a list drawn up of what she would need to take
along to her new life with her old man upon a desert,
beside an oasis, beneath the sun.

The two women walked, one old and the other
young, along the damp street. While Madeleine's recent
turmoils seemed to have dazed and wearied her, Sally's
finest feathers were flying as they always flew on
Fridays. Her intense enjoyment of this stroll made the
difficulty in finding the new café less important than it
might have been. She gilded the street with her whims,
gaily pointed at people, fixed her eyes on handsome
boys, nudged Madeleine knowingly with an elbow,
laughed loudly at whatever tickled her fancy. "I behave
just like a savage," she giggled girlishly and with a
delighted shame.

At last they found the café hidden between a bowling
alley and a pool hall, both which were closed at this
early hour. The café seemed to lack a name and it was
empty except for a waitress who sat at the back with a
movie magazine and a Coke. Engaged in filing her fingernails between yawns, she finished off her left hand
and lit another cigarette before calling to the women.
"You want something?"

"Two cups of your delicious coffee, please," cried
Sally in a festive voice. "This is just like a holiday," she
enthused to Madeleine. "I always say that only those
who stand by their home can truly enjoy an outing."

Six days a week Sally stayed inside her room and
drank while reading the newspaper. Both the morning
and evening editions were delivered to her door. She
owned six dressing gowns, each a different colour and
each worn in its proper turn on the six days of the week
she lounged and drank inside her room; in this way she
reminded herself exactly where she stood in time.
Everything in the newspaper interested her: the econ-
omy, the foreign policies and especially the Middle East,
her personal favourite. "There are a million angles to

that fascinating place," was Sally's dictum. "You could puzzle over it forever without finding your answer. East of what and in midst of where? Stand on your head and then see which way is which."

On the seventh day Sally didn't touch a drop until nightfall; instead of a dressing gown she donned civilian garb for her trek to the post office. Once outside her room she liked to make the most of it. She would bustle about the city in a handsome, energetic way, poking her nose into any business she happened upon, admiring her figure in passing store windows. The largest portion of the Friday was spent in the post office, where everyone knew about her expected letter and kept a sharp eye out for it. Sally knew all the postal clerks by name, interested herself in their intimate lives and joked with them for hours on end about nothing at all. No one, be he saint or be he sinner, could call her unsociable or unhappy, though she did like to stay inside. "It's the only home I've got," she explained to Madeleine as they watched the waitress saw at her right hand just as if she hadn't heard their order.

All at once the girl jumped up, threw down her file and filled two mugs with hot water from the tap. She carried these to their table along with a small jar of instant coffee, then stamped back to her seat across the room. There she amused herself by pressing tissues against her lipsticked mouth and imprinting kisses upon them. She arranged the kissed tissues in an orderly row along the counter and, just as with snowflakes, no two kisses were the same.

Madeleine and Sally looked silently at their mugs. Some of the hot water had slopped onto the table, which had been none too clean to start with. There were no spoons with which to mix the coffee. "May I trouble you for some cream, dear?" called Sally. "You're a pretty girl. What's your name?" The waitress pretended not to hear this and lit another cigarette.

"I take two sugars plus cream in my coffee," confided

Sally, "though some say it's too rich a taste. Lord, the price of sugar these days. It's a scandal! A million dollars to add a little sweetness to your life. Most people don't guess I'm the type for sweet fancies. I've built what seems to them a bitter little life for myself—but it's mine, however temporarily, and no one can take it away. I have my dressing gowns, my newspapers, my bottles. I know what people call me, but do I care? Heavens, don't look to me for the answer to the world's problems. It just isn't in me."

"But no one could fault you for staying inside," protested Madeleine. "Especially since you keep so well informed."

"But they do. There are thousands like me who enjoy remaining inside their room and the grinding mill of society looks down on us. They have a special unpleasant name for people like me—but damn them, I have my home and I'll fight for it. It's a God-given right and a privilege intended for all. We have a constitution, you know." Sally looked fiercely about, temper painting her cheeks. When she saw the waitress blowing on her nails to make the polish dry more quickly, Sally's anger left her.

"I wish," said Madeleine, "that I had the strength of character to remain inside."

"A watched kettle never boils. Yes, the world is full of waiting people and we all wait the best way we can," remarked Sally blandly. "We could discuss it until Judgement Day. Meanwhile, the post office has opened."

Just as Madeleine and Sally were gathering up their things to leave, the waitress strode to their table. "Get out of here!" she screamed. "Leave or else! You think you can buy my heart and soul for one dollar, but you can't. I'm better than both of you put together, and if you don't know that then you're more stupid than I guessed. I don't need you." The waitress slammed a pitcher of cream onto the table, then stalked to the back of the café, where she disappeared through a door.

Madeleine snorted and stuck her nose in the air. She had begun to flounce from the café when Sally spoke softly in her ear. "Sit down, dear. Just sit down." Sally's hand trembled on Madeleine's arm.

"Well," said Madeleine, arching her eyebrows.

Sally gripped Madeleine's hand tightly. "That girl doesn't hate us," she said sharply. Her voice softened. "Let me tell you something. Just one thing. The lot of a waitress is a difficult one—sore feet and back, hardly a word of thanks or a rusty penny for her trouble. People come into her café, they smile and talk with her as if hoping to become her best friends. Then she turns her back for one minute and they're gone. And there's no goodbye. This kind of treachery occurs countless times every day."

Sally's eyes misted. "I had the calling. Many years ago, when I was still a girl, I heard the summons and I obeyed the voice. I went to work in an all-night coffee shop on the I-9. Nothing fancy, just hot strong coffee. The place was combined with a gas station and stood in the centre of a long wide empty plain. There was nothing much around for a hundred miles or so in any direction. No towns, no farms, no houses, nothing. So when drivers saw our lights they were feeling pretty lonesome and tired. They were on a long journey and had no time to rest at night. They were the kind who dare to move from one place to another only in darkness, the kind for whom night is a sin that can be absolved only through high gear and headlights.

"I was obliged to live in a little cabin behind the café, for there was no nearby town from which to commute. During daytime I would lie in bed because there was nothing else to do. I would wait for my night shift to begin and I would think of the drivers maybe a thousand miles to the north who would reach the café later that night. It may have looked like I was pouring coffee and serving pie and nothing more, but I didn't see it that way. Each evening as I put on my white uniform I couldn't help but feel like an angel or a nurse. Without me and my coffee, how could the night drivers have carried on toward their destinations?

"I stuck out that job for as long as I did because of the hallowed feeling it gave me. On my two nights off each week I'd drive to the nearest city and look at one movie after another. It's a fact that waitresses attend the movies twice as often as anyone else. When you see that kind of thing—the four A.M. drivers—you don't want to think about it too much for fear that you'll become just as frightened as them. The next thing you know, you find yourself alone on the I-9 one night, driving in the rain with the windshield wipers casting their hypnotist's spell, and with the radio tuned to a country station's songs of family and home.

"No, you don't want to think about the sleepless drifters, so you go to the movies. The best ones are those with singing and dancing, laughs and a happy ending. They don't make many of that type any more, and only the Lord knows why. If I were still a waitress, I'd want to attend the movies every night of the week. But how could I? The prices! Besides, there aren't many real picture palaces left any more. Businessmen who don't understand pictures or people who need to see pictures now own all the modern chains. The new theatres are designed to make the real fans feel guilty if they attend alone and guilty if they sit through the feature twice. The ushers and popcorn vendors are hard-faced people who don't care for movies. Matinees are a thing of the past and smoking is prohibited.

"So you can see why our waitress friend is weighed down beneath her sorrows. Is it any wonder that the world's heart is so troubled and that others like me would rather look at our four walls than at the mess outside? If there are times when it's best to turn a blind eye, surely this is one of them."

"I never thought of it like that," said Madeleine. Now

the café seemed a soothing place, and Sally's words
sounded clear and old. They gave Madeleine the kind of
sleepy, peaceful sensation felt by a child whose mother
is reading her a bedtime story, lulling her toward warm
darkness, away from warm light. The chairs, tables and
walls of the café seemed to listen to Sally's words as
intently as Madeleine was. "Tell me more," she said in a
hushed tone.

Sally's voice blurred as she poured clouds of cream
into her coffee. "What more is there? They would push
open the café door and the scent of night would mix in
with that of coffee and french fries. Their eyes were red
and bleared, their voices tight. Often they'd been driving alone for so long that when they gave their order
their words sounded rusted and strange. I always gave
them free refills, though it was strictly forbidden. If they
wanted to drink their coffee and smoke in silence, I let
them—though I longed to hear about their journey and
the wide world beyond.

"Sometimes my head would become hot and heavy,
so I'd go and stand outside for a minute or two. I'd
smell the gas from the pumps and the grass from the
plain. I'd look to see if there were stars in the sky. I'd
look to the north and to the south to see if lights were
coming along the freeway.

"At dawn, when a wan girl with stringy hair relieved
me from my shift, I'd lie on my bed and one by one the
travellers I'd seen during the night would pass before
my eyes again. Like they hadn't gone on their way, but
remained inside me—here, in my heart. I could hear the
trucks roaring down the road and I could feel their
wheels rumble my bed."

Madeleine looked at the cold grey coffee inside her
mug. "But you did leave in the end. After all, you're sitting here with me now."

Sally laughed shortly. "One night a trucker entered
the café alone, left with me on his arm. I can't remember
his name, but I drove off with him in my white uniform.

Still wearing my uniform," she repeated as though to herself.

Suddenly Madeleine remembered riding in a car somewhere between two great cities, sometime between dusk and dawn. The world had seemed no larger than the interior of the car. Though it was late and she was tired, Madeleine hadn't slept. With the driver she had watched the headlights sweep along the freeway so quickly that the road was left behind in darkness at the same moment it was revealed. Now and then Madeleine had lit a cigarette, handed it to the pilot, then lit another for herself. The windows of the car were rolled up tight to keep out the cold, and the space inside was lit dimly by the glowing dials on the dashboard. Whenever a diesel approached around a bend, both drivers would dim their lights while they passed, like an unspoken greeting exchanged between two comrades who were travelling in opposite directions but at the same time were making the same journey. They had driven along mostly in silence, Madeleine and the pilot; but when they spoke their voices sounded sharp and lonely, like a calling across water. For long moments Madeleine had been able to forget that she was being taken away against her will, and was moving toward an unknown destination.

The table jarred and Madeleine jumped. Sally stood up with a sudden, jagged motion. Sticking a cigarette into her mouth, she pushed roughly at her hair. "I got no time for this. Damn rain makes me feel this way."

Madeleine looked at her new friend with troubled eyes. It was as though a curtain had quickly closed across the window of a room in which a precious jewel glittered and shone. The woman who had been speaking to her a minute ago was gone, and standing in her place was a stranger with a puffy face and a peevish expression. As she picked up her briefcase to follow Sally out onto the wet street, Madeleine turned and saw the waitress staring after them through the crack of a nearly shut door.

▰ Platinum Blonde

Frank slouched on the sidewalk in front of the Shanghai Saloon, through red-veined eyes staring down into the gutter before him. A rain as fine as mist drifted upon his bare head. One hand felt the hard heavy bottle inside the paper bag; his other hand fingered a smaller, lighter object hidden in a coat pocket. The man was unshaven and unbathed, and his suit was soiled and wrinkled. People passing along the sidewalk made a small detour around him.

Behind him the door of the bar opened and closed as customers entered or left the place. There would be a snatch of music or babbled conversation, then the sound of a car passing down the street or only silence again. Steve stood behind the counter of the Shanghai full time now, and another man had been hired to take his previous part-time place. A month ago Frank had suddenly announced an intention to take some time off, starting at once if Steve could step swiftly into his shoes. He hadn't explained why he was taking this break or how long it might last; no particular plan, such as taking a trip, was offered as a reason for it. "It's about time," people remarked about this decision at first. Now they said nothing, only watching Frank out of the corner of their eye or nodding in embarrassment when they passed him shambling down the street. Frank realized that he looked as bad as he felt, but he made no attempt to conceal his present state from others or even to show he was aware of it himself.

He continued to drop by the Shanghai every afternoon. He would sign cheques and inventory orders without looking at them, then sit at a table for a drink.

Knowing his presence made Steve and also some of the
old regulars uneasy, Frank wouldn't stay in the bar long.
He remained there only several minutes, feeling that the
place was more or less the same as it had been when he
was in charge. Steve seemed to be doing a fair job,
although Frank noticed that he was often curt and cold
toward customers. He hadn't mentioned the matter to
the man; they scarcely spoke. In silence Frank would
take a full bottle from behind the counter, stow it in a
pocket, then walk out onto the street.

There he wandered in all directions and he discovered
parts of the city unknown to him before. As he roamed,
he studied whatever came before his eyes, and there
was always now a puzzled expression on his face that
had before appeared considered and calm. Frank
watched children play in schoolyards and he watched
cripples roll by in wheelchairs. He saw women in furs
slide smoothly into limousines and he saw beggars
standing motionless in doorways and he saw lovers
entwined on bridges suspended high above cold water.
He entered churches and cafés, movie theatres and bus
terminals; and always he watched with the confused
eyes of a recent arrival to an alien planet, who has been
given insufficient information to enable him to interpret
visions which he has never seen on his own distant star.

Everywhere he went Frank encountered faces
haunted by loneliness. He was struck by the number of
people who so obviously had suffered silently and alone
for a very long time; their faces, deeply drawn and
etched by pain, swam always in his sight; and Frank
found himself unable to look into their eyes. He came to
feel that in this city alone there were thousands of ordinary people who lived lives of unbearable isolation, and
it seemed extraordinary that they managed to carry on
and sustain themselves by means of the smallest scraps
of pleasure, the most fleeting moments of happiness or
peace. It was this silent unquestioning acceptance of
such a condition that Frank found fantastic; and he

wondered if these people had achieved a measure of wisdom that lay a great distance along a difficult road before him. He wanted to ask them how they had managed to wander alone down this road for so long, and he wondered if he were strong enough to bear the journey himself.

At night, after he had wandered far, Frank would make his way home on legs tired from all the steps they had taken. His eyes brimmed with all that they had seen and his head was heavy from all that he had drunk. Entering his apartment, he fell into bed and slept at once. The next day he would waken at noon to find himself fully dressed, and with a head that hurt until he took the first drink.

Shifting on the sidewalk, Frank swallowed another mouthful of scotch. This month of wandering had seemed endless to him, yet every day on the streets he passed countless others who for years had wandered through long, lonely seasons. Their hands were pushed deep into pockets, their eyes glanced alertly into alleys; moving slowly along the sidewalk with no definite direction before them, they wondered if they would roam to Boston or to Denver when the season changed. If the season changed. This winter seemed to have lasted forever; but there were no visible signs that spring was nearing. Was the sky light for a few minutes longer each day? Did the rain fall less frequently and steadily now? Frank touched his hair. It was hard to tell.

He found it hard to tell about anything now. To discern verifiable evidence that there was a pattern to all he saw each day. It had always been hard to tell, everything had always been a question. But before, questions had seemed to expand and evolve and to hint at answers; once, they had grown richer with thought and had rewarded thought. Now these same questions seemed ancient and unanswerable and finally without use. They had turned into dark narrow alleys that led each to the same dead-end wall against which you

bashed your head until the brains oozed from your skull
and slid down the brick face to the ground, where they
were licked up by starving cats.

Frank fingered the small light vial of pills inside his
pocket. At this hour of late afternoon the street before
him appeared abandoned by everyone but himself. For
years he had lived alone, but only during the last month
had he felt the loneliness a ghost feels. Lately the neighbourhood around him seemed less densely populated,
home to fewer people, held significant by a smaller
number of hearts. At moments like this Frank felt that
even the lonely wanderers he had passed by only yesterday had moved a great distance away. People had
gone, and they had not come back. Frank wanted to go
away and not come back himself. He could roam to
Boston or to Denver. He could travel to an unknown
land—that enchanted island, or that mountain peak
where no man had stood before. Maybe he would find
everyone who had left these streets in that far-away
place. The nameless ones as well as the ones with
names. Sister Mary, who no longer shouted on the corners; the blonde, who no longer haunted the bar—
though once last week Frank thought he saw her turning the corner just ahead of him. "A new place," he
thought. "Somewhere we can all start from scratch.
We'll have learned from our mistakes here and we'll be
wise enough to avoid repeating them there."

Frank drained the last drops from the bottle, then let
it drop down the curb, where it rolled a few feet along
the gutter before coming to rest. He wasn't going to
wander the city this evening. He had wandered enough,
seen enough, questioned enough. Now it was time to
journey toward a new place where the knowledge
acquired here could be put to use. He felt ready. He
stood up, swayed and moved down the street. Soon it
would be dark.

Frank paused on a corner, then walked several steps
one way before turning back and heading in the other

direction. He walked with an uneven stride and in an imperfectly straight line; sometimes he slowed until he stopped, as if a spring inside him had wound all the way down. Then he would lurch forward again, his head bent toward the sidewalk, avoiding sight of what was around him.

Fitting correct keys into correct locks, he entered his apartment. He closed the door and felt his way through the dim rooms, neither opening curtains to let in the last of day's light nor switching on lamps. The place felt chilly; his hand adjusted a thermostat. He settled in his chair, still wearing his coat.

In a while he rose, felt his way to the kitchen, poured a glass of water. Back in his chair he removed the vial of pills from his pocket and spilled several onto the palm of his left hand. "I can't sleep," he'd lied to the doctor. "Business worries," he'd said, trying to grin while watching the hand scrawl a prescription. What were the pills called, anyway? Small, round, white. He swallowed one with water, then lit a cigarette. After stubbing the butt into an ashtray, he swallowed three more tablets. Isn't this the way a woman would choose to go? he wondered. Don't they typecast men to press a gun against their temple? According to the script, this is the final scene of a role played by an aging Hollywood starlet. *My heart is broken*, she writes with ruby lipstick on her mirror. *I can't go on*, she writes in the same hand she once used to fill high-school notebooks, then to sign eight-by-ten glossies. *Goodbye, so long, it was swell while it lasted.*

Frank swallowed the rest of the pills, one immediately after the other. Everyone wanted the last word. The chance to say one final thing while there was still time, because in a minute the long silence would begin. Frank felt the sea inside him turn heavier and more sluggish; the sound of its beating grew louder.

When he rose from the chair, his knees sagged and his legs nearly crumpled. He moved slowly and carefully, one hand holding onto the wall, the other feeling table tops for pen and paper. A rushing sound, like surf sweeping a shore, began to roar inside his head. His fingers clamped upon a pen and a sheet of stiff paper. Returning to his chair, he switched on the lamp beside it.

The piece of paper was an eight-by-ten glossy. One side was a shiny black-and-white photograph of a woman's face. A smooth, hard face. Perfectly lit and perfectly made up. More like the mask of a face than a face itself, Frank thought. The real face was hidden. Probably for good reason, probably for protection. Who was this young woman looking squarely into the camera, stretching the muscles of her face into a smile, waiting for the burst of light to blind her; with effort preserving the correct expression on the mask until the flash seared her mind like a sudden enormous current of electric shock. Immediately afterward there is a sense of relief and peace: it's over, it wasn't as bad as you imagined, you're still all right, aren't you? Yes, your face is still smooth, hard, perfect; your hair is still platinum blonde. It's only a short or not so short time later, when the camera's eye has turned away indifferently and for good, that you imagine that each flash of blinding light wiped out a little piece of your memory of what it was like before you assumed the mask. Suddenly it is always late at night, the room is always empty, the mask is turning ugly and old; but you can't take it off. You can't remember how you looked before the cameras first flashed their light into the dark secret places inside you. You can't remember what it was like before you were platinum blonde.

Sam, over at the Hollywood Palace, had given Frank this photo the other evening. He'd handed it over like it was a very valuable prize; in an excited voice he had spoken as if about an extraordinary thing. Frank hadn't listened to the man's words or glanced at the smiling starlet. He had walked quickly into the movie theatre, stood at the back until his eyes could see in the dark, then made his way to a seat near the screen. There he had watched and listened intently to a film without understanding the actors' words or interpreting their movements.

Was this a photo of Frances Farmer? Maybe that was who Sam had been chattering about; he was a big fan. Frank didn't know. He wasn't certain what the woman had looked like, how she had smiled into the camera. Frances Farmer. It was a name he had heard from time to time. The name of someone who people told stories about in sad bars and dim lounges. The subject of hazy recollections or distinctly recalled but disconnected scenes whose veracity could not be proved. Proof. That's what he'd looked for and never found in this world here. There were several lines of print on the flip-side of the photograph; perhaps they proved the identity of the platinum blonde. Later, near the beginning of the end—after the camera has raped her so often she is afraid to leave the room or to open the curtains, afraid of what any light will do to her—she sits in the darkness and tries to tear off the mask and fights to remember her true name. What is it? The letters wavered before Frank's eyes, slipped out of focus.

What did he finally want to say? In ten words or less. Light began to flash inside his head like brilliant fire-works or exploding stars, colours shooting and scatter-ing through the dark sky. Hurry up, Frank told himself. You haven't got all day.

"Wait," he suddenly said aloud. Hold on a minute. I think I've made a slight mistake.

He wasn't quite ready for this journey yet. He hadn't acquired enough knowledge; he needed to wander and to wonder for many more years before he could think of travelling to another world. Anyway, when he was finally able to make some sense of this world's confu-sion, he must stay here and put this knowledge to use right here. Yes. He wished to rise from his chair and to rush out into the street and to spray a message on the blank surface of every wall in the city. *Don't look for visible proof*, he wanted to paint in large letters everywhere. *Don't demand verifiable evidence*, he needed to let everyone know. Yes, that's what he must say now that he had watched and wondered for so long, now that he was prepared to speak. Don't ask for concrete confirmation that the world is sheltered by a powerful protector with a clear purpose and a sane plan, beneath whose caring eyes we may pass calm lives.

He'd made an error in judgement, committed an irreversible act. The platinum blonde looked at him steadily. Take it easy, baby, she seemed to say. You going my way or am I going yours?

He turned the photo over again, gripped the pen, lowered it toward the swimming white space that waited to be filled. Just a minute. Who were these words for? Dear Sister Mary. Dear Madeleine. Dear Frances. Dear Friend. Dear Anyone, damn you. Listen to me. "Is there anyone listening?" Frank called out as the pen slipped from his fingers and fell to the floor. The words he wished to write were being spelled by bursts of light that flashed inside his head. Technicolour signs illuminated the cold empty heavens. "Are you there?" Frank called out to the empty room. His head fell to one side. A moment later his body slipped slightly in the chair, and the side of Frank's face came to rest against the face in the photograph.

▰▰ Zimbabwe

"I know you happy here," said Lucille, setting down a basket of laundered clothes and plugging in the iron. "Though you won't say a word I know you glad to be here with me stead of in that cramped room above that

ugly pawnshop. My heart about broke when I found
you there, looking like you hadn't ate or slept or washed
yourself for so long, your Bible burned into black ash all
across the floor. It lucky you didn't set yourself on fire,
Sister. It lucky I came by when I did and brought you
back home with me. Sure you happy here, though you
won't say boo to me or no one else."

Mary stirred in her chair by the window. It was a
country you could find on a map, if you knew where to
look. It was a place here on earth that you could buy a
ticket for and travel to by airplane or boat or train. It
was somewhere you could go to right now. You didn't
have to suffer all your life before reaching there. You
didn't have to die in order to find Zimbabwe.

"Yes," said Lucille, waiting for the iron to heat up.
"The Lord sure do move in mysterious ways, don't He?
Here my Rufus up and left me feeling lonely and blue.
The very next day I go over to visit you and find you
needing me bad. I bring you back home and you fit
right into the space that old Rufus left empty. We both
been through a hard time, you and me, but now we
together again. We been separated all them long years
you was preaching on the street. Lord, I felt I'd lost my
only sister forever, I did. You was always discussing The
Spirit and The Light, I couldn't think of a word to say to
you. But now we here close together and giving each
other company and keeping away the loneliness.
Remember when we was little girls talking in bed after
the light was turned out? You girls go on to sleep now,
our mama would say. But we'd keep whispering till it
was late, we'd keep speaking all the things we had to
say to each other. Now we can talk that way again."

Yes, it was a country you could buy a ticket to, but she
didn't feel that it was necessarily such a particular place.
It was anywhere your people had come from long ago
and it was a beginning place where things hadn't gone
wrong. Somewhere old and new at once. Where there
was no crime or war or murder, no hunger and thirst

and sorrow. It was somewhere close and real that you
could touch with your hand and feel. Heaven here on
earth. Zimbabwe.

Lucille spat on the iron and glanced nervously at her
sister. "That doctor at the Free Clinic said there ain't a
thing wrong with your voice. He said you can talk as
clear and loud as anybody if you want to. And I know
you going to start speaking to me just as soon as you
good and ready. You take your time. We got all the time
in the world."

Maybe all she needed was to rest a little longer in
order to gain the strength to travel there. If Lucille
would just let her alone until tomorrow, she'd be able to
rise from this chair and start on her way. She would
leave in the first light of morning, when all the world
was still sleeping. Lucille would wake to find her gone
and to find the note she'd left behind. I've gone away,
she would write Lucille, you can follow me when you're
ready to find Zimbabwe.

"Things is going to get better," said Lucille, moving
the hot iron across clean cloth with large sweeping
movements. "I just got this feeling in my bones that
things going to improve considerable for you and me.
Soon spring come round again and we can walk in the
park and smell the earth wake up again. Course, this
neighbourhood ain't too safe, it dangerous for two
women to walk these streets after dark, them crack kids
crazy and killing anyone at all for no good reason. But
in the sunshine we be all right."

It would be a familiar land, though she'd never seen it
before. The same place she'd cried out about on the
streets day after day after day. Where the plants grew
green and the dirt smelled rich and strong. Where the
rivers ran clear and where the sea was full of salt. It was
how the world was meant to be. She didn't wonder any
longer why it seemed that the world right here was a
mistake. She was past puzzling over whether there was
a reason for all the suffering in her sight. Whether the

sorrow was part of a purpose and a plan. The Book had burned and The Word had turned to ash. Yet she still believed. Now she believed in Zimbabwe.

"I made us a plan," said Lucille. "I been meaning to keep it a secret and a surprise, but I think I tell you now and lift your spirits. I been thinking that if we combine our Assistance we might be able to move from these rooms to a better place on the West Side. If we plan careful and live in a saving way the next couple months, we might just manage. Over there it safer, nicer, prettier. They still believe in things that gives people half a chance. We could start over again, you and me. We ain't either of us so old. Why, you so smart you could be a brain surgeon if you cared for it. We could be anything we wished for with our hearts if we lived over on the West Side."

Or maybe she wouldn't have to buy a ticket to reach there. Maybe she could travel there without leaving this chair. Lucille would still be speaking to her from across the room, but she'd be gone over the edge of the horizon. She would be living in a house with a roof made of leaves and walls made of grass and a floor made of hard clean dirt. She would be teaching children how to build things and how to care for things and how to keep the land good and calm. Lucille would keep on speaking to her, but she'd be at the other side of the world, in Zimbabwe.

"I got it all figured out," said Lucille, folding the neatly ironed clothes. "We sell all this sad old furniture so we can move more easy. We just call us a cab and move over there with only the clothes on our backs. We won't need this or that or the other thing when we live on the West Side. I got a hunch we be happy there no matter what. You start talking and laughing again. We share the cooking and cleaning. We go to the movies and take books out of the library. We join us some clubs and make us some new friends. How about that?"

She could nearly feel herself travelling there now. She

could almost feel the light becoming clearer and the air turning warmer and the scent of flowers growing stronger. Lucille's voice sounded fainter. She was leaving, she was nearly half-way there, she would soon be in Zimbabwe.

Lucille pressed the clean, ironed clothes to her face. "This laundry sure smell sweet," she said, breathing deeply. Mary's hand lifted from the arm of the chair beside the window. It made a sign of blessing or a gesture of farewell or an invitation to follow. "You know what?" said Lucille, watching her sister's hand settle upon the arm of the chair again. "The funny thing is that it ain't really so far to the West Side as it seemed before. It just feel far off when you frightened and alone. But now we together again, we brave again and strong again. Now it ain't so far from here to there."

■ Blank Space

(Later it would seem as if there were blank spaces in her life, critical moments which the camera had missed recording. After she was gone, people would attempt to trace her movements, hoping to understand what happened to her and if what happened could have been avoided. They discovered mysterious weeks and even months—particularly in the last year of freedom—which could not be accounted for; by then her movements had become consistently erratic, abrupt, unexplainable, as if propelled solely by bursts of anger or fear. There would be found no records or evidence of where she went or what she did during the dark days when storm clouds were gathering overhead, massing black above a young blonde woman on the run. Afterwards, when she was always calm, she would keep silent about these gaps in time, perhaps because they had become empty spaces in her own hollowed mind. Or—the exact reverse—because they were all that was left to her: last secrets.)

How had it been before the director first shouted *action!* and the cameras started to roll and the carefully blocked out scenes began to unfold exactly as they had been rehearsed, with no room for improvisation and no space for inspiration? (Frances, just hit your mark and say your line.) For too long the soundstage lights had burned too brightly; they flared with radioactive force, destroying all life in a wide radius around them, melting delicate inner essences and leaving the brittle bones, the hard masks intact. (The hollowed eyes of Hollywood would brim with glycerine tears as they watched her swift descent through the sky.) Light searing her eyes so that when she tried to turn away from the camera's critical gaze the world appeared full of shadow, dusky even beneath the sun's golden glance. Now she was unable to make out even vaguely shapes which once had lain in completest clarity and sharpest definition before her. The white light bore into her brain and burned away whatever flickered and danced and wavered there—the daydreams of idle hours, the private passions of unwitnessed nights—leaving only bald disconnected facts to be screamed but unexplained in headlines of bold type. What had happened to the lost husband and lover and house on the beach? Where had her money gone and why was the studio suing her and what was the reason for the warrant? (Frances, you're guilty of saying the wrong words to the wrong people at the wrong time. Your crime is indiscretion and lack of caution and indifference to the rules or, shall we say, the script. Sentence: one lifetime.) And why were these phone calls slipping through the hotel switchboard and into her ear, these unknown voices burrowing into her head when she was trying to remember the sound of Michael's call rising through cold clear water and drifting with a breeze across the lake?

(Listen, Frances, the strangers advised in urgent whispers. You can still clear things up, there's still a way out, it's not too late.)

"Who is this?" she demanded of the black receiver, causing a click of disconnection to explode like a gunshot in her ear. Who was this young woman pacing a disordered hotel room in 1943, living another disconnected episode that she was unable to join to all the other disconnected episodes of a brief existence? If she could hide safely in a dark editing room for a day, a week, a month, she might be able to splice together the scenes, create a clearer sense of continuity, smooth the way for the difficult ending that was rushing toward her too quickly. When the telephone began to ring again, the young woman flung out her arm and sent the instrument flying from the table to the floor, where it buzzed like an evil insect as she sloshed more scotch into the glass.

"I want it all to stop," she said distinctly to the empty hotel room, over the sound of fists hammering against the other side of the door, over the noise of flat voices demanding entry. This film refused to halt, the camera kept photographing her flesh and bones with fire, imprinting x-ray images of her mind upon celluloid, evidence to be used against her later. Like hell there was still a way out. There was no back door or convenient window leading from this fucking hotel room. (Listen, Frances, you can still smooth things over, all you have to do is . . .) She drained the glass, pushed pages into a purse, opened the door.

"Cut," she said, shoving past a reporter, knocking a photographer against the wall. "Miss Farmer," called the desk clerk as she strode swiftly through the lobby, one hand trying to smooth snarls from her hair, smoke curling into her eye until she tossed the live cigarette onto the carpet, leaving her mark upon the Knickerbocker Hotel, where she would later return to be captured. She slid into a cab that idled at the curb, and an hour later was on a northbound bus.

(Later they would try to fill the blank spaces with a profusion of reasonable answers, a mass of sensible suppositions. They would suggest that just before the walls closed around her she made certain rash decisions and took certain unwise steps which ensured her doom. This unfortunate fate might have been avoided, they insisted; and they would speculate sadly upon why she apparently made no effort to divert or halt the gathering storm. What a pity, they would sigh. If only she had stuck to the script, they would lament.

The human heart cannot conceive of any god permitting certain events—torture, mutilation, degradation—to occur. There is a divine script that may be safely clung to, they gently protest, whereby A leads to B leads to C; fates may unfold as orderly as alphabets, one letter demurely giving way to the next until Z is meekly reached and any place resembling Hell is carefully sidestepped. Sacred storyboards outline every camera angle, close-up and cut exactly; there can be no blank spaces in the film; and the studio will be pleased to impose a happy ending upon the bleakest of stories. It was her fault, they would finally say, for disobeying the holy rules of Hollywood.

Frances Farmer disregards the director's cues, smashes the make-up woman's jaw, slips out of the camera's eye. She attempts to escape into a script she has written herself. Its pages are unnumbered, the camera set-ups are unplanned, and every scene leading to the inevitable ending will be improvised. Shooting title: *God's Peculiar Care.*)

Coming home, she dreamed of telegraphing Reeves as the bus rolled northward beneath dark clouds. Meet me at the ferry landing and we'll cross the lake together. And we'll climb the hill to where horses hide wild in the pines. But there are no more horses, remember? (Certain things are no longer present on this planet, Frances.) And Reeves is not waiting on the shore of Sunshine Bay.

Dear Movie Star, he had written two years before, at the same time that rage began to burn inside her, flames licking their lies, heat exploding the false scenes they insisted she live. (It's called arson, Frances. Sentence: one lifetime.) In the winter of '41, wrote Reeves, old man Harrod's big barn burned to the ground, and the season's supply of hay burned with it. After this the horses went hungry because Harrod was unable to buy more hay. The Humane Society brought about a court order instructing that all the horses be sold unless they began to receive proper treatment within thirty days. (What makes you think you can treat me this way, she screamed. How dare you think you can do this to me.) Harrod was unable to sell the horses as beasts of pleasure because they were poorly trained and in poor physical condition. (Frances, lay off the booze and pills and get yourself in shape. Frances, just do what the director says and keep your mouth shut. Frances, you give me no pleasure, I'm leaving you, goodbye.) He was able to sell the horses only as dogfood, for so many cents a pound on the hoof. (Frances, you're under contract, you have no choice, show up on the set.) They came in trucks for the animals one February day when snow was deep upon the ground and more snow was falling from the sky. The half-wild horses were frightened of the trucks and unfamiliar with the experience of being driven into a small enclosed space. (And it would be a dark space, too; and she would not go gentle into the night; and she would fight and rage, and cry out for help when she realized she could not win alone.) Attempts to herd the animals onto the trucks became less gentle with the passing of time and the failing of patience. The scene became confused as panic and fear spread from the horses to the men. (Someone help me! Why won't anyone help me?) Legs seemed to snap as

easily as twigs. Blood streamed upon the snow, crystal-
lizing as something black. In the growing disorder some
animals trampled others; brothers crushed brothers to
death. There was a continuous screaming that filled the
air like thick smoke from a fire burning out of control. It
was a very high-pitched sound, unlike the kind of
sound one would expect to issue from beings so large
and powerful. (Keep quiet, Frances. Don't scream. You'll
only make things worse for yourself. Haven't you
learned that yet?) This screaming faded only as the
trucks drove away and left the place to the silently
falling snow. Afterwards, wrote Reeves before he went
to war, Harrod sold the pasture land; it was subdivided,
all that open land across the water, into neat little pieces.
(They would make a single small cut into her brain,
quick and easy and clean, calming at once and forever
that wild stormy place.) Don't try to come back, warned
Reeves before he disappeared.

(Later, when she was suddenly remembered after having slept through seven silent seasons of Minneapolis
snow, they would work like detectives to piece together
the fractured frames of her life and to fill the blank
spaces with firm, solid facts. They looked to a certain
point, then withdrew with their conclusions. They
feared the blank spaces into which she leaped; falling
through vacuums of time and space to land, for
instance, on the bar stool next to someone who today
speaks freely of that encounter which occurred yesterday or forty years ago today, in a place called San
Antonio or Santa Cruz or the Shanghai Saloon. There
are witnesses whose testimonies have not been
recorded. There are whole lives which have been spent
in black space; thousands of struggles and searches
which have gone undocumented, unwitnessed,
unrecorded; passages through darkness which do not
seem, to the casual observer's eye, to illuminate the
darkness. A star appears one night upon an empty piece

of sky; the next night it is gone, and no one noticed it shine. However. Yet. But. Pages of the script that Frances Farmer tried to live still circulate slowly, seeming sometimes almost to disappear, then emerging in another city in another season, at the far side of another blank space.)

In evening the northbound bus arrived at a large city beside the sea. Frances descended to the ground, then wandered from the depot out into the street. The season was changing and soon it would be spring. Evening air drifted through her lungs; her body drifted through the evening, touched by the light of streetlamps, stroked by strangers' eyes, flowing forward. Only now, when she could already feel the handcuffs and straitjacket tighten around her, did she finally feel free.

The dark sky above was sprinkled with small points of light. There could be no slow graceful descent to earth for stars. There could only be a flashing fall, a shattering landing. It would be so quick as to be nearly unnoticeable. Suddenly there would be blank space in heaven where once light had shone.

Frances looked up and saw a sign before her. (Remember, she had told Reeves eight years before, I've always known exactly what will happen to me.) The left corner of her mouth twisted into a kind of smile. The perfect place. It would take them a while to find her here. (In fact, she would leave before they could find her here, she would vanish as if she had never been here, she would preserve this place as precious blank space.) Frances felt the weight of the pages inside her purse. She would win more time to work on the foregone conclusion to this script.

She threw her cigarette into the gutter; it drifted downward in slow motion. For a long time she stood and watched it fall as slowly as anything might fall; it was as if the frame were freezing, and in a moment would stand still. Taxis shimmered by, streetlights changed from green to amber to red, horns blasted into the night. Frances lifted her face, smiled, and quickly crossed the street. She entered the Holiday Hotel.

▄▄▄ Frances Farmer Lives!

Finally the day arrived. Sam was dressed in a new suit, with a red carnation fixed on his lapel. He glanced one last time around the lobby of the Hollywood Palace to make sure that everything was ready; he had worked through the night preparing the place until it was perfect. Now Frances Farmer gazed down from photographs and stills on the walls, her eyes looking at Sam from every angle and direction. He straightened one picture and wiped imaginary dust from another. Walking outside into the rain, he stood without regard for his new clothes and looked up at the marquee. *Frances Farmer Lives!* cried great shining golden letters. Sam returned inside. He had waited so many years for this day, and had lived through it so often in his dreams, that now he felt neither excitement nor anticipation.

He already knew how it would be. Between each show the audience would file into the lobby and fill it. The space would look different to them, just as they looked different themselves. Their faces would be white with excitement, they would fumble for cigarettes with hands made clumsy by this same excitement. At first they would be silent; but their eyes would burn with a fire that had not blazed in them for years, and now was new, leaping, roaring. The sound of their voices would rise slowly, gain urgency, then spread more and more quickly until one voice joined a hundred others and became a deafening cry. One word would become a thousand. People who for months on end had sat side by side in the dark Palace without exchanging a single word now would turn to each other like old friends, and they would speak together of all the dreams and desires which Frances Farmer had stirred within them. And though the need to speak pressed so urgently upon each person that he could scarcely listen to another's words, everyone would feel they fully understood and were understood just as completely in return. There would be some who walked slowly around the four walls of the lobby, encircling the ones pressed together in the centre; and they would pause before one or another of the black and white images, looking hard and searchingly at it, drawing strength from it. Sam himself would pass among the crowd, shaking hands and saying a few words to each newly wakened spirit; and he would see his own tears in the eyes of others. Later, after the end of *The Party Crashers*, the final Frances Farmer film, they would all march singing through the streets.

He waited by the door. The first Frances Farmer show, *Rhythm On the Range*, was just about to begin. So far only two people—a pair of shoppers ducking in out of the rain—had entered the theatre. Sam waited for the great stream of spectators that must surely pour through the door at the last minute. He watched workers hurrying back from lunch breaks, some holding umbrellas or folded newspapers above them, others with heads bared to the rain. Most of the passersby neglected to glance toward the Palace; not one lifted eyes to the marquee.

Something strange had happened the other day. Two cops had come by and asked some questions about a guy they'd found dead beside an empty pill bottle and an autographed glossy of Jean Harlow. On the back of the photo was written: "Presented to Frank Miller, the lucky 101 fan to buy a ticket to *Platinum Blonde* at the Hollywood Palace on Feb. 25, 198_." The cops had made out that Sam was somehow responsible for this poor guy's death. They'd acted like they were sorry they couldn't take him on downtown. What the hell did they think he was guilty of? Sure, he'd known the bartender,

just like he knew anyone in the neighbourhood who
came by the Palace now and then. And he felt bad about
what had happened to the man. But in the bustle of
organizing Frances Farmer's resurrection, Sam had
hardly given a thought to the incident. Now it came
back to him, as a dark omen, as a sign that something
was not quite right.

A few regulars—old bag ladies, drugged street
boys—straggled in and dug deeply into pockets or
purses for the price of admission. Sam told them that
there was no entrance charge today. But he couldn't
bring himself to make the little set speech he'd prepared
to greet each customer with on this special occasion. As
each regular trailed another set of wet footprints
through the lobby without noticing the pictures on the
walls, Sam's heart slowed another beat. Then he saw the
girl with long blonde hair hurry up to him. "I've got
something special for you today," he managed to say.
She smiled quickly, then walked straight into the theatre
as unseeing as the others.

By the time the first reel began rolling, the thought of
his dream made Sam feel sick. He didn't step into the
theatre to watch the show himself. Instead he began to
take the photos off the walls, one by one, until the lobby
was bare again. He pulled the red carnation from his
lapel and twirled its stem between his fingers. Standing
by the door, he looked out at the street. It was slowly
darkening. Rain continued to fall. Once or twice Sam
heard the sound of Frances Farmer laughing—but at
what, he didn't know.

The picture had already begun when Madeleine entered
the Palace. It took her several minutes to find a seat
because, though the theatre was nearly empty, most of
the seats were broken as well as worn. She didn't bother
to look immediately at the screen; that was hardly necessary. She knew well enough how the story would go:
a good blonde and a bad brunette would fight over a

man unworthy of the battle; he would be tempted temporarily to sin, but would resist in the end. Blondes had
more fun, plus they always got their man. Madeleine
smiled wryly to herself, then sighed. In such knowledge
was more than a little pleasure, yet it wasn't the time-
honoured progression of plots toward their automatic
endings that concerned her at this point. She was hoping for an entirely different kind of conclusion. "I think
I've seen this one before," she remarked conversationally to the darkness, though she still hadn't glanced at
the screen. Then she reminded herself once more that
the days of play and pleasure were part of a distant
past. Breathing in the stale smoky air, she huddled like a
refugee inside her coat.

She came to the Palace every day now. Since her
return to the city from Stella's suburb she had found
herself unable to spend many waking hours inside the
hotel. The place had changed. Ingrid's room was occupied at present by an ancient dwarf who bellowed arias
from Italian operas from dawn to dusk. She had never
glimpsed the woman who was now locked behind
Jeanette's door; the boy had not returned; and Sally was
always preoccupied with her bottles and newspapers.
Several weeks ago Madeleine had gone to the Goodwill
store and exchanged some of her most brilliant costumes for shapeless, colourless garments which gave no
indication of the role being performed by the person
inside them. She wore these drab clothes constantly, and
felt like a mere shadow of her former self when she did
not feel like a complete ghost. "I've stayed too long at
the fair," Madeleine would murmur, staring sadly at the
manuscript pages littering her room and wondering if
perhaps the story were really finished and she was
unable to see a conclusion even when it stared her
straight in the face. Still, she could not believe that her
mission was truly accomplished. Unable to take pleasure in the streets, the corners or the Shanghai Saloon,
she took refuge in the Palace, arriving there late each

morning and sitting through any number of features until evening. Often she did not pay strict attention to the scenes that flickered before her eyes, but devoted herself body and soul to the act of waiting, an activity demanding enough in itself. "After all," she reminded herself, "if one is in darkness, it should certainly be easier to notice the arrival of light."

She was sitting as always up in the balcony, where the house was darkest and the stars seemed closest. Most of the fervent fans chose to sit up there, and they frequently called to the stars, echoed their words, answered their questions. As Madeleine's eyes grew at home with the lack of light, she scanned the solitary figures who sat carefully apart from one another. They were either sleeping or concentrating intently upon the screen. Looking behind, she made out the shadow of two figures slipping from their seats and disappearing together onto the floor.

Small secret noises carried up from the main floor below. This was the preferred seating for those with little interest in the movies but still less interest in the rain outside. They were settling in for the day, taking off shoes so their feet could dry more quickly, rustling brown paper bags in search of pieces of food. Occasional nightmare screams mixed in with the love talk on the screen. Someone could not stop coughing.

All at once Madeleine jumped up. She had made a silly mistake. The seat she was in was the same seat occupied yesterday by a man who had caused a commotion. It had happened when Judy was repeating *there's no place like home, there's no place like home*, with closed eyes, chanting the prayer over and over again. The man had begun to scream at the screen: "Open your eyes, don't go back, they're tricking you, it's a lie, run farther and farther away!" Fortunately this scene occurred near the end of the picture; when Judy returned to Kansas, as she always did, the man had quieted down and only whimpered softly to himself.

Madeleine moved to another seat, and for the first time looked at the screen. The print was typically dusty and scratched, the sound was muffled. The show seemed familiar, though she couldn't quite place it. Shadows chased light and laughing voices rippled as they do in Heaven but never on earth. Blue-voiced angels whispered of what had been once upon a time and might be again but for all the broken promises and victims fallen through galaxies of hope. Though this was all very familiar to her, Madeleine viewed the spectacle with some interest.

Light flashed from behind as the door from the lobby swung open. A crowd fell loud and blind down the aisle and into seats. They giggled and whispered, and immediately began to call remarks—some rude—to the screen. Though they tried to disguise their voices, Madeleine recognized this gang of cheery friends at once. What times she had passed with them during those endless afternoons up in this balcony! They would sit in a long row, slouched in their seats, resting heads on shoulders and feet on chairs in front. They would pass boo and bottles up and down the line. Laughing, clapping, hissing, cheering—everything would be forgotten except what moved into their eyes. There was the way Slow Burn licked his lips whenever Claudette Colbert came on the screen. There was the way Blue refused to leave at the end of any Barbara Stanwyck picture. "I want to adopt that lady for my mother," he would stubbornly say. There were days and days of play, and when they fell red-eyed and dizzy onto the sidewalk afterwards they were always surprised to see how night had fallen behind their back. Arms linked and magic still sticking to the air, off they trooped to the Starlite Lounge or some other nearby bar. The fun had never ended then.

Madeleine twisted impatiently in her seat. She already knew by heart how the story started; it was the ending that interested her now. "What happened to

Sister Mary?" she suddenly wondered, as if recalling someone she had not thought about since a previous lifetime. "What will happen to us all?" She listened to soft voices behind her, above her, before her. The theatre was damp and chilly, as though rain filtered through its roof and drifted in a gauzy net upon the audience, falling around them and imprisoning them together in a single large cell when the comfort of companionship did not wholly compensate for a lack of liberty. The picture on the screen began to fade like something washed away by rain; its voices spoke from so long and far away that they could hardly be heard. Then the screen became empty and silent. Staring at the black space, Madeleine waited for the projectionist to repair the film, so an ending could unfold. "He's sleeping on the job again," she muttered irritably to herself.

The theatre was dark and silent. Then stars exploded red and blue and green through the darkness, like fireworks with falling souls. Light years vanished as comets dropped through blue rain before Madeleine's eyes. Tossed by God from Heaven, the stars splintered like glass across mountains and plains, into seas and streams, upon cities and towns. Fish and deer and other dumb creatures slowly approached the shining slivers in wonderment; but blind beings could not see the glass, they cut their feet on it and left tracks of blood as evidence of their circular searches, their confused and aimless wanderings. Thousands of light years lived and died; the stars melted into water and earth, and were born again. And would fall again.

Madeleine recognized the voice of one falling star as the voice she had been waiting to hear; unfortunately, Frances Farmer's scream was as wordless as any scream that sliced through the Holiday Hotel on any ordinary night. Turning to see if the group behind her were attentive to this spectacle, Madeleine saw them press their faces into each other's shoulders and turn away. Then only shadows filled their seats.

Slowly images began to darken the blank screen; just as slowly the words spoken by the images grew closer and clearer. But Madeleine neither listened to nor watched this happy Hollywood ending. She left her seat and walked quickly to the Ladies' Room, where she took shelter in a vacant stall until the bitter tears of disappointment stopped flowing from her eyes. "At least the flashing colours were pretty," she thought in consolation as, several minutes later, she remade her face before a mirror. "Perhaps I was not quite ready to receive her message," she deliberated, looking into the glass and wondering if her hair were not quite as golden as it had been before.

Emerging from her place of hiding, Madeleine spotted Sam standing by the front door of the Palace. He held a crushed flower in his hand. She was in no mood to listen to him blub and blab about Carole Lombard's natural wave, Jean Arthur's dainty feet, and who knew what else. He turned toward her; and though his eyes weren't shaded, they looked as if from behind dark glasses. For a moment Madeleine felt that she should say something about Frances Farmer. Then Sam turned back to the window. Surprised at her easy escape, Madeleine slipped past the man and out onto the street.

■ Something Cool

Madeleine slowly made her way to the Starlite Lounge, that pleasant blue-lit cocktail place with soft piano music running in the background. On the walls was painted the skyline of a large city viewed from its harbour. Above the rooftops and skyscrapers, all across the ceiling of the bar, small silver stars glittered against a dark night sky. It could be soothing to sit there with something cool after the movies; now that she had ascended several rungs of the ladder and left the Shanghai Saloon sadly below her, Madeleine depended upon the Starlite as a suitable sanctuary in substitution.

Harry, the bartender, was a still man who exuded such a sense of strength that Madeleine was always startled when he made some sudden move and she saw again that he was just one more of the walking wounded. And he was intuitive. On nights when Madeleine slid sideways onto her stool with a mind absorbed in meditations, he would serve her Cuba Libre and let her sip the drink in silence. On other evenings, when she appeared especially lonely, he would busy himself at the space before her and they would talk together. He reminded Madeleine so strongly of Frank— though there was really no physical resemblance to speak of—that sometimes she called Harry by that man's name, causing a frown to flash across his face before he quickly resumed his usual neutral expression.

"Where are all your friends tonight, beautiful?" he asked. "A girl like you shouldn't have to drink alone."

"Have a drink with me, Harry. Let me buy you a drink."

"You know I can't drink while I'm on duty. Most bartenders do, some of them are friends of mine. I could easily sip myself, since the owner is never around and wouldn't say a word even if he were. The owners like us to take a drink, in fact, because it's supposed to make us more friendly. And a friendly bar is a busy, profitable bar. It's dollars and cents to some, but for me it doesn't work that way. When I drink the blues come to visit. Once I had a girl, and she was as pretty as you. Well, I won't tell the story, but of course she left me."

"Tell me the story, Harry. Please, I'd like to hear it."

"That's just it. Bartenders aren't suppose to tell the yarns. They're supposed to do the listening. The average customer just wants me to listen, so I do. Not because it's part of the job, but because I like to listen when I'm not drinking or blue. It passes the time and I hear some

interesting things. You'd be surprised at what a person
will tell a bartender. Sometimes a complete stranger will
spill out all his problems, and I listen."

"You perform an invaluable service, Harry. Yes, you
fulfill a social need."

"Well, girl, often I end up feeling pretty bad. See, the
guy cries the blues and wants to know how he can fix
up his life. But I'm no doctor or no priest. So you know
what happens? After I've listened for an hour or two,
maybe ignored my duties and my other customers, the
guy gets abusive, obnoxious even. We run a nice quiet
set-up here and frown on rough language and that kind
of thing." Harry looked sharply around the lounge and
in one glance took in every detail.

"It's a nice place. Tell me, Harry, how do they get
those stars on the ceiling? Does someone stand on a ladder and glue them on one by one?"

"Funny, that's what most people think. No, they use a
machine, one of those gadgets that blows out air. When
the paint on the ceiling is still wet, they feed the stars
into the machine, point the hose upward, then shoot out
the stars. Some stick to the ceiling and some fall to the
floor. It looks more authentic when they do it that way. I
saw them do it once, and it was quite a sight."

"As you'd imagine a movie star wedding to be?" suggested Madeleine. "With silver confetti?"

"A bit like that, I guess."

Madeleine lit another cigarette and sipped her drink.
"Listen, Harry, who's that guy over there? He looks a little sad." The bar was shaped in a circle, with Harry and
his bottles in the centre and the stools placed in a ring
around it. This arrangement allowed the customers to
study each other easily, without obvious glances over
their shoulders.

"The guy in the blue leather jacket? Name's Tom.
Sure, he's got his share of troubles, they all do. But Tom
doesn't bend my ear with his, not like the rest of them.
He carries a switchblade inside his shirt against his skin,

in case any of his friends try to leave him. Everyone gets the blues when they got no one to care for them. No one to watch over them and to listen to their stories. That's why they come to bars. If they just wanted to drink, they could do that at home and save a bundle. It's cheaper that way."

"But the music is so nice here," said Madeleine, allowing herself to feel relaxed for a short moment.

"Yeah, we got the music and the lights and the skyline. It all brings them in, then they don't want to leave. They always come back. I'd come here myself even if this wasn't where I worked, it's that fine."

Madeleine looked at the painted skyline and the starry night above. "You know what, Harry? My grandmother always used to tell me that for each and every person in the world—rich or poor, sinner or saint—there's a single star that belongs to you and only to you. Your special star watches out for you and looks over you all your life." She stared up at the ceiling of the Starlite Lounge. At that very moment a silver star fell into her drink and floated there. Though she pretended not to notice this, Madeleine's heart began to beat very quickly. "What do you think of that?"

Harry also looked up at the ceiling, then slowly said, "Well, I always did have a special feeling for Judy Holliday. Most of the other guys liked Marilyn or Ava, but I preferred Judy right up to the very end. Did you ever notice her eyes? Even when she was cutting up and clowning, they were the kindest, gentlest eyes you ever saw. It hit me pretty hard the day she died. I guess I've never really gotten over it."

"I don't mean movie stars. I'm speaking about real stars. And my grandmother, she also used to say that if you had a loved one, like a brother or an aunt or anyone who cared for you and you cared for back, well, they wouldn't go to Heaven but to your special lucky star instead. They would float through the Milky Way forever. Even when you were sleeping they would look out for you, and whatever you did they would watch only with kindness."

Madeleine looked into Harry's eyes. "The problem is that most people notice only the first star of evening or the brightest star. They don't see the smaller, dimmer ones, and that's why they never find their star. But all you have to do is look. Of course, it doesn't help with all these spaceships and satellites they put into the skies nowadays. Oh, they wink and shine all right, but it's deceptive and it's counterfeit. You could spend your whole life praying to an airplane, and where would that get you?"

Madeleine stared into her fresh drink. Harry quickly gathered up empty glasses from the other side of the counter. As he washed them out, he thought, "No, they sure don't make stars like Judy any more."

He wasn't what he'd call a thinker. There were some fellows who got themselves tied up in knots until they choked with thinking and wondering and questioning. Harry had heard about guys in the business who fell apart because they got too tangled in the kinds of sorrows a bartender is naturally apt to see. He tried to avoid such speculation himself. He did his best to serve all his customers well, although of course he liked some of them more than others. Still, he was like every barkeep in the world in the way he'd close down, lock up, then sit alone at the bar and knock back a few at the end of a night. Often he sat beneath the blue neon until morning; however tired he was, he wouldn't feel anxious to limp back home and hit the sack: sometimes sleep is just a word. It wasn't that he thought about anything important during these late hours; he wouldn't have been able to answer if anyone asked what went through his head then. He sipped and he smoked. Small things would come to him that didn't mean much of anything, he guessed. He'd remember him and his sister waking early on Saturdays to tiptoe down to the basement with blankets and pillows. They would watch cartoons all Saturday morning in winter, until finally their mother put them outside. "You kids play out now," she'd say, stepping back inside the warm house and locking the door behind her. They would sit on the cold steps, he and his sister, and cry and cry to be let back in. Dark came early on those winter afternoons.

Sure, he'd be embarrassed to admit the crazy things that drifted through his empty head while he sat alone in the Starlite. It was like he was waiting for dawn, just as people wait by bedsides of dying people. You sit there even if the dying person is unconscious and unaware that you're near at all. You can't do anything really useful to ease the pain beside you. Still, you feel you must sit there and see this thing through. There's a duty and an obligation that goes beyond sense and that's more important than reason. There was no good reason for him to make a vigil out of the last hours of night in the Starlite. It was funny, but when he was most tired and his left leg most painful the empty lounge and vacant stools and blue neon would look different to his eyes. He almost felt that the place was going to speak aloud to him in the most ordinary, familiar voice. Like the voice of a loved one who is leaving the world. Like the voice that strains to speak through the pain and the leaving because it wishes to give some last message to you. Or because it just wants to ask if you remember sitting on those cold steps on Saturday afternoons in 1952.

"I've seen another night through," he'd think as the sky turned from black to grey. All across the city people were waking to a new day, reaching over to shut off alarm clocks, looking out from behind curtains to see if the rain had stopped overnight. "I guess I can go home now," he would think, taking his coat down from the peg. As if without him to witness it the night would not leave, the dawn would not arrive. "Sure, you're God's gift to the world," he would tell himself, making his difficult way through the early morning streets toward home.

The bar was quiet tonight. A dozen solitary drinkers watched ice melt in their glasses and drizzle fall outside the window. At about one in the morning the drizzle turned to real rain, and six or seven guys came inside. Harry fixed them up, while looking at the girl out of the corner of his eye. Her elbow was propped on the counter and her head rested in her hand; she was silent, and had a lonely look. "I've seen a million like her," Harry thought suddenly.

"What's the matter?" he asked.

"What's the matter?" echoed Madeleine, twisting the left corner of her mouth into a kind of smile.

"I think you've got the blues," diagnosed Harry. "Everybody gets them, they'll always be around, doctors or no doctors. You can only do two things when it all turns blue, and neither helps much. You can sit in a dark room and listen to sad songs. As you listen, you feel that sadness is just as good as anything else. You feel that someone else is just as blue as you, and for a while you and the singer are twins. That's why people feel like something's missing, like an arm or a leg, when they're happy. They miss their twin who stands nearby and watches them through tears. For some reason people always turn around and ignore the crying self before them, and so they feel complete only when they're blue. It's either incomplete or blue the whole life long, and no one knows why. It just is."

"What's the second thing you can do?" asked Madeleine.

"Drink. You can call a bunch of people on the phone and invite them all over for a big party. But no matter how much you laugh and drink the blues won't go away before their time. You can smoke all the cigarettes you want, but that won't help either. You just got to wait it out."

"I'm trying, Harry. Please turn down the lights. And pour me another drink."

"Sure, but make it a quick one, baby. It's almost two. Nearly time to go." Harry limped away to set customers up with last call drinks. Then he returned to Madeleine and said, "You know what you were saying about the star up there that belongs to you? Well, I was thinking, what happens if your only star falls?"

■■■ The Slow Development of the Spirit

Madeleine left the Starlite and hurried through the streets toward the Shanghai Saloon. There would be just enough time to share a drink with Frank before closing; even if it were already past two and no longer lawful to serve, he would still unlock the door for her and pour them both a shot. They would sit with their drinks at the battered piano and pick old tunes from the yellowed keys. Frank would be so glad to see her! She'd rattle off accounts of escapades and adventures; it wouldn't matter what she said, since any words would make Frank happy and set her own mind at rest.

Madeleine had felt uneasy about Frank and the Shanghai since ascending the upward path and leaving them below. She had a crazy idea that somehow she was guilty of the crime called abandonment, and couldn't help but think how every day Frank waited patiently for her to appear in the bar. As each client who entered was not her, he would feel a deeper sense of disappointment, though this emotion would not show on his face. Passing the bar and glancing into it of late, however, Madeleine had never glimpsed Frank behind the counter. Instead, in his place there stood a weasel-faced bartender who was, she instinctively knew, the kind of man who under-pours drinks and steals the profit for himself.

The Shanghai was just around the corner. Increasing her pace, Madeleine rushed past drinkers who were drifting slowly from closed bars and searching desolately for places still open. Then another worry beset her; this one was named Harry. Though he hadn't been able to say anything aloud, Madeleine was certain he had wanted her to remain a while longer with him in the Starlite. He would be turning off the lights now, delaying the moment when he'd have to walk home alone. Wishing for her shoulder to wrap his arm around and throw his weight upon. Hoping for her to help him hobble through the world.

"Madeleine," called a woman's voice from a darkened doorway.

She stopped and peered in the direction of the voice. Her local fame had spread more widely than was convenient; strangers who felt they knew her intimately accosted her wherever she went these days. Madeleine stepped closer to the doorway, yet was unable to see the figure clearly. "How are you on this fine evening of ours?" she asked pleasantly. "I think the rain will stop by morning, don't you?"

"Don't you remember me?" asked the woman in a voice somewhat familiar to Madeleine.

"Of course I do. How could I forget?" Madeleine tried to recall where this voice was from; at the same time, she wished to hurry on.

The woman moaned. A bottle rolled out from the doorway, dropped down two steps, then broke at Madeleine's feet. Stepping nimbly over the glass, Madeleine bent over the figure and brushed long hair back from a face. Eyeglasses caught at the light from a distant streetlamp. Madeleine stroked the face, then jerked her hand away upon feeling something sticky. The woman seemed to lose consciousness for a moment. When she stirred again, Madeleine breathed a sigh of relief.

"You are safe and dry here in this doorway. When the

dawn comes up, you will feel better," said Madeleine. "I promise you."

"Glitter and gold," muttered the woman, perhaps in a dream.

Madeleine pulled a mickey from her pocket; it was the emergency cache she always carried with her. "I'm sorry, I don't have that brand with me. Only this." She placed the bottle near the figure. "I have to run, I'm afraid. Goodbye."

Madeleine dashed swiftly away. As she knocked on the locked door of the Shanghai, the thought of Winston Churchill tumbled into her mind.

Inside the bar a man rose from a table covered with stacks of bills and coins. He walked over to the door and peered suspiciously through its glass window, perhaps fearing Madeleine to be the ringleader of a gang of thieves. Unlocking the door, he held it open an inch. "We're closed," he spat through the crack.

"I realize that. I'm terribly sorry to bother you, but I'm looking for an old friend, a certain Frank who is the proprietor of this fine establishment."

"No he ain't."

"But he is. Really, I'm very sure."

"Not no more he ain't." The bartender gave Madeleine a fishy look; he seemed to be trying to conceal a smile.

"You mean he's on holiday? I wouldn't blame Frank a bit for searching for some sunshine, especially after all this unpleasant rain we've had. I expect he went down to Mexico; it's grown popular lately. He's lying on a beach or beneath a palm tree right this second, perhaps with a big sombrero over his face. When will he be back?"

The bartender gave a short laugh, then shook his head slowly from side to side. The door closed and locked.

Madeleine walked away. "Frank deserves a holiday. He's such a hard worker. But why, I wonder, has there been no postcard?"

■ Too Long At the Fair

Upon returning to the hotel, Madeleine sat at her little table and composed a letter:

Dear Annemarie,

You must be quite settled into your European lifestyle by now. After all, you've been across the sea for some little time. Do you live in an apartment, a house or a hotel? Also, I wonder if Berlin is cold during winter? I expect you still follow the department store line of work. Please, I urge you not to abandon this channel, for a good department-store girl is but half a step away from the world of high fashion. You become a model, that is, and as the embodiment of everyone's dream your face looks down from immense billboards poised high above the greatest cities. And then, assuredly, the studio people are knocking at your door, waving contracts in your face, offering you starring roles. You know how it goes.

Here, of course, everything is still idyllic. I make excellent progress with my search, and fresh revelations occur daily. They are not, however, best described in a letter. They are more suited to Paris. Paris in the wintertime, to be exact, when it is cold outside yet warm inside. We stay at the top of a small old hotel in a cobblestone street. Big windows look past a funny little tree and over a bridge that stretches across the river. The bridges are nearly empty, for a cold wind blows up the river. Even though afternoon has come and gone, we have yet to leave our room. We wear blankets over our shoulders and drink iced white wine from glasses that hold a lot. There are happy voices ringing around and around the room, and they belong to you and me.

We talk for hours and hours about all that has

befallen us during our long separation, yet never draw nearer the end of what we have to say. Although we both speak at the same time, we also listen. I hear you and you hear me. Your eyes have never been so bright, and your bang falls over one side of your face, laying softly against your cheek. I see you so clearly.

Darkness falls over the city of light. You stand beside the blurred window and rub it clear. You wish to see if sleighs are drawing through the streets and if there is snow upon the rooftops of Paris. You want to know if what we saw long ago is still in view. I ask you what you see, but you are silent by the window, one hand holding the curtain aside, looking out as night spreads over Paris like it did when we were so much younger. What is it? I ask you. What do you see? And though we hear . . .

Madeleine sat still and thought about the lamp-poles that waited patiently on the bridges of Paris. Though her glass wasn't empty, she reached for the bottle and tilted it to her mouth. Quickly she reread the letter. It seemed to make no sense. "That wasn't what I wished to say," she thought. "It isn't Paris that I care about." She placed her hands upon her forehead, which was burning with heat.

Just then the sound of music cut sharply through the wall to her left, carrying with it aural evidence of objects being broken. The hotel seemed to tremble. Madeleine wondered what on earth her current neighbours were doing. For some time she had not known who resided on either side of herself; once an open book, the hotel was now a volume whose pages could not be cut and whose stories could not be read. The hallways were nearly always silent, and doors seemed permanently locked. It was as if with each day of the long winter inhabitants shrank farther and deeper into their rooms, like frightened or wounded or hibernating animals. As upon her arrival at the hotel, Madeleine again wandered often through its halls; the difference was that now she no longer knocked upon doors behind which her saviour might be hiding or expected these same closed doors to open of their own accord.

"Perhaps," she thought, "there is occurring beside me a dispute which I could settle by offering my objective point of view. Just as likely, an accident, catastrophe or some other unfortunate event which I am morally obligated to enter into is taking place next door. It could be that I have been roaming elevated altitudes while the world below has been falling apart without me; history affords many examples of gods whose scandalous neglect of lower regions leads to their tragic descents to still lower hells. Also," she added, leaving her room, "it is just as lonely at the top as Joan Crawford so wisely suggested."

Madeleine knocked upon the next door, from behind which both music and crashes continued to sound. When the door did not open, she entered the room uninvited and saw before her a young couple dancing cheek to cheek. Seeing Madeleine, they froze. "I'm afraid," she said, "that my watch has stopped. This couldn't have happened at a worse moment, because it is essential that I make an extremely important telephone call to Paris at a certain minute and not a second later. Do you know what time it is?"

"No," said the young man. Still in each other's arms, he and his partner observed their visitor with cool disinterest.

"Of course," continued Madeleine, "it is not the same time there as it is here. They live slightly in the past or the future—I can't recall quite which—in relation to ourselves. While we sleep, they work. While we die, they are born. And so on. Personally, I find the whole concept of time most alarming. Who is to say that at this very moment we are not living forty years in the past or in the future? We all know that calendars are completely illusionary objects created by capitalists as another money-making scheme. I must telephone Paris in order to know what is happening in that time zone; only then may I know what is happening as we breathe right here and now. Do you see?"

The young couple remained frozen silently together, apparently unenthusiastic concerning the topic of time.

"I am thrilled by your music," said Madeleine, speaking slightly louder. "Please continue dancing. It looks like you're having quite a party."

"No, we're not. We haven't invited any guests and there's no party. It's not for you or for anyone else that we play this music and do this dancing. It's for ourselves. We always like to dance for an hour or so before going to bed. It relaxes us, and we find that afterwards our sleep comes more quickly." Bits of broken glass and china lay scattered across the floor. The room wasn't large enough for even the close variety of dancing, yet the young couple hadn't tried to take full advantage of the space by shifting furniture. Madeleine wondered if each day they purchased new objects to replace those broken during the previous night's dancing.

"I know all this," she said, gazing at the girl. Her flesh looked very warm; Madeleine imagined it must feel even hotter to her partner's touch. "I am your neighbour, and so am as familiar with your habits as you must be with mine."

"We have a lot more dancing to do," said the young man curtly. "It's nearly midnight, and we always like to have a certain amount done by then."

Madeleine closed her eyes and swayed back and forth, as though she were about to fall. The young couple looked at each other with matched expressions of distaste; they were prepared to face the worst. When their neighbour opened her eyes and proceeded to speak somewhat desperately, the dancers' expressions did not brighten.

"Isn't that enchanting!" marvelled Madeleine. "You have been so enthralled by your dance of romance that you've lost hold of the hour. I envy you that; it's no longer so easy for me to escape the shackles of time. But, I'm afraid to say, it's already much later than midnight. I would say it's closer to four A.M.—but not in Paris, naturally."

"No, it's not," stated the young man firmly. His eyes flicked over Madeleine as he determined how to get rid of her with the greatest speed and the least ado.

Madeleine noticed that he hadn't bothered to check a watch or clock. "I hate to disagree," she replied. "But it really is much later than that. I wouldn't say so unless I were absolutely certain."

"You're wrong," said the young man with malevolent insistence. The couple began to dance once more. Oddly enough, their steps were stiff and clumsy, as though they were unused to dancing and unfamiliar with each other. They stepped very carefully over the slivers of glass already on the floor, but made no effort to avoid bumping into objects and causing additional damage.

"Good night," said Madeleine, after several minutes of watching the couple gaze deeply into each other's eyes. When she stepped from the room, they stopped dancing at once.

The page of her unfinished letter sat on the little table. *"And though we hear . . ."* She couldn't remember what she and Annemarie had hoped for in that other time zone into which they had unsuccessfully tried to escape. "An hour of human happiness? A holiday from our heavy loads?" Madeleine asked herself, unearthing the pages of her manuscript from beneath the pile of clothes where they had been lying idle for some weeks, hoping she would find in them the words needed for her letter. "There is still so much work to be done here," she muttered in a weary voice. "And time is running out."

Madeleine had added her own words to those written by Frances Farmer, and now she couldn't remember who had written what. Some phrases which seemed a part of herself were scrawled in an alien hand; others, completely unfamiliar to her, were in her own script. For the first time Madeleine noticed that perhaps the pages were a film scenario. She skimmed them faster and faster, searching for a hint as to what the story was about. But the quicker she read, the less sense the words made; rereading a page several times, she found that each perusal suggested a different meaning. "Is it about her or about me?" wondered Madeleine, failing to quell a sense of rising panic. "How can I ever finish it if I don't know that?"

God heard her prayer and inspiration rang bells in her head. She would write it as the memoir of a madwoman uncertain of her identity. There would be the usual rats gnawing at the flesh of chained virgins, the flickering torches dripping burning grease in clammy dungeons, the frightened screams echoing between cold stone walls from which there was no escape. All the madwoman books made the best-seller lists. It would be as easy as peach pie.

As soon as she began considering her ideas at greater length, they faded into nothing. Madeleine hid the papers beneath a pile of dirty laundry.

What was clear before her was the wallpaper of the room in Paris. Its pattern was one you could look at for a long time without really seeing. Then, one day, you suddenly saw that all the shapes were in fact umbrellas. Annemarie's voice faded as you watched the umbrellas dance across the wall.

The music in the next room fell silent. "Are you listening to me?" asked Annemarie, turning from the window. "I asked if you felt like skating on the pond in the park later." Some of the umbrellas were opened and some were closed. Madeleine wanted to reach out and pull one off the wall, then walk with Annemarie through the snowy streets of Paris, protecting them both beneath what she had finally been able to see. But, of course, you never really saw the umbrellas until after you found yourself in another place and time.

The hotel was very quiet. Madeleine sat in her shapeless, colourless clothes and gazed around the untidy room. She noticed that even after all these months she had never really finished unpacking her bags. "I should have placed some pictures on the walls," she thought regretfully, envisioning a cosy, comfortable space into which she could nestle forever. "Paris, Paris," she sighed sadly, then turned to the mirror and wondered if it were too late in the evening to bother redecorating her face with fresh paint.

Picking up her old purple address book, Madeleine turned its pages desultorily; they were filled with scratched-out names of people and places whose significance to herself she could not remember. "I must keep in mind," she lectured herself, "that it can be just as lonely at the bottom as at the top. Even as a little girl, long before my search began, I was mired in isolation. The other children hated me and stoned me, and they laughed at my attempts to raise discussion concerning salvation and saints and searches." Madeleine closed her eyes tightly and reached blindly for the tumbler of whisky. Her head hurt badly, and her heart was squeezed into a small tight knot from the evening's many swift descents to earth and equally rapid rises back to where the air was rarefied and empty and thin.

■■■ To Suffer for Our Sins or Those of Others

It was Sunday again, and rain continued to fall upon the city. Banks and businesses were closed; workers were free for the day. The hotel was filled with sounds of its inhabitants trying their best to while away the hours until Monday might arrive. By afternoon they were rereading the morning paper, looking for something more to wash out in their small sink, or laying out another hand of solitaire. Rather than prepare for revolution, they gazed out at the grey sky or stared at walls if their room lacked a window. Many people lay closed-eyed on beds. Radios played prayer programs.

Madeleine didn't look up as Sally entered her room unannounced. "Well, this is gloomy," the older woman remarked sharply, surveying with satisfaction the sight of the pale quiet girl on the bed. Last night's make-up was badly smudged across Madeleine's face, and she wore an old black negligee, much stained, with a torn hem and a broken shoulder strap fastened by a safety pin. She seemed to float becalmed upon a sad jumble of papers and clothes. Once possessed of a charmingly youthful and carefree quality, the room now looked simply confused, and without hope of ever being tidied.

Sally was out of humour, as was her wont of a Sunday. Although she did not believe the right to stay inside belonged exclusively to herself, she could not help but feel irritated when surrounded by so many fools at such a loss with being forced to spend twenty-four solid hours in the company of four familiar walls.

"Since Ingrid has gone, there's been no one to tackle my sloth," apologized Madeleine. She did not, however, make an effort to clear away the things piled on the only chair in the room. "It used to make Ingrid happy when I threw my clothes about with no thought of where they landed."

"I'm surprised," said Sally. "I tell you, I'm surprised. You used to have spunk. Everyone was afraid of you, including me, you were so full of your games and your tricks. There's one girl who'll get her nickel's worth, I used to think." Sally wrapped her blue housecoat more tightly around herself. Blue, blue, it must be Sunday. Her matching slippers were fuzzy, and looked like two blue rats huddled at her feet.

"Don't judge by appearances, please," said Madeleine. "If I dressed and made up, you wouldn't know me. I can be as deceiving as the best of them. I still possess my arts, but don't care to use them at this stage. I'm gathering together my power so that when my chance floats above me I'll have the strength to leap up and catch it. What time is it? All my instincts tell me that my hour is drawing near."

"Don't hold your breath," said Sally drily. She thought that Madeleine had lost all her style; her words sounded unconvincing, and her manner was false. "If you must wait, then you should do it in a brighter fashion. That's what time it is. Go to Woolworths. Fix up your room with novelties. They'll do the trick."

Although a general gloom prevented sight of the rain falling beyond the window, its steady splashing upon the bottom of the air shaft was as audible as that of rats swimming down in this dark pool. The water there was deep, and each day it rose higher.

Sally poked through Madeleine's things with a sneering expression. "Now you're just like me," she said, her pasty features sharpening. "Let's have a drink on it."

"Yes, let's do that," agreed Madeleine. She poured a pair of whiskies and switched off the light. "I want to show you something."

After a moment Sally said, "I don't like sitting in the dark. That's why they invented electricity. You can't close your eyes when it's dark, but you can't keep them open either."

Madeleine switched on the light. Roaches scrambled back under the bed and into the corners. When Madeleine fell laughing upon her pillow, Sally said, "Yes, I've seen that one before. It's a good trick." Blue half moons had suddenly risen beneath her eyes.

Madeleine refilled her glass, accidentally forgetting Sally's. "You look just like an elephant in a zoo," she chortled, without taking her eyes from the older woman's face.

"I'm not fond of the dark," explained Sally. "That's why I stay up all night with the lights on. When you

sleep during the day, you can always open your eyes
and see exactly what's around you. I prefer to cat nap
than to sleep. By the way, did you know I have a taste
for furnishings? I could make a living at it. Rich people
beg me daily to fix up their mansions and penthouses,
but I laugh in their face. This place gets me down. Let's
go up to my room. How much do you pay for yours?"

"One-fifty."

"That's too much. I pay one-fifty myself, and my
room is twenty times snappier than this. You should
change rooms. I could speak to Joe about it for you.
Maybe you could get a room with a window view right
beside mine. Then you could look outside and see
exactly what I see."

"I've had enough views for a lifetime," said
Madeleine. "I saw the pyramids when I was six. What's
left after that? A window would be wasted on me. Give
it to one of those moon-eyed dreamers who can sigh
over any dirty alley."

"From my window I have a view of a little world that
contains a bit of everything in the universe. I've seen a
few things in my time, girl." Sally shook her grey curls
wisely. "After all, there's more to life than sugar and
spice and foreign parts. Come and see. And bring that
bottle with you."

Sally's room was larger and brighter than
Madeleine's. Light from streetlamps and neon signs created a peculiarly luminous glow. Crepe-paper streamers
were twisted across the ceiling and walls, connecting
Japanese lanterns, coloured balloons, travel posters, and
flags from various ports. Sally proudly led the way to
the window. A fire escape slanted by on its climb to the
roof of the hotel; but the iron steps were rusted, and
appeared somewhat fragile for actual use.

Sally gestured expansively. "Feast your eyes and
count your calories. I gain a pound every time I glance
outside. You have your rooftops and your stores, your
cars and your pedestrians. At night I always leave the

curtains open, it would be a sin to close them. And see that bank across the way? I have the only view of a flag that flies on top of it." Unfortunately, this banner was not visible in the present obscurity.

"Are you having a party?" asked Madeleine, turning from the window without comment.

"Can't stand parties, never could. But I like the decorations all right. I can let you in on a little secret. My eye's on a cute pink lampshade that's just waiting for me in Fair Freddy's window."

"What's the secret?" wondered Madeleine. "Let's have another drink."

Sally seethed. "Some people wouldn't know a view or a secret if it hit them on the head. Yes, we can have another drink, but don't get the wrong idea. I didn't invite you up here for an idle time. I'll have no senseless cavorting or carousing in my room. Haven't the time for it. While you're here, you can make yourself handy. Listen to this letter I wrote. Some fellows next door were making a rumpus last night, and I couldn't stand it. So I made up this letter. All the words have to be right, they can't be wrong. First I'll read it straight through, then you can make suggestions. We'll have a drink after that, I guess. It goes like this:

Dearest,

I can't send you money. It isn't that I don't want to, I do. I just don't have any. Anything mine is yours, you know that, and it goes vice versa, I'm sure. Last week they cut off my cheque again. They want to see me beg and grovel on my knees, and I'll do it without giving a damn. After they've had their fun, they'll smile and sneer and give me more money. I'll twist a knife between their ribs and sweetly say: thank you, thank you very much. Then I'll twist it in some more. Let them think me another fool. I don't care.

But enough about me. Such is life, ha ha. You must

be in New Orleans by now. I send this letter to New Orleans because I know you always go there in the winter. Remember when you told me about New Orleans? We were in that little bar where we spent every afternoon during the time we lived in the two rooms across the bridge. That bar had heart-shaped tables and stools, and all the drinks were coloured red or pink. The bartender—what was his name?—always wore shirts striped like candy canes. The cocktail wait-ress even had red hair, though you said it was dyed. Remember that bar and the time you told me about New Orleans? You said it rains there in the winter, but you don't feel wet or cold even if you have no umbrella or roof over your head. You hear the rain like music in the night. It is a song that plays through the streets you walk down, it is something that sings all around you, but it comes from somewhere high above you. I can see you standing in the rain, your hair all wet and the iron gate beside you. New Orleans, you said, and I believed you.

I believed you, and now you haven't written to me for so long, not even a postcard or telegram or Christmas greeting. I say this, though of course you must already be well aware of the fact. Any letter I receive I tear up because it's not from you. I rip it to pieces before I open it. Yet who knows? A cheque for a million dollars could be inside any envelope that is not from you. This is no reproach. Heaven knows I'm not that type. I'm not the planning, plotting kind of woman. I know no tricks. I could have sent the police after you long ago, but I didn't. The thought never crossed my mind. I haven't the heart for the world and its games. Notice that I bring up this subject only in the middle of the letter. This shows you that the matter is only of secondary importance. In fact, I mention your neglect only in passing.

I waited for your letter. I waited forever. But it never arrived, did it? Now it's too late, so forget all about it. Don't give it a moment's thought. We sat inside, remember? We were young then. Rain splashed on cars and people passing outside. That was the only time for me. When we were inside, or when the sun was shining and we walked arm in arm down the avenue. Everyone stared because I wore that funny hat you liked. I wore it even though it made people laugh. That was the time, only not long enough, and passed now.

I can't help but think of Charlie when I imagine you in New Orleans. It's all mixed together. Charlie, poor Charlie, he would have died for you. And in the end he did. I hated you when you left him alone in the rooms for days at a time. Whenever you returned, he would be crazy with love for you. The longer you stayed away, the love-crazier he acted. But you only spoke strictly and shouted at him to stay off the bed. Then I came into the room, carrying coffee that smelled hot and strong. For a moment you didn't see me. You were hugging Charlie around the neck and whispering words I couldn't hear into his ear. When you saw me, you pushed Charlie roughly away.

What I want to say has nothing to do with New Orleans or Charlie or the Valentine Bar. I really want to say that I regret to inform you that I am too busy to write any more letters to you. I have a long list of things to do, longer than my arm, and more besides. If we met on the street tomorrow, I'd walk right past you. I wouldn't even take the time to stab a knife into your eye. I'm that busy. I don't have time to listen to your pitiful pleadings, so don't waste your breath. I have so many things to do, I don't know where to begin.

Sincerely, Sally

P.S. Don't try to phone me either. Also, I have no phone.

Sally looked up from the pages. "It took me quite a while to write it up," she said, gazing at Madeleine simply. "I wanted to use the right words."

Madeleine appeared white and numb. "I have a phone in my room," she lied. "I thought all the rooms had phones. I call long distance, person-to-person, collect, station-to-station. I'm devoted to telephoning."

"Oh, I asked them to take mine out," countered Sally. "I couldn't stand the thing, what with people calling up in the middle of the night with all their foolish problems. Once they get on a phone, people believe they have a licence to talk craziness. No thank you, thank you all the same."

"And there's nothing quite as difficult as letting a phone ring without picking it up, is there," responded Madeleine in a sugar-sweet tone. She began to look around at Sally's party decorations with an openly scornful expression.

"Tell me honestly. Should I alter any of the words? I want to be understood clearly and forever."

"The phrases are fine, if that's your taste. But don't ask me to mail that letter. I want no trouble with the law. Let's have that drink now. I want no trouble with anyone. Let them do their own dirty work, just leave me out of it. I'm the one who gets caught in the searchlight while they escape safely down the alley." Madeleine's eyes glittered feverishly as she took a long pull from the bottle.

"Please. It's the only thing I'll ever ask you to do," said Sally. "Take it. Mail it. Please."

Madeleine stuffed a hand over her mouth and started to laugh.

"What is it?" asked Sally.

Madeleine shrieked more loudly. "Your braces," she said when she could finally speak.

"I know. I should have had them taken off years ago. They've done their work," said Sally. "But I just don't have the courage to part with them. They're as precious

to me as my only child, a free-spirited girl who like her
father lives with the wind. Moves on whim and without
direction from this place to that place to the next place,
always aimless among strangers." Sally peered vaguely
about. "Now where did I hide those stamps? I know
they're around here somewhere."

A purple feather stood in a vase beside her chair. Sally
picked it up and said, "All these things fit into three
cardboard boxes. Would you believe it? I could move
seven days a week, if my heart wanted to. When you
splurge on a taxi, it's as easy as a fiddle. I know my
handwriting's terrible, but I don't have the strength to
copy the letter again. Please take it."

Madeleine watched Sally clumsily try to fit the pages
into an envelope that was too small for them. On the
envelope was written only *To Bert, New Orleans.*

Madeleine suddenly took the letter, then stowed it in
a pocket. "I have to go now," she said.

"I never wanted to see the world," said Sally. "I had
no desire to sail the Seven Seas." She looked past
Madeleine's shining eyes. "Oh, look! The moon's come
out from behind the clouds! I can see the flag waving
now!"

Madeleine strolled past the window. In the strange
light she appeared very young and beautiful for a
moment. "Thank you for the letter. Goodbye."

Sally jumped up. "Wait a minute. Get out, then.
Scram." As she shouted, Sally pushed Madeleine
toward the door; she was much stronger than she
appeared. "Get lost! Beat it!" Sally closed and locked the
door.

Madeleine stood in the hall and enunciated in a clear,
loud voice: "I'm not a bit like you. I'm gathering my
strength for come what may, not wasting it like cheap
perfume. I still have my telephone, thank God."

Sally fell trembling upon her bed and listened to
Madeleine's steps move far away, then fall silent.
Cradling the bottle, she rocked herself and sang softly to

the rhythm of her rocking. "Blue robe on Sunday, blue robe on Sunday. And yellow on Monday, tra la la."

■ Passing the Torch

Madeleine stepped inside her room and noticed, without surprise, that Frances Farmer was seated at the small table. She was so engrossed in the act of writing that she didn't look up from the page. Madeleine could see over Frances Farmer's shoulder and out the window to where the air shaft should have been. Snow was falling in large soft flakes, with nearly indistinguishable white butterflies drifting among them. The air had grown more mild, the sky had blued, and people were standing on the bridges once more. They leaned against the stone bridge walls and looked down at the water flowing below.

The window was open several inches, so Frances could breathe in the scent of snow and Sunday in Paris. Snow drifted inside the window and onto the page Frances was writing. There it melted, blurring the ink and creating puddles and streams of blue. Frances set down her pen, gathered snow like blossoms in her arms, and buried her face in the sweet clean scent. Holding the mass of blue-streaked white in her arms, she turned to Madeleine as if she had known she were there all along. "It's just beginning," said Frances in a harsh, deeply pitched voice. "It's only starting," she said, fixing Madeleine with a gaze that pierced like the pin that holds the butterfly in place. "If you try to fight alone, you'll lose." Her face appeared tense and tired and rough. The blue snow had melted, but Frances still held out her arms, as though offering a precious, fragile gift to Madeleine.

And though we hear the silver bells . . .

Madeleine could hear the old woman who always called down the hallway at night. "Is anyone there? Was that someone at my door?" she called monotonously, in a rough voice pitched exactly as low as Frances Farmer's. Shivering in her black negligee and bare feet, Madeleine stepped from the room. The hall was empty except for the old woman who leaned out her door at the other end. In the dim lighting it was difficult to see if her face were tired and tense, and if her gaze were piercing. "Is there anyone there?" she called over and over, her arms wrapped tightly around herself to keep her housecoat closed. After each call the woman paused and listened for an answer. None came.

Madeleine stepped back into her room, closed the door, and leaned against it. She didn't look toward the empty table, the dark air shaft, the shadowy mirror. Instead, she reached beneath her bed for the box she kept hidden there. Inside it were the few articles left behind by the boy, the soiled white glove given her by Frank, one of Ingrid's old tarot cards, a faded photograph of a youth found hidden beneath silken underwear in one of Stella's drawers, a sentimental and supposedly anonymous poem by Jeanette, and various religious and political pamphlets given to her by strangers in the streets.

Madeleine looked over these treasures, then added Sally's letter to them. Lighting a cigarette and humming tunelessly, she moved unhurriedly about the room, straightening up but not enough to make a real difference. "It's just beginning," she thought, tossing down the air shaft an old shoe whose partner she had lost long ago. As it splashed like a stone into the water, Madeleine smiled.

Though it was getting late, the hotel was noisier than it had been before. The guests had smoked all their cigarettes and finished all their liquor. Now they were searching pockets and drawers, looking behind dressers and beneath beds, for stray coins which might be awaiting discovery. If their search were rewarded, they would throw on a raincoat and run to the corner store. Those less fortunate would bump and knock around their room with blazing nerves until far into the night.

"Don't try to fight alone," a voice called down the air shaft. It sounded like the high clear call of a child, or like the chiming of a silver bell. The walls around Madeleine seemed to fade away, as in a film's slow dissolve, and a great expanse of water stretched before her, reaching far into the future. She stood on the shore, all her false and frightened words dropped somewhere behind her, and looked silently and steadily across the water. On the far side stood Annemarie and Ingrid and Sally. With other people they were forming a procession and preparing to march. There was Sister Mary and Rita, Harry and Joe, and Frank and Fingers too. They were studying Frances Farmer's manuscript to find out why they were going to march and to fight and to seize power. They all waited for Madeleine to join them. "There's strength in numbers," called Michael from beneath the water, promising that the bones of all the sunken ones would rise like a reef and allow the water to be crossed, the farther shore reached.

Madeleine blinked, and scarred stained walls closed around her again. The damp manuscript pages lay upon the table; they formed, she suddenly thought, a revolutionary text that offered good clear reasons for the necessity of an uprising, and a seizure of power from the hands of fools. Madeleine turned to her closet and began to go quickly through her clothes, wondering what a revolutionary would wear. Then she smiled bitterly and became still. She imagined the ragged band of marchers arguing over where they would march, what slogans they would shout along the way, and who would lead them. She saw them milling about in confusion, then wandering off in separate directions until they were each alone and lost once more.

Now there was only her own face in the mirror, rough

and unfinished and unlike the smooth faces she passed
on the street. First it was the face of a convict or an
addict, then it was the face of a child who all her life has
lived in the forest and the sky, and who arrives too late
in a strange place where nothing recognizes her and she
remembers only how it was in the trees by the creek on
the mountain. There were berries and bears, and the
roar of water.

"I know exactly what will happen to me," Madeleine
suddenly announced to the quiet room. Looking down
the air shaft, she saw two stars which floated at the bottom. One had six points and the other had seven. She
couldn't be certain if these stars were really there, or if
they were merely reflections of stars in Heaven.

■■■ Nina in the Afternoon

Nina waited anxiously in an elegant restaurant of the
type where the prices are high but the customers don't
care. She had sent the note early that day on lilac-
scented paper: "We haven't met, but I have something
to say that you will want to hear. I guarantee it."
Wishing to gain the upper hand so often ensured by a
late entrance, Nina had arrived for the rendezvous several minutes after the appointed time. Annoyed to find
her ploy thwarted, she quickly sipped several highballs
while she waited, despite the fact that drink made her
nervous. She hadn't slept for several nights.

A wet and wild-haired girl entered the restaurant,
causing a stir among the patrons. Nina waved to the girl
and noted her outlandish all-black costume of lace slip,
fishnet stockings, high heels and hat. "Sit down," she
graciously invited. "So you are Madeleine. Stella talks
about you all the time, but you know her ways. She
speaks in riddles she doesn't know the answers to.
You're not at all as I imagined, but your costume is

charming. Where did you find it?"

The girl seemed withdrawn and sedated, and she was much thinner than Nina had anticipated. She took out lipstick and applied it lavishly and carelessly. "It was advertised in a magazine. Near the back." She stared into her compact, then snapped it shut without seeming to notice that her mascara was badly smudged.

"You must find it chilly," Nina remarked warily.

"It's only when you get your feet wet that you feel the cold. In these heels I can walk straight through puddles. I didn't buy them. A stranger gave them to me, but I didn't ask for them. They nearly fit." She laughed through the cigarette smoke that swirled before her eyes. Her hat sat forgotten on her head. "I don't want anything to eat, but I could use a drink. You order yourself a big meal, eat all you want, it doesn't matter to me. I walked a long way to get here because I don't like cabs. They can kidnap you anywhere. I'm thirsty because I'm unused to walking. Before twenty miles was nothing, I wouldn't feel it. Lately I haven't done much walking because I've been licking my wounds at home."

"I see," replied Nina.

"Who are you and what do you want?" Madeleine asked roughly.

Nina was taken aback. "I'm Stella's best friend. I admire her immensely, though she is a bit foolish now and then. I look out for her, protect her interests. Someone's got to do it, but why me? It's a thankless job. Marriage has changed Stella for the worse. It does that, either improves your character or swallows you whole. Stella has become petty, I'm afraid. I believe you were quite close to her?"

"I barely remember her. She was as foolish as a drunk schoolgirl." Madeleine ordered another drink from the waiter. "They're the most dangerous kind, sly and dumb enough to try the worst tricks with the least chance of succeeding."

"As I say, she's changed recently. A good deal of her sense has left her. I still keep in contact, though, because she needs me more than ever. She has a trick way of making me feel responsible for her, while all the time darkening my days and ruining every one of my possibilities."

"I'd forgotten her altogether," said Madeleine, her manner becoming more vivid. "It doesn't matter to me. I've brought thieves and murderers to their knees. I'll bring the whole world to its knees before I give up. Let them call me what they will, I've been called worse before. This is just the beginning." The male diners, who had been eyeing Madeleine frankly to this point, now turned nervously from her feverish gaze.

"No one is calling you anything," soothed Nina, "though I do suspect that Stella worries about you. She says nothing out loud because the subject is too painful for her, but from the safe harbour of her domestic bliss she looks anxiously at those dashed upon the rocks."

"Tell her I've gone to Hell or to Hollywood. Tell her I'm in mourning for my dream. Tell her they haven't beaten me yet."

"I've noticed," remarked Nina, "that there are those who pretend they fight to save their noble souls when really they're serving a mean and ugly spirit."

"Why not?" cried Madeleine. "They push your head under water, then laugh when you struggle for air. I'd sell them all to the devil, then burn the money. I would reach, reach through the flames."

"Remember that Elizabeth Taylor movie? The boy drowns the girl so he can carry on with Elizabeth Taylor. That was a good one."

"He said it was an accident, but it wasn't," shouted Madeleine. "That boy had dark hair and dark eyes. They always say that."

"Monty Clift had blue eyes, eyes blue as blue," disagreed Nina. "They photographed him in a trick way so his eyes would look dark. They weren't, but that's Hollywood for you."

"Black or blue, it makes no difference to me. What time is it? I'm late. Hurry up and tell me what you want to say."

"I've heard wild stories about you, each crazier than the other. I didn't believe any of them, I'm not so easily fooled. I'm like you, smarter than they are. Robert, that's Stella's husband, goes moon-eyed at the mention of your name. He's a fool, like Stella. When her back is turned, he tries to kiss me. But I won't let him."

Madeleine addressed the young couple at the next table, who were gazing nervously down at their empty plates: "This place stinks. Let's go for a real drink. I know this bar close by."

"Wait," Nina said desperately. She seized Madeleine's hands. "I still haven't told you why I arranged this meeting. You see, I feared you had the wrong impression of me. I know how Stella can twist things around. She's short-sighted and too vain to wear eyeglasses. Like you, I've been falsely accused. People blame me for their own bad luck. How can I look after their interests by turning a blind eye to my own? I would do them little good six feet under."

"I have never been the first to strike in battle!" shouted Madeleine.

"I see through your lacy lies. I've heard about these false mediums and their rigged meetings in the dark. Candle flames don't fool me. They drown bees in pools of their own honey, it's in the paper every day."

"I will do anything to be saved!" cried Madeleine.

"Save indeed!" snorted Nina. "You deposit people in your bank account, draw interest on them until you've saved enough to pay for all your sins. I have a chequing account, thank you very much."

Madeleine became more emotional: "I look at people like you and they run in fear behind locked doors and drawn curtains. I laugh and walk on toward the sun."

"Spare me," Nina said acidly. "I'm about to open up my own beauty salon. I've got this man tied around my baby finger. He'll set me up with a fashionable address and all the most advanced fittings. As a matter of fact, I must leave this instant to place my signature on certain vital documents. I'll have a good laugh about this later."

The restaurant manager, disturbed by Madeleine's excited manner, approached the table. After a few whispered words with Nina, he offered to help Madeleine to the door.

"I'll go!" she cried, bumping into several tables on her rough passage to the door. Her eyes were black, and the brim of her hat cast a dark shadow across her face; she glared at the diners who were watching this scene with covert curiosity. "Don't touch me! I'll go and go and go until the day I reach across the gap and feel like standing stone, with everything safe inside from poisoning eyes and hands that squeeze your heart to death. Take your hands off me, I said!"

They closed the door behind her. The wet street looked silvery and smooth, as though she could slide over it forever without feeling tired. For a moment everything seemed clear.

Soon the spirit of battle deserted her, and it was only Madeleine and benny, a friend inside. She strolled past the Shanghai Saloon, the Starlite Lounge and the Hollywood Palace, scarcely noticing them but feeling that there was something faintly familiar in the scenery, as if it formed the background of a film she had once seen as a child. A group of friends, clustered for warmth around a lamp-pole, called to her. Madeleine walked on without turning her head.

It began to rain harder and the streets became emptier. Black dye washed out of Madeleine's hat and into her hair; the black slip became drenched and stuck to her skin. Shapes wrapped in rags and newspapers huddled in doorways. Figures also dressed in black danced alone across intersections and stood crying on corners. Others bent like black crows over trash cans, digging into them as furiously as mothers who struggle to retrieve children suffocating beneath the earth. These black figures didn't seem to hear or see one another; nor did they notice Madeleine. When the rain began to fall with still greater force, they started singing and laughing in the middle of the street, spinning and twirling with their faces turned up to the sky.

Madeleine's heart beat faster. "Excuse me," she asked one black figure, "but why are you singing and dancing?" From close by a siren screamed, and the figure fell with a shriek upon the sidewalk. Madeleine reached down and touched its shoulder, and black cloth beat like a moth's wing in her face.

Then the sea was before her. At this point of shoreline there was a boardwalk lined with grass where the public liked to frolic in finer weather. Madeleine spotted several cigarette butts and candy wrappers on the otherwise deserted shore. The sea rolled up against the boardwalk in large deep waves. Through fog and rain and growing darkness she saw the lights of a freighter a short distance out on the bay. The lights were red and green. "The night is just beginning," thought Madeleine.

She tried to remember her vision, and how it had once been as bright as a searchlight. She went over it again: the journey is away from home and toward the dream. There are times when both home and dream seem far away, and the search just a lost space in between. But this is only natural, and part of the trial. The world is an outlandish place, and the end you must keep like a shining jewel inside.

Madeleine envisioned waves pushing up from deep beneath the heavy mass of sea before her and all the other seas upon the spinning globe. Immense powers went unharnessed, enormous forces were ceaselessly at work. The old hopeful mood fell upon Madeleine, the curtain fluttering like an angel's wing, and behind it a moment in a dream.

The fog suddenly thickened, the ship was no longer visible. It had left for another port, or sunk in this one.

■ Menthol Cigarettes

Ingrid was standing in the middle of Madeleine's room. "The man downstairs gave me the key. He still remembers me. Isn't that kooky?" Her voice was louder and flatter than before, and she was dressed in a skin-tight jumpsuit made from some shiny, artificial material. "Don't they have any heat in this place? I can't believe I ever lived here." Ingrid ran a finger along a dusty ledge.

Madeleine stripped off wet lace and pulled on a robe. "Actually," she remarked, "I've resided here longer than I intended. In the old days I never remained in one place for more than several months. It was the motto I lived by and it never let me down.

"But the truth of the matter is this: I have several interests here which prevent me from leaving immediately. I shouldn't say anything because it's all still very hush-hush, but I've lined up important meetings with editors, agents, studio people and the like. It's imperative that I be here for these conferences."

There was a long silence while Ingrid strode between the scarred walls. "I can walk without a raincoat even while it pours and still not get wet in this outfit," she said. "The water just slides right off." She picked up objects then set them down unexamined, as though looking for something she didn't care if she found or not.

At last Madeleine spoke. "Now tell me about your friend. Bill is his name? Sally tells me he's in business."

"Oh, that one. He got put in jail a long time ago. Now I go with this photographer guy. He's going to make me into a movie star. He wants to take me to Hollywood as soon as he finds the cash. He says that it's always summer there and that I can swim in the ocean whenever I want to. They call it Santa Monica, which is Spanish. I've always been nuts to live in a place with a Spanish name, just to see what it's like."

"I've been to Hollywood," said Madeleine, "but I never cared for the place despite the good offers I received there. What happened to the unknown reaches of your soul, Ingrid? I believed you carried the lamp of mystery."

"Oh, that. It was a dumb game, wasn't it? But I brought the cards along anyway. Since this is our last chance, we may as well do one more reading. Do you like my hair?"

"Very bright red is a nice colour. What last chance?" asked Madeleine.

"I guess I just told you. I won't be coming back here no more. Lou says we gotta go south because things are easier there. They got the money, the glamour, the works. I didn't like this hotel even when I lived here. It's creepy."

"It used to be your home," pointed out Madeleine.

Ingrid lit a menthol cigarette. "Have you ever tried these? They taste like candy."

"Remember that afternoon we were bored so crazy we climbed the fire escape to the roof of this hotel? It was a foggy day, and the buildings below looked like ships bumping lost on water. Remember how we pretended that if we covered our bodies with Krazy Glue we would stick to the fog? And when the fog lifted we would be carried with it out over the bay? Didn't you feel like an explorer looking at an undiscovered land?"

"No," said Ingrid, laying out the cards. "I don't remember that. By the way, this will have to be a quick reading. I'm late and in a hurry, so I can only stay for one more menthol cigarette." She muttered in exasperation. "These cards. Before I could see everything so clearly. Now it hardly seems worth the trouble, they blur so much."

"I've missed you," said Madeleine.

"Now, before I do the reading, you have to tell me your plans. That way I can set my mind in the right direction."

"Well, Ingrid, now that you mention it, I do happen to have several plans. For example, I've been meaning to write to my good friend Annemarie, who dwells in Berlin. You must remember her. She and I share a feeling."

"Look," interrupted Ingrid. "Is it show business or the steno pool? The fair or dark handsome stranger? You know how it goes." She glanced undisguisedly at her watch.

Madeleine went to the little table by the window and poured herself a drink. "Do you care for one?" she inquired. Before Ingrid could answer, Madeleine quickly said, "Annemarie was such a funny girl. Her favourite things in all the world were peanut brittle and wading in streams. One afternoon we discovered a shady stream we had never found before, although we knew that mountain well. It was a hot day, even for July. We jumped from stone to stone up the creek, and the air turned cooler and greener as we rose higher. The redfish were running up from the lake then, to mate and lay eggs in their place of birth. They had to fight their way against the current to climb the creek, and many didn't make it all the way back to where they'd started from. The fish were red, but on that afternoon they looked golden. The peanut brittle came wrapped in silver foil. . . ."

Madeleine didn't turn around when she heard the door close. The air shaft was deep, and muddy water glimmered at its bottom. The creek had been crystal clear; then the light changed, and the fish became silver. They followed the stream higher and higher as it roared down through the trees.

The unread cards were arranged neatly on the bed. When you looked into the forest on either side of the creek, the light was dim and full of shadow. Suddenly, she had seen a bear dancing in a glade. It moved stiffly and solemnly, like an old general waltzing his millionth waltz. "Look," she cried to Annemarie; but the stream sang so loudly that her friend couldn't hear her. Madeleine leaped up the creek, following Annemarie.

■ Night Must Fall Come What May

Dearest Sister,

I don't know what has happened to me here. I only know that once all the answers lay within my heart, waiting to be drawn out one by one like jewels of blood. My heart beat strong and hard, and sang a song of soon, soon. True, my dream lay far beyond tomorrow's sunset, but tomorrow is just one day after today and night must fall come what may.

Everything was inside me, dark and unknown. All I needed was one moment in one place for the world to stand still and its secrets to shine before me. I believed this was the moment and the place, but every hour here has proven me wrong.

For now all is different. I listen and listen so hard the earth cracks open, but my blood is silent as it awaits the footstep on the stair. My body aches and the dream cries out for release. It is still inside, waiting for the touch that will turn the key. Somewhere hides a Saviour who looks like anyone else and talks like anyone else, but who is the Only One who can hear my call and answer with one glance that breaks the spell. All the hurt pours out like blood until you hold your beating heart like a baby in your hands.

Some day. This city is too large. The Saviour could walk down one side of the street as I walk down the other. I turn one way; the Only One turns another way, and is unseen and lost forever. A million such tragedies occur daily in every city upon the globe. The world is too large.

So many here have called to me with drowning voices and clutching arms, believing me to be their Saviour. My face was stone as I watched water fold smooth upon them until the sea became one vast unmarked grave. Their cries did not touch me, for I was listening for another call and searching for another hand; it would lead me onto the boat that would sail across the sea, above the drowned ones with seaweed-streaming hair.

I know you are in such torment you cannot write to me. Your hands are crippled and your eyes blind and your mind encaged. I hear your dying call. I would come to you if I could. Now it is springtime once more. Now I must leave this city for a place where no ghosts laugh in my face and touch my shoulder. Their laugh is real and their touch is real, but they are not there.

Please don't grieve that I have abandoned my search. Know instead that I have learned that it is just beginning and that it will be more difficult than we ever imagined. You who stood so tall beside me and looked into the future with eyes both clear and bold, you can understand that the tunnel through the rainbow may be dark. Now that you have fallen it is doubly important that I see this task through to the end. It doesn't matter that I am tired. Once I find my Saviour and see an angel watching from behind two dark eyes, the door to my dreams will unlock and all the secrets inside will in their true voices speak to me. This I know. Also, the clouds will roll away.

I will write to you from wherever I happen to end up. Don't worry. Hang on. You will see that one day we shall both sail away on our ship to the place beyond the farthest horizon. It will be sooner or later, but it will be. This I also know.

Madeleine

The blonde girl reached for her Bible and flipped its pages to where an old, deeply creased map served as a bookmark. It was the map and not the Scripture she studied. "Let's try again, Frances," she said, speaking to the ghosts of all the searchers who had paused in this room before continuing on their paths. Madeleine closed her eyes and moved a finger in a circle above the map. Then she stabbed it.

It took her five minutes to pack. She filled her beach bag with whichever objects were nearest at hand or caught her eye; when the bag was full this meant that the remaining objects were to be left behind. Going through her wardrobe, she dressed in a layered combination of a number of costumes, then stuck a feather in her hair. She examined her face in the mirror and plucked three grey hairs from her head. With a finger she tried to erase smile lines at the corners of her eyes and mouth.

There was nothing left to do. The walls were blank. Unchosen clothes were strewn across the bed and floor in strange, twisted shapes; pages were scattered like fallen leaves among them. The manuscript would offer instruction to the next person in need of its teachings, and then to the one after that, and on and on. "It will never be finished," thought Madeleine, digging deep into her purse to see how much worldly wealth she had to finance the next step of her journey. $6.29. After a moment's consideration she decided to invest one cent of this sum in good luck, and dropped a penny down the air shaft since no wishing well was at hand. The splash echoed, then faded into a silence that spread through the hotel. No doors banged, no music played, no footsteps sounded, no one coughed or shouted. For one second the world was perfectly silent, and in that moment Madeleine tilted back the bottle and swallowed its remains. Then there was nothing left.

■ Union

It was Harry's night off. He'd taken the opportunity to visit the woman he'd recently started seeing; Sherri lived with her small son in a room above the bowling alley where she worked a concession stand Monday through Saturday. They'd sat out on the landing of the fire escape that ran past her window, so they could talk without waking the boy asleep on the fold-out bed inside. They sat close together while they talked, he sometimes leaning on her, she sometimes resting against him. For spells they were silent, and looked at the lights of the streets and buildings around them, or turned their faces up to the stars. Sounds of cars and radios and laughter stirred through the air, like evidence of the world turning around. The rain had stopped the night before, and the evening was fresh and warm with spring.

Harry didn't know how this new thing would work out. Sherri was kind of a frightened woman, on account of what had been done to her by the man she'd finally made herself leave. Harry found himself moving quiet and slow around her, making no sudden sounds or motions that might startle himself as well as her. He'd also been around the old block a time or two; his heart felt tender and tough at once. Still, he had a good feeling, a hopeful feeling. "We rhyme," said Sherri, speaking their names together.

Now he was walking through the neighbourhood where he worked. He didn't feel like going on home yet, though his bad leg felt stiff and sore. He felt like staying out in the crazy mixed-up world. Harry glanced toward the darkened windows of the Starlite; the place was closed this one night each week. Passing the Shanghai Saloon, he frowned without realizing the cause for this expression or even that it crossed his face. As he approached the Hollywood Palace, the marquee suddenly switched off: the words *Come and Get It* glittered and shone with blazing light, then fell into darkness and seemed to disappear. Sam emerged from the theatre.

"How's it going?" asked Harry, pausing on the sidewalk and lighting a cigarette.

"Can't complain," said Sam amid the jingling of turning keys. He pushed at the door to make sure it was securely locked, then took out cigarettes and lit one with the manner of a man who has finally finished a long shift of work and may now start to relax.

"What's this I hear about you shutting down?" asked Harry. "You leaving the business?"

"What?" asked Sam, his eyes turning in surprise to the other man's face. "Where'd you hear this?"

"Can't remember," Harry cautiously replied.

Sam looked up at the darkened marquee for a long moment. *Come and Get It* was her best film. She had a dual role, first playing a good woman who's abandoned by the man she loves, then playing this woman's daughter, a girl gone bad who's loved by the same man who left her mother. Hell, it wasn't the greatest picture ever made, but it was pretty good. It didn't reveal much about the woman who was its star—how she had lived and struggled, suffered and died. The point to her existence? The story behind her story? There were a few flashes, maybe. A few hints in her eyes for those looking for them. Not too much more. Still, Sam guessed he'd show the picture now and then; it gave an audience pleasure.

"No," said Sam, slowly shaking his head. "Don't think I'd ever close up the Palace. I couldn't find my way to doing that. You come by in fifty years and you'll see a withered old guy shuffling like a ghost through the lobby. That'll be me."

"Sure," said Harry. "And I'll be the ghost in the Starlite who fills up glasses on the sly. So they're never empty, always full. What a life."

The two men looked at each other and smiled.

"Which way you headed?" asked Sam.

"Down to the bay to look at the lights on the bridge. You know, after staring all week at the skyline painted inside the Starlite, I kind of get an urge to see the real thing. The view's good from down by the water."

Sam flexed his sore fingers and remembered his banjo. He'd bought it early in the winter from a beat-up pawnshop nearby. Crazy. Didn't know how to play the thing, didn't know why on earth he'd bought it. He'd forgotten about the instrument at once, and hadn't noticed it sitting on top of the refrigerator until just the other week. Funny. He'd had it tuned at a music store, then bought an instruction book. Now he was learning to play the banjo, a new trick for an old dog. Sam felt foolish and proud at the same time. He could already handle some simple chords and was improving with each night of practice. There were a few easy tunes he was just able to manage. He played them over and over late at night, until he felt peaceful and sleepy and ready to turn off the lights. The banjo was painted with a moon and five stars.

Standing on the sidewalk with Harry, Sam felt that he would be alone for thousands of nights in the future, strumming his banjo in his dim quiet room while out in the sky beyond the window all the stars he'd ever wished upon flashed and flared. He had a sudden strong yearning to look up and see real stars after watching their symbols seven nights a week in the Palace. Sam lifted his eyes above the buildings around him. With a shock he realized that sometime recently it had stopped raining. Now the sky was clear, and it was possible to see far into the night.

"Want some company?" he asked.

A sharper needle of pain jabbed Harry's left leg. This year the end of the rain hadn't meant an easing of that pain. Maybe from now on his leg would hurt him equally through clear and rainy days. But as long as he felt that hurt he'd know he was still alive, still searching.

OK. All right.

"Sure," Harry replied evenly, though he'd have preferred to be alone; he wanted to think over the things he and Sherri had talked about on the fire escape, and to ponder the possibility of their lives joining up. "Let's go," he said.

The two men walked slowly together down the street.

▬▬ It's a Wrap

One March night at three A.M., when there was little movement in the Holiday Hotel, Joe leaned upon his desk and added one column of figures after another. Two numbers became one. He worked slowly and methodically, stretching out and savouring his pleasure in the work. When the lobby door burst open and footsteps ran toward him, Joe looked up irritably from within the small circle of lamplight.

The boy was breathing hard. His arms hung straight down and ended in two clenched fists. "Where is she?" he asked.

Joe looked down at the figures again. One more calculation would balance the hotel's accounts for the entire month. "Who?" he asked.

"Madeleine. Where is she?"

"Who is Madeleine?"

"324. The room to the left of the landing."

Joe recalled the last time he'd seen the blonde. She had walked slowly across the lobby as though afraid of falling over at any step, a beach bag striped red, white and blue dangling from one hand. "Excuse me," he'd called. She'd walked on as if she hadn't heard him, her eyes fixed straight ahead and an eerie smile on her face.

Joe reached for his black book and pretended to search through its pages. "Room 324 is empty, but the rent's been paid until the end of the month. The party left a while ago, but her things are still there. We're just about to clear them from the room."

"Where'd she go?"

"I don't know. She just left." After a moment Joe said, "Here's the key. Take anything you want."

The boy unlocked the door. The room's light bulb was burned out, but enough light shone from the hallway to reveal that everything inside was turned upside down. The boy quickly gathered up all the pages he could find, stowed them inside his jacket, then left the room.

Seeing the boy approach once more, Joe cleared his throat. "You might want these. No one else does." He pointed to a bundle of letters stamped heavily in a foreign language. "They've been returned to the party."

The boy threw down the key and walked away. The lobby door closed behind him. Joe looked down at the numbers before him. He could figure in his head the final sum that they would make, but he didn't write it down. Instead, he opened the first letter.

■ Part Five

"That night I knelt and thanked Him, who led me out of the exile of despair and gave me another chance. I shall always thank Him. . . . I am very much in love and think that, from now on, life is going to be wonderful."

Frances Farmer, 1959
(post-lobotomy)

After the End

Shit, boy back in Hollywood, where else? What now? Fun and games and the fucking street dying before his eyes and saying: we take you with us, kid. Everyone gone or hiding or dead in unmarked graves. It cold and dark and empty and there no place to go but a has-been bar known from ugly times before. Empty inside except for bartender, remember him, listening to some burned-out baby at the back. Right away bartender say: get outa here, ain't nothing for you here tonight, beat it.

The old bird drool into her fifth drink and look over boy with eyeballs smeared lipstick red. "Let the kid stay. He's my brother or my son, I forget which. Ain't you?"

"He's a pretty boy. Ain't you a pretty boy?" say Nick.

"And you're a stinking liar, Nick. Come over here, baby. I'll buy you a drink and make you a star. Hows about some Southern Comfort? Hell, Monroe was in my speech class, and was that tramp jealous of my southern accent. They were all jealous of me, every one of them."

"Shut your mouth. Marilyn was just a lonely kid," say Nick.

"Are you a lonely kid, pretty boy? Let mama tell her boy a bedtime story. Let's see, how does it go? How did it go? It was back in the good old days, way back when. There was a party, the kind they used to throw in the great old days, where bad young girls like me were given a chance to meet someone who might help us out. For a price. All fair and square, the price-tags clearly marked. What's there to lose? I think. So there I am, after the party's over, riding up the Coast Highway with some guy. He's the quiet type, thank God. At least that kind don't tell you you're garbage but only look at you that way. Radio playing some song, can't remember what it was, just some song, and I wasn't feeling too bad for a change. Anyhows, we get to the motel, one just like all the others, some joint called The Ebbtide or Hightide

289

or some damn name. I get undressed and into bed fast cause it's cold or maybe it's just the way it makes you feel. But the guy, he just stands at the window and looks out, staring at the moon or stars or I dunno what. We had a real moon and real stars in those days, not cheap no-talent trash like today."

"Says the expert on the subject," interject Nick.

Ginger don't hear him. She swirl her drink around in her glass. "The beach was right there across the highway, and in between the noise of the lousy traffic you could hear the waves. Come here, baby, what's up, I says to him. But he just standing there with his back to me. I had drunk too much, I guess, and all of a sudden was feeling pretty bad."

"Some things don't never change," say Nick.

"That's right, you asshole. I was born with class and I'll go with class. I won't die in this crummy joint like you."

"Watch it, Ginger. Your stories make me sick and I don't much like feeling sick," speak Nick.

Ginger look deep into the smoke of her cigarette. "Then he begins to talk and he don't let up. I was feeling tired, tired of it all, tired of the nothing that ain't never gonna end. Just wishing he'd come to bed so maybe I can catch a few hours shut-eye afterwards. But this guy, what the hell was his name, who gives a fuck, talks on and on, and it's all about that Frances Farmer. Remember her, Nick?"

"Sure I do. She was crazy or a dyke or a red. Everyone had a different story. What happened to her anyway?"

"Makes me sick to think about it," say Ginger. "She had it made, then threw it all away. But I knew enough to keep my mouth shut. The big boys were out to get her and they did. What the hell, I didn't feel sorry for her."

"You're a sensitive gal, Ginger. Miss Sensitivity, 1922," say Nick.

"On and on this guy talked, all about how they mur-

dered Frances Farmer. He said it was a frame job, they
drove her crazy, dumped her in the sewer, then threw
away the key. He spent one night with her, and when
she spoke it was like an angel smiling inside your heart,
he said. She was hiding out in some downtown hotel,
locked in her room trying to get off the stuff, trying to
write some kind of book. She was too smart for her own
good."

Nick pour himself a shot. "I saw her once on LeBrea
and knew she didn't have a chance," he say. "1940? '41?
She wasn't like the others, who looked like shit off the
screen. I only glimpsed her from a distance, but to me
she looked like . . . like . . ."

"A lonely kid?" spit Ginger. "Ain't you a lonely kid,
pretty boy? Lonely? Hell, she was crazy. How do I feel,
there in bed while this guy's talking about some crazy
broad. If it wasn't that he'd promised to introduce me to
some shit-faced agent—hell. His back is to me, he talks
out to the dark. On and on about how Frances Farmer
makes him want to die, she's the mountain-tops and the
sea, and she says nothing but it's like making love with
God. A fucking queer, just like all the rest.

"He turns to me and says, do I know what he means?
And his face is sloppy and wet and I think, Jesus, the
guy is crying. Beat that. What do you do with a crying
man? Don't cry, baby, it's gonna be swell, I say. Then he
comes over to the bed, and I'll tells you, I thought it was
the final reel for yours truly, and me used to rough trade
how in this town you gotta be. But it ain't so easy to die,
worse luck, and the next morning I wake up and the
bastard is gone. Me stuck in this dive motel with no car,
no cash. Ain't life lush? I was lucky, though, cause the
dirty manager of the joint let me be nice to him and then
he helped me out. The world's full of nice guys."

"So what happened?" ask Nick.

"Ha! A happy ending. The two-bit heel goes and gets
himself knocked off before he can introduce me to any
agent. What did he expect, talking around about the

Farmer broad like that. Any frame job they paint over nice and pretty with poison and silence, and you better look the other way, mister.

"But listen now. Listen to me and I'll tell you something. I had no pity for the Farmer girl, but even so I think she deserves better than what she's getting now—this crummy town turning her into some kind of marquee saint, lining their pockets and consciences with silver. She'd spit in their faces. Hell, maybe that ain't rain out there after all."

"The book. What happened to it?" wonder Nick. "They ever print it?"

"Not a chance. Disappeared or something. Vanished like everything's got a habit of doing."

"No, it didn't," say boy and he begin to walk away.

"What's that?" mutter Ginger. "Come on home and I'll sing you a lullaby. What's the matter? It was just a damn story."

"Let him go," say Nick, throwing back another shot.

"Burn in hell," slur Ginger as she slowly slide off her stool.

The boy walk out into Frances Farmer's tears.

THE END

1981—San Francisco; Santa Cruz de Miramar, Mexico; Hollywood; Vancouver; Toronto; New York; Paris; Berlin; Sevilla, Spain—1989